SHE MOST
FEARS...AND
DESIRES

Temptation...

He smiled, and her traitorous heart skipped a beat. She had not imagined yesterday how handsome he was. . . .

"Miss Lafon, I imagine you believe you have many reasons to dislike me. I'd like for you to give me a chance to prove myself, if you would."

He said it so charmingly that Rosalie started to smile back at him. She caught herself just in time. He was dangerous. Dangerous and unpredictable, and Rosalie wished with all her heart that Papa had not brought him home. "I am committing myself to no one but God."

"If you're truly meant for God, Miss Lafon," he said, "there's nothing I can do to change that, isn't that so?"

Slowly she nodded.

"Then how can it hurt to humor me just a little? Give us a chance to get to know each other. If it turns out we're not meant to be together, at least you'll know for sure."

Rosalie got to her feet. "Excuse me," she said quickly. "I have forgotten . . . something."

She heard his laughter follow her as she rushed to her room, to prayers and safety, away from challenging blue eyes and a wicked laugh that made her think of things she should not know about.

BOOKS BY MEGAN CHANCE

Fall from Grace
The Way Home
The Gentleman Caller

Published by HarperPaperbacks

HarperChoice

The Gentleman ❧ Caller

MEGAN CHANCE

HarperPaperbacks
A Division of HarperCollinsPublishers

🏰 **HarperPaperbacks**
A Division of HarperCollins*Publishers*
10 East 53rd Street, New York, NY 10022-5299

This is a work of fiction. The characters, incidents, and
dialogues are products of the author's imagination and are not to
be construed as real. Any resemblance to actual events or
persons, living or dead, is entirely coincidental.

ISBN 0-06-108704-1

HarperCollins®, 🏰 ®, HarperPaperbacks™, and
HarperChoice™ are trademarks of HarperCollins Publishers, Inc.

Cover illustration © 1998 by John Ennis

First printing: December 1998

Printed in the United States of America

Visit HarperPaperbacks on the World Wide Web at
http://www.harpercollins.com

❖ 10 9 8 7 6 5 4 3 2 1

For Cleo,

*who makes everything twice as hard
as it has to be—and twice as wonderful*

I love you

Love, we are in God's hand
How strange now looks the life he makes us lead
So free we seem, so fettered fast we are!

—Robert Browning
Andrea del Sarto

❦ Chapter 1

June 1856—New Orleans

Corinne Lafon tiptoed across the upper gallery, wincing at every creak of the cypress-planked floor. Papa had such sharp hearing; if he were to find her sneaking around outside his sitting room . . . The humiliation of it was too extreme to think of, so she didn't. She had no other choice than this, since he'd already told her that he didn't want her hanging on his every word like some silly bird, and that she should trust him to make the decision that was best for her.

She wanted to obey him, she truly did, but she couldn't stand sitting there in the parlor alone, chafing in the humid, overcast heat while she waited for Papa to decide her future. Rosalie had already gone to the infirmary, and there was no one else to counsel her to be patient, and so here Corinne was, flattening herself against the plastered wall so a shadow wouldn't give her away. The French doors of Papa's sitting room were open onto the gallery—she had never doubted they would be, it was so hot. The soft gauze of netting lay limply against the frame. That morning's breeze had died away; there was a storm coming, she could feel it. The change in the weather seemed propitious somehow; it was a good day to decide her future. The thought made her heart beat faster as she eased as near to the doors as she dared. She held her breath and leaned close to hear.

She heard Reynaud first, that rushed, anxious voice he had when he was tense and uncomfortable. Corinne winced. She had told him and told him that he must be calm, that Papa would find any weakness in him. She had told him to think of her when he spoke, to persuade Papa the way he so easily persuaded her, with reasonable words and that soft confidence that shone from his big brown eyes.

But his voice was scratchy and high. "This is not so sudden as it would seem," he protested. "Corinne and I knew we were destined for each other the moment we met. Each hour we spend together since then only strengthens our love."

"Your love?" Corinne flushed at the contempt she heard in Papa's voice. "Love is irrelevant to me, Reynaud, as it should be to you. Marriage is a business."

"*Monsieur,* how you cheapen it!"

"Love fades like a cut flower the moment the water runs dry—you understand my meaning, *oui?*"

Hesitation. Then, "I cannot say I do."

"Ah, I suppose you do not."

There it was again, that contempt. She had heard it too many times to mistake it. Corinne prayed for Reynaud to stop faltering like a shy child.

"How do you intend to provide for my daughter?"

"I make a decent living," Reynaud said. "My paintings—"

"You expect to support my daughter on a few mediocre portraits?" Papa asked in a low, soft whisper that didn't soothe the blunt brutality of his question. Corinne pressed her hands hard into the wall, imprinting the brick-patterned plaster into her skin. She knew that whisper; she had spent a lifetime hating it.

"*Monsieur,* I am an artist. I will find a patron—"

"Ha! Not in New Orleans."

"With your support, I can—"

"But you don't have my support, Reynaud, eh? Do we understand one another?" The squeak of a chair, the low choke of a wheeze. "You come here and you say you love my daughter, but why not be honest with each other? My riches will gain you the life of ease you're looking for, *n'est-ce pas?* That is why you are here, asking for permission to marry my daughter."

"*Monsieur!*" Reynaud's voice shook. "I love Corinne. This has nothing to do with money."

Papa's laugh was low. "You will understand if I disagree. Surely you must realize that I must refuse your suit. I cannot allow my daughter to marry you."

Corinne felt Reynaud's will breaking; she felt him crumbling, even though she couldn't see his face. "Oh, be strong, *chéri,*" she whispered under her breath. "Remember that you love me."

But no amount of strength would help him now.

It was over. She had had too many conversations like this with her father—she even knew the way Papa was looking at Reynaud now, as if he were an irritating fly Papa was too lazy to kill—oh, it was over.

She blinked away the start of tears and pushed

away from the wall, uncaring now who heard her. It wasn't until she reached the wrought-iron benches surrounding the fountain in the center of the courtyard that Corinne let her frustration surface. She sat down hard on one of the benches, glared up at the open doors of her father's sitting room, and clenched her fists so hard, her nails bit into her palms.

If only Maman were alive. Maman would understand how she felt about Reynaud, the things she couldn't put into words except in her own head. Reynaud made her feel as if she mattered, and Corinne's hungry soul drank up the adoration in his eyes. To Reynaud, she was perfect, and she wanted to be perfect once in her life. She wanted to see pride in a man's eyes instead of the disappointment she saw continuously in her father's. For that, she could put up with Reynaud's loud, threadbare vests, his pink stockings, and the tarnished watch chains looped across his chest.

Sometimes she thought she disappointed Papa simply by being alive. She'd tried to make him happy; she'd flirted with the sons of his Creole business partners, thinking such a match would please him, but he'd only chastised her for encouraging them. She'd tried to comfort him when he was ill or tired, the way she'd seen Rosalie do, with soothing touches and calm words, and all she got was irritation and an order to "Wash your face, girl, you smell like a brothel." She'd tried everything she could think of. But the only time she'd ever seen affection in her father's eyes was when he looked at Rosalie.

It was not good to feel such jealousy toward her sister, and Corinne tried to fight it. But the nasty little feeling bit harder and harder, until finally she had no choice but to give in to it. It was the only way to control it, she knew. If she gave it free rein now and again, then when she pushed it back into its box, it stayed.

Though she knew it was sinful, there were days when Corinne dreamed of Rosalie's going away, joining the Ursulines the way she'd talked sometimes of doing. But no, Rosalie stayed here, caring for their widowed papa, basking in the adoration of the entire Vieux Carré. St. Rosalie, she was called. An angel of mercy. Surely there'd be a reward for her in heaven.

Well, Corinne would never know. She lifted her face to the bright but overcast sky, closing her eyes to imagine a cool breeze blowing the shadows of the banana leaves, rustling through the urns of boxwood and the twining wisteria. She colored her imagination with the smells of sweet olive and rose geraniums and citronella. The perfumes filled her head, cleansing her, washing away her jealousy and her anger the way they always did. She loved smells. She loved the way they claimed the air, the way the breezes sharpened them, the way the rains made them softer and at the same time more intense. When she was married, with a home of her own, she would plant her courtyard with masses of flowers. She would have them blooming all year long. She would have this fountain copied, and she would surround it with mimosa and sit beneath it until her head spun from the sheer beauty of it.

She opened her eyes and took a deep breath.

She trailed her fingers in the warm water of the fountain and looked up into the brittle bronze smile of Narcissus, bending low to look at his reflection in the water, and told herself her dream was coming true.

Certainly it was possible that Reynaud was convincing Papa, wasn't it? She played a game with herself, the same game she'd played since she was a child. She imagined going to her father, convincing him of the match. She imagined him taking her in his arms and saying, "*Oui, oui,* of course, my darling child. Whatever you wish. How proud you make me."

She heard soft footsteps on the flagstones near the house. Corinne looked up. Reynaud. The sight of him made her forget her game. He looked tired and dejected. The bright green vest she'd thought so cheerful glinted dully in the light, and his shoulders were slumped forward, the dark shining curls of his hair falling into his face—even the heavy macassar oil could not contain them.

She said nothing. She waited for him to see her, and she watched his face when he looked up and spotted her across the courtyard. There was desperation in his expression, and despair, but as he came closer, those things faded into a brittle smile, into brightly glittering eyes.

"Corinne, *chérie,*" he said, holding out his arms to her. She rose from the bench just as he reached her, and he grasped her arms and pulled her so hard into his chest that she felt the scratch of the metallic threads on his vest and the cut of his watch chains.

"He refused me," Reynaud said with a heavy sigh. He let her go when she eased away, shaking his head sorrowfully. "He does not understand our love for each other, *chérie*. He is just an old and bitter man."

"Oh, Reynaud." Corinne stepped back and sank onto the bench. She brushed against the mimosa, dropping fragile blooms to the flagstones, where Reynaud's shiny buckled boots crushed them into the walk.

He sat and put his arm around her shoulders. His heavy, flowery cologne filled her nose, the perfume of macassar in his hair.

"*Chérie*," he said in her ear, and his breath was as hot and moist as the humid air around her, wet against her skin. "Your father is cruel to try to keep us apart. But our love will prevail, *n'est-ce pas?*" His smooth, easy hands caressed her shoulder. "Come away with me, Corinne," he whispered. "He will have no choice but to approve the match once we are married."

For a moment she thought about going away with him, about marrying him. She thought about how his hands on her body made her feel, how passionately she had loved him. But already those feelings had faded; she could not remember them. Papa's voice was so loud in her head: *I must refuse your suit. I cannot allow my daughter to marry you.*

Corinne looked into Reynaud's big brown eyes, the same eyes that had made her feel like the most beautiful woman in the world only an hour before. But the luster was already gone; she saw only her own reflection.

"He will not approve it," she said with a sigh. "It won't matter to him if we marry or not. He will never approve."

Reynaud's brow furrowed. He reached for her hand. "Don't be a fool, Corinne. Of course he will approve!"

She jerked her hand away. "I cannot, Reynaud."

"You don't mean it! *Chérie,* our love . . . you cannot just throw it away."

"I'm sorry," she said again. "I can't marry you."

For a moment she thought he would protest again, and her heart tightened in embarrassment for him. But he said nothing. His eyes clouded and he looked away. His hand went to his vest, smoothing his watch chains, before he looked at her again.

"I did not tell him about the nights we have spent together," he said slowly. "You think he would change his mind if he knew his daughter was no longer chaste?"

"You would not!"

"No, I would not. I may be poor, but I am still a gentleman." But his eyes were hard, his mouth tight. "But I think . . . perhaps I will abduct you. Perhaps I will come to your room at night and take you away from here. Perhaps then you would see what I know— that your papa keeps you like a perfect jewel beneath glass. If you do not defy him, you will be an old maid like your sister, catering to his every whim."

His bitterness made her feel nothing. Her affection for him was already gone, so fast . . . strange how it should be so fast.

"Well, Corinne?" he asked. "Should I take you away?"

"I would fight you," she said softly.

He left her then. Without a word, he walked away and motioned for Robert to bring his horse from the stables. She watched him mount and go, disappearing into the tunnel of the porte cochere that led to the street. She heard the heavy creak of the carriageway door as it clanked shut behind him.

Corinne sighed. She looked up at the sky, at the purple-gray clouds beyond the courtyard, and felt the too-heavy air that seemed to match the heaviness in her heart.

Rosalie Lafon straightened on the hard stool and drew her hand back from her patient's forehead. The man was sleeping at last, his breathing slow and calm, and she felt a gentle satisfaction that she had helped to make his last hours peaceful ones.

The little infirmary was full today—temporary beds had even been set up in Father Bara's office, crowding around his desk so he could not use it. The cholera had already hit—it was early this year, after a particularly wet spring—and in a way Rosalie was glad for it. It meant there were more hours to spend here, more hours to bury herself in her work, more hours not to think about how Papa had been so very ill. . . .

No, best not to think of that. Better to think of the decision she'd made only a few days ago, of the life that awaited her. Yes, think of that.

It did not quite bring the reassurance she wanted it to. Instead, she remembered Papa's thunderous expression yesterday, his insistence that she could not know what she was doing. She had so wanted him to understand, but she had stumbled over her words, and there was so much she couldn't tell him. How could she explain that his illness had made her afraid? That when he was gone there would be no purpose to her life, no reason except for the few daily hours she worked here or at St. Anne's? A few hours were not enough.

The truth was that she did not want to be alone. When she was alone, she thought too much, and she did not want to think. She did not want to remember. . . . Rosalie closed her eyes. Deliberately she willed serenity and calm. She murmured an Our Father until the words filled her head.

"Rosalie." The soft touch on her arm startled her. Rosalie's eyes jerked open. Sister Angelina smiled. "Forgive me," she said, "but Father Bara is outside. I know you wished to speak with him before he left."

Rosalie nodded. "*Merci.*"

She rose from the stool. It was past noon already, and hot. The heavy serge of her gown was unbearable, and the canvas apron she wore over it trapped the heat against her skin. Though the windows had been opened to let in the breezes, the thin curtains lay limply against the window frame, and the smell of blood and illness was undiminished. It was miserable, and the rooms were small and mean—there was hardly money for more. But Rosalie found a forgetfulness here that she treasured, a peace few other places held, and she did not like to leave.

But Father Bara waited. Rosalie untied her apron and hung it on the hook near the door. She took her veil, hat, and gloves from the table there and paused, looking out the doorway to the orange tree guarding the street. There was still time to change her mind—in fact, Papa had insisted she not talk to the priest today, that she wait. But she felt sick at heart when she considered the delay. There was no other choice for her—deep in her heart she'd known that every single day of these last ten years. She had already delayed too long.

Rosalie put on her hat and veil and stepped from the little house. There was a straggling herb garden fighting for life near the front steps, and it was there she found Father Bara. The priest was kneeling among the spindly herbs, weeding. He looked up and gave her a tired smile.

"Rosalie, my child, I wondered when you would give up for the day."

He looked worn. His dark eyes had circles beneath them; his gray-streaked dark hair was mussed, as if he'd run his hands through it many times. He was not an old man, perhaps only forty, but he looked old now. His face was heavily lined, and he had the pallor of one who spent most of his time in the dim indoors.

He sighed and motioned to the plant beside him. "I think the thyme is dying," he said. "No matter what I do, it seems to wilt."

Rosalie stepped down. She settled herself on the edge of a stair and slapped her gloves lightly against her hand. "Perhaps the soil's too stony here."

"I've thought of that," he admitted. He sat back on his heels and grinned wryly. "Or perhaps God has decided I've had thyme enough."

Rosalie laughed lightly. "Time enough for what, *mon père?* Not for sleep, I would say. When was the last time you rested?"

"I can't remember. Yesterday, perhaps."

"For an hour at least?"

"Oh, if it could have been that."

"*Mon père*—"

"Time races away, does it not?" Father Bara sighed. "It was good of you to come, Rosalie. I know your father has been ill. There are many things pressing on you."

"*Oui.*" Rosalie was quiet. She watched Father Bara dig in the dirt again, shoving little rocks out of the way, nudging the thyme back to standing, bolstering it with tiny mounds of soil.

"*Mon père*, I . . . I have been praying."

He looked at her in mild surprise. "I would hope so. A dialogue with the Lord is a necessary thing."

"*Oui.*" Rosalie nodded. "I have been . . . These last years have . . . ." She trailed off, looking at the gloves in her hand, the soft kid frayed at the edges, the stained seams.

"Is something troubling you, my child?"

Rosalie took a deep breath. "I want to join the order, *mon père.*"

The words came rushing out, finally said, finally done. Rosalie closed her eyes in relief. When she noticed the silence, she opened them again to see that Father Bara was sitting back on his heels, a dirt-encrusted spade dangling from his hand and smearing mud on his clothing. His brow was furrowed; she could not miss his concern.

"You have told your father this?" he asked.

"*Oui.*" Rosalie nodded.

"And he approves?"

She felt cold. "Shouldn't this decision be between myself and God, *mon père?*"

"God has given you a father on earth to protect and love you, my child. Certainly his feelings on the matter should be consulted."

"He thinks . . . he thinks I'm too young."

"Do you agree?"

"I'm twenty-six years old, *mon père.*"

"Still time for marriage, for a family," he said slowly.

Rosalie jerked up to meet his gaze. "God is more than enough for me."

"Is He, Rosalie?" Father Bara dropped the spade to the ground and sighed as he brushed mud distractedly from his tunic. "Will you be happy never having a husband for yourself? Will it be enough to have only the orphans at St. Anne's as your children? Can you be satisfied as a bride of Christ?"

"It's what I want," she said, leaning forward. "I've prayed for this, *mon père.* I've fasted. I've asked the Lord for guidance. I haven't made this decision lightly.

For years I've considered it, and now . . . now the time is right."

Father Bara's gaze was searching. "Your father has been ill."

"He nearly died." Rosalie felt tears start. "He is not a young man. Dr. Wiley says there may only be a few years left. Perhaps only months."

"And when he is gone, you will be alone."

Rosalie went still. "*Oui.*"

"Rosalie," Father Bara said gently. He laid his hand on hers. "This is an important decision. It does no one good if you enter the order simply because you are alone or lonely. You are useful to us even without the veil. Your nursing skills are invaluable. You are a comfort to us already. Those things will still be true if your father dies."

"I want more than that." Rosalie's hand tightened on her skirt. "It's not enough for me simply to do charity. I want to follow Christ. I want to feel His hand upon me—"

"His hand is there already."

"I want His kiss, *mon père*," she said desperately. "I want to be His, body and soul. I feel alone when I leave here, when I go home. I want Him all around me. I want to breathe Him in the air, and instead all I have are my own candles, the silence of my room. . . ." She stumbled over her words, and her vision wavered. The tears were coursing down her face now; she could not stop them, she could not help herself. Rosalie squeezed her eyes shut, but still she felt Father Bara's gaze on her face.

It seemed forever before he sighed. "Very well." Rosalie's relief filled her chest so that she could hardly breathe. Such simple words, but how good she found them. She blinked away her tears. "Oh, *mon père*," she said in a rush. "*Merci. Merci*—"

He held up a hand to stop her. "Rosalie, you will be a credit to the good sisters, I know—"

"I will try."

"—and there is no one I would rather have by my side in the infirmary. You are a true comfort to the sick."

She opened her mouth to thank him, but he silenced her with a shake of his head.

"If this is truly what you want, my child, you shall have it. But I must ask you to do one thing."

"Of course," she said.

"I want you to take three months. The rest of the summer. I must ask you to think about this further, to pray for guidance. If at the end of that time you still wish to take the veil, we will proceed."

Rosalie stared at him in stunned surprise. "You doubt my conviction?"

"Not your conviction, Rosalie," he said softly. He leaned forward with a quiet smile and laid his palm against her cheek; she felt the warm roughness of his skin. "Just your reasons."

"But *mon père*—"

"Three months," he said. "You will thank me for this, Rosalie, my child, I promise it. If this is truly what you want, it is only a moment in a lifetime." His knees creaked as he got to his feet and stepped away. She watched him go.

Only a moment in a lifetime. Yes, it was that. Only a moment. But she did not want to wait. The thought of waiting made her feel a little desperate, unsure. As if her decision could somehow be taken from her . . .

But that was ridiculous, wasn't it? She had prayed for this, she had spent years considering it. It would not disappear in only a few months' time. She would do as Father Bara suggested. She would use these three months to strengthen her conviction, to prove to the priest, to her father, that this was indeed her calling, that it was the voice in her heart. They could not refuse her then. They could not turn her away. In three months she would have peace at last.

It seemed an eternity.

❧ Chapter 2

It was late in the afternoon, the sky darkening both with twilight and an approaching storm, when Jackson Waters stepped out of the Lafon carriage and onto a street he hadn't seen or thought about for three years.

"You got luggage, *monsieur?*"

Jack glanced back at the young Negro Garland Lafon had sent for him and shook his head. He held up a flimsy drawstring bag. "I've got everything," he said.

The man—Robert, he remembered suddenly—looked disconcerted for a moment, but then he nodded and climbed down from the seat. "You'd best go in there," he said, nodding to the front door. "They be expecting you."

Jack said nothing. He waited, listening to the doors of the porte cochere groan and wheeze as Robert pulled them open, hearing the slow rhythmic *clop clop* of the horses and the creaking carriage wheels as they disappeared into the carriageway.

Jack stared at the house in front of him and wondered again how this had happened; how had he come to be standing here in front of Garland Lafon's house on St. Louis Street? It seemed too sudden, unreal. He'd walked by this house probably hundreds of times without paying much attention to it. Who would have thought that one day it would be his future?

He gripped the bag in his hand, smelling the mildew of his clothes, the sharp tang of his own sweat. It was certainly not how he would have imagined his arrival at a home like this. But then, he would never have believed he would be invited, either.

Jack had known little of Garland Lafon except what the old man had told him, but somehow the words "I am a very rich man" had not prepared him for this house. It was one of the larger homes in the Vieux Carré, and though Creole, it spoke of Lafon's American preferences, with its obvious center hall and front doors recessed behind elaborate arches and Ionic columns. French doors lined the upper gallery, and the lower story had double-hung windows with shutters that gleamed green against plastered brick painted a soft pink.

It was the kind of house whose doors Jack had expected to be closed to him now, and the sight of it made him break out in a sweat. He took a deep breath. It was time. He'd promised to be here by seven, and it must be close to that now. He walked to the porch and climbed the four flat steps to the front door.

It opened before he even reached it, wide open, so Jack could see past the servant standing there to the back of the house, where doors opened onto a green and shadowy courtyard.

"*Monsieur*." The servant smiled; her teeth flashed, and her dark eyes swept over Jack in idle curiosity. "He been expecting you."

She stepped back to let him by, then closed the door behind him, enveloping him in the dark cool of the foyer. The house was in summer dress; the gilt mirrors lining the hall were cast in mosquito netting to protect them from flyspecks, the floor covered with matting, the paintings draped, but Jack had the sudden and lasting impression of expensive furniture, gleaming trims and rich woods, the smells of beeswax and citronella.

"The master's in here, *monsieur,*" she said, leading him down the hall with crisp efficiency. She paused at a doorway. "Monsieur Waters," she announced.

Jack's stomach knotted. He licked his lips and stepped forward, then let out a long, slow breath. "Mr. Lafon," he said.

Garland Lafon smiled and his face broke into a thousand wrinkles as he shook his head. "*Non, non,* Jack, you must call me Garland, eh? We do not stand on formality here, not now." He came forward, taking Jack's hand. "What is your preference, *mon ami?* Bourbon, perhaps? Brandy?"

The warm greeting relaxed Jack only slightly. "Bourbon," he managed. When Garland went to pour drinks, Jack set his bag down behind a chair, shoving it out of the way with his boot. He sat on the edge of the seat, sliding a little on the hard horsehair.

Garland turned, a glass in each hand. "*Non, non,*" he said, shaking his head. "Not there by the door. Come, come, over here, where I can show you off." He motioned to one of the chairs flanking an elaborate marble fireplace, and obediently Jack rose and sat

where the old man wanted him to. Garland handed
him a drink and sat in the chair opposite with a heavy
sigh.

"I thought perhaps she would be waiting with
you," Jack said.

Garland chuckled. "All in good time. It is not good
to be so impatient when it comes to women, Jack.
Patience is a virtue, eh?"

Jack tensed again. It made him uncomfortable
that she wasn't here. He wondered why—he wondered if Garland had given her a choice, if she were
angry, if she were happy. He wanted to know exactly
what he had to cope with.

"She will be here soon enough. I have said that I
have an announcement to make at dinner."

Jack started. "You mean . . . you haven't told her?"

"There is a time for everything, Jack." Garland
smiled, but the look in his eyes was measuring. "It is
something to remember—a key to success."

Jack nodded warily. He was nervous again—or,
more accurately, because he had not stopped being
nervous since Garland Lafon had left him in an
American coffeehouse that morning, he felt it more
intensely.

But Lafon seemed relaxed, and so Jack tried to do
the same.

"It is good to have an American in my`house,"
Garland said, taking a large sip of his drink. "I confess
I tire of my compatriots. Tell me, *mon ami*, have you
ever thought to wear pink stockings?"

Jack swirled the bourbon in his glass. The scent of

the liquor filled his nose, raising a longing so deep inside him it was all he could do to keep from downing it in one gulp. He took a small sip; the taste burst to life on his tongue. He wanted to close his eyes against it—he had forgotten the taste, it had been so long—but instead he turned to Garland and shook his head. "Pink isn't my color."

Garland laughed, almost a snort. "Pink stockings . . . My daughter has some strange ideas—"

"Which daughter are you talking about, Papa?" came a voice from the doorway. It was light but strong, and there was a question in the expression of the woman who came into the parlor, a smile in her dark eyes.

Jack rose so quickly he nearly spilled his drink, and she looked at him with curiosity and surprise before she threw her father a questioning glance.

"Rosa," said Garland, "this is Jackson Waters. Jack, my elder daughter, Rosalie."

Rosalie. Jack tensed; for a moment his disappointment was so crushing he could barely manage a courteous nod. She looked to be exactly what he'd been hoping she was not: a society spinster who spent every spare moment martyring herself to good works and religion. Rosalie Lafon had clean features, a strong face, a nicely accented jaw, but whatever claim to attractiveness she held was countered by the stern chignon of her dark blond hair, the severity of the pale gray gown she wore. A rosary hung from the chatelaine she wore at her hip, the crucifix dangling against her skirt as she came forward.

She was exactly the kind of woman who would disapprove of him, he knew. When he saw her gaze scan him, his gut tightened. He knew what she was seeing: his too-small, out-of-fashion coat and his shaggy hair. She could probably even smell him. He waited for the distaste to come into her face, for the patronizing courtesy that barely veiled outright rudeness.

But neither of those things happened. Her gaze stayed open and a little curious; she came forward and offered her hand. "Monsieur Waters. You are a friend of my father's?"

"In a manner of speaking." He glanced at Garland, waiting for the old man to explain. But Lafon shook his head slightly, so Jack took her hand; the quick clutch of her fingers was soft but strong. There was still time for her to dismiss him—she was close enough now to really smell him. He waited for it.

"How intriguing," she said. "Papa, such a mystery."

Garland smiled indulgently. "I meant to warn you, *ma petite*," he said. "But this was unexpected. Monsieur Waters is to be our houseguest for the next few months."

If the news distressed her, she didn't show it. "I'll have a room in the *garçonnière* made up."

"Mattie's taking care of it already," Garland said. He took another sip of his drink and then motioned for them both to sit. "You make me feel old, the two of you, standing that way, eh?"

Jack sat, and she took a seat across from him,

smoothing her skirts, sitting with a comfortable elegance. Her hand strayed to the rosary; she drew the beads through her fingers with the nonchalance of an old and familiar habit. "We'll try to make you comfortable, *monsieur*," she said with a smile.

The smile, her kindness, disconcerted him. It seemed out of place; it was not what he expected. Even when he'd accompanied his highly respectable uncle, Creole women had never deigned to notice him. He was an American, after all, and in trade, and he was not acceptable. He expected that reaction from her. He expected more than that, given his appearance. But she was doing her best to make him feel comfortable, and it surprised and confused him. He was on edge, waiting for her to become what he expected, waiting for her sneer.

"I'll try not to inconvenience you, Miss Lafon," he said stiffly.

Her smile widened. "But of course you must inconvenience me," she said. "I should think I'm not being a proper hostess otherwise."

"My house is at your disposal," Garland put in. He rose and went over to the liquor decanters, pouring more bourbon into his glass before he refilled Jack's. "I expect you to use it as you will, Jack, *oui?* Rosa, you will see to everything he needs."

"Of course, Papa," she said. "Monsieur Waters, are you one of Papa's business associates?"

Jack took a sip of his bourbon. "I guess you could say that."

"Jack and I have just entered into an agreement,"

Garland said with a chuckle. He lifted his glass. "To the future!"

Jack followed suit. He saw the puzzlement in Rosalie's eyes, but it faded quickly, and her composure never wavered. That was it, Jack thought suddenly. Garland did business with many Americans, and no doubt Rosalie Lafon was used to catering to them. But such a smile, such warmth . . . She was an asset Garland was right to be proud of. She made Jack feel as if he belonged here, as if she were glad to see him, as if her whole existence depended on pleasing him.

He'd never known anything like it. Not with any of his uncle's business partners, not even in his uncle's house. It gave him hope—perhaps she would not be so disappointing after all. But he told himself to be careful; she didn't yet know who he was.

Then her dark eyes turned to him, liquid kindness and approval, and he went warm with a strange, formless longing. There was something in her he liked—it was more than he'd anticipated, given how Garland had described her.

"The future," she said quietly, smiling. "Well, then, this is a celebration?"

"It is too hot to breathe," came a voice from the doorway. "I sincerely hope—oh, *pardon*."

Jack turned to see another woman step into the room. She was dressed in pale green that accented her blond hair, fine skin, and dark eyes. She stopped short, staring at him in surprise and curiosity.

She was one of the most beautiful women he had ever seen. He forgot Rosalie Lafon completely.

"Ah, Corinne," Garland said, rising. "Jack, this is my other daughter, Corinne. Corinne, this is Jack Waters."

Jack rose when she came forward. She extended her hand, and the tips of her fingers caressed his palm when he took it. "Monsieur Waters," she said in a smooth, melodic voice. She smiled so blindingly it hurt his eyes. "It is very good to meet you."

She let her hand linger, let her gaze stay on his face for several moments before she pulled away and took a step back. It left him slightly stunned, and hungry. It had been a long time since he'd allowed himself to think of women, but when he looked at Corinne Lafon and breathed deeply of her rose fragrance, he itched to touch her, to run his fingers through her fine, gleaming hair, over her mouth, her cheekbones. He followed her with his eyes as she moved to the window and looked out on the purple twilight. He drank her in until he noticed the silence.

He took a quick sip of bourbon. Garland clapped him on the back, nearly causing him to choke.

Garland laughed. He set aside his bourbon. "Corinne, come away from the window. Converse with our guest."

Corinne turned. "It's going to storm."

"Yes, well, let us hope it does not drench the color from poor Reynaud's vest." Garland laughed again. He bent close to Jack and whispered in his ear, "The pink stockings."

It took Jack a minute to make the connection—Corinne's latest love interest. Yes, Garland had told him about that, among other things. He saw her face darken prettily as she came away from the window.

Garland smiled. "Come, come, missy, you know it was for the best, *oui?*"

"I would prefer not to discuss it," Corinne said tightly.

"Corinne!" Rosalie's scold was gentle, and the look she turned to Jack was apologetic. "Corinne has just had a terrible disappointment, you see."

Corinne laughed lightly. When Jack looked at her, she smiled at him. "Why, *monsieur,* surely you cannot want to hear about my 'disappointment.'" Her eyes sparkled, and he read her flirtation in the way she tilted her head. "And perhaps there is a reason for everything, don't you agree?"

"God has a plan for us all," Rosalie said serenely.

Corinne did not look away. "Why, Rosa, I am beginning to think perhaps He does." She gave Jack a smile that speared him neatly to the chair. "What do you think, Monsieur Waters?"

Garland snorted. Jack tore his gaze away from Corinne to look back at the old man, who threw him a warning glance. Garland lumbered to his feet. "Enough foolish talk," he said sternly. His large hand clasped Jack's shoulder, pulled him tightly into his side. "Come, let us go in to dinner. As I have said, I have an announcement to make."

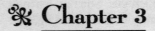

❧ Chapter 3

T he dining room was no cooler than the parlor, though the French doors were open onto the courtyard. Sunsets were so fleeting in New Orleans—here, then gone—and the purple twilight had already given way to approaching night. Even the darkness brought no relief from the heat. In the distance, thunder roared.

Rosalie shuddered involuntarily at the sound. She did not like storms. She did not even like remembering that once she had, that there had been a time when she and Corinne had run down the gallery stairs to stand in the middle of the rain and the wind, letting it wash over them and sting them and pinken their skin, laughing at the servants who shook their heads and predicted, "The two of them will come to a bad end, that's for sure. Two foolish girls, *n'est-ce pas?*" while Papa chuckled and Maman shouted for them to come out of the rain.

The rain had felt good then, warm and clean, and the thunder had cleared her head. The slapping of the trees against the side of the house and the gallery railings had sounded like a hundred laughing spirits, and she had felt free, as if the world and everything in it waited for her.

Rosalie shivered. It had been a long time ago, and

she was no longer such a foolish girl. She had learned how treacherous those laughing voices could be, and now storms made her uncomfortable and nervous— something she could not afford to be, not today, with Papa's mysterious business partner sitting across the table from her—and an important partner, too, she guessed, given the way Papa was treating him.

But that was another unsettling thing, and the past few weeks had been unsettling enough. Only last night her announcement that she was joining the Ursulines had made Papa so angry, she'd thought he would end up back in his sickbed. He had never been the kind of man who calmed easily. She would have thought he would still be furious with her, but he was smiling and talking to her as if there had been no dis-agreement between them. It wasn't like him. It made her as nervous as the impending storm. He had not told her he was expecting a houseguest—certainly not one staying for an extended time—and that was odd. He hadn't told her of any special announcement, either, and that was also surprising. He was hiding something, she was sure.

It had something to do with the man sitting across from her. The moment she'd entered the par-lor to see him sitting there, with his fierce blue eyes and his smile and his handsome face, she'd known her father was up to something. Jackson Waters looked to be a man who'd had some hard times. His coat was too small and frayed at the edges, and his hair needed trimming, but still, she'd been jolted by the sight of him. His smile had caused a sinking feeling in her stomach, a heat that was too familiar and wholly unwelcome after all this time. Because as handsome as he was, as warmly unexpected as his smile was, there was something else there, too, a hunger she recognized. It was no wonder he and Papa had entered into some kind of agreement. Papa liked desperate men.

But he had never involved his family with those men, and to bring such a young, handsome one here as an extended houseguest, and declare that he had an announcement—

"Crawfish vol-au-vent," Papa said with a smile as Mattie brought the first course. He broke a serving spoon through the pastry, collapsing it, and took a deep breath. "Ah, there is nothing sweeter than a summer crawfish, eh, Jack? I like them plain. Too much sauce here—one cannot reach in and suck their heads."

"It is not so messy this way," Rosalie said.

"Oh, a breeze." Corinne fanned herself delicately, looking toward the French doors. The netting draping the windows had not stirred. "I'm sure I felt a breeze. Oh, where is that storm?"

Jack Waters spooned the crawfish stew onto his plate. "It's coming. I can smell it."

Rosalie gave him a puzzled look. "You can smell what?"

Corinne leaned forward eagerly. "Oh, don't mind Rosa, *monsieur*, there is no poetry in her soul. But me, I love that smell—all that green, and the flowers and the wet flagstones—"

It was hardly a criticism. Rosalie would have described herself in much the same way. Strangely, though, tonight Corinne's words, coupled with Jack Waters's curious glance, made Rosalie feel . . . lacking.

She pressed her lips together, irritated with herself. The day had left her feeling sensitive and alone. First Papa, then Father Bara . . . It was the only reason her sister's comment bothered her. Nothing Corinne said ever really mattered.

"You see if you're so happy about the storm tomorrow, missy," Papa said, "when that mud ruins one more gown."

"I love storms," Corinne said, ignoring Papa, smiling at Jack Waters. "Why, sometimes I'll stand out in one and let it drench me to the skin. It makes me feel alive. Do you know what I mean, Monsieur Waters?"

There was an intensity in Corinne's eyes that added vibrancy to her entire bearing, that made her sparkle, and Rosalie knew without looking what expression Jack Waters wore. She'd seen it on a hundred men, that stunned, enraptured look. Rosalie imagined it was how sailors looked as the Sirens lured them to their death, and she'd never understood just how Corinne did it, whether it was deliberate or if it was simply how she was.

An hour ago Corinne had been whining over Reynaud Broutin, and now he was forgotten, replaced by another handsome face, a charming smile. Another suitor, so easily captured; it exhausted Rosalie to think of it, to have to go through one of Corinne's romances again. She knew each step: Corinne's growing interest, her questions, the late-night visits to Rosalie's room: *"What do you think of him, Rosa? Do you think he cares for me?"* There would be a few weeks of flirtation, and then Papa's refusal, and it would start all over again.

The vol-au-vent pooled untouched on Rosalie's plate. She put aside her fork and reached for her wine. She glanced at Jack Waters just as he took a bite, and found herself caught by the look on his face, a look of pure . . . what was it? Revulsion? No, not that. More like . . . like joy. Yes, she decided. He was savoring each bite of crawfish as if it were his last.

It fascinated her in a morbid sort of way. It made him oddly vulnerable, and she felt the sudden urge to be kind to him.

She smiled at him, her gracious smile. "So you're a bachelor, Monsieur Waters?" she asked.

Papa laughed. He pointed his fork at Waters. "Rosalie, she is a smart one, *oui?* You must watch her every minute, Jack, that she does not get the best of you."

Jack Waters caught her glance, and she saw immediately that she'd made him uncomfortable. "Oh, *pardon*," she said. "It is too personal a thing to ask—"

"No," he said. "I'm not married."

"It's just that . . . I assumed you had no chef. You enjoy the food the way a bachelor does."

"Yes. It's very good."

"Jack has not been eating well, eh, *mon ami?*" Garland chuckled. "We will change that, not to worry. A few meals and you'll be fat as an old man. Our cook, he is a French master, *n'est-ce pas*, Rosa? What is his name?"

"Monsieur LaFleur," she said. She gave Jack Waters an apologetic smile. "He has not told us his given name, you understand. He is from Paris. But I would call him whatever he wishes to keep him here."

"If he lasts through Papa, it will be a miracle," Corinne said, gently teasing. "Yesterday it was the sauce on the fish, Monday the red beans were too salty—"

"My palate is too discriminating," Papa said pointedly. "Perhaps you should develop one of your own, eh, missy?"

Corinne sighed. She leaned forward, her breasts thrusting against the soft green of her gown, and her smile to Jack was small and apologetic; it held a you-see-what-I-must-cope-with intimacy.

Rosalie glanced at their guest. That look was on his face again; he was well and truly captured. She felt a sharp little pain that pierced her heart and stayed there like a sliver, working deeper. Her hand went back to the soothing beads of her rosary.

Papa cleared his throat. He wiped his lips delicately with his napkin and glanced around the table. "I said earlier that I have an announcement. Perhaps now would be the time to make it."

"Oh, yes, do," Corinne said. She put down her fork and fanned herself again. "It's too hot to eat. And hurry, Papa. I am expiring from the heat. Perhaps later you would walk in the courtyard with me, Monsieur Waters?"

"Jack has other plans tonight," Papa said.

"Well, then, after that, if it is not too late—"

"It will be too late, Corinne."

Papa's voice was stern and chastising. Rosalie saw her sister flush. "I'm sure Monsieur Waters doesn't wish to sit here and listen to us argue," she said soothingly. "Papa, your announcement?"

Her father looked momentarily distracted; then he smiled and sat back in his chair. "Ah, yes, my announcement. As I was saying, I think you will be pleased."

He laughed, and Rosalie went cold. She didn't like the look in her father's eyes, and she didn't like his voice. She knew him too well; she would not like his announcement today. "What is it, Papa?" she asked slowly.

His smile widened. "I have been looking for someone to lead my family into the future. After all, I am old, *oui*? God will not be content to have me live forever, however much I wish it.

"But I can make my peace with that now. Today I went to Jack Waters with a proposition, and he has accepted."

Corinne straightened. "What sort of a proposition?"

Papa looked away from her. He looked at Rosalie, and the chill inside her grew; she could not even breathe as he smiled at her. "Rosalie, I would like you to meet your fiancé."

For a moment she thought the storm had started. There was thunder in her ears. It was so loud she could hear nothing else. But then he spoke again, and she realized the storm was not there at all, that it was just the pounding of her own heart.

"Come, Rosa, you do not smile, you do not laugh. You will make Jack think you are not happy with this arrangement."

Corinne was frozen, her fork suspended in midair. "Not . . . Monsieur Waters?"

"Who else?" Papa laughed. "Come, *ma petite,* say something."

Rosalie looked at Jack Waters. He sat there calmly, taking in their reactions with a pale-eyed gaze that gave nothing away, and it was that calm that gave her back her voice, that melted her shock into a horror so overwhelming she could not keep it from her voice as she confronted her father. "You can't mean this."

His expression was chilly. "But I do mean it, Rosa." Though his smile was still in place, there was a hardness in his voice Rosalie recognized.

"This is not for you to decide," she told him.

"Who then, if not your father?"

"God!" Rosalie could not help herself; she was shaking as she rose. "I have promised myself to Him—"

"I am unpromising you," Papa said.

"Papa, please . . . you don't understand."

"I understand too well." Her father's eyes were blazing. "*Mon Dieu,* as long as I have life left in this body, I will not let you waste yours."

Rosalie's legs were so weak, she had to brace her hands on the table. "Papa, surely you must see how ridiculous this is—"

"You are embarrassing me in front of our guest, Rosalie," he said softly.

"You cannot mean this. I don't even know this man."

"An easy thing to remedy, *oui?*" Papa shrugged. "I need an heir, you need a husband. In Jack we have everything."

Rosalie felt sick. "You have made him your heir? Oh, Papa. You have been ill, you are not thinking clearly—"

"Rosalie!"

"You cannot mean this. You cannot mean to buy me a husband."

Papa went still. "You misstep, Rosalie. This is still my house. I will not allow you to offend my guests."

Rosalie turned to Jack Waters, whose expression was as implacable as ever. "*Pardon,*" she said stiffly. "I do not mean to offend you, *monsieur,* but I plan to spend the rest of my life in God's service. My father knows this. He has known it since yesterday."

"Really, Rosa?" Corinne asked. "You have decided, then?"

Papa frowned at Corinne. "Quiet yourself. This has nothing to do with you."

Deliberately Rosalie turned to her sister. "*Oui.* I decided yesterday. I talked to Father Bara this morning."

"And I will talk to him tomorrow morning and tell him you are to be married like a good Creole girl."

It took all Rosalie's strength to meet her father's gaze. "You will have to drag me to the altar, Papa," she said. "And even then the only vow I will take will be to the Lord."

Papa didn't waver. "You are my daughter, and you will do as I tell you." Then he looked at Waters, and his smile was tight. "You see, Jack? It is as I have told you. You will have your hands full with this one."

Rosalie felt his dismissal like a slap. She watched her father pick up his wineglass and take a sip, and the tension of the moment grew and spread.

"Well." Corinne sighed. When Rosalie glanced at her sister, Corinne was picking up her own glass with a thin smile. She turned to Waters. "Welcome to the family, Monsieur Waters."

He smiled back at her, and with that smile a sudden wind gusted through the French doors, filling the netting that took the place of drapes. Outside, the leaves of the banana tree rustled and snapped. The storm hit. The rush of sudden raindrops came fat and heavy on the wind, and Papa laughed. "The storm is here, eh? It is like God's smile."

Rosalie could stand it no longer. "*Pardon*," she muttered. She raced from the table so quickly she knocked over a wineglass. She heard the shatter of glass and Corinne's gasp, but Rosalie didn't look back. She hurried to the sanctuary of her room, to peace, to prayers, but her hand trembled as she lit the votive candles, and her breath extinguished the light that had been dancing on the plaster casts of Saint Mary Magdalene and Saint Catherine. In the heavy darkness she felt the trap of her father's will closing around her; she felt the lure of Jack Waters's smile clear into her bones. Her instincts were right. Jack Waters was a dangerous man.

Jack stood just inside the door of his room. It was above the kitchen, on the second floor of the service wing, at a right angle to the main house—the *garçonnière,* or bachelor's quarters. It opened onto a shared gallery overlooking the courtyard, and just outside there was a broad-leafed banana tree shaking in the storm.

The room had been used chiefly for storage; even now, trunks filled the empty spaces, and the furniture was spare and utilitarian: a simple armoire, a narrow bed, a washstand. He had few enough things of his own to fill it, so none of that mattered to him. Jack laid his bag on the bed, where it sank and rumpled, a dingy gray spot against the blindingly white coverlet.

This room was small, but in three years he'd never been alone in a space this big. When he sat on the edge of the bed, it sprang and crunched beneath his weight. The mattress was stuffed with Spanish moss, a luxury he'd forgotten. He imagined crawling naked between clean, cool linen sheets, imagined the feel of them against his skin, crisp and stiff, the fragrance of perfumed lye soap, maybe rose—Corinne's scent—and that brought to mind Corinne lying beside him, pressed against him, her breasts and her softness and her hair in sharp contrast to the sheets, the hot rose smell of her . . .

No, not Corinne. Jack pushed the image away and

thought instead of this morning, when Garland Lafon had waylaid him in the coffeehouse near his uncle's cotton brokerage to propose this deal. He thought of the old man leaning across the table, giving him back the future Jack had gambled away three years ago.

Yesterday, when he'd stepped from the gates of Parish Prison, it had seemed a bleak future indeed. His aunt and uncle were not there to greet him, and he had not supposed they would be. In the three years he'd been in prison, he'd never received a visit, not even a letter. He told himself he understood. Some things were hard to forgive.

But he had gone to his uncle's office anyway—he had no real choice, there was no place else to go. Perhaps things had changed over the last years; perhaps Uncle Charles might be willing to give him another chance.

But all Jack got for his efforts was a "What makes you think you're welcome here, Jackson?" and a reminder that he was not—had never been—a worthy heir to the Waters fortune. "I won't give you a single thing, do you understand me? I'm not putting a penny into your worthless hands."

Lafon's proposal had seemed a gift from heaven. It still seemed like a dream, not quite real. This morning he'd been an ex-convict with no future, and now . . . now he was Garland Lafon's heir, he had riches at his disposal, the chance finally to work toward the dreams he'd buried all these years. If this kept up, perhaps he would start actually believing in God.

Jack laughed lightly to himself. Unfortunately,

nothing in life was free. He'd known when he came here today that the price he was paying was a hard one: marrying a woman he'd never seen, a woman who was on the verge of consecrating herself to God. He'd been prepared; nothing about Rosalie Lafon had surprised him.

Almost nothing.

Jack rose from the bed and went to the closed doors, pushing aside the limply hanging muslin to stare out at the storm. It was raging beyond the doors, the wind whipping the trees, the rain heavy and dark. He thought of what Corinne had said at dinner, about standing in the storm, drenching herself to the skin. His mouth went dry.

He forced himself to recall Garland's caveat: "I would not have Rosa marry someone who would not care for her. Do we understand each other, Jack? If you want my fortune, you must make her happy. I will settle for nothing less."

Jack had agreed readily—he'd never known a woman he couldn't charm, and as devout as Rosalie Lafon was, he was sure he could charm her, too. He would have agreed to charm a toothless hag for the fortune Lafon promised him.

But he'd had no idea then that Lafon's other daughter was like Corinne, and even if he had known it, he would never have believed she could make him this . . . hungry.

It had been three years, he reminded himself. Perhaps longer; it was hard to remember. A quick, surreptitious visit to the levee, a few coins to one of the women there, and this problem would be solved. Corinne Lafon would not be a threat.

He shrugged out of his frock coat and pulled off his vest, unfastening his shirt so he could breathe again. Damn, he was hot. He pulled off his boots and walked onto the gallery barefoot, his shirt blowing back from his chest, the air soft against his skin. The door slammed shut behind him, but he barely noticed. He lifted his head to the drenching rain, felt the soft, heavy drops on his skin and his lips, tasted them. His shirt was plastered to his shoulders. The rain was warm, the wind without bite. The vines below his room scattered and dropped bruised, drenched petals, and their fragrance was soft and subtle, mixing with the scent of green and the clean wash of flagstones, taking away his prison stench.

He closed his eyes and stood there, imprinting the night on his mind. Never before had he understood what freedom truly felt like. It was this, this sense of living, this knowledge that the future was his and it was a good one, with opportunities enough to fill his hungry soul. Everything he had ever wanted—

Laughter carried on the wind. He opened his eyes and saw Corinne. She was across the courtyard, on the upper gallery of the main house, with the halo of her bedroom light behind her, the mosquito netting of her curtains blowing from the open French doors. He was hidden in darkness, he knew, and so he felt safe watching her, watching her spread her arms and fling back her head. He saw her loose blond hair, a heavy shadow down her back. She was dancing and laughing, twirling in the storm along the gallery railing, and her thin, wet nightgown clung to her body. He could not see the pinkness of her skin, but he saw the outline of her lush breasts bouncing with her movements, the swing of her hips, and he stood there in the rain and watched her and hungered for her until his senses were so sharp with want that he tasted the smell of her on the wind, felt the hard press of need, imagined the warm wetness of her skin beneath his hands.

His senses were on fire; he saw the rush of rain in the darkness, the movement of shadows. He heard the soft click of a door, and Jack jerked his gaze from Corinne to another room, a room farther down, at the end of the house.

He saw which door it had been immediately, saw the soft sway of mosquito netting, the tender glow of light shimmering across a shadow drawn back and huddled against the edge of the door. Rosalie. Watching the storm. Watching her sister. And he found himself remembering her early kindness, her warmth, and then how her face had tightened with disapproval and anger when she found out who he was, what he meant to her. The memory disappointed him in a way he couldn't explain.

She drew back from the door. A light went out, darkening the French doors, and she was gone. He wondered if she heard the storm whispering, if she ever paid attention. *Rosalie. Rosalie, come out to play. . . .*

No, he decided. She had not even known there was perfume in the rain.

❦ Chapter 4

Rosalie hardly slept. When dawn broke, she was already awake, kneeling at the altar in her room, murmuring prayers and lighting candles. She'd spent the night praying for guidance, for wisdom, but she was no nearer to those things now than at the start.

She sat back on her heels, sighing as she blew out the candles, and watched the faint smoke curl against the blue satin draping her altar. Throughout the night, Father Bara's questions had not left her. *Can you be happy without a husband, children? Can you be happy as a bride of Christ?*

She had a husband staring her in the face now, and Rosalie clung to her plans for the future more tightly than ever. Throughout the night she'd tried to comfort herself with the reminder that this was only one of God's trials. Father Bara had told her He would test her; she just had not expected it so soon. And she had not expected a test like Jack Waters.

Rosalie took a deep breath and rose. Last night she had been too angry to reason with her father; today she would make him understand that marriage to Jack Waters—or anyone else—was out of the question.

The morning held a tentative coolness that would be gone within the hour, when the heat of the day made its way through the mimosa and sweet olive. Rosalie stepped onto the gallery and looked down at the courtyard, at the scattered, rain-drenched flowers wilting on the flagstones. The air felt good on her face, refreshing, a little damp, God's kiss. She raised her face to it, and her gaze went to the service wing, to the still silent *garçonnière*. Her panic from last night came back, withering her pleasure in the morning. Deliberately Rosalie turned away, hurrying down the gallery stairs to her father's office.

He was there already, as she'd known he would be. Even illness had not kept her father from his work. When she stepped through the door, he looked up with a frown.

He looked old this morning. His white hair was coarse and dull, and there was a fine sweat on his skin in spite of the coolness of the morning. He seemed feeble and pale, and she had the sudden, sickening thought that he wouldn't live much longer.

It shocked her. For a moment she foundered, she forgot why she'd come here, what she had to say. But then his frown melted into a smile, and it changed his face, that familiar smile, those familiar wrinkles, the twinkle in his eyes. No, he was not that ill; there was nothing to worry about. . . .

"Rosa!" he said, and then he hesitated and gave her a sheepish smile. "You are not still angry with me, *ma petite?*"

She was used to smiling at him. It took effort not to. "I am furious with you, Papa."

"Ah, as I thought." He sighed and leaned back in

his chair. "You have not changed your mind during the night, I see."

"*Non.*"

"I do not like to insist when it comes to you, *chérie,* you know this."

"Then don't insist," she said. She crossed her arms over her chest. "You should have talked to me about this first, Papa. I would have told you my mind was quite made up. We could have saved the embarrassment of last night."

"Hmmm." Papa regarded her intently. He motioned her to a chair. When Rosalie sat, he said, "You do not find him attractive in the least, then?"

"Papa, that is not—"

"Answer my question, Rosa. Does he repulse you?"

The question needled. Rosalie sighed in exasperation. "He's attractive enough, I suppose, but—"

"And smart. He is a clever boy. He has little experience with banks, but I can teach him. Who knows, he may even turn out to be a genius."

"Papa—"

"He has had an unfortunate adolescence, of course. But I am convinced that his wastrel days are behind him. A little responsibility will do him good—"

"Papa!"

Her father stared at her in surprise.

"I am not marrying him," Rosalie said.

"You dislike my choice this much?"

"I would dislike any choice, and you know this. I told you what I intended. Why can you not believe that marriage is not what I want?"

He was quiet for a moment. His gaze was searching, a little uncomfortable. "I want to see you happy, *ma petite*."

"I have told you what would make me happy."

"A cloistered life? A life of prayers and nuns? Now this I cannot believe."

"You should believe it, Papa. It is what I want."

"Why, Rosa?" He spoke the words in a whisper, and the question was all the more disturbing for its quietness.

"Does it matter?" Rosalie's voice was sharper than she'd intended.

Her father lifted a brow. "Those who join the church do so out of love for God. Why is it I do not think that is your reason, *chérie*?" His gaze was unsettling, too knowing, too wise. "Rosa, look at me. I am an old man."

"Not so old. Dr. Wiley believes—"

"That fool. He would say whatever he thinks I want to hear. But I know this, Rosa." He thumped his chest with his fingers. "I feel this heart fading, eh? I feel the skipped beats. I am not long for this world."

"You mustn't say such things."

"It is the truth. You know this, too. And I will tell you something, *chérie*. I am not afraid to die. I have lived a good life. Your *maman* waits for me in heaven. But I worry. I have no heir. Who will take care of my fortune when I am gone?"

"If you are so concerned about it, marry Corinne to this Monsieur Waters."

He snorted. "You are cleverer than that, Rosa.

Think of this: If I marry Corinne to Jack, all those dollars will go merely to increase her wardrobe, instead of to any of the charities that could benefit from my money. Is that what you want? Eh?"

Rosalie shook her head. "*Non*, of course not. But—"

"And I will not choose Corinne's husband until you are safely wed, Rosa, you know this. I have made it plain before. But there is something else. Something I have not told you." He sighed and played with the heavy silver paperweight on his desk, rubbing his finger over the etching of the First Bank of New Orleans.

Dread started in Rosalie's chest. She could not bring herself to say a word.

Her father glanced up with a small smile. "Your *maman*. You remember her last days?"

"Of course, Papa."

"So much pain." He shook his head. "And she was worried too. Not for herself, but for you. For Corinne, too, but not so much. Corinne will always land on her feet, eh? But I tell you she was right to be worried. Even then you were so serious. Your catechism you knew, but you could not spare a glance for the boys in church."

"I was thirteen, Papa."

"Old enough to be interested, *chérie*. Your *maman*, she said to me: 'Do not let Rosa turn so much to God. She thinks He will make her happy, but I know her. She needs a husband. She needs children.' I vowed to her that I would see you had those things."

"Papa—"

He held up a hand to stop her. "I have been selfish these last years. With your *maman* gone . . . well, I admit I have not always thought of you. You have made things easy for me, serving as my hostess, running my house. I did not want to lose you. But now, Rosa, I am thinking of you. I am fulfilling the promise I made to your *maman*."

"I am not thirteen any longer, Papa. I have had time to understand my own mind. I know what I want."

His gaze was so sharp it seemed to go right through her. "Do you, *chérie?* Do you really?"

"*Oui.*"

"It seems to me there was a time—"

"I was a child, and that was a mistake." Rosalie jerked to her feet. "I know you mean well, Papa, but you must believe me when I say I don't want to marry anyone. Not ever."

Papa's expression hardened. She had never seen that look on his face for her, and Rosalie's dread grew until she could taste it. Her father straightened in his chair. "I must insist, Rosalie. Trust me. You will thank me for this one day."

"I've heard those words before," she said tightly.

"And was I not right then, too? Eh, Rosa? Was I not right?"

Rosalie felt the blood drain from her face. "You can't do this, Papa."

"I can, and I will. You had best get used to it. We will plan the wedding for the fall. For the start of the season."

For the first time in her life Rosalie felt she might

faint. She stumbled back against the wall, hard enough that her elbow banged into it. The pain brought her back to herself. Her protests died in her throat. She looked at her father, at the stern expression on his face, an expression that until now she had seen on his face only for Corinne, and Rosalie knew he would not change his mind. No matter what she said, he would marry her to this man—and he would do it without her permission, if he had to.

There were other ways to handle this. Steadily, Rosalie regarded her father. "As you wish," she said quietly.

He looked stunned. Then slowly, as if doubting he'd heard correctly, he said, "*Bien. Bien.* You have always been a reasonable girl, Rosa." He paused. He fumbled again with the silver paperweight. "You will let him court you, *oui?*"

"What does it matter?"

"I would like you to be happy, *chérie,*" he said. "I think you will like Jack when you know him better."

Rosalie turned to go. "Is there anything else?"

"One thing," he said. "I would plan a *déjeuner de fiançailles,* but Jack is American, and his family will not understand a betrothal breakfast. It is more customary for them to hold an engagement ball."

Rosalie's throat tightened. "Not a ball, Papa." She barely managed the words.

He frowned. "You have agreed to this betrothal. Why should we not announce it?"

"Not a ball," she said again. The more people who knew, the more embarrassing it would be for her father later. "I would prefer nothing at all."

"Rosa—"

"A soirée, then," she said.

He said nothing for a moment. She felt his gaze on her face, measuring, watching. Then he sighed. "A soirée. *Oui*, that will do."

Relief made her weak; she was glad of the wall behind her. The office felt too close, the air suddenly too heavy to breathe. Rosalie excused herself and left her father so quickly, he could not have the chance to call her back. She could not breathe again until she stepped into the courtyard.

You will let him court you. . . .

Rosalie closed her eyes and took several deep breaths of the rapidly warming air. She had no intention of letting Jackson Waters court her. She had no intention of marrying him. But her father was set on it, and she did not have the power to change his mind. The only person who did was Jack Waters.

Rosalie glanced up at the *garçonnière*. It was quiet. Waters had not yet shown his face this morning. She looked at the closed door of the guest room and wondered about him. What kind of a man would agree to marry a woman he'd never seen? What kind of man would accept the offer her father had made?

An unscrupulous man. An opportunistic man. A man like her cousin Gaston, who would leave the woman he said he loved because he'd been paid enough to do so. . . .

Rosalie shook away the thought. No, she would not marry him. She would make this courtship so uncomfortable for him, he would withdraw. If Jack

Waters decided she was not worth marrying, certainly Papa would have no choice but to agree.

It should be easy enough to achieve. What man had ever wanted to marry a nun? Still, as Rosalie turned into the house and readied to leave for her morning rounds at the infirmary, she felt nervous and ill at ease. There was something about Jackson Waters that told her it would not be so simple after all . . . but she shook off that thought and told herself it was nothing—her own discomfort, nothing more.

But she knew deep inside that it was something more than that. Something even more threatening. Something harder to define. And though she remembered his pale blue gaze, his charm, and that seductive smile he'd sent in her sister's direction, there was something else Rosalie remembered, too: the burning want in his eyes, the steady desperation.

Yes, she remembered his desperation most of all.

It was late when Corinne stretched awake—nearly nine o'clock. The morning was her favorite time; she was usually awake soon after sunrise. But the heat this summer was draining, and she had felt tired and listless. Even last night's storm did nothing to invigorate her.

There was a coolness in the sunlight, the heady scent of roses beaten by the storm. But there was no promise in the morning. Papa's announcement that Jackson Waters was meant for Rosalie chimed through Corinne's head again. Resentment and envy gathered in a tight little knot near her heart. Her father's favoritism stung more than ever.

It was not that Corinne begrudged Rosalie happiness. She loved her sister and wanted her to be happy. But Rosalie did not want a husband, and Papa knew it. This declaration of his that Rosalie must be married first was absurd. Rosa didn't need a husband. She had God and Papa. Corinne had . . . Corinne had nothing. If he was so anxious to marry one of them off, why not choose her?

It had been two days since Papa had turned down Reynaud, and though Corinne did not miss him, she did miss the passion of being with him, the love she had fooled herself into thinking she felt. When she'd seen Jack Waters sitting across the table, she had thought, *I could love him,* and the possibility had been so . . . exciting. She had breathed in his charming smile and seen Papa's approval shining upon him, and in that moment Corinne had understood what it was she'd longed for all these years, what she had wished for.

A husband her father approved of. A courtship sanctioned by her family. It was something she'd never had, never even thought to wish for. Since she'd been old enough to have suitors, Corinne had tempted fate often. She had met with men alone and reveled in the forbidden freedom of it. She had let them kiss her and more—she flushed when she thought of her secret meetings with Reynaud. But now she was tired of the rebellion; there was no point, it would never win her father's love.

Suddenly the thought of a classic courtship seemed so intriguing. She imagined the mystery of discovering the man she was to marry beneath Papa's watchful eyes. How romantic it would be: lingering, smoldering looks across a crowded parlor, the subtle tension between herself and her lover as he whiled away the evenings playing cards with her father, the prick of her embroidery needle on her finger as she caught his eye. The traditions were so precious, and she wanted them all now. She wanted the big ruby engagement ring and the celebratory breakfast that brought two families together.

A real courtship . . . Corinne closed her eyes and thought of it. Of her father's smile, his gaze warm with approval. *Ah, Corinne, you are the daughter I always wished for. . . .*

The vision faded before her, scattering before she had a chance to grab on to it. Corinne opened her eyes, staring into the gathered yellow silk above her head. It was so unfair, Rosalie having what she didn't want, Corinne not having what she did . . .

The thought made her tired. It was all she could do to wash and dress. Corinne went downstairs and into the dining room. She saw her father's back and the gold of Jack's hair where the sunlight slanted across it. She paused in the doorway, and when Jack turned to see her, she felt her heart move into her throat, felt the pounding in her head like driving music. She was suddenly disoriented, dry-mouthed, *covetous*.

She stumbled as she came into the room. She could not help smiling at him as she made her way to the table. When Papa turned from his newspapers to grunt a good morning to her, his unenthusiastic greeting didn't hurt the way it usually did. She barely heard it.

"*Bonjour, monsieur,*" she said, pulling out the chair next to their houseguest.

He glanced at her father, who was buried again in his paper, and then he smiled at her. "Good morning, Miss Lafon," he said before he turned back to his breakfast, figs and cream cheese and corn muffins. Her stomach twisted in sudden nausea, and his disappointing silence took her appetite. She fought it; he was Rosalie's fiancé, she had no right to want him. But she couldn't help herself. She couldn't control her hunger for his talk, for his smile.

"Did you sleep well, *monsieur?*" she asked. "The *garçonnière* was to your liking?"

"Well enough," he said. His voice was quiet—like her father's, really; one had to strain to hear. He slanted her a glance.

"You must tell me if you have need of anything—"

"Stop chattering, Corinne. It is too early for such nonsense." Papa folded his paper and laid it neatly aside. "Jack, I have discussed with Rosa my plan for a soirée to announce your engagement. What about next Tuesday?"

Jack shrugged. "As you wish."

"That should give you some time to get to a tailor, *oui?* You look like a convict." Papa laughed shortly. "We cannot have that. Marceau et Fils in the Vieux Carré know my requirements. You will go to them."

"Of course," Jack said.

"I would have you make a good impression on my friends. Most of them cannot understand that the future of New Orleans lies with the Americans. They will be disapproving that I am marrying my daughter to an outsider. They may not take to you right away, *mon ami*."

"I cannot imagine why," Corinne said. She blushed when Papa frowned at her. "I mean, Monsieur Waters is—"

Papa turned away abruptly, dismissively, and Corinne's words broke into nothing. She swallowed tightly and reached for her napkin, spreading it on her lap carefully in an attempt to hide her embarrassment.

Papa took a sip of his café au lait, setting it aside as he rose. "Now I must go. Jack, amuse yourself while I am gone. Tell Rosa if you need anything."

"I won't let him be bored, Papa," Corinne said. She turned to Waters. "Perhaps we could walk in the courtyard—"

"You've better things to do, missy," Papa said sharply. "And so does Jack." He looked at Jack, frowning. "You should go to the tailor now. Tell him to put it on my account."

Corinne went hot, and she looked away quickly, feeling like a chastened child. Jack pushed back his chair. He was on his feet instantly, and she didn't look up at him, embarrassed and confused at Papa's tone. Then she felt Jack's touch—soft and reassuring—on her shoulder. She glanced up in surprise, but he was already turning, following Papa out the courtyard doors. He did not look back at her.

But she recognized the touch as one of comfort and sympathy, and his kindness nearly brought tears to her eyes. He was the man she'd always dreamed of, handsome, charming, compassionate, and the injustice of life weighed heavy on her heart. He was Rosalie's, she told herself. He was meant for her sister. But she could not silence the yearning that burned inside her as she watched him go. And she could not help wishing: *If only he weren't Rosalie's. If only . . .*

Chapter 5

It was late in the afternoon when Rosalie went to the courtyard. Corinne was taking a nap, and Rosalie would have done the same but for the fact that she couldn't close her eyes without thinking of her father's words, without wondering how best to make Jack Waters withdraw his suit.

So now she sat alone in the heat and stared unseeingly at the bright flowers in the parterre. Her mind was so occupied with Jack Waters that when she heard the heavy clunk of the porte cochere door and saw him striding into the courtyard, she was not surprised. It was almost as if her thoughts had leaped from her head to create him there before her.

Such a walk. So self-assured, so confident. He'd been here less than a day and already he seemed so at home, as if he belonged, as if he already owned the flagstones beneath his feet. *So familiar*—everything about him was so familiar.

Rosalie tensed. Suddenly she could not think of what to do or say. She wanted to run fast and far away, as far from him as she could—someplace where his smiles could not affect her, where his charm had no power. But she forced herself to remember her purpose. She was half hidden by overgrown greenery at the edge of the garden, but she knew just the moment he saw her: He straightened, his expression sharpened. He paused just a second and then came toward her.

Rosalie's heart went into panicked racing. It was all she could do to stay seated.

"Miss Lafon," he said smoothly, stopping before her. "Good afternoon."

He smiled, and her traitorous heart skipped a beat. She had not imagined yesterday how handsome he was, even in a too-small suit with his blond hair badly cut.

Rosalie swallowed. "*Monsieur*, won't you have some lemonade with me?"

His smile broadened. "Of course," he said, and sat on the bench next to hers. In his movement she caught his scent—a little spicy, shaving soap and sweat.

She felt stiff and uncomfortable. There was nothing but a small iron table between them, and she wished he were farther away. But she lifted the bell to ring for Lucy.

He'd been carrying a hat, and he laid it on the bench. The shiny beaver glinted in the sun. It was too fine a hat to wear during the day, too new.

"You've been shopping," she said.

He nodded. "Your father sent me to his tailor this morning. I've just returned from there."

"Marceau et Fils?"

"Yes."

"They're very good."

He nodded.

Rosalie lapsed into silence. She could not think of another thing to say except *Leave me alone. Tell my father you won't marry me.*

Lucy came hurrying from the kitchen then, pulling at her tignon, a little breathless. "*Pardon, mademoiselle.* You rang the bell?"

"Lemonade, Lucy. *Merci.*"

Lucy hurried away again.

Jack Waters picked up the beaver hat, turning it idly in his hands. "I didn't see you this morning at breakfast."

"I was out."

"So early?"

It was strange; she felt reluctant to tell him where she'd been. But that was absurd, wasn't it? It was best if he knew the true depth of her commitment. "I was at the infirmary," she said.

He raised a brow. "The infirmary?"

"I try to help out a few times a week," she explained. "Father Bara's . . . over on Toulouse."

She expected him to nod, to murmur some platitude about how good she was to give her time to charity—she had heard such words many times before. But he only looked at her, and there was a curiosity in his eyes that made her nervous.

"Why?" he asked finally.

Rosalie looked at him in confusion. "Why?"

"Why do you go to the infirmary? There was talk in town today of cholera. I assume it's come to—Father Bara's, you say?"

She nodded.

"I've seen men dying from cholera. I've seen what it does to them. Why do you risk it?"

The question took her aback. Rosalie answered with surprised honesty. "Because it's God's will that I help, *monsieur.*"

"God asks you to risk your life?"

"God has given me a life," she said. "I thank Him however I can."

His gaze was steady. "Miss Lafon, you are too good to be true."

She tried to read his expression; she searched for the implicit criticism in the words, for sarcasm. There was none. He said it matter-of-factly. Perhaps there was even admiration in his tone. Still . . . she was nervous again. Rosalie fumbled for the bell. "Where is that Lucy?"

"There," he said calmly, nodding toward the kitchen at the side of the courtyard. "Here she comes."

He'd barely finished before Lucy was there, setting a tray of lemonade on the table between them, and some little cakes iced pale yellow and pink. Rosalie reached for her glass. It was wet with condensation; it slipped in her fingers so she nearly dropped it.

He was watching her, and he didn't look away as he reached for his lemonade and took a sip. "I've made you uncomfortable," he said slowly. "I'm sorry."

"*Non, non,* of course you haven't," Rosalie said. The lemonade was too tart. It seemed to fill her throat, so it was difficult to speak. She wanted to leave now; she did not like anything about this moment, not how he looked sitting there as the sun dappled over his shoulders and tangled in his hair, not how he reminded her so strongly of someone else. She wanted him to be nobody important; she longed for politeness that held no underlying reason.

But that was impossible.

Rosalie put aside her lemonade. She cleared her throat and met his gaze. "I wanted to talk to you."

"Yes. I imagine you do."

She squirmed, thinking of last night, of her unforgivable outburst. "You must understand. My resolve not to marry has nothing to do with you. Marriage has never been my intention."

A little smile came to his lips. "Why?"

"I had intended to take the veil."

"That wasn't my question."

Rosalie frowned. "You asked me why—"

"I asked why you never intended to marry," he said, leaning back into the bench. "Why would such a pretty woman want to dedicate her life to God?"

She stared at him in confusion.

He smiled, the same smile she'd seen him give Corinne last night at dinner: slow, seductive, spreading over his face as it spread its heat deep inside her. "Don't tell me no one's ever said that to you before."

His words sent a chill through her. "Are you trying to make a fool of me, *monsieur*?" she asked quietly.

"Oh, no," he said, and the fervor in his voice surprised her, as did the quick shake of his head. He put aside his lemonade and leaned forward, resting his forearms on his knees, holding her gaze. "On the contrary. I admire you."

"Now you *are* making me the fool."

He smiled. "Is it so hard to believe I would find you attractive, Miss Lafon? That I would admire you?"

His question took her aback. She felt churlish, and Rosalie disliked the feeling. "Why would you care anything at all for me?" she asked, more sharply than she'd intended. "You hardly know me."

"I'd like to change that."

"I would not."

"I'm not interested in a marriage of strangers."

"I am not interested in marriage at all."

She spit out the words in an angry panic and then was surprised when he didn't seem perturbed by them. He sat back again in his chair and picked up his lemonade. For a long, slow moment he said nothing at all. He looked down into his drink, tracing his finger along the rim of the glass, sending rivulets of condensation dripping onto his pant leg. When he spoke again, it was with a disarming little smile, a frankness that lit his pale blue eyes. "Miss Lafon, I know you're not happy with your father's decision. I imagine you believe you have many reasons to dislike me. I'd like for you to give me a chance to prove myself, if you would."

He said it so charmingly that Rosalie felt herself start to smile back at him. She caught herself just in time. He *was* dangerous. Dangerous and unpredictable, and Rosalie wished with all her heart that Papa had not brought him home. "I am committing myself to no one but God."

He looked at her. "You love Him that much?"

"*Oui.*"

"You would follow whatever He told you to do?"

"Of course."

He nodded shortly, put aside his lemonade. "What if this marriage between us is God's wish? What if this is the path He's chosen for you?"

"It isn't—"

"But what if it is, Miss Lafon?" he asked insistently. "How would you know?"

His words confused her. Rosalie didn't trust herself to say anything.

"Don't you at least owe it to yourself to find out for sure?"

"I know already," she said. She could not bring her voice above a whisper.

"What if this is a test?" he asked.

The words mirrored her own thoughts so exactly that Rosalie was surprised into silence.

"If you're truly meant for God, Miss Lafon," he said, "there's nothing I can do to change that, isn't that so?"

Slowly she nodded.

"Then how can it hurt to humor me just a little?"

"Humor you?" she managed.

"Give us a chance to get to know each other. If it turns out we're not meant to be together, at least you'll know for sure. You can cloister yourself without a doubt."

It was as Father Bara had told her, and the fact that Jack Waters was saying the same thing disconcerted her. It all sounded so reasonable, so logical.

But still . . . there was a trembling fear inside her, an instinct that told her to keep away from him. Men like Jack Waters were her weakness, she knew that already. She did not want to get to know him. She wanted nothing to do with him at all.

"We could start with breakfast," he said. "Tomorrow morning, here in the courtyard."

She stared at him.

He chuckled. "If nothing else, perhaps we could even become friends."

Rosalie got to her feet. "Excuse me," she said quickly. "I have forgotten . . . something."

"Of course. Don't let me keep you," he said politely, but there was amusement in his eyes.

She hurried away. Behind her, he called, "Don't forget. Tomorrow morning."

She heard his laughter follow her, and Rosalie rushed to her room, to prayers and safety, away from challenging blue eyes and a wicked laugh that made her think of things she should not know about, that made her wish for innocence.

The thought of Jack Waters haunted Corinne. She watched him all through the evening, through an interminable dinner during which she had been unable to eat a single bite and then after, while she played the piano in the parlor. He rarely looked at her, but when he did, she treasured the glance. She felt sick at the thought of him with Rosa, even as she warned herself not to care.

But Rosalie barely acknowledged him. Corinne played a game with herself. If Rosalie smiled at her fiancé, Corinne would put the thought of him aside. If Rosalie touched him even once, Corinne would resign herself to having Jack as a brother-in-law and nothing more. But Rosa did none of those things, and as the evening grew, so did the possibilities.

The tension of the game wore her out, and she had excused herself early, too tired to keep pretending nonchalance. She could not keep on like this. When she heard Rosalie's footsteps only moments later, Corinne opened the door and motioned for her sister to come into her room.

Rosalie entered with a frown. "What is it, Corinne?"

"I've a touch of the headache," Corinne said. "Do you think you could—?"

Her sister hesitated, then nodded. "*Oui*, of course."

Corinne went to sit at the mirror, and Rosalie took up the brush and stood behind her, gently undoing Corinne's hair, pulling the brush through it. For a while after Maman had died, Rosalie had brushed Corinne's hair nearly every night, a hundred strokes, but it had been rare since then for Corinne to seek such comfort. Now she closed her eyes and leaned her head back, but she could not relax. The question she longed to ask burned in her head.

"It's going to rain again," Rosa said. "The air feels heavy. Perhaps it's that giving you a headache. Or . . . you hardly ate a thing for dinner."

Corinne put a hand to her stomach. "The fish did not look good."

"You're not ill?"

"*Non.* Only a little tired."

"I hope this helps."

"I already feel much better." Corinne watched her sister in the mirror. Rosalie looked as tense as Corinne felt. Rosa's jaw was stiff, as if she had been clenching it so long she'd forgotten she was doing it. "Perhaps I should be doing this for you instead," Corinne said.

Rosalie's hand stilled.

"You look troubled."

Rosalie shook her head and took up brushing again. "*Non.*"

"You cannot fool me, Rosa. You have not been the same since Papa announced your marriage."

"There will be no marriage."

"*Non?*" Corinne raised a brow. "You have told Papa you won't marry, and he understands?"

The brush jerked. Corinne let out a small cry of pain.

"*Pardon,*" Rosalie said with a sigh. "I am afraid Papa is . . . insistent."

Corinne smiled into the mirror, her gaze catching Rosalie's in the reflection. "Ah. But Rosa, be honest. It would not be so bad to be married to him, would it? He is handsome—even you must admit it."

"Handsome doesn't make a marriage, Corinne. I know nothing of him."

"Does it matter? Think of the things you can discover about him. How romantic it is!"

"It is not romantic at all."

"You've spent too much time praying for the souls of orphans. You've forgotten what it means to love."

Corinne saw her sister flinch and look down, and she pressed on, determined to find the truth of Rosalie's feelings. "You must dream of it sometimes. Remember when we would look in the mirror on Good Friday to see the faces of our future husbands? Don't tell me you don't think of that now and then."

Rosalie shook her head. "No. Never."

"Not even a little bit?"

Rosalie stepped away, letting Corinne's hair fall. "You must be feeling better. I haven't time—"

"Wait, Rosa, don't go." Corinne twisted on the seat. "*Pardon,* I did not mean to tease. It is just that . . . I want to make sure I understand. There are worse things than marrying Jack Waters. Perhaps, just a little bit, you want him—"

"I do not want him."

The vehemence in Rosa's tone took Corinne aback. "But . . . to be a nun . . ."

"I can think of nothing that would suit me more," Rosalie said. She put the brush down—Corinne thought she would slam it onto the tabletop, but at the last moment Rosalie laid it down so softly it barely made a noise.

"*Bonsoir,*" she said, and then she paused. She looked as if she would say something more, but a moment later she turned abruptly and went to the door. "*Bonsoir.*"

Corinne let her sister go, and as the door closed

again, shutting out the night, she could not help the hope that grew once again inside her. She had spent a lifetime being jealous of Rosalie, but the truth was that she loved her sister. She wanted Rosa to be happy, and it was obvious that what would make Rosalie happy was a life devoted to God.

Corinne felt suddenly as if she'd been holding her breath for days, and now she could breathe again. She would never have pursued Jack had Rosalie wanted him. But now . . . Papa wanted Jack as his heir. He wanted Jack to marry into the family. Why shouldn't she be his wife if Rosalie was so unwilling?

Corinne should never have doubted that her sister would refuse to marry Jack. She knew Rosalie well— Rosa was immune to love, to romance. She had been ensconced in church life and infirmaries, in the tales of nuns, since she was a girl. She didn't know how it felt to find a man's eyes suddenly on you, to feel as if your insides had melted to nothing. A kiss would be foreign to Rosa—the way lips held such soft warmth, the moistness of touch, the taste. Had Rosalie ever sat in the sun and felt its caress yet burned for something more, something else? Had she ever looked at the breadth of a man's shoulders and wanted to hold him tightly to her?

No, Corinne thought. No, Rosalie would not even know to want those things. She was a woman of rosaries and prayers; the altar in her bedroom dripped with hardened wax. There was no passion in Rosalie's soul.

Rosalie would never have a husband and children,

never know the warmth of her own family. She had
Papa's favor now, but that would be cold comfort
when Papa died.

For that, Corinne pitied her sister. In the end
Rosalie would throw away this last chance, and
Corinne felt sorry for the long nights full of prayers
and the cold plaster faces of saints that would be
Rosalie's solace. For the first time in her life, Corinne
felt the more blessed, and the feeling made her pause,
made her blink; she felt a sadness in her heart for her
sister, and an emptiness that seemed to echo the bleak-
ness in Rosalie's sad, sad eyes.

Rosalie stepped out onto the gallery just as the rain
started. It was not a real storm, just wind and fat raindrops and cooling air, but just the same she didn't like
the feel of it on her skin. She didn't like the way it
made her *feel* her skin. She didn't like Corinne's words,
or the memories, and when she got to her room she
shut her doors against the outside. She breathed deep
of the candle-scented air and felt herself again.

But Corinne's words stayed with her, bringing
back to her the dream she'd once had. She had not
even remembered it until Corinne reminded her of
Good Friday superstitions and reflections in mirrors,
until she had said, "You have forgotten what it means
to love. . . ."

His face came into her mind then, a flicker of
movement like a dream, hard to remember, hard to
place. Gaston. Rosalie squeezed her eyes shut and

shook her head, blowing it away. The past could not be undone. She had decided her future.

She was only feeling maudlin. By tomorrow she would feel better again. It was just that Corinne's words had dredged up the old memories, the old expectations. How hard it was to give up adolescent dreams; they stayed and haunted, they teased. *You wanted to be this, you wanted that, and look at you now. Look at how you've failed . . .*

Rosalie went to the door and watched the night through the glass. The rain made the darkness darker, a heavy veil between her and the world, and she felt alone in her room, the plaster statues of St. Catherine and St. Mary Magdalene only statues, the scent of the votive candles waxy and old. She wrapped the rosary beads around her fingers, but they held no solace this time; they were only beads.

It was nothing, she told herself. Corinne's words, old dreams . . . they had no place in her life now. All they'd ever caused her was misery. If sometimes she thought about them, if sometimes she wanted her sister's youthful innocence, it was only in passing. A wish for a past that had never been. A life that was not hers.

❧ Chapter 6

When Jack woke, he saw Rosalie was already there in the courtyard. It was obvious she was not waiting for him. The little iron table held the remains of her breakfast—a nearly empty cup of café au lait, half a brioche, a pool of rapidly melting butter, and shiny globs of what looked like strawberry preserves. She had pushed the dishes aside to make room for a ledger, and she was bent over its open pages, the picture of concentration. She did not even seem to sense him as he approached and stood behind her at a little distance, half shaded by a pale pink climbing rose.

He watched the way the sun played over her light brown hair, gilded the little wisps at the nape of her neck. From behind, he could almost pretend she was attractive. He could feel a hunger rising deep inside him as he imagined himself kissing her there, that spot where her jaw met her ear, imagined blowing against those little hairs softly so they trembled in his breath. But then she stirred, raising her head so her back went ramrod straight, and he remembered her stern piety, the patronizing faith that left him cold.

Married to a nun. Jack sighed. There were worse women to be chained to than Rosalie Lafon, he supposed, though at the moment he couldn't think of any.

Even fat Ursula, the cook at Parish, had been passably pretty when she smiled.

The thought brought another vision into his head—the first time he'd met Rosalie Lafon, the kindness in her eyes as she welcomed him into her home. Before she'd known who he was or why he was there. He wished now he'd never seen it, because he already felt its loss.

It was ridiculous, of course. Her kindness had been so ephemeral that he should be able to forget it. But it had been so long since anyone treated him with kindness that the memory of it stayed with him like a festering wound. He'd even had the fleeting thought that he could like her, that this devotion to religion was just the passing interest of a longtime spinster, easy to put aside once the chance at marriage presented itself.

But her devotion was real, and it was the worst kind. It withered him almost where he stood. It had taken all his will yesterday to flirt with her. If it weren't for the fact that Rosalie Lafon held his future in her hands . . .

She bent again over the ledger, and Jack took a deep breath and stepped from the climbing rose.

"Good morning," he said. "I see you haven't forgotten our breakfast."

She started. She jerked to face him so hard that her elbow hit the delicate china cup, sending it skittering across the table. Jack caught it just as it teetered at the edge. He smiled and set it back down. "I've startled you. I'm sorry."

"*Non, non,*" she said, but she was obviously flustered. Her hand went to her hair, smoothing it back even though there was not a strand out of place, and then to the crucifix around her neck. She played with the chain until the heavy jet cross was even between her breasts.

Smoothly Jack pulled out the other chair and sat in it. He swept his gaze over the table and gave her a chiding look. "You started without me."

"It . . . it was late. I was . . . hungry."

"I forgive you, then." Jack reached for the rest of her brioche and took a bite. "Very good."

"*Oui.* Our chef is—"

"French. Yes, I know." He leaned over the table. "What are you doing?"

She drew back, as if his encroaching even an inch into the space between them was impossible to bear. "The bills," she said. It seemed even those few words were an effort.

"Doesn't your father take care of that?"

"*Non.* He has no interest in running the house."

"I see."

"I give him the ledgers once . . . a month . . . to see."

"But you take care of everything."

Her expression held a question.

"I was just wondering what there might be for me to do," he explained.

"To do?" she asked in surprise—and then, acidly, "Why, *monsieur,* you will be a man of leisure."

There it was: what she thought of him in a single

sentence. He read the meaning behind it easily, and he knew what she was accusing him of. Marrying her for money. He couldn't take offense; after all, in a way it was true. But there was more to it, things she knew nothing about, and her assumptions irritated him, so he spoke before he thought.

"I didn't realize God had given you the right to judge."

She looked at him. "Then you must tell me I am wrong—if you can."

He worked to rein in his annoyance. He meant to smile, but the effort was, at last, too much. "Your father's holding a soirée in a few days," he pointed out. "Shouldn't you at least pretend to like me?"

She went pale. She pulled a rosary from the pocket of her skirt, drawing it nervously through her fingers. The beads were as black as the crucifix dangling between her breasts, and they looped heavy and ugly against the white of her skin. It was only one more thing to put him off. Looking at her put a chill so deep inside Jack that he felt cold even in the warmth of the morning.

Find something, he told himself. He was marrying this woman. There must be something about her he could like. He tried to remember that moment two days ago that had made him think this marriage would work; he tried again to remember that kindness he'd seen at their first meeting. But he couldn't, and there was nothing in her face to help him. There had to be something attractive about her, something—

"*Monsieur,* forgive me for being so blunt, but I am

afraid I have nothing to say to you this morning. It is clear we . . . we will not suit. . . ."

Her mouth. She kept on talking, and he didn't hear a word she was saying. He stared at her mouth, at the way she spoke. He didn't know what it was—a slight lisp, perhaps, or maybe it was simply the way she barely moved a mouth that was made for mobility. Yes, he could lose himself in that mouth. He could even imagine a smile—

"*Monsieur.*"

He glanced up. She was frowning at him, her dark eyes cold and disapproving.

He smiled at her. "Forgive me," he said. "I was thinking of something else."

She snapped the ledger closed, started to her feet. "I have other duties, *monsieur.* I expect you will hardly mind, as I seem to be boring you."

She had not been able to resist the jab, he thought, and then he saw the regret flash across her face, the wish she had not given in to the urge. For one who professed not to care at all for him, she was curiously annoyed at his inattention. Jack could not help it; his smile widened. "I was thinking of you," he said.

She picked up the ledger and turned to go. "I am busy, Monsieur Waters—"

"Of your mouth," he said.

She hesitated. He saw the way her shoulders stiffened, he felt a change in the air around her. A pause, a softening—but it was fleeting, gone almost before he noticed it, and she was turning away completely.

"*Au revoir,*" she said.

He let her go, feeling a vague sense of satisfaction as he watched her walk rigidly across the courtyard and disappear into the house. She was not immune to him—it was enough to strengthen his resolve to win her over. Garland had been right; his daughter was not meant for the veil. She just didn't know it yet.

But she would. Jack would make sure of it. He took the last piece of her brioche and dabbed it into the puddle of butter and jam, and when he took a bite he thought again of the way her mouth moved, the fascination of it. Wondering what it would be like to kiss her consumed him for a good few moments. Longer than he would have thought possible.

Corinne woke feeling ill. Last night she had only been half feigning the headache she'd asked Rosalie to soothe away, and this morning it was there with a vengeance. Too much wine last night, she thought, though she'd had only a few glasses and they had not seemed to affect her then. She stretched and got out of bed, feeling a little nauseated as she washed and dressed.

Breakfast did not sound at all appealing, but the thought of Jack Waters was, so she hurried down the stairs to the dining room. No one was there. It was obvious everyone had already eaten. Corinne stopped, staring at the remains of breakfast, the last few spoonfuls of *grillades* and grits, a single brioche, and then at the dirty dishes on the table still waiting to be cleared away.

How could she be so late? She glanced at the clock, startled to see that it was nearly ten o'clock. She'd slept the morning away—why hadn't Paulette awakened her?

"Oh, *mademoiselle* . . ."

Corinne turned to see her maid standing in the doorway.

Paulette inclined her tignon-covered head. "I just be going to wake you, *mademoiselle*."

"As you can see, I'm already awake." Corinne said. Her disappointment over missing Jack Waters made her voice sharp, but Paulette only shrugged—the woman was not even twenty, yet she was as immovable and calm as a rock.

"You sleep so sound, *mademoiselle,* I have not the heart to wake you this morning. You be so tired lately, I thought—"

"Don't think next time," Corinne said. "I do not care how tired I seem."

Paulette only looked at her calmly. "*Oui, mademoiselle.*"

Immediately Corinne felt churlish for being angry. Paulette had a way of making her feel more the servant than the mistress—more than once Corinne had considered letting her go. But Corinne liked the maid, and Paulette was closemouthed and secretive—qualities Corinne had needed when she was sneaking out at night to meet Reynaud.

"Some breakfast, *mademoiselle?*" Paulette offered.

"*Non,*" Corinne said. She went to the sideboard and looked at what was left. "I am not that hungry."

"But you must eat something."

"This, perhaps." Corinne picked up a brioche and went to the table. She pulled out a chair—Jack's place—and sat down, setting her brioche on his jam-and grillades-smeared plate, liking that she was touching something he had touched.

Paulette grabbed the serving dish of grillades from the sideboard. "Some of these, too, *oui?* You do not eat these last days, *mademoiselle.*"

Paulette began spooning out the grillades onto the plate, a big, congealed spoonful of meat and gravy that spattered the brioche. Corinne caught the smell—the dish was heavily seasoned, as her father liked it—and her stomach flipped. When she saw the grease gathering in big, translucent pools, she pushed back the chair, running for the courtyard. She made it to the climbing rose at the edge just before she vomited.

The maid was there beside her in an instant. "*Mademoiselle*—"

"Water," Corinne gasped. She sat back on her heels, pushing back her hair, wiping at her face. She truly had had too much wine last night. Or she was ill. Good Lord, there was cholera in the city—hadn't Rosalie said it just the other night? Cholera . . .

Paulette was beside her again, pushing a glass of water into her hand. Corinne took it gratefully, but the rusty, alum-flavored water only threatened to turn her stomach inside out again. She took one sip and handed it back.

"Help me up," she said, leaning into her maid. When she was on her feet again, she felt weak. Her head was pounding, her stomach rocked. She sagged into Paulette.

"You best be in bed," the maid said.

Corinne shook her head. "*Non. Non,* I am fine. It is just a passing illness. . . ." She caught the skepticism in Paulette's dark eyes. "It is not the cholera," she said rapidly, her heart pounding. "I cannot be—"

"Me, I do not think you are sick, *mademoiselle,*" Paulette said.

"The wine, then."

"Not wine." Paulette sighed—the prelude to some dire prediction.

Corinne knew the sound. She pulled away, fell into a nearby chair, and put her hand to her eyes. "I am not interested in your voodoo wisdom, Paulette."

"I think you be with child, *mademoiselle.*"

The bold, matter-of-fact words slammed into Corinne's head. She gasped and jerked up to look at the maid.

"What did you say?"

"You heard me fine." Paulette shrugged. "You think on it, *mademoiselle.* All them meetings with that boy. Then you have the headache. Then you cannot eat—what, do you wish to be thin? You already skinny as a snake. Sleeping all the time. You tell me—you been bleeding?"

Corinne's mind whirled. She tried to concentrate on what Paulette said, but instead she saw Reynaud before her, leaning down to kiss her, slipping the buttons of her gown through their loops, laying her back on his shoddy little bed while Paulette waited in the street outside and the sun slanted through to glisten on his dark, oiled hair. *This is proof that you love me,* he'd said. *This is proof that it is me you want.*

The afternoons and nights spent with him cluttered her mind, memories of days similar but for the weather. The smells of his turpentine and paints, his talk of her posing for him—that was how it had started. He had wanted her to pose, and she'd taken off her clothes and sat draped in a sheet because she liked the notoriety of it; she liked being so desirable that a handsome artist would beg her to help make him immortal . . .

Immortal, yes, but this was not the way she'd intended. Not by having his child—

"The last time, *mademoiselle,*" Paulette was saying. "When the last time?"

"A week ago," Corinne said weakly. "We met—"

Paulette snorted. "Not when you lay with him last. When you last bleed?"

Corinne tried to think. When had it been? Oh, not for so long; she couldn't remember. Weeks ago. Weeks and weeks. She was late now. . . . If it hadn't been for Papa's dismissal of Reynaud, and then the arrival of Jack, she would have thought of it, she would have remembered.

"April," she said in a small voice. "It was April."

Paulette nodded. "You be about six weeks along, then."

Six weeks. Corinne did not question it; it explained too many things. Her exhaustion, the way her breasts felt so tender, the sickness. She had watched her friends over the years, married at sixteen or seventeen, pregnant soon after. Most of them had two or three children by now. She knew the signs; Lorraine Minot had whispered the details only last year, when she had discovered she was expecting her first.

Six weeks. Corinne closed her eyes. *Six weeks.* What was she going to do? When Papa found out—

She moaned aloud. Paulette patted her shoulder.

"We figure this out, *mademoiselle.* No need to worry."

But worry came into Corinne's head and would not leave. Papa would hunt down Reynaud and force him to wed her. Then he would disown them both—

"I find this boy," Paulette whispered. "I bring him back to marry you."

"*Non.*" Corinne shook her head vehemently. "I don't want to marry him! I don't love him. Papa will set us on the streets—"

Paulette frowned. "What choice you have?"

"I won't marry him. He's a fortune hunter. Papa hates him."

"And better for you to be outcast?"

Corinne buried her face in her hands. The climbing roses beside her and the smell of her own perfume made her head spin. This could not be happening. This was all a dream, and she would wake up soon. On the count of three, she would wake and it would all be gone. *One, two—*

"*Mademoiselle,*" Paulette said, and her voice was low. "There be a potion to take care of this. Mammy Zaza, she—"

Corinne looked up in horror. "*Non.* I could not."

Paulette regarded her gravely. "What will you do, then?"

Perhaps it was the question, or the way Paulette looked at her with such sorrow, as if the future was too bleak to contemplate, that gave Corinne the answer. She hardly knew. All she knew was that when Paulette had said, "What will you do, then?" a vision rose from her desperation. She saw a face, a man. She saw Jack Waters.

"*Mon Dieu,*" Corinne whispered, because what she was considering was so unthinkable. But once the thought was there, she could not lose it. It was so perfect; it solved everything.

She looked up at Paulette. "I need a love charm."

The maid frowned. Then, suddenly, from the middle gallery of the service wing, outside the *garçonnière,* came a whistle, a low and ragged tune. Paulette looked up, and Corinne followed her gaze to see Jack Waters coming from his room, his blond hair glistening in the sun.

"I need the charm today," Corinne said quietly.

Paulette looked down at her, and though the maid said not a word, Corinne saw the measuring look in Paulette's eyes, the slow understanding.

"The charm, it take two days," Paulette whispered.

"I don't—"

"While I make it, you do this, too: Write his name on a piece of paper. Your name on another. You pin them together like a cross, with your name on top."

Corinne nodded. She glanced toward the gallery. Jack had disappeared into the stairwell. "Then what?"

"You put this in some water with sugar and orange water. In a glass—you hear me? It must be a glass. Then you burn a red candle before it for nine days."

"Nine days," Corinne repeated. "I can't wait that long."

Paulette smiled. "You will not have to, *mademoiselle*. The love powder, I make it strong. Two days, and he will look to you, no mistake. The candle only a spell for good measure."

Paulette straightened. She looked toward the gallery. Then, in a voice so low Corinne had to strain to hear, she said, "There be another charm, too, if you want it. If there be a rival—"

"*Non*." Corinne looked up in alarm. "*Non*, not that. There is no need."

Paulette raised her heavy brows.

Corinne shook her head. "There is no need."

"So you say, *mademoiselle*."

"She wants to be a nun," Corinne said desperately.

Paulette shrugged. "So she says now."

"It won't change."

"Not unless he make it change."

Corinne glanced at the maid, but Paulette's expression was suddenly enigmatic, and before Corinne could question her further, Jack Waters was in the courtyard, striding toward them with a smile.

"Miss Lafon," he said, inclining his head. "Good morning."

Corinne's throat constricted. It was all she could

do to nod. She was acutely aware of the pool of vomit at the base of the climbing rose. She prayed he didn't notice.

He frowned. "Is something wrong?"

"*Non*." Corinne worked up a smile. She felt the hard strain of it, felt Paulette's hand clench on the back on her chair. "Are you just waking, *monsieur?*"

"Actually, I've been up for some time. I had breakfast with your sister. Have you seen her?"

"Rosalie." Her sister's name felt heavy on Corinne's tongue. She looked up at him, trying to sparkle, and she felt the desperation of her flirtation in every move she made. "Now, why would you be looking for her, *monsieur,* when I am here now to entertain you?"

Something flickered in his eyes—an interest she was not imagining. Corinne's heart jumped. But then he looked away, stepping back with a small shake of his head. "Have you seen her, Miss Lafon?"

"*Non,*" Corinne admitted. "Not this morning."

"My search continues," he said, and then, with a smile, he was gone again, moving past her into the house. She heard the muffled thud of his footsteps on the mat-covered floor.

Paulette's knuckles grazed Corinne's shoulder blade. When she glanced up, there was a question in Paulette's eyes.

"*Non,*" Corinne said again. "I know what you are thinking. Leave Rosa alone."

Paulette nodded. "*Oui, mademoiselle.* But this be a mistake, I warn you."

"Then it will be my mistake."

Paulette muttered something beneath her breath and walked off, and as Corinne watched her go, she felt desperation harden within her. She had to win Jack Waters, and soon. She had no other choice. Rosalie would forgive her—even thank her. After all, Rosa did not want a husband. She had said so many times. Corinne had no reason to think that sentiment would change.

Not unless he make it change.

Corinne pushed Paulette's words from her head. She would not think of that, not now. It would not happen.

It could not happen.

❧ Chapter 7

I t was that most perfect of all things: a balmy summer evening in New Orleans. Jack sat on the gallery outside his room and breathed in the growing night, the warm breezes, the smells. Jasmine and sweet olive, roses and oranges. He had missed those smells; he had missed the leisurely nights, the rhythm of New Orleans, which made a man lazy and unafraid.

He braced a foot on the railing and leaned back in the wrought-iron chair, staring up into the deep purple sky. It was too early yet for stars, and the moon hadn't risen, but the sky was beautiful still, and he wondered if he'd ever get enough of it, if staring at it long enough and hard enough would ever make him forget the years when he'd never seen it at all.

It was not that it was peaceful; New Orleans nights had never been peaceful. But there was something in them that stirred his blood, that felt like music running through his veins—a sense of impossibility, of magic.

And this was all impossible still, his being here—a fairy tale where all his wishes had come true. But even in fairy tales there was someone determined to foil the hero, and this situation was no different.

Jack sighed and stared up at the sky until the hard

iron of the chair pressed painfully into his back and neck, until he saw the flickering lights in the dining room dim. He'd deliberately missed dinner. He wasn't hungry and he thought it would do them all good to have at each other when he wasn't in the room. Garland could press the issue of Jack as his heir, Rosalie could protest, and Corinne . . .

Now, Corinne was something else entirely. Jack frowned. Yesterday morning he'd felt sorry for her; the way Garland belittled her reminded him too much of his own relationship with his uncle. Because of that, he felt a kinship with her, and that was dangerous enough, because she was so beautiful he couldn't look at her without wishing, *Why not her?* Then this morning, when he'd seen her and her maid sitting together in the courtyard, he'd had the disturbing sense that she was flirting with him.

He discounted it; she knew he was her sister's betrothed, and though he hadn't seen real closeness between Corinne and Rosalie, neither had he seen rivalry or dislike. He told himself he was imagining the depth of Corinne's smile, the sparkle in her eyes.

But his body believed it. As much as he told himself he was supposed to be seducing Rosalie, he could not control his dreams, and he'd dreamed of Corinne last night and awakened hot and sweating. His chest tightened; immediately the image of her dancing in the rain came to him. It would be much easier if she would keep her distance, if she followed her sister's lead and took it into her head to dislike him. The temptation of her smiles, her sweetness, every damned beautiful movement she made . . . He would go insane before the week was out if he didn't do something about it.

But what he would *not* do was encourage her. He'd regretted touching her shoulder since he'd done it yesterday morning. He'd meant only to reassure her—he had not liked watching her deflate beneath her father's sharp words. But touching her . . . what a mistake that had been. A smart man would stay the hell away from Corinne Lafon, and Jack was planning to be very smart. He would not lose this chance because he could not keep his hands off his fiancée's sister.

He heard the sound of music on the night air. Corinne's piano. Jack sat up, ran his hand through his hair, and dragged his suit coat from where he'd draped it over the edge of the gallery rail. He'd given them time enough to argue about him. Now he would make himself one of the family.

He went down the stairs and across the courtyard into the house. The remnants of dinner were being cleared away by the servants, and the music grew louder as he approached the room where the Lafons were gathered.

The second parlor was divided from the first by a *porte á coulisse*—folding doors that were closed now, separating the family from the room meant for company, and when Jack entered it he felt instantly enveloped in an intimacy that was foreign and familiar at the same time. The scene before him looked much the same as the nights he'd spent at his uncle's home so long ago: Rosalie embroidering in the corner, the way his aunt had done, Garland smoking as he read the newspaper, very much like his uncle.

But his uncle's house had never held such a charming sight as Corinne bent over the piano, the sleeve of her gown slipping just barely off her shoulder. When she caught sight of him, she fumbled over the keys, and then she smiled—a dazzling smile—and the music stopped abruptly.

"*Monsieur!*" she said. "You have come! When you didn't come to dinner, I thought perhaps you were ill."

He shook his head. "I had no appetite."

"You're not ill?"

"No, no," he assured her. He saw Rosalie and Garland looking at him, and he nodded a hello.

"*Bonsoir,*" Rosalie said, glancing up from her embroidery, some elaborate pattern of leaves and roses. There was a guard in her eyes, and when he smiled at her, her fine mouth tightened before she inclined her head and went back to her sewing.

Garland gestured to a chair. "Jack, Jack, *mon ami,* come sit down. Have a cigar, eh? Some port?"

It sounded good, and the parlor felt good, too. Jack smiled as he accepted a glass of port and seated himself in the chair beside Garland's. When he took a sip, it warmed his tongue, his throat. He felt its trail clear into his stomach.

Corinne began playing again, some sentimental tune, and Jack leaned back in his chair, swirled the wine in his glass, and felt a comfort he remembered from long ago, a rich, well-heeled comfort. He took in the portraits draped with mosquito netting, a bowl of wax fruit, a rarely used fireplace, its mantle boasting the requisite glass dome holding wreaths and flowers made from human hair. In the corners stood palmetto fans in sand-filled vases, and they waved a little in the smoky air drifting from the open hallway, as did the soft gauze of netting. The whole effect was peaceful, somnolent, a little decadent.

There was a pause in the music; he looked up to see Corinne turning the pages in front of her before she continued. Jack took another sip of port before he noticed that Garland was staring at him with a quietly assessing look.

Garland blew out a mouthful of smoke. "The tailor treated you well, *oui?*"

"Perfectly. At least one suit will be ready next week."

"*Bien. Bien.*" Garland nodded. He threw a glance at Rosalie, who was ignoring them steadily as she concentrated on her embroidery. "Do you hear that, *chérie?* There will not be time for a new suit for Jack before the soirée. We must have one of my old ones altered for him, eh?"

Rosalie's jaw tightened. "As you wish, Papa." She pulled a thread taut, and her hand knocked the glass chimney of a nearby flycatcher, trembling the fly carcasses floating inside so they looked weirdly alive.

The music stuttered.

"Oh, it is so difficult to turn the pages myself," Corinne sighed from the piano. She looked straight at Jack. "*Monsieur,* do you think—"

"Jack is busy now," Garland said sharply, and Jack felt pure relief at the old man's words. Corinne and Rosalie looked surprised at their father's vehemence. "If you want a page turner, find a new beau."

Corinne flushed. "Papa—"

"Imagine," Garland went on, "a beautiful girl like that, and the best she can do is a traveling house painter."

"He was not a house painter, Papa." Rosalie supported her sister quietly. "He was an artist."

Garland harrumphed. "If you can call pictures of cows art. I would ask where you met him, missy, but I already know. He has the nose, eh? Like a hound for the fox, a nose for gold. Corinne, stop looking at me as if I am the devil himself. Play something."

"I would love to, Papa," Corinne said. She was pale, a little flustered, but when she looked pointedly at Jack, he felt the impact of her deep brown eyes like a hard blow to his chest. "But I need someone to turn the pages."

Jack felt skewered. He could not refuse without looking churlish, and so he said, "I'd be delighted."

He carried his port over to the highly polished piano and set it on an embroidered runner. Corinne's smile cut through him, so dazzling, so completely mesmerizing, he felt himself neatly harpooned.

She eased over on the seat. "Sit beside me, *monsieur?*"

He glanced at Rosalie. She was steadfastly ignoring him, but Garland was glowering, so Jack declined with a shake of his head. Corinne seemed undaunted.

She merely edged back so he felt her shoulders against his pelvis. He was trapped; if he backed away, he would be too far to turn the pages. She looked over her shoulder at him, and her eyes were catlike—almond-shaped, liquid brown.

"'Oft in the Stilly Night,'" she said.

He reached over her shoulder. She pressed back against him, and he exhaled sharply, fumbled with the pages. The music slipped between his fingers. It seemed forever until he turned to the page she wanted.

She leaned forward, but every key she hit caused her shoulders to move, to brush his hip. The yellow silk she wore gaped a little between her shoulder blades, drawing his attention to the fine hair at the nape of her neck, the down revealed by her loose chignon. Her fragrance drifted to him, hot and deep, the spice of roses.

He was dizzy. When the tune ended, he barely heard her request to turn to another song. She had to repeat the title twice.

He didn't think he was imagining the deliberateness of her. Corinne was the kind of woman who knew exactly her effect on men. He'd seen the look in her eyes that told him that, the little smile on her lips whenever she cast him one of those shy, slanted looks. She knew he wanted her, and he knew also that she wanted him. He had not been away from the world so long that he misinterpreted the way a woman seduced a man, and Corinne was doing just that. If she had been in love with that painter who'd asked for her hand, she had already forgotten him.

Jack felt Garland's gaze like a burn. He reminded himself to take care, to stand back, to keep from twining one of the loosened strands of her golden hair around his finger, to keep from trying his breath against the fine down at the nape of her neck. He tried to remember why he was here, to remember his fiancée's mouth, but even though Rosalie was just across the room, she was suddenly fuzzy before him, undefined. He could barely bring her into his head.

Corinne finished the tune. She twisted to smile at him, and the movement sent her arm brushing against the piano, tumbling the sheet music to the keys.

"Oh," she said, grabbing for them, but the music scattered beneath her hands and littered the floor. "Oh, I am so clumsy," she laughed, bending low to retrieve the pages, looking up at him so he saw the swelling of her breasts above her décolletage. "Could you help me, *monsieur*? I am certain I can hardly manage to gather these myself."

He could hardly refuse. Jack bent and scooped together the papers, and when he went to hand them to her, she slid her hands over his, easing the papers from his grasp, staring into his eyes and holding his gaze for one split second—there was a frankness there that amazed him—before she looked away again and swiveled on the bench, shaking out the thin sheets of music, reordering them in a calm, unhurried way.

"Another song?" she whispered. That accent, the rounded French, the trill of her words. Such a hot little voice. It curled inside him like a fever. "Do you prefer 'Twilight Dews'? Or perhaps something else, perhaps ''Tis Midnight Hour'? I am quite fond of that one myself—"

"Perhaps something less sentimental, missy," Garland said from the corner. There was steel in his words, anger in his eyes when Jack looked at him. "A lullaby, perhaps. It grows late—perhaps you should find your bed, Jack, *oui*? There is much to do tomorrow." It was not a request.

"Oh, Papa," Corinne pouted. "But—"

"Your father's right," Jack said. He smiled at her and then at an expressionless Rosalie. "I am feeling rather . . . tired. I think I'll bid you all good night."

"*Bonsoir*," Garland said. "In the morning, then."

"In the morning." Jack nodded and stepped away from Corinne, from the scent of roses. It would be a long night, he knew as he left the parlor and went down the hallway to the courtyard. He stood there in the darkness, listening to the whisper of the flowers and feeling the night breezes stroke through his hair like the fingers of a lover.

Rosalie watched him go. Even after he'd left the room, his presence stayed behind. His smile, his steady gaze, were still in her head, as they had been since the morning, when he'd told her he'd been thinking of her mouth.

She yanked a thread so hard it broke, and Rosalie stared at it disbelievingly, for a moment not understanding what had happened. Her hands were trembling; she hated that he should bother her so much.

"You look ill, Rosa," Corinne said.

Rosalie glanced at her sister. Corinne was watching her with the oddest expression, a too-intent gaze.

"I'm fine," Rosalie said.

"Of course. It is just that . . ." Corinne paused. "You seem distressed."

"And why should she not be?" Papa demanded, blowing smoke through his pipe. "She has just watched you play the coquette with her fiancé. You watch yourself, missy. I will not have Rosa's future thrown away because you cannot keep from flirting with a man who should mean nothing to you."

Corinne flushed. She twisted back to the piano, plunking a finger on a low, soft key.

Papa turned to Rosalie. "We will plan the soirée for Tuesday, Rosa. I will give you the list tomorrow. Only a few people, eh? No need to overdo. As I said, we will not wait for Jack's new clothes. Bring Paul in to alter one of my suits."

Rosalie felt sick, but she nodded agreeably. "As you wish, Papa."

"I want him to look presentable."

"He'd be presentable even without the suit," Corinne put in.

The comment silenced their father. Rosalie winced as Papa drew himself up fully and directed his sharp gaze to her sister.

"Did I raise you in a brothel, to notice such things about men?"

"But Papa—"

"Keep your eyes to yourself, missy," Papa said harshly. "Watch yourself, or I will send you straight back to the convent. I have a mind to do it anyway."

"Come, Papa, Corinne was only noticing Monsieur Waters's appearance," Rosalie said gently. "It is no crime to notice."

"It is not the noticing that worries me," Papa said grimly. He threw a disparaging look at Corinne before he heaved himself from his chair. "You listen to me, missy, eh? I will not have it. Ah, this conversation wearies me. *Bonsoir, mes enfants.*" He took the few steps to Rosalie, leaned over and kissed her tenderly on the head, and then he left the room. Rosalie saw the way Corinne leaned forward for their father's kiss, then the careful way she sat back when he left the room with nothing but a wave in her direction. Corinne turned back to the piano.

But she didn't play. She leaned forward, idly turning the pages of music. "Why not just tell Papa you don't want him, Rosa?"

Rosalie looked up at her. "It is not so simple."

"Perhaps you should run away, then. Join the convent without telling him. If you do, he will have no choice but to end your betrothal."

It was what Corinne would do, Rosalie knew. But she was not Corinne, and Father Bara had asked her to wait. Three months was not so long—what had he said? *Only a moment in a lifetime.*

But she did not tell Corinne about Father Bara's request. There was nothing to be ashamed of, but

still . . . She did not want to see the question in
Corinne's eyes, and she most certainly did not want
to have to answer it. So instead she said, "I could
not do that to Papa."

"Of course you could not," Corinne said.

Rosalie heard the faint sarcasm in her sister's
words. She rose. "I think I will retire as well."

Corinne glanced up at her. "Tell me again, Rosa . . .
you do not want him? Not even a little?"

Rosalie shook her head. "Not even a little."

She saw the little smile come to her sister's face,
and she turned away, suddenly exhausted. "*Bonsoir,*"
she whispered before she left the room.

The house was dark and silent as she went to her
room, and once she was there she threw open the
doors and stood in the doorway to feel the cool of the
night. The evening played itself out in her mind:
Corinne's relentless flirtation, Jack Waters's careful
response to it. Rosalie had not missed it, and though
she told herself not to care, there was a part of her that
remembered this morning and his words to her: *I was
thinking about your mouth.*

Such a little flirtation, but it brought to mind other
times, other places, another man. Rosalie swallowed.
After all this time, it was impossible that the yearning
should still be there, that the lies a man told should
still have such power. What had happened to her, that
simple flirtations had suddenly taken on such dark
meanings? Where had her innocence gone?

She knew, of course. She knew exactly when it
had left her, but that did not bear thinking about. She

closed her eyes, wishing for forgetfulness. Her longing for the comfort of the Ursulines was so strong it was as if something were pulling at her heart.

Slowly she turned back into her room. But she left the doors open as she took down her hair and went to her altar to light the candles. And she fell asleep as she prayed, until she woke in the small hours of the morning to find her fingers covered with cooling wax and the hard shape of her rosary imprinted into her cheek.

❧ Chapter 8

The day of the soirée celebrating the betrothal finally arrived. It was to be a supper dance for a few of Garland's closest friends—a quiet affair, only twenty people. A small orchestra had been hired to play, and the *porte à coulisse* was opened to make room for dancing.

There had been a rain shower a few hours before, but it had only washed the evening clean. Now the sun was shining, steam rising from the flagstones. Jack stood on the gallery outside his room, the cypress planks slick beneath his boots, and watched the bustle as the household readied for the party. The fragrance of turtle soup wafted from the kitchen, and one of the scullery maids hurried across the courtyard carrying an ornate sculpted nougat cathedral, the *pièce montée* for the table centerpiece, a Creole tradition.

When the carriages began to arrive, he didn't move, but stood there, watching the guests appear— breathless and refreshed from the cooling rain, the ladies in their mud-spattered boots holding fine silk shoes in drawstring bags that hung from their wrists. Today solidified his future. The invitations had gone out bearing the news of their engagement. There was no way Rosalie could wriggle out of it now without causing her family great embarrassment. He could not imagine her doing such a thing.

But still Jack watched the carriages arrive with a tiny prick of foreboding, a formless nervousness. He told himself it was because it had been so long since he was in polite company; he was not sure how to behave. And though that was part of it, there was something else, too, something he could not quite put his finger on.

Jack waited until the party started before he made his way into the parlor. He paused outside the open dining room doors, standing out of the way of the servants who rushed in and out carrying trays and dishes.

It was a small group, as Garland had said, but the women had dressed in dazzling colors, silks and flounces, the men in formal black frock coats. Jack eased his shoulders back, feeling an unaccustomed freedom in the cut of Garland's made-over coat. The fabric was old and rich; it smelled of money, it smelled of the life that had once been his, and for a moment he wondered if there was anyone here who might recognize him, any American businessman who'd had dealings with him at his uncle's brokerage, or worse, any plantation owner who had rented convict labor from the lessor of Parish Prison. He dismissed the thought as ludicrous. Garland had not mentioned anyone Jack knew from his days with his uncle, and if any of these people were plantation owners—well, they had never come near the convicts working in their fields; better to leave that to the overseer hired by the prison. Besides, it had been a long time since Jack had been allowed to work in the sunshine. Two years.

He tensed again, and then he saw Rosalie Lafon, and the sight of her, the serene smile on her face, her steady grace, made him feel instantly unworthy and coarse, the proverbial sow's ear. She looked cool and elegant in a restrained gown of pale blue silk, her dark blond hair smoothly caught up in a chignon. She was the epitome of a gracious hostess, milling through the crowd, offering merise, wine, lemonade. He watched her for a moment, marveling at the change. No one looking at her now would think she was anything but the perfect hostess, a kind and gentle soul. The cold, spinster martyr he knew had disappeared.

It reminded him of the first time he'd met her, and that memory made him vaguely uncomfortable, bringing with it as it did that strange yearning for her acceptance. Jack turned away, edging past the dining room table with its extended leaves, the pristine tablecloth, the sparkling wine glasses, and the nougat cathedral shimmering in the candlelight. The sideboards were already groaning with dishes for the first course, the scents of turtle soup and vol-au-vent and oysters mingled with a dozen perfumes. The rain-fresh breeze coming through the open windows and doors could not compete. There was the rapid chatter of French and laughter and the discordant tuning of instruments, and Jack poured a glass of bourbon and held it tightly in his hand as he stepped into the room.

Rosalie had disappeared again, but Jack saw Garland at the far wall, gesturing to another gentleman, telling some story. When he caught sight of Jack, he motioned him over, and obediently Jack went to stand beside the old man.

"My future son-in-law, and my heir," Garland said, clapping Jack heartily on the back. "Bertram Minot, may I present Jack Waters. This is why we celebrate, eh?"

Bertram Minot was small and dark and exceedingly polite, too well-bred to snub the American relation of his business partner, but Jack saw the faint distaste in the man's eyes, and the snub was there in the way he murmured a "*Bonjour*" and lapsed again into French. Garland did nothing to include Jack in the conversation, and after a few moments Jack excused himself and wandered off. He nearly bumped into Rosalie as she came around the corner.

"Monsieur Waters," she said. Her tone was chilly. Whatever charm and elegance he'd seen earlier was gone—at least for him. "I wondered if you planned to make an appearance this evening."

He smiled at her, broadening it when he saw how taken aback she was. "Now, darling, you know I wouldn't miss this for the world."

"How unfortunate," she murmured. Then she glanced around the room. He saw the distance in her eyes as she raised her voice and lapsed into careful politeness. "I've heard the streets are nearly impassable. I imagine your uncle will be late in arriving."

Jack nearly choked on his bourbon. "You invited my uncle?"

She looked at him in surprise. "Why would I not?"

Jack swallowed the rest of his bourbon in one gulp. He could only guess what his uncle's reaction would be to an invitation. "I could have told you not to waste the effort," he said, and though he tried, he could not erase the bitterness from his voice.

He saw the puzzlement in her eyes. "But . . . do you mean he does not approve?"

"Let's just say my relationship with my uncle is . . . strained."

"Oh. Papa didn't tell me."

Jack glanced across the room, to where Garland was entertaining a group of his cronies. Jack had not expected this. To invite his family . . . what could be the purpose of it?

He glanced back to Rosalie and saw that she was watching him carefully. With effort, he shuttered his thoughts and smiled again. "Well, now you know," he said. "I don't expect he'll be attending this little party." He emptied his bourbon and looked around for something to put the glass on, then decided to hold on to it; he could use another.

"I'm sorry," Rosalie said, but there was less sorrow in her tone than confusion. Then she glanced over his shoulder and frowned. "He must not be that angry with you."

"Why would you say that?"

"Because he's here." She nodded toward the front door. "At least, I assume it's him. I know everyone else. And your aunt, too, it seems. They've come after all."

It felt as if the floor went out from beneath him. Jack watched Rosalie push by him, saw the gracious smile instantly on her face, and it seemed as if the room—the colors, the scents, the motion—tilted, blurred. He could not place himself, he could not find his bearings. His uncle had come. His aunt . . . He hadn't seen her in three years, and the yearning that came at the thought of her pulled everything from him.

Slowly he turned. He met Garland's eyes. The old man smiled and raised his glass in salute, and suddenly Jack remembered how bound his uncle was to the First Bank of New Orleans. Charles Waters would not risk offending Garland, regardless of whether he'd disowned his nephew.

Jack watched Rosalie make her way through the crowd, and then she was there, greeting his uncle, instructing Mattie to take his uncle's coat and his aunt's wrap. Rosalie gestured back toward him, and Jack could imagine her words: *Jack's just inside. I know he will be anxious to see you.*

Anxious, yes. Afraid. Angry. *Longing.* Jack was rooted where he stood. He could not tear his gaze away from the couple who had been the only parents he'd ever known. Instantly the images from that last day in court flooded back to him: his uncle's absence, his aunt crying softly in her seat, her inability to look at him, the pain in her voice.

Jack's throat tightened. Now, dressed in finery, smiling as she made her greetings to Rosalie, his aunt seemed almost a stranger. There was more gray in her hair now, and her skin had contoured to the bones of her face. She had not been youthful when he'd gone into prison, and the years since had not been kind to her. The only thing he recognized was the color she wore, the pale yellow that was her favorite shade.

She was the only mother he really knew. His own mother was nothing but ghostly shadows and vague fragrances, memories so old they were almost those of a stranger. He waited for her to turn, to catch sight of him. He felt an anticipation so strong it made his skin hurt. Uncle Charles might not want to see him again, but Aunt Agatha . . . He'd been worming his way into her affections since the day she'd taken him in. He was hungry for her smile.

Rosalie leaned close and said something to the both of them. His uncle straightened and looked around the room. Jack felt his uncle's gaze brush by him, then stop. He felt that piercing look—it had skewered lesser men to the spot—and Jack went hot. Then he saw his aunt turn. Jack started toward them.

Aunt Agatha turned away.

It was so startling Jack stopped. She hadn't seen him yet, he thought. Perhaps if he raised his hand . . . But the truth was a hard, bitter tightening of his gut. His aunt left his uncle's side, disappearing through the crowd, and Jack saw the disbelief on Rosalie Lafon's face, the confusion.

His aunt had snubbed him. It was deliberate and slow, and he would not have believed it but for the obvious embarrassment on Rosalie's face. Now, suddenly, he remembered the truth of his aunt's tears at his trial, the averted gaze that stemmed from anger and betrayal—not pain, as he'd wanted to believe.

He felt a surge of anger, humiliation, and fear that he swallowed quickly when he saw his uncle working toward him. They had both disowned him, but of course Uncle Charles could not leave well enough alone. The bitterness Jack felt at the thought was so overwhelming, it was all he could do to stand there and wait for his uncle to reach him.

Charles Waters stepped through the people like Moses parting the Red Sea. When he reached Jack, he stopped and jerked his head toward the courtyard. "A word with you," he said curtly.

Jack wanted to refuse, but a lifetime of obeyance held; he found himself grabbing a decanter of something from a servant's tray as he turned to follow his uncle.

The night was blue and balmy now after the rain. The courtyard was lit with candle lanterns that glowed softly on the flagstones and the banana leaves. There were others out there, too—a night for romance, it seemed. He heard quiet whispers in the air, the hum of mosquitoes, low talk—somewhere a giggle.

His uncle didn't look back once to see if Jack followed, and Jack was angry at the assumption, at the confidence, even as he came. Charles Waters didn't stop until he was fully in the middle of the courtyard, and then he stood there, staring into the darkness, until Jack came up beside him.

"How nice of you to make an appearance," Jack said acidly. "I didn't expect to see you."

His uncle stared straight ahead. "You must know I had to come."

"Ah, yes. Can't risk offending the great Garland Lafon."

His uncle slanted him a glance. It was strangely knowing, a little curious, and it discomfited Jack so he knocked the decanter against his glass when he poured. The smell of cherries wafted up to him. Merise. Ah, well, at least it was liquor. He took a long, deep sip of the sweet cherry wine and grimaced.

"I have to say I was surprised to learn of your recent good fortune," Uncle Charles said slowly.

"Surprised? Or displeased?"

"A little of both." Charles Waters inhaled deeply. "I'd thought you were too smart to get involved in something like this."

Jack laughed shortly. "Is that a compliment?"

"Oh, come now, Jack, I've never thought you weren't smart. Too smart, perhaps. Too clever. There wasn't a situation made that you didn't find all the angles to it. I'm just wondering if . . . perhaps . . . you're not seeing all the angles here."

"What do you care?" Jack winced. Such little-boy words. But that was how he felt. It was what his uncle always managed to reduce him to: a chastened little boy, a worthless child. He drained his glass. The merise did a tingling burn down his throat. He poured another. "What, have I disappointed you, Uncle? Sorry that I'm not going to be living under the wharves with the other derelicts? Well, I've landed on my feet in spite of you."

"Oh, yes, you've landed on your feet all right," Uncle Charles said lightly. "Out of the frying pan . . ."

Jack stopped in midsip. "What is that supposed to mean?"

Uncle Charles turned to face him fully. His spectacles reflected the candlelight; it was impossible to see the look in his eyes. "This only proves what I've always told you, Jack. You didn't learn a thing working in the brokerage—and now it seems Parish hasn't taught you anything, either. An engagement, an inheritance . . . What is it Garland expects from you? Have you wondered what the price will be?"

"I can see you've never met my fiancée."

Uncle Charles ignored that comment. "Who initiated this little deal of yours? Did you search out Garland? Or did he search you out?"

"He found me."

"Ah." Charles nodded as if Jack's answer satisfied him. "He's heard me say you were clever, but I'm warning you—he isn't me. He won't tolerate laziness. He will expect you to make something of yourself."

Jack took a step back. "And you think I can't do that—"

His uncle's hand on his sleeve stopped him. "Listen to me, Jack. I know you don't believe this now, but I have your best interests at heart—"

"Oh, yes, the 'I'm doing this for your own good' speech." Jack shook his uncle's hand loose. "Pardon me if I don't care to stay around and hear it again."

"You'd better listen this time." Charles Waters's voice was low and so intense that Jack did stop. He looked into his uncle's face. In the dimness, the man could have been a stranger. Only the voice was familiar, only the voice held him. "Your aunt and I took you in when you had nothing. When you threw that kindness back in my face, you disappointed me beyond reason. For that, I don't care if you spend the rest of your days twisting in the wind. But that woman in there has cried every night since you were arrested. Because of her, I promised myself I would talk to you tonight and do my best to keep you from ruining yourself again."

"Ruining myself?" Jack asked tightly. "Or making a success of myself? Which bothers you more, Uncle?"

Charles Waters laughed. "Believe what you want, Jack. But this I will tell you: I don't know what you think you're doing with Garland Lafon or what game you're playing this time, but you'd better watch yourself. This is your last chance. You ruin it, and you're finished in New Orleans, do you hear me?"

Jack raised a brow. "Aren't you overdoing it just a bit?"

His uncle stared at him. Jack could only see himself—his shadow—reflected in his uncle's glasses. But Charles Waters was still, and his mouth was tight, and Jack had the uncomfortable and wholly familiar sensation that his uncle was sizing him up, and that he was—once again—failing miserably.

"My God, boy," Charles whispered, "be truly clever for once in your ill-conceived life."

The words were worse for the softness of them. Jack felt them settle hard into his gut, stealing his replies. He could do nothing but stare helplessly as his uncle turned abruptly away. Charles Waters strode back to the house without another word.

Jack could not help himself; he followed. He stopped just inside the dining room, and the clank of dishes, the talk, the music filled his ears; the smoky heat from the candles nauseated him. He saw his uncle's height through the crowd, saw him go to Garland, murmur something, and then leave. His aunt was waiting for him at the archway separating the parlors. She took his arm, and the two of them left. A short visit, an appearance. She had not even looked back to say goodbye.

That woman in there has cried every night since you were arrested. Jack glanced down at the decanter in his hand, at his empty glass. Then he put the glass aside, half dropping it to the table near him, and took a long, stinging gulp of merise from the decanter. Two gulps. He drank it like water, and it choked him and curled in his gut and squeezed. He thought of her motherly hugs when he was a boy, the pride in her eyes when he'd achieved some minor accomplishment. He thought of her touch. His imagination was so vivid he could actually feel the warmth at his shoulder, the press of her hand—

"Why, *monsieur*, I have been looking everywhere for you!"

The bubbling voice was jarring. Jack jerked around. The smell of roses hit him full in the face.

Corinne Lafon.

❧ Chapter 9

He did not know why he didn't walk away from her. It was stupid. She could ruin him. But she had come upon him when he felt empty, and the touch of any woman would do. When Corinne sparkled at him, his insides dropped, and the scent of her filled his nostrils along with the fragrance of cherry wine, the deep, rich heat of roses, and something sexual, a muskiness, a singing in his blood. He could not look at her without imagining how she would feel against him.

"Are you enjoying yourself, *monsieur?*" Corinne asked.

He met her gaze. "Oh, yes," he said.

She tilted her head. The candle lanterns caught her glow; the light played on her soft blond hair, her breasts rose above the low-cut neckline of her gown. She leaned close. "Come with me. I have something to show you."

The promise in the words caught him. His mouth went dry. She led the way through the courtyard, toward the service wing, and he heard the warning ringing in his ears and ignored it. He followed her until she stopped against the wall of the service wing, until she leaned breathless and laughing against the brick.

"Here," she said. "Ah, I love it here. Do you know why, *monsieur?*"

He glanced around. He could see nothing in the darkness. "Why?"

She laughed again. "Because—" She lowered her voice and leaned close, "this is where I had my first kiss."

He could not fathom why she would tell him this, and it made him feel fuzzy and disoriented until he realized suddenly that she was playing a game with him. A dangerous game.

She is not for you.

Then she touched him. She laid her hand flat upon his arm, and he felt his vulnerability in a slow ache, the yearning for a human touch, for some comfort, for . . . whatever he could get. Whatever would soothe him.

"First kisses are so delightful, are they not?" Her voice was silky and low. The lantern cast her face in shadows; he saw the way strands of hair had fallen into her face. Her lips seemed fuller, her eyes slanted and promising. In the seductive light, she was irresistible, and when she smiled at him he forgot why he was keeping his distance, only that he was.

He was off balance; she pulled his hand a little and he fell forward, catching himself just before he touched her. He planted his hand on the wall just beside her head, and she giggled—no, not a giggle; a low, throaty sound that cut through his heart and lungs and stomach and drained him.

"Oh, Jack," she said. His name was laden with

meaning when she said it, heavy with promise. "We are alone at last. I've wanted this to happen. Haven't you?"

She laid her hand on his chest, and it rested there, moving slightly with his breathing before she let it fall. She trailed her fingers down toward his stomach, and he found himself wishing for nakedness—he could not feel her through his vest and his shirt. The motion mesmerized him, the promise of where those fingers might go, what they might do.

"I've seen you watching me," she said. "I know what you want, Jack."

He could hardly think when she was so close. "Do you?"

"Would it surprise you to know I want the same thing?"

"And what would that be?"

"Love."

They were nearly touching now, merely a hair's breadth away. "I thought you were already in love," he managed. "With your pink-stockinged painter."

She angled her head back; he saw the reflection of candlelight in her eyes. "That's over," she said.

"Love is so fleeting?"

"How could it be love? He was just a boy. Not a man. Not like you." She said the words on a breath that seemed to lodge in his chest. "He knew nothing of romance."

"What makes you think I do?"

She smiled again. "Oh, you do, I think, *monsieur*. I am sure you do. I see you with my sister, and I know.

You want flesh and blood, *oui*? A real woman, not a nun."

It was true; he could hardly deny it. He couldn't remember why he wanted to.

Corinne lifted her face; her lips parted, and he felt her moist breath, warm with the scent of sherry. "Tell me what you want, Jack. Whatever you want. I can make you forget Rosa."

He was reaching out to touch her when she said the name. *Rosa*. Rosalie. It stopped him dead; his mind came back to him. This was disaster. Corinne Lafon could ruin everything.

He stepped away, and he heard the hush of Corinne's breath as she realized what she'd done.

"*Non*," she whispered. "Don't think of her. Think of me."

"She's my fiancée."

"But she doesn't want you, Jack. She wants only God." Corinne stepped close again. The smell of her roses was all around him, touching him, clinging to him.

It took all his strength to say, "She hasn't told me that."

She stopped. She looked up at him, and there was an arrested expression on her face that he didn't understand. Desperation, thoughtfulness, calculation . . . It was too dark to tell, and he wasn't thinking clearly enough to know for sure.

"But if she did tell you that, if you were not betrothed to my sister . . . would you . . . want me?"

A dangerous question; even in his befuddled state,

he recognized it. Jack said nothing, but she must have read his gaze, because she nodded and smiled. And then, just then, there was laughter on the other side of the sweet olive, too close for comfort. Corinne tilted her chin and threw him a look—a promise that took his breath—and then before he knew it she was gone, just a rustle of belled skirts in the darkness, a sudden burst of mimosa as she brushed against the branches. He sagged back against the wall, looking up through the trees at the night sky. Relief washed over him so strongly that he felt cold. What he had almost done . . . what he wanted to do . . .

He stared up at the stars, at the darkness, until he could breathe again, until the quick laughter and hum of talk filled the silence in his ears. Thank God for intervention. He had almost ruined himself.

But it wouldn't happen again. He felt his control seep slowly back. Jack straightened. His uncle was so damned certain Jack would fail—well, he would not. He would resist Corinne Lafon with his last breath. He would win Rosalie, and with her, the riches he'd dreamt about. He would not allow himself any weakness at all.

She should not be in the garden.

Rosalie knew this. She should be inside, rearranging nougats on silver trays, summoning servants to refill glasses, charming Papa's guests the way she'd always done, the way Maman had done before her. Yes, she should be doing all those things, and the fact that she was not brought a guilt that made her furtive, that made her hide in the shadows, beneath the stairs of the gallery and the vines of a climbing rose.

She wasn't even sure why she was here, why she had obeyed the instincts that had made her follow Jack Waters and his uncle into the courtyard. It was none of her business what they said to each other; she didn't care. But she had not imagined the surprise on Jack's face when Charles Waters had shown up at their door, nor had she missed his distress in the moments before he covered it up. Jack Waters had something to hide, something to do with his uncle. Why else would Agatha Waters have said, "Don't call him over," in that brusque and rude way when Rosalie had offered to bring Jack to greet them?

It had made Rosalie suspicious. It filled her full of questions, and each one was unwelcome, disconcerting. What could Jack be hiding? She wondered if Papa knew, and decided he did not. Perhaps he didn't know his heir as well as he thought he did.

Rosalie had not been ably to resist following them out, hiding in the shadows of the huge, bushy climbing rose, but now she heartily regretted it. There was such a thing as knowing too much, Maman had once told her. For the first time, Rosalie understood what that meant. Because though she had not been able to hear all of Charles Waters's words, she'd heard enough to put her on edge: *There wasn't a situation made that you didn't find all the angles to it.* Oh, yes, she had suspected that. *I don't know what you think you're doing with Garland Lafon, or what game you're playing, but you'd better watch yourself. You ruin this, and you're finished in New Orleans.*

That had surprised her so much that she hadn't heard the rest. She'd stood there in shock and dismay as Charles Waters left his nephew, striding by her in an angry rush. She would have gone inside then—it was obvious he was leaving, and she should be the proper hostess and see him out—but just as she'd started from the roses, Jack had walked by, and she found herself held in place, at first because she didn't want to risk discovery, and then . . . then because there was something in his face that stopped her, that reminded her of when he'd first come into the house and she hadn't known who he was. She saw that vulnerability again, a flash of it, across his face. An inestimable sadness.

Before she could prevent herself, her compassion went out to him. She'd started from the bushes, she'd thought to say something—

And then there had been Corinne, and Rosalie had stayed hidden in the roses.

They had disappeared so that Rosalie could not see them, but she had not missed the flirtation between them, and she could not move from her hiding place. Her emotions were tumbling: anger, dismay, and . . . fear. Fear was the worst of it. Whatever compassion she'd felt for Jack Waters disappeared—he was exactly what she'd thought he was. He belonged to women like Corinne, whose hearts were so easily repaired. That vulnerability was an act meant to disarm her. It was not real. She should not make it real.

He was dangerous—she felt it in the ache of her heart, the tug of his charm. She could not look at him without remembering, without longing . . . *No*. Not longing. It was simply that she had a weakness for men like Jack Waters, charming, dangerous men who masked their danger with need. She would not be fooled again. It helped, in fact, to know this about him. It would make her determination to resist him so much stronger.

Carefully Rosalie backed out of the shadows of the rose, moving again into the light.

"Miss Lafon."

She jumped at the voice behind her, snagging her gown on the roses, whirling around to see Jack Waters standing there with a slight smile on his face.

"You should be more careful of your hiding spots," he said. He came forward, reaching into the bushes. With a touch too gentle for a man, he freed her silk skirt from the thorns. Then he stepped back again. "Did you enjoy your little foray into voyeurism? Or perhaps you've done this before. Perhaps you aren't so sanctimonious after all."

"I am sanctimonious," Rosalie snapped, and then flushed when she realized what she'd said. "That is . . . I was . . . I wasn't—"

"No, of course not," he said smoothly, though she heard the irritation in his voice. "I imagine it's quiet there; perhaps you were only reading."

She was well and truly caught. The more she protested, the worse she looked. She remembered what she'd overheard, and that gave her the courage to look up at Jack, to confront him with the truth.

"I'm sorry for eavesdropping," she said. "But not sorry for what I heard."

He frowned. "What did you hear?"

"Enough to know I need to talk to my father."

He tensed. "Talk to him? About what?"

"About ending this farce of a betrothal."

His gaze touched her face, and he said nothing for a moment. "Why?"

She struggled for a reason to give him. Something more than the truth—it was too dangerous to admit that she'd known a man like him once, that she knew what he was capable of. "It's clear you're simply after my father's fortune."

He looked surprised, and then he laughed. "Why, Miss Lafon, that's hardly a secret."

Of course he was right. He had never pretended otherwise. Rosalie flushed and looked down at the ground.

"But I'm willing to have it not be the only reason," he said softly. When she looked at him, he gave her a little smile. "I'm willing to fall in love if you are."

Rosalie stepped back from him. "I'm already in love."

"Ah, yes. With God."

"*Oui.*"

He sighed. "Such a pity."

"And if I weren't, I would hardly pick such a man as you to fall in love with."

"Why is that?"

"It's obvious you're playing some kind of game

with my family, *monsieur*. I don't know what it is or
what you've done—"

"What I've done?"

"You must have done something, otherwise you
would be safe in your uncle's employ. I assume you
would inherit his business. You would have no need of
my father's money. Or of me."

His expression was quizzical. "You've been thinking too much, Miss Lafon."

Rosalie met his gaze. "It is clear your family has little use for you, *monsieur*. It is clear they haven't seen
you for some time. Why is that? Where have you
been?"

His shoulders flexed. He looked away. "In a deep,
dark hole," he said, and then he laughed bitterly and
looked back at her. "Does it matter?"

She made a sound of disbelief. "Of course it does."

"You disappoint me, Miss Lafon. I thought you
were a religious woman."

"I am."

"Isn't forgiveness part of your faith?"

"*Oui.* Of course."

"Then I would assume that whatever I've done is
irrelevant. You would be ready to forgive me for it."

"I can't grant you forgiveness. Only God can.
Perhaps you should ask him."

"But you have God's ear. Why, you even know
what His will is, or so you've said."

"I would never presume—"

"Certainly you do," he said. "You told me it was
God's will that you help at the infirmary, didn't you?

How do you know that? Did He tell you?"

She stared at him in confusion. "Through prayer, *monsieur*. I know it through prayer."

"Then perhaps it wouldn't be so hard to pray for me, would it? Go ahead, ask Him if I'm forgiven. I would surely like to know."

"Why don't you ask Him yourself?" Her words were sharp; she didn't like the way he made her feel, the way he twisted things around. She remembered the other day, in the courtyard, when he had changed from one mood to another, lightning quick. She never knew what he would say next, and she did not like people like that. She did not like him at all.

He was gazing at her, and she was wondering what it was he saw in her face when he suddenly looked away. He sighed, and she felt the air change between them, felt something fall away, a slackening, before he turned back to her and held out his arm. "Walk with me?"

She stared at him suspiciously. "Why?"

"So I can apologize," he said softly.

"For what?"

"Come with me, Miss Lafon," he said. "Let me explain."

He reached out and took her hand, placing it on his arm. His hand was warm and strong. The touch was vaguely disconcerting. He held her there so she couldn't pull away. When he started to walk, she had no choice but to walk along with him.

"It's a pretty night," he said as he led her down the dimly lit flagstones, into a pool of light created by a lantern and then out again, into the shadows. It was so dark that she could feel him and smell him but could barely see his face.

"I suppose it is," she said. Then, bluntly, "If you expect me to change my mind about you, *monsieur*, I must tell you you're wasting your time."

He chuckled. "You're a little like a bulldog, Miss Lafon. Has anyone ever told you that?"

How flattering. "*Non*," she said stiffly.

He laughed again. "It wasn't an insult."

"Of course not."

"I've rarely seen a woman who knows her own mind so well."

She wasn't sure if she was being insulted or not. Rosalie stole a look at his face. It was too shadowed to see his expression.

"But I wonder," he said, "if you've thought about what your father will do if you decide to take the veil."

Rosalie hesitated. His question brought a tight sadness into her chest, and she felt again the uncertainty that had haunted her these last weeks since Papa's illness. "*Oui*, I have thought about it."

"He'll be lost without you."

"I know."

"You've been taking care of him for a long time."

"Since Maman died."

"How old were you then?"

Rosalie inhaled deeply. "Thirteen."

"A child yourself."

"*Non*." She shook her head. "I was always old for my age. Maman used to call me her *petite assistante*.

She used to say that she could depend on me to take care of everything."

"Hmmm." His voice was low and thoughtful. "Who took care of you?"

She felt a sudden, deep ache. "I didn't need anyone."

"Not even your mammy?"

"Papa dismissed her just after Maman died. He was afraid she was taking Maman's place in our— Corinne and my—affections." It made her sad to think of it even now. She remembered the day Mammy Titi had left, her dress hanging on her bony body, her tignon sagging. Rosalie had not been able to forget it for a long time. Along with the memory came a sick regret, the sense that she could have stopped it from happening. She had meant to visit the old woman, to comfort her, but she never had. Two years later she'd received word of Mammy Titi's death, and though she'd meant to go to the funeral, something had happened—she couldn't remember what now, but she hadn't gone.

"And now you have God."

He startled her a little; she had been wrapped alone in the memory, and his voice was an intrusion.

But it seemed as if he didn't expect a reply, and so she didn't answer him. They were at the back of the courtyard now, near the kitchen. The stables were just beyond; they were close enough to hear the horses nickering to each other. In the cooling pond behind the cistern, the water trickled softly.

The music of the soirée seemed quiet and far away,

another world. Here there were only the horses and the water and the soft hum of insects, and Rosalie found herself relaxing, lulled by the softness of night and the sounds, by memories that had nothing to do with the man beside her. When he led her to a bench near the sweet olive tree, she went without protest and sat beside him.

"I like this courtyard," he said. "It reminds me of . . . home."

She glanced up at him. "Home?"

"My uncle's house." His sigh was soft, barely there, but she heard it nonetheless. "My parents died when I was quite young. I don't remember them. I was . . . three, I think, when I went to live with my aunt and uncle."

"They were your parents, then."

He laughed shortly. "Ah, yes. Such a loving pair."

The compassion she'd felt earlier came back to her; it felt harmless to give in to it a little. "I'm sorry."

"About what?"

"Your aunt," Rosalie said.

"Don't worry about it," he said gruffly.

"She really is your *maman,* isn't she?"

"Was," he told her. "Not anymore."

"I see." Rosalie took a deep breath. "Perhaps it is you who does not believe in forgiveness, *monsieur.*"

"You think I should?" He glanced at her. "I've been disowned and rejected. Pardon me if I'm feeling a little angry."

"Perhaps they're angry, too."

He choked a laugh.

Rosalie hesitated. "I will ask you again, *monsieur.* Why . . . why are they angry?"

He went very still.

"A personal question, I know," she said quickly. "It is just that—"

"Ah, yes. You were eavesdropping."

His voice was hard. Well, she deserved that, certainly. "I apologize. But I—" She wasn't sure how to word it. How did one say, *Is he right about you?* Would she even believe what answer he gave? "You must realize, *monsieur,* that you are a stranger to me. I am only protecting myself and my family; certainly you would do the same. Forgive me if I'm a little overzealous in my attempt."

He nodded. Then he was silent for what seemed like a long time—long enough so that when he spoke again, the sound of his voice surprised her. "What is that over there, by the kitchen—night jasmine? I smelled it even in my dreams."

Rosalie looked to where he pointed. It was dark, but she had a vague memory of some viney plant snaking up the gallery post near the *garçonnière.* "I don't know," she admitted. "I'm not much of a gardener, I'm afraid."

"No? What a pity."

His voice was low and soft, and there was a sadness in it that surprised her. There was the vulnerability again, and she wondered why. What was so sad about the flowers? What was he remembering?

"I used to garden myself. A long time ago."

"So did my mother," Rosalie said.

"The bougainvillea over there is a rare color," he said. "I noticed it this morning."

The bougainvillea. Rosalie looked blankly into the darkness. She didn't remember bougainvillea; where was it? A pink flower, wasn't it? How was it that she couldn't remember? Certainly there had been a time when she wondered how it got to be such a brilliant pink, when she had delighted in the delicacy of jasmine, when the mimosa and wisteria had enchanted her with their fragrance. She could not remember it, but she knew those things in some deep place inside her. She knew that once she had noticed.

The thought brought a strange emptiness, and she leaned back against the bench, feeling the elaborate iron hard against her shoulder blades. Suddenly she remembered what she'd come out here to say to him.

"*Monsieur,*" she blurted, "I really must ask you to give up this idea of marrying me." She felt his surprise in the darkness, and she knew her words seemed abrupt, too cold for the conversation they'd just been having. "You must understand, I have made a vow to God—"

She broke off when she saw the way he was looking at her: a long, slow look that was strange and disconcerting. It made her feel tight and embarrassed. She squirmed beneath his gaze until she saw his faint smile, until he said, "You've said that before, Miss Lafon. Who are you trying to convince? Me? Or yourself?"

He got to his feet then. "Good night," he said, and then he left. He simply disappeared into the darkness before she could say a word, leaving her breathless and unsettled behind him. It was minutes before she truly realized that he didn't mean to come back, that he'd left her alone with her thoughts, with his question.

Rosalie looked blankly into the courtyard. The lamplight from the house glowed into the night, shadowing the magnolias and the orange, softening the mimosa. The music floated on the air along with the scent of melting candle wax and citronella and roses. Roses as strong as her sister's perfume.

She turned and realized the bench was in the roses, and there were fat blooms near her shoulder, their heavy heads sagging. Slowly she reached for one and snapped it from the stalk. She could not remember the color, and in the darkness she couldn't tell. There was only the shadow of it before her, the feel of it, the perfume. She brought it to her nose, inhaled deeply—and sneezed. The bloom was overripe; it disintegrated in her hand, petals falling in a cascade to her skirt, littering the flagstones.

Rosalie tossed what was left of the bloom into the flower bed. She got to her feet, treading on the petals, and hurried back to the party, to the safety of small talk and refilling glasses and arranging nougats just so on a tray, away from the night and its flowers, away from questions she did not want to answer.

❦ Chapter 10

It was two days before Corinne saw Jack Waters alone again. Late in the afternoon, she returned from the milliner's to find him in the courtyard. At first she thought he was a servant, because his back was to her and he was on his hands and knees, digging in one of the parterre beds. She started to go to her room—she was exhausted and nauseated from the rocking carriage and the too-hot day, and a headache was threatening. But then she saw his hair glinting gold in the sun, and her heart stopped. She glanced around the courtyard. Rosalie was nowhere to be seen, and there was no one else around. Corinne drew back into the butler's pantry, among the giant clay ollas, to gather herself. She jostled one, and a ruffle on her skirt trailed into the drinking water.

Corinne closed her eyes and took a deep breath, trying to banish both the pain in her head and the queasiness that threatened to bring up what little breakfast she'd eaten. She could not let this opportunity pass by, regardless of how she felt. There was too little time—a man might believe that a baby that came one month early was his, but two months . . . She knew little of Jack Waters, but one thing she did know was that he was not a fool.

She had made some progress with him the other night at the soirée, and for that she was relieved. Paulette had sprinkled the love powder she'd concocted onto his breakfast—it was why he'd been so receptive to her that night, Corinne was sure. She had been longing for the opportunity to press the advantage.

She waited a few more moments, and when he rose from the garden and sat on one of the nearby benches, she caught her breath at the sight of him. In shirtsleeves, he was quite the most handsome man she'd ever seen. Such broad shoulders, strong arms where the shirt clung to the sweat on his skin. He angled himself so the wrought iron seemed to caress his whole body, and then he closed his eyes and sighed. *Oh, this is perfect—it could not be more perfect.*

Corinne stepped from the shadows. She crept over to where he was, careful to keep her skirts still, and clapped her hands over his eyes. He jumped, muttered a curse, and tried to twist around, but before he could, she leaned down close to his ear and whispered, "Guess who?"

He tensed, then she heard his sigh. "Corinne," he said. He grasped her wrists lightly, pulling her hands away from his eyes, and turned to look over his shoulder.

"Ah, and I tried to disguise my voice!"

"It's your perfume," he said. "Roses. It's hard to mistake you."

She smiled. He'd noticed her perfume; could one be more sure that he was enraptured? "You looked so peaceful, I couldn't resist. Were you dreaming, *monsieur?*"

"I wish."

Corinne gave him her dimpled smile. "How nice, to wish for such a thing. Tell me, what do the dreams of Jackson Waters hold?"

His look was wry. "Running, mostly."

"How intriguing," she said. "When I was at the convent school, I used to have a recurring dream that someone put a rat up my skirt. What do you suppose that means?"

"That you're afraid of rats?"

She smiled again, warmly. "What about you? Is there something you're afraid of? Or . . . wait . . . perhaps it isn't seemly for a man to admit to fear. Sister Bertrice used to say: 'Men's purpose is to take care of the weaker sex. They must fear nothing but God.'"

"She was a nun," Jack said.

Corinne laughed. "Of course. I did not think of that." She lowered her voice teasingly. "So what are you afraid of, *monsieur?* Something other than God?"

Jack's face darkened, but for just a moment, too short a time for Corinne to regret the question. Then he smiled up at her. "I'm afraid of charming women who wear roses for perfume."

She came around the bench and sat beside him, hoping as she arranged her skirts that he noticed how prettily they fell, the way the lace crumpled just so around her hand, highlighting her slender fingers. The bench was small, and she felt the brush of his shoulder against hers. "Then you must let me teach you not to be afraid. Let me see, how to amuse you? Ah, I know—the weather."

"Too hot," he said. "Discussion over."

"You take all the fun out of it, *monsieur.* You see, I must fan myself and lean back and sigh dramatically, and you must reassure me that the rains are coming soon."

"Too much melodrama. It sounds like a romantic novel."

"Then perhaps an observation instead: It is far too hot to be working in the garden, and below your station as well. We have servants for that kind of thing, you know."

"I was bored. And no one else seems to be taking care of it."

"*Non,*" she sighed. "The man who tended it died a few weeks ago. They said it was a fever, but Paulette tells me he was"—she lowered her voice to a whisper—"overcome by a voodoo curse."

He gave her a quizzical little smile. "Who's Paulette?"

"Our maid."

"And she would know?"

Corinne leaned close. "Don't tell Papa, because he would dismiss her in a moment—he is intolerant on this point—or Rosa, either, but Paulette's aunt is a voodooeine."

"Ah. What about Paulette?"

"She knows a few spells. Mostly . . . love charms. And the like."

He smiled. "Miss Lafon, what need would a woman

like you have for a servant who can make love charms?"

Corinne smiled and thanked the Lord for Paulette. "Such a compliment, *monsieur*. You must be careful or you will turn my head."

His smile flattened slightly. He leaned his head back to look at the sky, and the mimosa overhead dropped a dying petal into his face. She leaned over and brushed the petal lightly away, and he jerked beneath her touch and sat up quickly.

She took it as a sign that he was not immune to her. He too must have felt a shiver at the simple touch. But he looked out at the garden, to where he'd been working. There was newly mounded dirt around one of the roses, with thorny clippings and faded blooms scattered on the walk. "You say Paulette tends to your sister, too?"

Warily, Corinne nodded.

"But Rosalie doesn't know about this voodoo?"

Corinne laughed. "Do you think she would countenance it? Rosalie?"

Jack chuckled; the sound warmed her clear through. "That's true enough."

"She would be praying for poor Paulette's soul every night." Corinne pressed her hands together and looked heavenward, mocking her sister. "'Oh, dear Lord, please save Paulette from the devil. She is dancing along the path of evil!'"

He sat up, and there was something in his eyes when he looked at her, a new interest. "You do that very well. Perhaps you should be on the stage."

"Me? You mistake me, *monsieur*. I am just a poor

girl destined to marry and have children. Such grand schemes—" she tsked in mock dismay— "they are not for me. Perhaps for Rosalie. She could play Saint Joan."

He laughed. "You know your sister well."

"I have spent my entire life with her. It is hardly surprising." She leaned forward and lowered her voice. "After years of study, I have come to an important conclusion."

"Which is?"

"I hate to tell you this, *monsieur*, but I believe Rosalie is not meant for marriage. The convent is the best place for her."

"Why do you say that?"

Corinne didn't bother to hide her sarcasm. "Have you not noticed? She spends her days at church or helping the poor and pitiful. She spends her night in prayer. Rosalie has dedicated herself to God. She wastes her time here at home; why, think of how much good she could do at the Ursulines."

He raised a brow. "Seems to me that what your sister could use is a lover."

He said the word slowly, thoughtfully.

It sent a shiver through her—Corinne could not decide if it was merely the sound of the word on his lips and the visions it brought into her head, or if it was because he was her sister's fiancé and the thought of them together was . . . distressing. Corinne felt a touch of panic. She tried for nonchalance. "Rosalie does not want a lover. She has never wanted one. You should have seen her at her debut; such a shy girl. She hardly tried to catch a man's eye. It was as if she didn't care."

Corinne remembered it well. She had been eleven when Rosalie was sixteen, and she remembered how Rosa had changed that summer. The girl Corinne knew, the sister who had run about the courtyard with her, who had spent afternoons making love charms and naming their future children, had become someone she didn't know at all.

Rosa had never courted the attentions of the young bachelors at the Opera that season. She'd drawn inside herself instead, trading adolescent whispers and flirtatious smiles for rosary beads and Our Fathers.

"Let's not talk about Rosa now." Corinne smiled her best smile at Jack and saw the dazzle of her expression in his eyes.

"All right," he said. "Let's talk about you. You seem to be an expert on what is best for everyone, Miss Lafon. What about yourself? What's best for you?"

Corinne caught his gaze and held it. "Why, *monsieur,* it is a simple thing. What I want is true love."

His eyes darkened, and Corinne's heart skipped a beat. He was going to kiss her, she knew he was—but he didn't. He leaned back a little, and the muscles in his arm tightened against the back of the bench as if he were holding himself in check.

"You mean you haven't found it yet?" he asked, and there was a tease in his voice.

Corinne felt herself flush. "It is not nice of you to remind me of him. I've told you, he was a boy, not a man. Not like you."

"Me?"

"You know what true love is, Jack, I think. You are a romantic at heart—you cannot tell me you aren't. Why else would you be here with me like this, unchaperoned?"

"Oh, we have a chaperone," he said. He inclined his head toward the house. When Corinne glanced through the veil of mimosa to the house gallery, she saw the glint of sunshine on dark blond hair, the bright flash of an embroidery needle.

Rosalie. She seemed as calm and serene as ever, the very picture of a woman taking the evening air, innocently embroidering. But just as Corinne looked, Rosalie glanced up—once, quickly—and then down again, as if she saw Corinne's study.

Corinne felt the hot rush of embarrassment. "*Mon Dieu*," she snapped, unable to help herself. "Why does she spy on me this way?"

"I don't think she's spying on you," Jack said quietly.

She looked at him, and he touched her lightly on the arm and smiled. "I should leave you," he said.

But she read the promise in his eyes; she understood the message he was giving her. They would meet again. Sometime soon, and alone. Her heart jumped, and she felt a relief that made her smile. "*Oui*, of course," she said. She dipped her head and said in a soft voice, "You know Rosa goes to mass every day. In the morning."

He nodded and got to his feet, and though his movement looked quick, she felt the lingering heat of it, the way he let his hand fall across her shoulder as he rose. His smile was warm and intimate; it seared itself into her heart, branded her there. If she had not been his before that moment, she was then.

"Good afternoon, Miss Lafon," he said, and then he paused and looked toward the *garçonnière*. There was a puzzlement in his face, a curiosity. "That jasmine . . . I can smell it clear over here."

Then he was gone, striding across the courtyard. She watched until he opened the door of the service wing stairs and disappeared into the darkness. She heard the door latch, and watched for him to appear on the upper gallery.

She waited until he was in his room, and then Corinne closed her eyes in satisfaction and leaned back against the hard bench. She took a breath of air, trying to smell the jasmine the way he had said. When they were married, it would be a shared memory—years from now, she would say, "Do you remember how the jasmine smelled that afternoon?" and he would reply, "Every time I smell it I think of you." But the jasmine was not so strong—here among the sweet olive, in the cloud of her own rose perfume, she could barely smell jasmine at all.

When she saw them there in the courtyard, Rosalie felt the pinch in her chest, so tight she couldn't breathe. She'd been in her bedroom, glancing through the French doors, when she'd noticed them, Jack Waters's dark blond head and Corinne's golden one close together, with the sunlight playing upon them like God's blessing. He was leaning too close, he was flirting . . .

Rosalie went hot. She felt like a fool for even caring—no, she did not care. As long as he was not flirting with her, she didn't care at all. It would be better if he fell in love with Corinne, if he married her, if he left Rosalie alone.

Who are you trying to convince? Me? Or yourself?

Rosalie looked down at her embroidery, willing the words away. Instead, she forced herself to remember other words, the ones his uncle had said to him, but those words, too, made her uncomfortable. *There wasn't a situation made that you didn't find all the angles to it.* Yes, she'd known that about him already; her heart had known it, her heart had recognized him.

The thought unsettled her; she looked again down at the courtyard, heard her sister's laughter. Jack Waters was Gaston all over again. One touch, one moment of ecstasy, and it was over, it was eternity.

Rosalie's fear settled in her heart like an old wound. And then suddenly she thought of a way to end this farce. For once she was thankful for Corinne's flirtation—it would convince Papa once and for all that Jack Waters did not belong here, that as a husband he would not do. Surely her father would not force her to marry a man bent on a liaison with her sister. Surely he would throw Jack Waters into the street. . . .

The plan brought immeasurable relief. Rosalie's fingers tightened on the tapestry in her lap; she murmured, "Thank you, Father, for staying beside me in this time of trouble."

Almost in response to her words, Jack Waters rose. He nodded to Corinne, said something, and then walked away. Rosalie made herself stay seated until he was gone, until he had sprinted up the stairs and disappeared into his room. Then she gathered up her silks and stuffed them into the basket beside her, barely noticing when the needle pricked her finger. She hurried down the stairs to her father's office. She knew he'd come home early today, and he was exactly where she'd expected to find him, seated at the big desk, bent over papers with a glass of *bière dolce* at his elbow. He glanced up when she paused at the door.

"*Chérie,*" he said with a smile. He put down his papers and motioned to her. "Come in, come in."

Just as it always did, Papa's smile reassured Rosalie. He would listen to her this time, she knew he would. She stepped fully inside, settling in one of the hard-backed chairs that flanked his desk.

"You look worried, Rosa," he said, squinting at her. "What can be troubling you today?"

"Papa, about Monsieur Waters—"

Papa frowned. "This topic wearies me, Rosa. I have told you, I am not changing my mind about him. You had best put this nonsense about the Ursulines behind you. I am determined that you will be a bride in the fall."

"Perhaps you will not be so sure when I tell you this, Papa," Rosalie said calmly.

Her father's frown deepened. "Tell me what?"

"I am afraid Monsieur Waters is not acting the part of a betrothed man."

"Well, you should encourage him, *chérie*. How can he tempt you if you do not allow him to do so, eh? Take my advice, Rosa—let him flirt with you, encourage a kiss or two. The best way to keep a man close is to keep him interested."

"Oh, I think he is interested, Papa," Rosalie said wryly. "Just not in me."

"What are you saying?"

"I think he has developed a . . . *tendresse* . . . for Corinne."

"For Corinne?" Papa looked puzzled.

"She's been flirting with him, and—"

"Ah that—that is nothing." Her father exhaled in relief and waved his hand dismissively. "Corinne would flirt with a tree stump if it wore the right clothes. She will soon forget if she's not encouraged."

Rosalie took a deep breath. "Today they were together, in the courtyard. And Papa . . . it looks as if . . . that is, I think perhaps he is encouraging her."

Papa stared at her as if he had not heard her correctly. Rosalie licked her lips. "I'm not imagining it, Papa."

Her father held up her hand to quiet her. His mouth tightened. "You are sure?"

"*Oui.*"

He exhaled slowly. "*Mon Dieu,* that girl. Would that *she* longed for the convent! I will admit, I saw the way she looked at him, but what is a father to do with a beautiful idiot like that? Corinne may have all your mother's beauty, but she has no brain in her head. Not like you, eh, Rosa? I thought Jack would have the sense to stay away from her."

"It didn't look as if he was staying away."

"He bent close to her? He kissed her?"

"They looked—" Rosalie struggled for words. "—intimate. And Corinne knows of my aversion to this marriage. Perhaps she thinks she is better suited to him."

"She hasn't the reason God gave a flea." Papa snorted and shook his head. "You have done well to bring this to me, Rosa. *Merci.*"

"I was right, wasn't I, to think you wouldn't condone such a match?"

Papa laughed shortly. "Condone? *Mon Dieu,* I would not! He is meant for you."

"But if I don't want him," Rosalie said carefully, "and he would rather have Corinne—"

"*Chérie,* do not worry. Leave this to me."

Rosalie tried for nonchalance. "You will talk to him?"

"I will do more than talk to him," Papa said, and there was a threat in his voice that reassured her.

Rosalie bowed her head, working to keep the smile from her face. "I knew I could rely on you, Papa."

"*Oui, oui,* that you can." Her father came around the side of the desk, sitting on the corner across from Rosalie. He leaned forward. "Rosa, I promise you I will take care of this."

Rosalie smiled. Papa motioned her forward, and

when she came to him, he kissed her softly on the top of the head and patted her shoulder. She could not hide her relief. Jack Waters would be gone by tomorrow night, she was sure of it.

But as she left her father's office, she was struck by a sense of déjà vu, the memory of the last time she had asked for her father's aid this way. The memory was old and worn, but it was there, an unwelcome reminder, a bitter weight.

Rosalie paused in the hallway. She leaned back against the wall, closing her eyes until that memory was tucked safely away. That time, too, Papa had done the right thing. He had saved her from herself, and now, years later, she told herself she was grateful for it. But deep inside there was a dissatisfaction that still lingered, a fear she could not ignore. She wished suddenly that she had told Papa in no uncertain terms to send Jack Waters away.

It was early the next morning when Jack heard the knock at his door. He rolled over and slitted open his eyes—the dawn was barely there, it was still just pale purple light—and mumbled for whoever it was to go away, but the knock was persistent, and Mattie's voice was squeaky with insistence.

"You must come, Monsieur Waters. He askin' for you."

He slid out of bed and padded to the door in his underwear. Mattie quickly averted her eyes, but her discomfort was barely punishment enough for waking him so early. Jack raked back his hair and squinted into the hazy morning light.

"Who's asking for me?"

"The master, sir," she said. "He's waitin' in his study."

The summons was urgent, then, and Jack didn't dare ignore it. He nodded at Mattie, then closed the door and washed and dressed.

Except for the birds, the courtyard was quiet when he went out onto the gallery. But the smells of breakfast were already drifting up from the kitchen below, and he saw the kitchen maid's slight frame at the huge cast-iron cistern at the end of the service wing, drawing water into big clay jugs.

He turned away and started to the house. The rooms were quiet on the upper gallery, windows still hazed by drawn netting, dark beyond the paned glass. No one else was up, and he wondered why Garland was, what was so urgent that Jack had to be called from his bed at this ungodly hour of the morning.

Garland's study was on the bottom floor, a small room, utilitarian in decor, without any of the fancy plasterwork or furniture of the rest of the house. Plain white walls were unadorned but for a black and white sketch; a fireplace against one wall held liquor-filled decanters and glasses on its mantel; the chairs were plain, straight ladderbacks. Everything bowed to the huge maple desk in the middle of the room and to the man who sat there—which was, Jack was sure, exactly as Garland Lafon intended.

Garland looked up as Jack entered. The French doors leading onto the courtyard were open, and the pale morning light filtered into the room, glancing across the many papers on his desk, illuminating the plate of figs, burnishing the silver café au lait pourer. Garland was still clad in his nightshirt and his robe, and his face was drawn, as if he hadn't slept well, but there was a sharpness in his eyes that belied any sign of fatigue.

"*Bonjour*, Jack," he said. He motioned to the coffee and raised his brow in question, and Jack nodded and waited for Lafon to pour him a cup of coffee. When he took it, it was lukewarm—Garland had obviously been here for some time.

"Sit down, sit down." Garland sighed and leaned forward over his desk. "You slept well?"

Jack sat. He cradled the delicate china cup in his palm. "Until I was awakened in the middle of the night."

Garland chuckled. "*Oui*, well, some things cannot be avoided, you understand. I wanted the chance to talk to you before my daughters woke."

"Oh? Why is that?"

"There are things we must discuss that are not for their ears."

Jack's chest went tight, but he met Garland's eyes, feigning unconcern.

Garland smiled. "Did you ever work on the chain gang?"

It was all Jack could do to remain expressionless. "No."

"No, eh? A pity, in a way. Such hard labor would make you appreciate the Lafon lifestyle more than you do, I think."

"I appreciate it fine," Jack said.

"Do you? I wonder. More coffee? *Non,* it is too cold, *n'est-ce pas?*"

"I assume you have a point."

"Ah, you are direct, Jack. A perfect American. Tell me, how do you find your days now as a man of consequence?"

Jack said nothing.

Garland fixed him with that assessing, hard gaze. "Perhaps you take it for granted a little too much, eh?"

Jack took a long, slow sip of his coffee. It was cold against his tongue, the chicory too bitter, but he swallowed it and took another, trying to ignore the heavy feeling in his chest, the warning prickling the hairs at the back of his neck.

The old man sat back in his chair. He played with the handle on his cup, and Jack didn't miss the symbolism of it: the gilded china that looked too fragile beneath Lafon's strong, blunt fingers.

"This life satisfies you? To be the heir of a fortune, to be affianced to a woman like Rosa . . . there is little else for a man to want, *mon ami,* is that not so? And you do want it—in this I am not wrong, *oui?*"

It was not a simple question; Jack understood that. But he answered as if there were nothing else beneath it, as if it were not the trap he sensed. He gave Lafon a wry smile. "I want it."

"So I thought. Then why, *mon ami,* do you risk it all by pursuing my daughter?"

A blind panic stabbed through him. Jack struggled for calm. "Your daughter?"

"Corinne. Rosalie has told me she saw the two of you in the courtyard yesterday, and that you looked . . . well, let us say that it did not appear innocent. I have seen the glances that pass between you—I am not a blind man."

"So you're spying on me?"

"I have eyes everywhere, *mon ami.*"

Jack laughed. He hoped it sounded wry, unconcerned, though in reality he was anything but. That girl. Damn that girl. Damn his own inability to resist her completely. He put his cup on the edge of Garland's desk and sat back against the hard wood chair. "You don't trust me."

"Can you blame me? With your past?"

"You chose me, old man."

"And I have rarely erred when it comes to knowing men's natures. But you surprise me, Jack. You have everything here, and yet you tempt fate this way." Garland sighed, his brow wrinkled in what looked like confusion. "I have asked you to court Rosalie, to make her love you. It is an easy enough task, *oui?* Not difficult for a man with discipline, one would think. And I tell you, Jack, tending to a fortune as great as mine requires discipline."

Garland sat back, and Jack saw there was a sharpness in the old man's bearing—he was not as relaxed as Jack had first thought. Garland was too composed;

the slant of his body and the flattening of his fingers against the surface of the desk were the clues. Jack had grown adept at reading men's bearings, and he knew the old man was only pausing. He steadied himself for Garland's next words.

"I spoke to your uncle yesterday."

Jack had not expected that. He felt the freeze clear into his soul. Jack met Garland's gaze evenly. "I imagine he had a few choice things to say about me."

"He is concerned about you, *mon ami*. To hear him tell it, you do not have a reputation as a—how to say this?—a man who bears responsibility well."

There was cleverness in Lafon's eyes, and amusement, and it made Jack itch. He sensed the next question before Garland even asked it.

Garland stroked his chin. "But a few reckless nights hardly make a father disown a son, eh? Which makes me wonder, *mon ami*, what it is you did to your uncle to make him dislike you so. I ask myself, perhaps there is still that wildness in you, eh? Perhaps, if you could betray the man who made you his son, you could betray me."

"I'm not the man my uncle thinks I am."

"Of course not. Three years in Parish have a way of changing a man, *n'est-ce pas?*"

Jack's throat went tight. "Yes."

"So I thought, so I thought. It is just that—" Garland shrugged. He smiled again, and there was poison in the expression. "Well, it is of no matter, is it? It is just that I do not forget it. I remember everything. Tell me, Jack, how you liked Parish Prison. Is it everything they say it is?"

Jack heard the warning in Garland's tone, the implicit threat. *Leave Corinne alone or you'll be on the streets again.* It did not have to be clearer. The memory of his homecoming was still sharp in his mind. Sleeping on the loading dock of his uncle's warehouse, waking before dawn to avoid the workmen. Walking because there was nothing else to do. Listening to his stomach growl.

Damn her, damn her, damn her.

Jack got to his feet slowly.

"Perhaps it is only ennui that makes you reckless," Garland continued. "Well, then, we will try to keep you too busy for idle flirtation. Next week you will come to the bank with me. It is time you found something to do with your days."

"What about Rosalie?"

"Court her at night," Garland said. He chuckled, but there was a meanness in the sound, a warning. "There is little that cannot be accomplished beneath a New Orleans moon, eh?"

Jack nodded tightly. "I understand."

"Do you, Jack?"

Jack didn't bother to answer. He turned and left the chill of Garland's office, and he felt the old man's gaze on him as he strode through the French doors into the courtyard.

He kept walking, clear to the edge of it, until he was hidden by overgrown plants: climbing roses twining about the cistern, split and frayed broad banana leaves. The soft morning air brought sweat to his face, and the smell of flowers was pure and cleansing. This was all too familiar—a threatening conversation with an old man, an escape into a courtyard. It made him think of home, of his uncle. Jack took a deep breath.

What was familiar, too, was this dangling of dreams before him, the yearnings that ached inside him until his blood danced with the urge to move, move faster, be smarter, be better. The last time he'd felt this way, it had won him a spot in Parish Prison. He heard his uncle's voice again: *This is your last chance.*

Corinne's face rose in Jack's mind, and he felt the tightening in his gut, the churning desire. He wanted to curse himself for yesterday, for allowing her to sit next to him, to talk to him so intimately. He should have walked away the moment he'd seen Rosalie sitting on the gallery, watching them, but he'd been caught up in Corinne's smile; she was so effortless, so much easier than Rosalie.

Rosalie.

He thought of her yesterday, with her head bent over her embroidery, her furtive glances. He thought of Garland's words: *Rosalie saw the two of you in the courtyard yesterday.* And suddenly Jack understood what had happened. Rosalie Lafon was determined to get rid of him, and he was playing into her hands. He was giving her reasons to walk away from him.

He'd been stupid. Giving in to even a few moments of pleasure could put him on the street. *Be smart,* he told himself. Rosalie was the one he needed. Garland had told him in no uncertain terms that he had tied his fortune to her—and to Jack, that fortune meant more than money. It meant his chance to make his dreams come true. If Jack could not get Rosalie to abandon her plan to join the convent, he would lose his future.

He'd been too confident, thinking that he'd made strides the other night. She was still wary, and he'd known that. He wanted to kick himself for forgetting it. He had to devote himself more fully to the quest. Like every other woman, Rosalie Lafon had an Achilles heel.

All he had to do was find it.

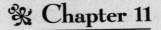

Chapter 11

R osalie was stunned to find Jack at breakfast Sunday morning, and even more surprised when he announced that he was going to mass with them.

"Why?" she asked.

"Tsk, tsk, Rosa, such a question, eh?" Papa grinned, pulling his vest down over his prominent stomach. "Religion is good for a man."

"Of course. I just didn't realize Monsieur Waters believed in God." Rosalie couldn't even look at Jack Waters as she spoke.

"When did I ever give you that impression, Miss Lafon?"

"Few people are as devout as you, Rosa," Corinne said. She wiped her lips delicately with her napkin and put it aside. "It hardly means they don't believe in God."

Corinne threw Jack Waters a brilliant smile. He turned away without smiling back, and Rosalie realized with a sinking heart that Papa *had* talked to him. Instead of putting him out on the street, her father must have reached some sort of agreement with him. In frustration she gripped her fork, forcing herself to lay it down gently instead of throwing it across the table.

Her appetite disappeared. The eggs she'd already eaten settled hard in her stomach. Rosalie excused herself and hurried from the table before the others, suddenly more desperate than ever to get to church, but Papa stopped her before she reached the doorway.

"Wait for the rest of us, eh, *chérie?* We will go to the cathedral together."

It was the usual routine for Sunday, and normally Rosalie enjoyed it. Though she took comfort from her days alone before the altar, when quiet engulfed St. Louis's Cathedral, Sundays reassured her, too; the crowd inside, the murmurs, the hushed stillness of the congregation as the mass began. She felt soothed in the company of her family; there was a sense of belonging that made her feel—if only for a few moments—truly virtuous. And after, they would buy *calas* and café au lait, perhaps go to a friend's house or to the opera when it was in season.

But today, as Rosalie pulled on her gloves and fastened her veil over her face, the comfort she usually took in Sunday mass was hard to find. But she got into the carriage with the others and struggled to remain serene. Already the morning was hot. She was perspiring beneath the band of her hat, and the air under her veil was close and heavy. The ride along the rutted roads to the cathedral jostled her into Corinne, and more than once her knees bumped Jack Waters's where he sat across from her. Rosalie kept her gaze on the view outside and tried to ignore him. By the time they had traveled the short distance to the cathedral, her jaw ached from clenching her teeth, and a headache pounded behind her eyes.

She knew most of the people she saw entering the tall wrought-iron gates of Jackson Square, but it was an effort to smile and nod, and as they walked the exquisite parterre, she stood back and let Papa and Corinne greet the people they passed. She felt Jack Waters at her side, constantly there, never wavering in distance or speed even when Corinne smiled and beckoned him forward.

He was at least taking Papa's warning to heart, for he was noticeably colder toward Corinne. Rosalie had been right about him after all. He was nothing more than an opportunist. Like Gaston.

It was odd, but she found she had wanted to be wrong. She had wanted him to have the courage of his convictions. But men like Jack Waters had no convictions—that was one thing she knew. Men like Jack Waters were dangerous because they cared only for themselves.

Rosalie took a deep breath and let her gaze travel up the length of the cathedral's spire. She'd often thought it was the most beautiful thing she'd ever seen, a testament to God, but today it was just a spire.

"It's impressive, isn't it?" Jack Waters asked.

His voice seemed to come from her own thoughts. It was vaguely startling. Deliberately, Rosalie shrugged. "*Oui*," she said simply.

"Oh, come, Miss Lafon," he murmured. He leaned close; his voice was warm in her ear. "Surely you can do better than that."

"You've said it more eloquently than I ever could."

He laughed. It was a low sound, a rumble from his chest that was warm and intimate, strangely appealing. She felt its draw, the way her heart seemed to leap toward him. *Dangerous.* Rosalie focused on Papa walking ahead, on the bell of Corinne's blue striped skirts as she called a greeting to Annette de la Croix.

"I've never been accused of being particularly articulate when it came to God," Waters said.

Rosalie kept her gaze straight ahead. "Monsieur Waters, I have no idea what your relationship is to God. Nor do I particularly care."

He was quiet. He wasn't going to answer her; it was what she'd hoped for. Perhaps he would even take his leave now. Rosalie quickened her step to encourage him to do just that.

But he didn't lag. He stayed with her. "Not so fast," he said softly. His hand closed over her elbow, a warmly intimate touch. Rosalie jumped, and her heart raced.

She jerked to a stop, looking pointedly at her arm. *"Pardon, monsieur."*

"What have I done to make you so angry with me?"

The question was blunt, unsettling. It left Rosalie's next words withering on her tongue. Her gaze jerked to his and then she wished—oh, how she wished—that she hadn't looked at him at all. His eyes were intense, compelling, and in that moment she felt too close to him, too touched by him, her arm, her gaze . . . Desperately she stared at his hand gripping her elbow. "Don't touch me."

He released her instantly. "This is about the other day, isn't it?"

"I don't know what you mean."

"What you saw between me and your sister. What can I say to convince you it was an innocent meeting?"

"Nothing," Rosalie said. "I wouldn't believe whatever you said."

"I'm sorry for that." He paused and let out a long, low breath. "I wish you had talked to me about it yourself instead of going to your father. Now he's under the impression that I'm carrying on a flirtation with your sister."

"Is he?" Rosalie shot a look at Corinne and her father. They were still talking animatedly to the de la Croix family. "Perhaps it was your tête-à-tête in the garden that gave you away."

"Ah, but a well-chaperoned tête-à-tête, wasn't it? Tell me, do you really believe I would have a liaison with another woman while my fiancée was watching?"

"Perhaps. I hardly know you. I have no idea what you're capable of."

"Don't insult me, Miss Lafon. It's below you."

She looked at him sharply.

He gave her a knowing smile. "Use some common sense. I would have to be a fool to carry on an affair with your sister while you were watching."

Rosalie looked away. "I only know what I saw, *monsieur*."

"And what was that?"

She frowned at him.

"What was it you saw that led you to believe I was flirting with your sister?"

Rosalie faltered. She thought back, remembering the scene, detail by detail. The way he had leaned forward, his smile. There had been laughter, too, hadn't there? And he'd touched Corinne . . . or had he? "Things . . . I . . . things."

"Things? Well, then, perhaps you heard something?"

She'd heard nothing; she'd been too far away. Still, she could not admit it. She could say nothing at all.

"Ah, Miss Lafon," he said. "What have I done to make you distrust me so much?"

There was sadness in his voice, that vulnerability again. Rosalie felt suddenly unbalanced, wrong. But no, she knew what she had seen. He was twisting her words, deliberately distorting things, and this compassion he made her feel—it was her weakness. She was simply drawn to that low voice and that little-boy sorrow, and he knew it. She understood that quite suddenly, quite completely. He knew just what to say to persuade her.

"Monsieur Waters! Join us!" Corinne called. She stood a short distance away, and she was laughing as she spoke to Annette de la Croix. "I would like you to meet someone!"

He glanced up. For a moment he looked torn, as if he might go. Then Rosalie saw him glance at Papa. "Excuse me, Miss Lafon," he said. He strode away, but not to Corinne, as she'd expected. He went to Papa and whispered something to him, and the two men walked over to a suddenly frowning Corinne.

Rosalie felt breathless and uncertain. She was surprised to find that she wanted to believe him. Suddenly she didn't want to be there any longer. She didn't want to look at the confusion on her sister's face and know she was the cause of it. She didn't want to be Jack Waters's morning entertainment.

It was a breach of etiquette to move on. Rosalie should stay. She should greet Annette de la Croix and her family. But instead Rosalie left her family there. They would find her in the Lafon pew, and for now she wanted to walk into the cathedral alone.

It was just like any other Sunday mass, with the close press of people entering the church, the soft reflection of holy water, the scent of God: incense and beeswax, musty vestments, the tang of wine. But instead of reassurance and solace, Rosalie felt the weight of guilt pressing down on her with every step. It didn't leave her as she touched the holy water; she felt its darkness in the dim light of gas lamps struggling against dark wood and veined marble and the pure vastness of space. What a fool she was, that even the reminder of her unworthiness didn't cut dead that yearning inside her, that need to believe him, to like him.

Rosalie paused at the end of the family pew and crossed herself quickly before she went to kneel at her place. She folded her hands on the back of the pew before her and bowed her head to the bright, immense beauty of the marble altar with its painting of St. Louis above. Rosalie took a deep breath and worked to clear her mind, to open her heart. She listened to the sounds until the familiar echoing whispers soothed her. Then she opened her soul to God.

And God whispered back to her: *Do not believe him. Why should you want to believe him?*

Rosalie's eyes snapped open. Her father was at the end of the pew, ushering Jack Waters in to sit beside her, taking his place next, leaving Corinne at the end. Rosalie tensed as Waters settled beside her.

"Is this what you always do?" he asked her, leaning forward to whisper in her ear. "Do you pray as soon as you sit down?"

Rosalie rose and sat back against the hard pew. His shoulder brushed hers. "I am making my greeting to God," she said stiffly.

"You mean He doesn't know you're here?"

She heard Papa's chuckle. Rosalie stared straight ahead. She studied the colors in the portrait of St. Louis, the words in Latin that had been translated for her: *My Blood is drink indeed; I am the Way, the Truth, and the Life.*

"When the service starts," Waters whispered to her, "perhaps you could translate? I don't understand Latin. Or much French either, for that matter."

There was little point in telling him she understood no Latin herself. But she understood the prayers; she knew them by heart. She nodded to him, but once the service started, she was too distracted to translate. The Latin words jumbled into a toneless hum, and the words in the hymnal wavered before her eyes. She heard him beside her, the low murmur of his voice as he prayed, his solid baritone. She felt the heat of him, and now and again the burn of his gaze.

For the first time in her life, Rosalie was glad when mass ended.

As they rose to leave, Rosalie reached past Waters and tugged her father's sleeve. "Go on without me," she said. "I'd like to make confession."

Papa's brow furrowed. "Confession? *After* mass? *Chérie,* what ails you?"

Corinne was staring at Rosalie as if she'd just lost her mind. But then Corinne looked past her, to Jack, and she smiled and said, "We'll have coffee without you, then."

"We will wait," Papa suggested.

"*Non.*" The word came out too abruptly—Rosalie knew it the moment she said it. Papa looked worried. She tried to smile, but the effort was strained. "I'll walk home when I'm done."

"I'll wait with you," Jack said.

Rosalie shook her head a little desperately. "Please, I won't hear of it."

Papa regarded her intently. Rosalie was afraid he would insist on her joining them, but he only said thoughtfully, "We will leave you to yourself, then."

"*Merci,* Papa." Rosalie smiled in relief. She stood back and let them go. When they left her, she sagged back against the pew.

The smell of incense filled her head. She watched a few people light candles, listened to their brief prayers, and waited as the hum of talk gave way slowly to silence.

She rose. She heard her footsteps on the hard, patterned floor echoing in the high arches, the swish of her gown, and the whispers of those who remained in the great cathedral as she made her way to the confessionals, with their highly polished wood reflecting the lamplight. The door clicked softly behind her as she went into one and knelt. She saw the shadow of a priest behind the wooden screen between them. She murmured the prayer of contrition: "O my God, I am sorry for offending You. . . ." When it was over, she couldn't speak. She stared at the wall until she heard the rumble of the priest's voice, close and somber.

"I am here, my child."

Father Bara. It was impossible not to recognize his voice.

She saw his face in her mind, his too-large nose, the close-set eyes, the kindly smile.

Rosalie closed her eyes. Her throat squeezed tight; she blocked his image. Whatever she had been going to confess escaped her; in that moment she was not even sure what she had planned to say.

"My child?" the priest said.

She felt foolish and confused. Hastily she rose—so quickly her rosary fell from her pocket onto the floor. She grabbed it and pushed open the door, stepping out, meaning to hurry away before he had a chance to see her, to recognize her—

"Rosalie?"

She had gone barely a few feet. His voice stopped her; the soft quiet of it stripped her will to be gone. She felt weak, suddenly, and was ashamed of it. She had no idea how she would explain.

Slowly Rosalie turned to face him. Father Bara stood on the edge of the step, the confessional door open, revealing the shadows beyond. His expression was worried. "Rosalie?" he asked again.

She tried a smile. It was weak and wavery. "*Pardon, mon père.* I am . . . not myself today."

He looked at her for what seemed like a long minute, and then he nodded. He gestured down the hall, the winged sleeves of his robes fluttering. "Come, walk with me awhile."

Familiar words. She heard another voice saying them; she felt the soft, balmy darkness of the courtyard; she smelled the fragrance of flowers and the waxy smoke of candle lanterns. *Who are you trying to convince? Me? Or yourself?*

Rosalie hesitated. But Father Bara waited, and so she went to him, moving beside him as he walked with a measured step past the rows of lit candles.

"Have your prayers not answered your questions, Rosalie?" he asked softly.

Her rosary was still in her hands, spilling between her fingers, the beads pressing into her skin in hard little knots.

She twined them through her fingers. She stumbled over her words. "I—I have thought upon this at length. I have prayed every moment. My determination has not changed, *mon père.* I would . . . I beg you, ask me to wait no longer. I am ready to take the veil—today, if need be."

The priest looked at her. She tried to read his eyes, but they were shut to her; she saw only a vague compassion. "If you are meant to be a nun, Rosalie, the wait can only increase your conviction."

"I don't need any more conviction!" The words flew out; immediately Rosalie wished she could take them back. When Father Bara glanced at her in surprise, she flushed, looking down at the floor. "*Pardon,*" she said quietly. "It is . . . this has been a most trying week."

"And why is that, my child?"

She managed to whisper, "My father is not happy with my decision. He is determined that I marry this . . . one of his business partners."

"And you have refused him."

"*Oui.* But Papa is most insistent." Rosalie fumbled with her rosary. The beads clicked and rattled through her fingers. "And I . . . this man disturbs me, *mon père.*" When the priest nodded, she raced on. "Oh, it's not what you think; I am not tempted. But I . . . he reminds me of—that is, I should care nothing for him. But there are times when . . ." She trailed off, unable to say the words, not even knowing what they should be.

There was a long pause, a condemning quiet. Then, "My child, when Adam and Eve first came to this earth, they were free from sin and suffering. They were graced with control of their appetites and the knowledge of all things."

Rosalie looked at him in confusion.

He sighed. "Even they could not resist temptation. We are fallen children, Rosalie. Human nature is not a perfect thing. Our wills are strong. Few of us are completely accepting of God or of His judgment. Sometimes it takes a lifetime to understand what it is He wills of us."

"What are you saying, *mon père?*"

"Rosalie, my child, have you asked yourself if perhaps you are meant to have a husband?"

She froze. Her fingers were like ice. "I have no wish for a husband."

Father Bara nodded. "Of course. But perhaps you long for a family . . . just a little? It is not a crime. I confess, there are times even now when I myself yearn for the soft touch of a woman." The priest smiled wistfully and shrugged. "But those times are only God's test for me. What I am saying, Rosalie, is that you must trust Him to show you the way. Listen to God's will instead of bending to your own. He will bring you happiness in whatever way He deems best."

He meant the words kindly, she knew. He meant them to soothe her. But all she felt was a mindless panic, a desperation that made her say bluntly, "So you are denying me, then."

"Rosalie." He took her hand and patted it reassuringly. "When you are sure that God is your destiny and not simply your solace, come to me again. Remember that He guides you in all things."

Rosalie swallowed. Her disappointment rose in her throat, but she gave him her best smile, and when he released her hand she bowed her head and said, "*Merci, mon père.* You have comforted me."

She left him then. But when she reached the candles, she hesitated. The glow of flames blinded her, and she stared at them until they separated into a hundred orangey glows, a hundred prayers, a hundred souls. The candles smelled of sadness, of loss and grief, and Rosalie filled her lungs with the scent and felt her own fear as a hard, full ache deep in her chest.

Slowly she approached and lit a candle for her mother, watching the flame burst to life beneath her hand. Rosalie stared at the flickering light, and in the glow Maman danced before her. On her face was a soft smile, a kindness, that brought tears to Rosalie's eyes.

She squeezed her eyes shut. "Maman," she murmured, "as you love me, help me now." But it was all she could say aloud; the rest of the words unfolded mutely in her heart. *You were wrong about me, Maman. Marriage is not the answer. I do not want a husband. I do not want* him. *Tell me you understand.*

There was no answer—only the flame gaining strength, pooling wax. Only Rosalie's dark sense that those words, too, were a lie.

Corinne tossed and turned. It was a warm night, and she was too hot beneath the heavy watered-silk coverlet. Finally she rose from the bed and paced. In the dark, everything was shadows; the faint movement of her own reflection in her vanity mirror was the only sign that anything was alive—that she was alive.

She'd spent the last few days wondering if perhaps she had somehow disappeared. She felt herself: her own skin, the fabric of her gown, the stiff lace collar against her throat. She heard herself talk and laugh, and certainly everyone responded as if they heard her.

But in the only place it really mattered, in Jack's eyes, she had vanished. She did not know what could have changed. Only a few days ago he had been her charming, romantic courtier—she had not imagined that he had laughed with her in the courtyard. She had not imagined the way he'd looked at her or how they'd touched. He'd wanted her. How could that change in so few hours?

It had, that was all she knew. The Jack Waters who greeted her now was a chilly stranger. She had tried her best today, but he had not even smiled at her at breakfast; he had barely looked at her when their knees bumped in the carriage on the way to church. Through Jackson Square, he had walked behind (with Rosalie; that was not lost on Corinne), even after Corinne had beckoned him to join her. The admiring looks she'd grown used to, the shared smiles . . . they were completely absent.

She tried to tell herself it was nothing. He was tired, perhaps. The nights were hot; it was difficult to sleep. She had been sure that once mass ended and she and Papa and Jack went to walk the levee, without Rosa, her Jack would return. But the walk was a failure. She had put her hand in the crook of his arm, and he had disentangled himself almost immediately, professing interest in some steamer in the distance. Corinne had thought of a hundred reasons why he would not want to walk so close to her: the sun was hot, the smells coming off the river were heavy and nauseating, Papa held him in conversation. Things would change when they went to the de la Croix house for dinner, she'd told herself.

But dinner . . . ah, it had been all just the same. The man who'd had eyes only for her had suddenly gone blind, and she had no idea why.

Desperately Corinne glanced at her bedside table, at the love spell Paulette had instructed her to make. In the darkness it was only a blacker shadow, but she knew it was nothing now but a lumpy mass of dissolving paper and ink in a glass of gray water. All that was left of the red candle before it was a hardening pool of orangey wax and a blackened piece of wick. She had done everything right; she had followed every step of the spell so carefully. And Paulette swore by the powder she'd sprinkled over his food. But it did not look promising.

Corinne went to the French doors and stared out the paned windows at the darkened courtyard. She tried to see beyond the darkness, through the shadows to the *garçonnière*, to Jack's room. She willed him to be there, to feel her calling him. But there was only silence, and the only movement came from the nighttime breeze through the wisteria.

She turned away so fast her nightgown tangled about her legs. She swished past the mirror, and there the movement of her reflection caught her eye. Corinne sat at the vanity and lit a candle. She rested her elbows on the tabletop and stared into the mirror, trying to see what he saw. Was there some flaw in her? Something he'd suddenly decided he didn't like? But what was not to like? She was beautiful, she knew—men had told her that since she was old enough to smile at them. The candlelight was especially flattering; it turned her golden hair into a halo and made her lips look fuller. It brought mystery to her eyes.

She looked at her body beneath the thin night rail. Her breasts were painful to the touch, and they seemed larger, but there was no difference at all in her stomach or her hips, nothing to show she was increasing. Nothing to repel him.

"Jack, Jack," she whispered, "what have I done to displease you?"

The reflection before her had no answers. She peered beyond herself, trying that same game she and Rosalie had played at midnight on Good Friday, trying to find a glimpse of him there, her future husband. But it was past midnight, and it wasn't Good Friday, and the only other thing she saw in the mirror was the huge shadow of her bed beyond.

Corinne sighed. She squeezed her eyes shut and felt the panic inside her like a burning flame, growing brighter with every little doubt. She could not let him slip away; she could not breathe when she thought of what would happen if she couldn't bring him to her bed. She could not bear to think about it.

Corinne opened her eyes. She had never yet lost a man she wanted to keep, and she had no intention of starting now. Not now, when it was so important. She didn't know why Jack had stopped wanting her, or why his glances and his smile had suddenly become so restrained. But he was a man, and a man who had wanted her once could be made to want her again.

If she couldn't win him with winsome glances and teasing words, she would win him with the things Reynaud and the others had begged for. She would use her body and her kisses. She would seduce him.

She had been taking her time, but she would not do that any longer. Corinne smiled; the woman in the mirror smiled back at her, and in the darkness the smile was filled with mystery, with secrets, with knowledge that made Corinne's mouth go dry and raised a hunger deep within her. In the end, Jack Waters would be hers, and once he was in her arms, she would make sure he was so glad to be there that he would never turn away from her again.

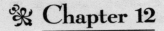

Chapter 12

Rosalie dragged herself out of bed, feeling too tired even to wash. She coiled up her hair and put on a black dress. Within seconds it was too hot to wear in this heat, but there was no time to change. She stepped onto the gallery as quietly as she could, hurrying down the stairs and across the courtyard to the carriage house. Robert was just waking, but he roused instantly when she ordered the carriage.

"One moment, Miss Rosalie," he said, turning his back to fasten his braces. And then, as if he read her hurry, "I be with you soon, you know it."

She walked out of the carriage house and paced, casting worried glances toward the house, toward the service wing. She saw Lucy go to the cistern and heard Monsieur LaFleur cursing in French as he lit the cooking fires, but those were the only people awake yet. The sun was just coming into the sky, but the day was hot already, and promising to get hotter.

Rosalie pulled at her collar. It seemed forever before the carriage house doors opened and Robert led the horses out, but she knew it had not been so long. She didn't give him time to help her inside; she was up the step and settled on the stiff leather seat before Robert even saw her. He smiled an apology and shut the door, and she felt the carriage bounce as he climbed into the driver's seat.

"Wait!"

The voice came from across the courtyard. Rosalie stiffened. She leaned out the window to see Jack Waters striding quickly toward them.

"*Non,*" she said, hitting the side of the carriage with the palm of her hand to get Robert's attention. "Do not wait—"

"I need a ride to the tailor's," Waters called.

"Very good, Mr. Jack," Robert said.

"I'm sorry, but you'll have to wait until Robert gets back," Rosalie called out. "I'm in a hurry."

"But I'm ready to go now." He smiled and reached for the door, and she jerked back. "I won't hold you up."

"I'm sorry, but I must insist."

"You do a lot of insisting, Miss Lafon," he said.

He opened the door and waited for her to move so he could climb in. Rosalie didn't budge.

His grin broadened. "Unless you want me to sit on your lap—"

Rosalie scooted back. She squeezed herself into the corner, making herself as small as possible as he climbed in beside her. He seemed too big for the carriage, his presence overwhelming; his spicy scent stole all the air.

She breathed a sigh of relief when he didn't touch her, but then the carriage started off, and the jerky motion of it had them both adjusting for balance. His thigh pressed against hers, and she felt his arm against her shoulder.

She looked out the window. "It is a short distance to Marceau et Fils. I would have thought you would prefer to walk."

"I was a little tired this morning," he said. "I didn't sleep well."

The interior of the carriage darkened as they went into the porte cochere, and for just that moment she was afraid. In the darkness, it was easy to imagine Jack Waters was the devil beside her. She felt the heat of him, and again she felt that tiny, insidious longing rising inside her, the memory of touch, of temptation that she'd thought she'd long forgotten.

But then they were out of the carriageway and into the light, and things seemed easier again. She stared out at the Rue de St. Louis. There was a mangy spotted dog trotting along the banquette, and she kept her gaze fastened on the animal as she searched for some casual small talk, something to break the uncomfortable silence.

"You look stern today," he said.

His voice startled her. Rosalie looked at him, but it was a mistake, and she knew it immediately. He was watching her with that lazy, speculative gaze that made her heart race, and she had the impression that he'd been doing it since they left the house.

"Black?" he asked, gesturing to her dress. "Your penance must have been particularly harsh."

Rosalie turned back to the window. The dog stopped to sniff at something in the gutter, and the carriage left it behind. She felt curiously abandoned.

"I would like to see you in silk," he said. "A light color. I understand pale green is in fashion now."

Rosalie didn't look at him. "I didn't realize you knew so much about women's clothing, *monsieur.*"

"There's quite a bit you don't know about me, Miss Lafon."

"I would prefer to keep it that way."

"Why?" he asked, and there was a quiet intensity in his words that made her turn to him. "Who knows, you might even grow to like me."

"Perhaps," she said. "But I cannot help thinking—" She broke off. He was looking at her so strangely. She could not remember her words in the face of his gaze. "That is, I . . ."

He smiled gently, and that smile raised a longing in her that was so sharp that it hurt clear into the core of her. Rosalie felt trapped; her breath caught in her throat.

"Poor Rosa," he said. "You should learn to relax, to enjoy life. Not everything needs to be such a strain."

The carriage jerked to a stop. Robert yelled down, "The tailor's, Mr. Jack!"

Rosalie felt breathless, disoriented, and so when Waters said to her, "Where are you going?" she didn't think to put him off.

"St. Anne's Asylum," she said.

He leaned out the window. "Go on," he called to Robert. "I'm accompanying Miss Lafon to St. Anne's."

The carriage started again. Rosalie stared at him. "What are you doing?"

"Going with you," he said. "I've a hankering to see what you do with your days."

She felt that breathlessness again, the shiver at his glance, and she turned away. She had been ruled by her passions once before. She knew how dangerous they were, how completely irrational they could be. Rosalie made herself think of the Bayou St. Jean, of Spanish moss trailing like ghosts in the dusk, of bubbling water and a fetid smell. She made herself think of a little house hidden there beneath the twisted branches of cypress. . . .

Her dress stuck to the sweaty skin between her shoulder blades. It itched unbearably, and she forced herself to bear it, to hate it, because the physical discomfort helped her focus, helped her remember who Jack Waters was and why she should be wary of him.

He said nothing else in the few blocks to St. Anne's, and it was a relief, whatever the reason. When they reached the asylum, a converted Greek Revival mansion at the edge of the Vieux Carré, Rosalie felt her confidence return. She fixed the Ionic columns and wrought-iron gate in her gaze and felt settled again. She was in her element here. Here, among the destitute and helpless, Waters would not be able to shake her.

The carriage stopped. He was staring out the window at the building.

"This is St. Anne's?" he asked. His voice was toneless. He was unusually still.

"*Oui.*" Rosalie waited for him to open the door, to step down, but he didn't move until Robert opened the door for them.

Waters shook himself a little, and then he stepped

out, turned, and held out his hand to help her down. Rosalie grabbed the side of the carriage instead. She tripped a little coming down the stair, but it was better than touching him. She expected some comment from him, some little joke, but he looked oddly disconcerted, and she had the feeling it had nothing to do with her.

They walked to the gate, and his whole body seemed tense. His jaw was clenched.

"What is it?" she asked. "Is something wrong?"

He exhaled, and then he shook his head. "No," he said, and then, "How long has this been St. Anne's?"

"A year or two now," Rosalie said.

"And the family who lived here?"

She looked at him in surprise. "You knew them?"

He was expressionless. "In a manner of speaking."

"I am sorry, then, to tell you this. The yellow fever—"

His gaze jerked to hers. Rosalie stumbled a little and then went on. "It took them all except for the oldest son. He donated the house to the church and asked that it be used to ease the suffering of those who lived. Then he . . . went away." She felt a moment of compassion for Waters, of grief that he should suffer. "I am so sorry. Did you know them well?"

He gave her the strangest look. He was staring at her as if he didn't know her—or no, not that, exactly. It was more as if he were really looking at her for the first time, rediscovering something in her face.

It made Rosalie uncomfortable. She turned away. "*Pardon,*" she said. "It is not my concern."

"I didn't know them well," he said bluntly. "They owned a plantation on the river road."

Rosalie shrugged. "Perhaps. I don't know much—"

"They did," he said. He turned away and looked back at the asylum, and he was quiet for a moment. She felt him thinking, imagined he was wondering how much to tell her before he said, "I worked there once."

She did not know what to say. His words did not seem to match the mood that came over him. She felt there was some hidden meaning beneath them, something she should understand, but she did not.

He was quiet for a moment. His gaze shifted to her, and she felt its intensity like heat on her face. Then he turned away and lifted the latch on the gate, and he was himself again, the Jack Waters she knew. Arrogant, a little sarcastic, too confident. He opened the gate and stood back with a little flourish, motioning her inside.

Rosalie stepped through the gate and expected him to leave her there and felt a dizzy relief that he would do just that. But he didn't, of course. He closed the gate and followed her inside.

There was nothing she could do about it, so she didn't try. She tried to ignore his presence as they went inside the asylum, and within moments after stepping into the entry hall, she felt like herself again. St. Anne's was an asylum for destitute women and their children, and there was an orphanage as well. Rosalie had spent so much time inside its walls that she was familiar with almost every face.

She lifted her veil and stripped off her gloves as she came inside, and turned into the office. Sister Mary Catherine looked up from a scratched and beaten desk and smiled. "Mademoiselle Lafon. It is good to see you."

Rosalie laid her things aside. She nodded toward Waters. "I've brought someone to visit, Sister," she said. "Monsieur Waters is a guest at our home. He was anxious to see for himself just how downtrodden our poor women are."

Sister Mary Catherine nodded. She rose and reached for a bell. "Your interest is greatly appreciated, *monsieur*. I'll summon Sister Theresa to escort you."

Waters stopped her just as the sister began to ring the bell. "Please don't disturb Sister Theresa. Miss Lafon's escort is enough."

Sister Mary Catherine put down the bell with a small frown and threw a questioning look at Rosalie. "As you wish," she said.

"I'll be going into the sickroom," Rosalie told him. "You would be better off to tour the building with Sister."

"I'm not afraid of sick people, Miss Lafon."

"Oh?" Rosalie raised a brow. "Are you afraid of cholera, *monsieur*?"

He smiled and gestured toward the door. "Lead the way."

She had not expected that. She'd hoped he would be a proper gentleman and tour the asylum with the nun. Whatever peace Rosalie had been hoping for dissipated as she led the way to the sickroom and felt him beside her. She'd been wrong to think Jack Waters wouldn't be able to shake her here. She was jumpy and ill at ease, and confused, and she wanted him to leave. She wanted the chance to sort through her emotions, because there was no one feeling that she could point to and say, *Yes, this is it, this is how I feel about him.*

Rosalie's first steps into the sickroom distracted her. Every bed was full. They were all women and children. There were no men allowed at St. Anne's except for priests and the occasional visitor. Most of these women were escaping cruel husbands or fathers, and St. Anne's was their sanctuary. The sisters worked hard to make sure it stayed that way.

Rosalie went inside, moving to the rhythm of murmured prayers. Near the corner, a nun crossed herself as she knelt by the bedside of a woman; the sweet and musty odor of sickness filled Rosalie's nostrils.

Looking at the sister and the labored breathing of the woman she prayed for, Rosalie forgot Jack Waters completely. There were children in the sickroom, too, and their drawn, pale little faces twisted her heart. She was never sure, when she was nursing, whether it was compassion or empathy she felt—perhaps it was both, or perhaps they were the same thing. But she felt ill as those were ill; she felt for their families, for a mother's pain and a child's need. Her relationship with God was never so great and her prayers never came so easily as when she tended to the sick.

She came to St. Anne's once a week, and so she knew exactly what to do. She tied on an apron as she went to the first bed. She saw the sister at the far end of the room nod an acknowledgment, and then Rosalie forgot her, too. She went from bed to bed, soothing hot brows with a cool cloth, feeding broth to those too weary to lift their heads, changing poultices.

As always, the time went quickly. It was afternoon before she finished with the last patient. She turned from the bed and saw Jack Waters leaning against the wall, his arms crossed over his chest. She'd forgotten him so thoroughly that she jumped at the sight of him; her heart leapt in her chest.

It surprised her that he was still here, that he hadn't left in boredom hours ago. But there he was, and his gaze was avid.

Rosalie's shoulders stiffened. Slowly she untied the apron and walked over to him. She forced a smile.

"You're still here," she said, hanging the apron on the hook by the door.

He pulled away from the wall. "Where's the court-yard?"

"Through the hallway," she said. "But it's late. We should—"

"Walk with me for a moment."

Rosalie stopped short of taking the arm he offered. Her chest tightened so she could barely breathe. "We should go home," she said again.

"And run back to your responsibilities so soon?" He shook his head. His smile was beguiling. "Take a rest, Miss Lafon. Walk with me a little while."

It seemed too much effort, suddenly, to fight him. She had not the skills for it, and the last hours had left her without the energy to try. So she nodded; she took his arm and let him lead her down the hallway, through the voices that cried and explained, the shouts of playing children and their harried mothers, the beseeching whispers echoing from the chapel.

The courtyard was not empty. There were nuns moving among the flower beds, and women sitting alone on painted wooden benches. In the far corner, children played hide-and-seek under a magnolia tree. Rosalie felt a measure of security in the noise; he could not confuse her here, she would not lose control of herself.

She saw an empty bench by a hedge of roses, and she thought he would lead her there, but he didn't. He simply walked, and there was an aimlessness to his motion; she had the sense that he didn't see the other people in the courtyard, that he was distracted. Rosalie didn't know whether to be grateful for it or afraid.

It seemed a long time before he spoke, and she felt the coming of it like an impending storm, the heaviness in the air, the dark anticipation. Yet when he finally said something, the words seemed so insubstantial that she was almost disappointed.

"You seem to enjoy nursing."

Rosalie looked at him in surprise. "*Oui.*"

"You have a talent for it."

"What talent does it take, *monsieur,* to tend to the sick? They need comfort more than anyone."

"Perhaps," he said. He was looking away, toward

the children under the magnolia. "Or maybe it's just that their need is more obvious."

The words puzzled her. They seemed oddly sad, not in character for him, and she felt again that strike of compassion; she saw that vulnerability in him that raised her instincts.

"It is plain that this place disturbs you, *monsieur.* We should go."

"You think that's what it is?" he asked. "This place?"

"You are not yourself."

He laughed a little. "And what is that, Miss Lafon? What kind of man is it you think I am?"

Such a philosophical question. She was uncertain again, on edge. She was not sure what to say to him.

"Tell me something," he said, and his gaze was thoughtful. "You don't like me—don't protest, Miss Lafon, you know it's true. I frighten you. I can see your instincts screaming at you to stay away from me. Like this morning, when you didn't want to hold the carriage for me."

It shamed her, to be reminded of that—not so much that she'd done it, but that it had been so obvious to him. "I—"

He put up a hand to stop her. "No, don't apologize. That, at least, I understand." He stopped. They were at the bench, the hedge of roses, and he brought her around to face him without releasing her. "I'll ask it again: What kind of a man do you think I am?"

She swallowed. The scent of the roses was suffocating. "Are you trying to confuse me, *monsieur?*"

He shook his head. "An honest answer. That's all I

want. And I don't mean the standard one. You think I'm taking advantage of you and your family—that I already know. Tell me the rest."

"I—I'm not sure I understand."

"It's easy," he said, and there was an intensity in his eyes that made her want to step away, even as she could not. "This morning, outside this place, you looked at me as if you understood. It was the same look you gave me when we first met—do you remember? You smiled at me, you made me feel at home. You treated me like a welcome guest."

"I—"

"Why?"

Rosalie tried to pull away. The words jumbled on her tongue; her dress itched; discomfort prickled her skin. But he held her so tight that his fingers hurt where they pressed into the tendons of her hand, and not once, not even for a second, did he look away. "You—you were a guest, *monsieur*. I hardly knew—"

"Not that. There was something else there. What is it you think you know about me?"

She didn't even understand what he was asking her. "You—you're a man like any other man," she said, stumbling over the words. "You—you are talking of—of charity. There is no other secret. God asks it of us all—"

He barked a laugh. He released her hands so suddenly it was as if he'd flung them from him, and Rosalie stumbled back, almost losing her balance.

"Charity." He bit off the word; it was derisive and bitter, and with that one word he was back again, the

Jack Waters she knew, the man like Gaston, the man she had always been afraid of. And suddenly she was not afraid of this man at all. It was the Jack Waters of a moment ago who frightened her more, the one who asked for so much, who needed so much. He was the danger.

"Is that what I am, Miss Lafon? One of your charity cases?"

Suddenly it was too much for her: his bitterness, the way he pushed her, the way he kept her off guard. "Of course not," she said, and she didn't try to disguise the tartness in her voice, the anger. "You have no need of me. You have everything."

"Everything?"

"You have my father. You could have Corinne if you wanted her. What more could you want?"

His jaw tightened, his lips clamped shut, and for a moment she saw something behind his eyes, that little boy again, that vulnerable man. But just for a moment. Then his eyes shuttered; she saw nothing but blankness. He turned away.

"Let's go back," he said. "You have responsibilities."

He held out his arm, waiting for her. Rosalie took it. It was stiff, and he was cold, and she felt a barrenness in him that she'd never felt before, a place she couldn't touch, that called to her, that pleaded, *Save me. Help me.*

It was God's voice, and it came to her in a burst of sound and feeling; it shook her into her bones. And though Jack Waters was silent as they went back through the asylum and to the road, Rosalie's ears were ringing as if every bell in the city had chimed out at once. She understood finally and completely why he had been sent to her, what his real purpose was in coming to the Lafon house.

He was hers to save, if she would. It was God's mandate. It was the only way to explain the yearning for him that filled her very soul.

Jack put Rosalie into the carriage and directed Robert to take her home, and then he left her. He turned away from her surprised glance, from the curious little frown that creased the skin between her eyes. He didn't answer her "Will we see you for dinner, Jack?" though the words startled him. It was the first time he could remember her using his given name, and the sound of it on her lips hit him so hard, he nearly stumbled in his haste to be away. He didn't like her voice all over his name. He hated the intimacy of it, because it was just one more intimacy to add to the things he was growing to hate about her.

It was that intimacy that drove him to walk the streets in the intense heat of the afternoon. Her voice rang in his mind, *Jack, Jack, Jack,* in time to his footsteps, until he walked in the dust of the street to muffle the rhythm. He dodged carriages and drays and the curses of drivers, and made his way to the levee, where the air was wet and hot as it came off the river, where the odor of sewage baking on the *batture* was sweet as it mixed with the scent of overripe fruit and West Indian rum and fermenting molasses.

He stood on the edge of the levee, looking down toward the wharves, where the steamers unloaded, and he stared unseeingly at wispy bunches of loose cotton floating muddy and sodden on the water. A sudden blast from a steamship horn startled him, and he shook away his uneasiness and walked on.

But the uneasiness didn't leave him. He felt uncomfortable in his own skin, and Garland's made-over suit chafed at his neck. He was hot and sweating, and yet he couldn't stop himself from walking faster, farther. It wasn't until a mule cart dashed in front of him, stopping him short, that he realized where he was, where he'd walked to.

Waters's Cotton Brokerage.

It was just a block away, and Jack realized with a little shock that it was where he'd been heading. He paused and took a breath, and then he steadied himself and kept walking until he was standing across the street from the long, flat building that was his uncle's business.

He remembered that once the sight of the brokerage had filled him with longing, that when he was thirteen and his uncle had told him he was old enough to work there as an errand boy, Jack had been overwhelmed with pride and happiness. The first day he'd gone to work, he'd worn new gray trousers with braces and a vest, and his aunt had sent him off with his lunch packed in a basket. He could still taste that lunch on his tongue—smothered chicken and biscuits and a thick, creamy slice of his aunt's coconut cake.

He'd felt like a man that day, and he'd run himself ragged trying to keep up with his duties. That night, at dinner, when his aunt had asked how the day had gone, Uncle Charles grunted and said, "You need to be a little faster next time, boy. Those papers were late getting to Stevens."

The joy had started to go out of it then, just a little, like a balloon leaking air, and that balloon had kept leaking, until after a year there was nothing left of Jack's confidence, until he wondered what point there was in trying so hard—he could not live up to his uncle's expectations.

He had drawn away a little then. His anger and bitterness toward his uncle had strengthened until they were a hard knot in his chest that never went away. His uncle could not tolerate idleness and waste, so Jack did his best to achieve both. As he grew older he found friends as dissolute as he was. His days never started before two o'clock, his nights never ended before dawn. In the hours between, he nursed hangovers and listened to his aunt's lectures.

It had gone on like that until Jack was twenty-seven and a particularly belligerent night of drinking had resulted in a berth at Parish Prison.

His uncle had told him—often—that he would never make it in this world, and in some dark place inside himself Jack believed that and was afraid. Opportunities seemed to seep through his fingers like melting ice, there and solid one moment, in the next nothing but wetness and the memory of cold. He had never been clever enough, or worthy enough.

He glanced again at the gray building before him, and Jack thought of Lafon's rich home, the soft pink brick, the pillars. His legacy now, if he could hold on to it. His chance to have everything he'd ever wanted.

But today he'd felt it melting away.

Rosalie.

Jack thought of her this morning, ordering Robert to hurry on, as though she were some regal matron. He wished that was all there was to Rosalie: subtle reproach, obvious disdain.

But there was so much more to her. This morning she had stood in front of St. Anne's and looked at him with a compassion in her eyes that made him remember the first time they'd met, that night when she'd smiled at him and offered her hand and made him feel as if he belonged. And as it had before, that compassion hooked him.

It was why he had stayed with her at the asylum—that building where his memories were so raw and bitter. It was why he'd walked down that hallway—barren now, and smelling of musty clothes and sadness, but he remembered standing there with the other convicts while a servant ordered them to take off their shoes so they didn't muddy the fine carpets.

They'd been transported then to a lavish plantation. There had been no chains attached to his ankles there, but he had worked like a slave in the sun, and the rattle of chains had been loud in his mind.

Those memories stayed with him as he'd followed her inside to the sickroom. The smell of the place had never left his nostrils, so that when Rosalie took him back to that little room, he'd smelled citronella and cigar smoke and fine perfume instead of vomit and unwashed bodies. It had taken him a long time to forget those things, long enough that he could not have said how long he stood there remembering the humiliation of being leased out to the man who had died of yellow fever in that house.

But then, suddenly, he'd been struck by something Rosalie did. He'd been half watching her, too involved in his own musings to really notice her—what was to watch, anyway? A few wet cloths on foreheads, a whispered prayer, a smile. She was like the rest of those society matrons who deigned to visit the poor and heap well-heeled comfort upon them.

Until she'd reached one bed. It held a woman who was obviously near death. Her eyes were glassy and her breathing was labored; her thin chest shook with the effort. When Rosalie sat down next to her, the woman tried to lift herself up to say something, and the effort was too much for her. She gasped and vomited all over herself, and it was foul, the way cholera vomit always was.

He had expected Rosalie to call the nun and move on to some other poor suffering soul, but she had not. She'd grabbed a pail of water and a cloth, and then she'd gently bathed the woman. All the time the sympathy in her eyes, the care, had radiated, and Jack felt its warmth where he stood.

Remembering it now still shook him; he was embarrassed to admit how much. He knew absolutely that Rosalie's compassion was genuine and that when she turned it on him, it was no lie.

He almost wished it were. A liar he could handle, but true goodness frightened him. It made him ashamed of the things he'd done, the man he was. Rosalie Lafon saw inside him, and yet he knew she didn't understand what she saw. She had no idea of the truth of him; she didn't know him at all.

Yet he found himself wanting her to understand. He longed to see that compassion in her eyes for the man he truly was; he wanted her to think that he was worthy. He wanted to *be* worthy.

God, it was absurd. She could not know him; he had not told her the truth about himself. But today he'd wanted her to look at him and see not the fiancé she didn't want, her father's despised heir, but Jack Waters, convict, fool, dispossessed. Because if she saw those things in him and could still care for him, he would know he was not unredeemable. He would know there was something worthy in him. . . .

Jack raked his hand through his hair and turned away from Waters's Cotton Brokerage with a broken curse. Such a stupid delusion. Rosalie would never know how he felt about anything, and that was how it should be. He didn't want her to know.

But that was the real lie—there was a voice inside him whispering it, teasing him from the shadows, and Jack walked faster, until he was far away from the American sector and his uncle's business, past the damp and boggy median of Canal Street.

He walked for a long time, until he found himself again in the Vieux Carré, on Royal Street, where he'd spent so many nights—so many days—shut away from the sunlight, bent over a drink and a deck of cards.

Jack stopped and looked at the buildings, at one gambling hell he'd known too well, and suddenly it seemed as much a prison as Parish had; years without seeing the sun, without tasting fresh air. So much wasted time . . .

He took a deep breath, and the smell on the air caught him. Jasmine. His body recognized the scent. Rosalie.

He spun around, expecting to see her, but she wasn't there—only a sad and crippled vine twisting over a courtyard wall, its few small flowers wilting in the sun. He had a sudden vision of jasmine twining outside his room, and realized in that split second that it wasn't jasmine there at all. It was wisteria. It was wisteria, and yet he'd smelled jasmine for two weeks, everywhere he went. It was in his head, and in his dreams, and he'd thought it was from that damned vine beneath his window. He'd thought—

But it was Rosalie.

The scent memory punched him. She'd been walking beside him today, down that hallway at St. Anne's, and he'd smelled it. Sweet jasmine in the midst of sickness, jasmine where there was no plant to smell.

Jack's stomach twisted. Her face wavered before him: that mobile mouth, her eyes dark with compassion, and he found himself—suddenly and completely—longing to bring her down to his level, to show her with his mouth and hands just exactly why she wasn't the saint she thought she was.

And hating himself for wanting it.

Chapter 13

J ack woke late the next morning. He pushed back the thin bedcovers and sat up. He hadn't come home until everyone had already gone to bed, and it felt strangely as if he'd somehow lost a day. The feeling only increased when he found the water Mattie had left outside his door was cold, as though it had been sitting for a long time. It felt good as he washed, but it was so muggy, he was sweating by the time he was dressed. The café au lait was cold as well, but he drank it down in one swallow, grimacing at the bitterness.

When he finally finished, he stepped onto the gallery. The courtyard was deserted, and it made his sense of losing time stronger before he saw with relief that the garden wasn't deserted after all. Garland was at a table beneath the mimosa, enjoying a late breakfast. The old man looked up and waved him down.

"Come, *mon ami*, come to breakfast! I am waiting for you. I have decided today is the day to introduce you to the First Bank of New Orleans."

Jack felt relief. He'd forgotten Garland's decision to teach him the banking business, and the days were beginning to drag on before him. He was already tired of idleness; the last three years had stripped him of the habit. Quickly he made his way down the stairs and over to where Garland sat.

Garland poured a cup of café au lait and motioned for Jack to drink. "You look as if the devil himself bit you last night, eh?"

Jack heard the veiled implication. "I was walking."

"Ah? Not playing encarté? Drinking with your old friends?"

Jack shook his head. "I haven't seen them since I went into prison."

Garland surveyed him critically. "*Non?* Well, that is good. From what I hear, *mon ami,* your old friends are men you would be best to stay away from."

Jack's gaze flew to his. "Who told you that?"

"Who would not think it who knows your past?" Garland shrugged. "Nothing about you is a secret to me, Jack. But that is not what worries me today. I was . . . concerned . . . when Rosa came back yesterday without you."

There was a question in the statement, a small censure—it was not the gentlemanly thing to abandon a woman, even to her own carriage. Jack wondered what the old man was asking, what he was being held accountable for, but in the end he pretended there was nothing behind the statement; he explained his action as if it were Garland's only concern.

"I think your daughter preferred to be alone."

Garland raised a brow. "She would prefer to spend the rest of her days surrounded by nuns. I did not bring you here to grant Rosa's preferences."

Jack nodded.

"One other thing," Garland said. "About Cor-inne—"

"I've stayed away from her," Jack said quickly.

"*Oui, oui,* I can see that. I was only about to com-pliment you, *mon ami,* on your great strength of will. It has restored my faith in you."

Jack felt only slight relief. "Good."

"She is no longer a temptation for you, eh?"

Jack gave him a steady glance. "She never was."

Garland laughed. "As I thought." He clapped his heavy hand on Jack's shoulder. "Now, come with me, Jack. I have things to show you, and the day moves quickly."

Robert had the horses already harnessed, the car-riage waiting, and they were inside and on their way before many minutes had passed.

Garland settled back into the seat, the leather creaking with his movement. "Ah, the smell of the Vieux Carré," he said, taking a deep breath as the car-riage rocked and swayed through the streets. "Do you not smell it, Jack? It used to be the smell of money, but now . . . now it is not that so much. Now it is just the smell of life."

Jack looked out the window. The leather shades were drawn back, but what little air came in didn't ease the hot mugginess of the carriage, as laden as it was with dust and the smells Garland talked about—horse manure, baking bread, the heavy scent of flow-ers, and the festering sewage in the drainage ditches lining the narrow, intimate streets.

The roads were rutted so badly that Jack's muscles

hurt from tensing against the constant jostle. The world outside shuddered before his eyes. Sunlight slid into shadows between the narrow buildings, glinting off open windows where women leaned on the sills and gossiped to each other, disappearing into the dark passages of carriageways. Every now and then the contents of a chamber pot cascaded from a window and splashed through the green velvetlike scum growing on the surface of the gutters.

Looking at it now, with its growing vacancies and fading colors, it was hard to believe the Vieux Carré had ever smelled of money. But Jack was willing to try to make it smell that way again. He remembered the night of the soirée, his uncle's admonitions, and roughly Jack pushed them away again. He was going to succeed at this despite his uncle's words to the contrary. Maybe because of them.

Garland leaned forward. "Ah, here we are. The First Bank of New Orleans."

The carriage slowed. The bank was no great distance from the house, a few blocks only, walking distance for a healthy man, though the heat was especially oppressive today. The First Bank of New Orleans was impressive, but Jack knew that already; he'd seen it almost every night on his way to the gambling hells of the Vieux Carré. Three stories, with a courtyard at the back, arched windows, and an elaborate iron gate with the letters N and O entwined in the design.

It was obvious that Garland had sent ahead to say they were coming, because the moment the carriage door opened, a man rushed from the bank. He was small and thin, with a dark mustache that twitched the same way his body did. He reminded Jack of a little bird; there was that same look about him in the eyes too, dark, alert, darting.

"*Monsieur*," he said to Garland as the driver helped the old man down. "Everything is ready, as you asked."

"*Bien, bien.*" Garland smiled and turned back to Jack. "Jack, this is Etienne Toledano. Etienne, my soon-to-be son-in-law, Jack Waters."

Toledano inclined his head. "Monsieur Waters," he said. "*Bonjour.* Welcome to the First Bank of New Orleans."

His voice was as slow and deliberate as his movements were quick; it was oddly disconcerting. Jack stepped down from the carriage. After the sweltering ride, the hot, muggy air felt almost cool. "Mr. Toledano," he said, taking the man's hand. "It's good to meet you."

"I am going to show Jack around this morning," Garland said. "You will cancel my meeting with Monsieur Wiggins, *oui*? Tell him we will talk tomorrow."

Toledano nodded. "As you wish, *monsieur.*"

They spent the next hour touring the building. The old man was obviously proud of the bank, and justifiably so. The building housing the First Bank of New Orleans was of restrained design, but it had an impressive vaulted ceiling topped with a dome, and an elegant curved wall that enclosed a courtyard filled with bright green wisteria. Mostly it felt secure and safe. Jack felt an immediate affinity for it; he could barely rein in his longing. For a moment he had the image, a quick fantasy, of himself taking his rightful seat in the director's office, welcoming the businessmen of New Orleans into his bank.

"We will give you an office here, upstairs," Garland said. "Small to begin with, eh, Jack? Until you learn the banking business. Then, we shall see, we shall—" His gaze fixed on something beyond Jack, and he frowned suddenly. "What is she doing here?"

Jack glanced over his shoulder, and the minute he saw her his stomach clenched so hard he thought he'd groaned aloud. But Garland gave no sign that he heard. The old man was already walking past him, crossing the lobby.

Corinne stood just inside the door, folding the pretty pink parasol that matched her walking dress. She had the requisite veil covering her face, the gloves and hat no Creole woman went anywhere without, but on Corinne those things did not have their intended effect. Instead of looking demure, she looked mysterious. Instead of seeming innocent, she brought to mind a hundred different indecencies.

Garland was saying something to her in a low, angry voice. Jack licked his lips and walked slowly over, and he knew she was aware of his every step; he saw the way she tensed when he reached them.

"Jack," she said, speaking through her father's words. She gave him a smile that wavered for a second before it gained strength. "Mattie said you had come here this morning. I was just telling Papa that I had hoped the two of you might have time to take a lady for coffee."

"And I was just telling my wayward daughter to go home," Garland said crossly. "You grow more foolish with every passing day, missy. This is a business, eh? We have things to do here. When have I ever had time for coffee with you?"

Behind the fine lace, the smile wavered again. She blinked and looked at Jack. "Perhaps, then, you—"

"Jack is busy," Garland spat. "*Mon Dieu!* Etienne! Etienne, see if Robert is still outside."

"I already let him go," Corinne said. "He was leaving as I came up the steps."

Garland cursed beneath his breath. "Where is that errand boy . . . what is his name? Georges?"

Etienne came up beside them. "He has gone to take papers to Monsieur Swann, as you requested."

Another curse. "I have no one to take you back home, Corinne. So you will sit here and wait until Etienne can find someone to run for Robert." He turned crossly to Etienne. "A secretary, *oui?*"

Etienne nodded quickly and moved away. Garland scowled at Corinne. "Do not think this has endeared you to me today, missy. This was a foolish little trick."

"*Oui*, Papa." Corinne's voice was barely there. She had dipped her head to look at the floor. "I had not thought. . . ."

"When have you ever?"

Corinne visibly sagged. Jack saw the spirit seep out of her, the way her face shadowed behind the lace veil. He felt a moment's anger that Garland would treat her this way, a familiar resentment. It was like his uncle all over again.

Jack started to step forward, to protest, and then, remembering himself again, he held back. He clamped his lips together.

Garland motioned down the hallway. "Wait in my office," he ordered Corinne. "I—"

"*Pardon, monsieur.*" Etienne was at Garland's elbow again. The man had the most uncanny way of anticipating Garland's every move. "If you please, Hermann has a question for you."

"Can't you take care of this?" Garland said.

"He would be happy to go for your carriage," Etienne said in his slow, deliberate voice. "But he has a concern he wishes to discuss with you."

Garland's exasperation was palpable. "Show my foolish daughter to my office, Jack," he said. "I must take care of still another imbecile."

He was off then, marching across the lobby toward the poor secretary who had jumped to obey him. Jack watched him go, and then he turned to Corinne.

"It was a nice thought," he said quietly.

She looked up at him. "What was?"

"Coffee."

"Ah." She sighed. She glanced toward her father. "He is right, it was foolish. The two of you are busy."

"It was a nice thought," he said again, and then wondered what the hell he was doing when she gave him a radiant smile that the lace of her veil barely concealed. His stomach jumped as the smell of her perfume surrounded him, and suddenly he could barely think. He needed to keep this girl far away from him, not give her reasons to come closer.

He felt weak. Garland had asked him to take Corinne to the office, and already Jack knew he was in trouble. Abruptly he turned away from her and gestured down the hall.

"This way."

Before he could take a step, she was beside him. Though he had not offered his arm, she took it anyway. She clung to it as she slid into step beside him. "You've already made me feel better," she said. "You are a kind man, Jack."

"It's an aberration in my character," he said gruffly.

"Oh, I think not." She tsked. "Though I will admit that the last few days, I have not thought so kindly of you."

"Oh?"

"I thought perhaps I had done something to offend you."

"No." He shook his head. He felt the shape of her beside him, the dress shifting into his hip, away again. Her perfume made his head pound. He was tight all over. "It's not you."

"Perhaps you have . . . other things on your mind," she said.

"Yes," he said. "Yes."

"It is not easy to be a betrothed man." There was a smile behind the words. Jack did not dare look for it.

"I suppose so."

"Have you managed to talk Rosalie out of the convent, then?"

Jack stiffened. "Hardly."

"She may not ever change her mind."

Jack glanced down at her. She was leaning into his arm, but she was looking straight ahead. Her voice was disarmingly nonchalant.

"Perhaps, if you are looking for entertainment . . . you will come to me?"

The words startled him. He thought he heard a distinct invitation in them, and his imagination ran riot. Her voice was low and hot—they were talking of nothing, and yet a hundred different images came into his head, all of them with Corinne Lafon in various stages of undress.

In that moment, the urge to kiss her was so strong he had to turn away. They were at the door to Garland's office. He opened the door and stepped back, gracefully moving away from her.

"Wait with me?" she asked quietly.

He shook his head. "I shouldn't." *I can't.* "I have to get back."

"Of course," she said with a smile. "You are my father's brilliant new protégé. But you will remember my offer, Jack?"

He liked the way she said his name, the softened *J*, the drawn-out *A*, a whisper rushing headlong into the hard wall of the end consonants. He lingered at the door. "I'll do that," he said.

"*Au revoir*, then," she said. She stepped into the

office with a slanted look over her shoulder, another clear invitation.

Jack grabbed the handle and pulled the door shut, a solid object between them, something to blind his vision of her.

He leaned his forehead against the door and took a deep breath. The smell of roses lingered in the hallway. "My God," he murmured beneath his breath. The trouble he was in . . . he'd had enough of enduring it. After dinner he would sneak out and pay a visit to the levee. Lust could be conquered for a few picayunes.

This was all harder than he'd thought it would be, this business of securing a future. There were traps set all along the way. He had the sudden vision of yesterday, of Rosalie Lafon's compassionate eyes. The fancies of yesterday—the smell of jasmine that haunted him, the secrets in her eyes—still unsettled him. Between his fiancée and her sister, he felt twisted in a hundred directions. His instincts were screaming at him to be careful.

"Jack? Jack, are you ill?"

Garland's voice projected down the hall, loud and startling. Jack jerked back from the door, shaking his head, smiling.

"I'm fine," he said. "Tired."

"You look ill," Garland observed. He came closer. "Perhaps you should go home when Robert comes, eh? Get some rest."

The thought of being alone in the carriage with Corinne was too much. Jack shook his head. "No. I'd like to see the rest of the bank."

Garland smiled. He clapped Jack on the shoulder. "You are the best investment I've made in years, eh? Etienne will show you to your new office, *mon ami*. Go on up there now and take a look. I cannot be with you again for an hour."

Jack nodded and took his leave. The last thing he heard as he hurried down the hall was Garland opening the door, his "Well, missy, I hope you're satisfied," before the door shut firmly behind him, closing off all sound.

Jack felt a moment's sympathy for Corinne, a minute of understanding. Then he closed off every thought and went to meet Etienne Toledano.

Garland did not make it up to Jack's office the rest of the afternoon. Jack buried himself in the loan books, familiarizing himself with every transaction made over the last year. He felt ownership in the smooth polished wood of the desk beneath his hands; every thick page he turned spoke to him of possibility.

At his uncle's brokerage, he had felt the same way for a time. Brokering had seemed made for him; he liked the ins and outs of it, the feel of money in his hands. And now the First Bank of New Orleans was like a chastity-belted old dame with challenge in her eyes and a siren call. *Make me yours, lover, show me what you can do. . . .*

He worked until his eyes began to blur and the sun was hot and blinding in the little room. Jack put aside the books and stretched. A breath of fresh air would feel good; it would invigorate him for the next few hours. Certainly Garland would understand—the old man had probably forgotten him. Jack yawned and stepped away from his desk to the door. No one gave him a second glance as he went through the bank and to the front door, and Garland was nowhere to be seen.

The air felt good when he finally walked outside, as hot and muggy as it was. He felt free standing there on the stoop of the First Bank of New Orleans. He went down the few steps to the banquette and inhaled deeply.

He saw her hurrying down the street almost the moment he hit the walk. Jack stiffened and cursed beneath his breath. First Corinne, then Rosalie—it was almost as if God was determined to steal his confidence today. Perhaps he could slip back up the stairs, disappear inside until she passed . . . but he hesitated too long. Before he moved a step, she looked up and saw him. The only saving grace was that it was obvious she wasn't anxious to see him, either. Her step faltered for a moment before she lifted her chin and took the last yards between them. Samson facing Goliath, he thought. Before yesterday, he might have found the comparison amusing. But now it made him wary and tired.

"*Monsieur,*" she said with a nod.

"Miss Lafon," he managed.

She was as bundled up as Corinne had been on this hot day: hat, veil, gloves, a gown that fastened high at her throat. But whereas those things had only served to make Corinne more enticing, on Rosalie they kept a man at bay. *This is a virgin spinster,* they screamed. *Hands off.*

She motioned to the small bag hanging from her wrist. "Papa forgot his medicine today. I thought I would bring it to him."

"You take such good care of everyone," he said. He had not meant it to sound caustic—or perhaps he had; he barely knew his own mind anymore. Still, it surprised him when she flinched; it made him feel mean, and he disliked that feeling too.

"He forgets to take it," she said pointlessly. Then she hesitated. She looked as if something had just given her courage, and when she looked up at him, her gaze was softened only by the smudge of her veil. "I was going to church after I deliver this to him," she said. "Perhaps you'd like to join me?"

Church. It was such a startling thought, he stared at her in surprise. "Why?"

"Because confession is good for the soul," she said. Anyone would have sounded prim uttering those words. On Rosalie Lafon the effect was exaggerated, more than prudish—it was impossibly righteous.

Jack couldn't help it; he laughed. "I don't think so."

Her lips came together, a tight dark line behind the faint shadow of fine lace. "I see. I misunderstood, then."

"Misunderstood what?"

"The other day, in the garden at St. Anne's, it seemed you were looking for something, *monsieur.* I had thought perhaps God could fill that emptiness inside you."

Jack stared at her in stunned disbelief. He felt turned inside out again, that fear that she knew too much, that she could see . . . Deliberately he hardened his voice. "Now, Miss Lafon, why would I need God? I'm the man who has everything, remember?"

He thought she flushed; he couldn't be sure. She bowed her head, instantly contrite. "I apologize. What I said was unforgivable."

"Not unforgivable," he corrected, and then he remembered what those words of hers had done to him.

"You must let me show you how sorry I am," she said.

"I don't want to be one of your charity cases, Miss Lafon."

Another flush. Then she looked at him earnestly. "Monsieur Waters, I have been unaccountably rude to you since you arrived in my home."

"That's not true," he reminded her. "There have been times—"

"I have been," she insisted. "And you must forgive me. I was . . . afraid." She paused, then rushed on. "For my family."

"And for yourself," he said.

Her glance darted; it was strangely telling. It made him feel a little weak.

"No, of course not for me," she said sharply. "I have dedicated my life to God. I am not tempted by the offer of a husband."

There must have been a breeze, though he didn't feel one, because suddenly her jasmine fragrance was alive and filling his nostrils, filling the air all around him. "Miss Lafon," he said slowly. "What exactly are you saying?"

"Until yesterday I did not understand that you are searching for redemption, *monsieur*," she said. "I would be sorry if my incivility kept you from it."

Such self-assurance, such patronizing faith. He could not help himself. He took her arm and saw the surprise in her eyes when he drew her around the corner of the building, into the shadow of the courtyard wall. He felt the flutter of her pulse in her wrist.

"Let me tell you about redemption, Rosa," he said, and saw her start when he used the nickname. "God doesn't save those who don't want to be saved, or didn't you know that?"

"E-Everyone wants to be saved."

"Oh? You haven't tasted enough of life if you believe that."

She stared up at him. The fine lace smudged her features; her expression was hard to read. It took all his control not to tear the veil from her face.

"You only say that because you're afraid," she said. He heard the shake in her voice, saw the force of her control. "But God forgives even the worst sinners, *monsieur*."

"Come, come, Rosa. Do you really believe that?"

She was shaking. He felt it in the birdlike tremble of her bones beneath his fingers. "I do. I do. I . . . I have to."

The words were a whisper. The mystery of them

startled him so that Jack dropped her wrist. Her hand went immediately to her pocket. He heard the clicking of her rosary beads as she fumbled with them. He stepped away.

"What is it you wish forgiveness for, Rosa?" he asked. "Such a prim little soul you must have. How is it you've offended God, hmmm? Did you forget to say a prayer before breakfast?"

She snapped from a trembling, frightened woman to anger just that fast. "What do you know of contrition, Jack? When have you ever done anything except exactly what you wanted? Do you think you have nothing to answer for?"

The words hit him hard. "At least I haven't buried my sins in martyrdom."

She laughed shortly. "*Non,* you revel in them instead. You take advantage of innocent people—"

"God helps those who help themselves."

She shook her head. "You are a wonder, Jack Waters. I think your uncle was right. Which angle are you playing when you speak to me, I wonder?"

There wasn't a situation made that you didn't find all the angles to it. The memory of his uncle's words withered Jack's response. He stared at her hard. "Tell me, Rosa, how often am I going to hear those words thrown at me? Am I just wasting my time hoping you'll trust me? Tell me now, so I can stop trying."

"Don't tell me you would not think the same," she said angrily. "If a stranger came into your family and threatened everything—"

"I would hate him outright," he snapped back at

her. "He would know how I felt every minute of every day. But you—there's no telling with you. One minute you treat me like a friend, the next I'm an enemy, the next I'm your latest social project." He stepped close again. "Hate me, Rosa, if you want to. At least then I know where you stand."

"I don't want to hate you," she said softly. She looked up at him. Then, so softly he barely heard her, she said, "What I want is for you to be a better man."

He froze. Her gaze seemed to sear right through him; again he had the wild and improbable thought that she could see inside him to that spot that held all his uncle's words, that spot that held his fear. *A better man.*

"You self-righteous little prig," he said, and in his anger he enunciated each word, gave each equal weight until she seemed to shrivel beneath his eyes. "What gives you the right to judge me?"

"Oh, Jack," she said, and suddenly she wasn't shriveling at all, she was looking at him with compassion and understanding. "God will understand, don't you see? He will understand."

Jack laughed shortly. "My God, your sister was right about you."

She frowned.

"She said you belonged in a convent. All this talk about God—Tell me something, Rosa. When have you ever lived life? Do you know anything about it at all?"

She swallowed. "Of course."

"Oh? What passion have you ever felt?"

"I've . . . I . . ." She took a deep breath and looked away. "My passion for God is all I need."

"Maybe your spirit is satisfied, but what about your body? Are you human at all? Don't you ever wish for passion of another kind?"

"*Non.*" Her answer was loud, brittle, a little desperate.

"I don't believe you."

"I don't care what you believe."

She backed away, and he realized with surprise that they had been pressed together, that his leg was pressed hard into her skirts. He could feel the solid weight of her body against his hips. It made him think of yesterday, of his wish to show her how unsaintly she could be. How had he stepped so close to her? Only moments before, he'd been turning to leave.

"You know nothing about me, Jack Waters," she said. "You think you do, but you have no idea of my life. You have no idea what I want or what I feel."

"Then we're even," he said.

Whatever it was she heard in the words, it stopped her. Her chest was heaving, but she straightened, she calmed. Her rosary beads silenced. "I was trying to help you," she said.

"You spend too much time worrying about other people," he said. "Perhaps you should worry about your own life."

She took a deep breath and uttered a little, breathless laugh. "Believe me, that's the last thing I want to think about."

The words were strange, and they affected him oddly. What was left of his anger melted. He felt her vulnerability hovering between them, the palpable sadness of it. *Don't ask,* he told himself. *Don't care.* But the word came out anyway. "Why?"

She seemed startled. "It doesn't matter. What matters is that I—I have vows to keep. I've made promises. . . ." Her voice faded off, and she glanced away.

"I see," he said quietly. "How lonely you must be."

Too much of a push; he felt it. She was quiet. He felt her withdrawal even though she hadn't moved.

"Not lonely," she said. She gave him a tight smile—or maybe it was only the veil that made it seem so.

"No," he said. "You have God."

"*Oui.*" She nodded. "I have God."

Then she made her excuses and left him standing there. He watched her until she disappeared around the corner, and when she was gone he glanced at the brightly colored bougainvillea that had dangled over her head, and felt . . . what?

Their exchange had not been what he'd expected. She was too important to him; he couldn't afford to have her hate him. But he was left with the strange and vaguely uncomfortable notion that she didn't hate him, that in spite of the angry words they'd exchanged, something . . . something had changed between them.

And as he walked home in the hottest part of a New Orleans day, he heard her words, *What I want is*

for you to be a better man, and he felt, instead of anger
or pain, a deeply disturbing intuition, a sense that she
understood that worthlessness inside him because,
deep inside Rosalie Lafon, there was a place like that,
too.

❧ **Chapter 14**

C*orinne Waters.* Corinne tried the name on her tongue. She drew it into the air. Corinne Waters. She liked the way it felt. It had a nice sound.

Soon, she told herself. *Soon, soon.* He would be hers, and they would be together, and Papa would no longer dismiss her the way he'd dismissed her this morning, chastising her in front of Jack . . . even now, the humiliation of it heated her cheeks. But then she heard Jack's voice: *It was a nice thought.*

A knock on the door startled her. The maid murmured, "Dinner, *mademoiselle.*"

"*Merci,*" Corinne called back. She rose from her chair, looking out onto the courtyard, at the intense, flickering sunset that would fade to darkness in moments. From the corner of her eye she caught her movement in the mirror, the shimmer of golden silk. She had chosen her gown with care. She shivered when she thought of how Jack Waters would look when he saw her in it.

Anticipation surged through her, and she hurried from her room and down the stairs to the dining room, where the others were gathered. Rosalie was the only one in the dining room. She was lingering by the sideboard, and she looked pale and wan. Corinne had no time to question her before Papa and Jack entered the room.

She caught Jack's eye and gave him her best smile. "*Bonsoir,* Jack," she said.

Papa raised his eyebrows, and Jack looked away. The moment she'd hoped for was gone. *He* was gone. It was as if his kindness today, his smiles, had been only an illusion. She struggled to lose her disappointment, to ease her sudden, overwhelming desperation. Her Jack was there, somewhere. He was only distracted.

"Let us go into dinner," Papa said. "I feel rich as Croesus today. I hope we are having oysters."

Rosalie sighed. "Oh, Papa, you should have put in your order this morning when the fish man was here."

"Ah, well." Papa smiled and put his arm around Rosalie, leading her to the table.

Corinne stepped in beside Jack. "You must sit near me," she said, and she hoped the desperation she felt wasn't showing. "I have missed you today."

She touched his arm, felt him tense; the breath he took was hard. Then he glanced down at her, and she felt almost dizzy with relief when he said, "Of course, Miss Lafon," in that formal, polite way that she knew hid his true passion.

She smiled and led the way, but when she was nearly to her seat, Papa frowned at her.

"Corinne, you must not monopolize Jack. Jack, sit over there, near your fiancée. You do not spend enough time together, eh? Ah, well, I suppose it is my fault. I should not have taken him to the bank today, Rosa."

Corinne smiled a little desperately. "I imagine it

was better than digging in the dirt, was it not, Jack?"

"I have to admit I missed the weeds," he said, taking his seat beside Rosalie.

Corinne reminded herself of his smile earlier. He *did* care for her. He would admit it soon—either that or Rosa would put an end to this and insist on the convent. In either case, he would be free. He would be hers. She tried not to think of the passing days, her expanding waistline. Only this morning Paulette had been unable to fully tighten her stays.

Dinner was strangely quiet. Corinne hardly felt it; she was consumed with watching him, with waiting for a sign, another smile, a look, something to tell her he hadn't lost interest in her, something to give her hope. She memorized his few gestures, his quiet words. Watching him made her feel breathless and anxious.

The second course was served. Corinne watched how he smiled at Mattie when the servant leaned over to pour the second wine. She imagined that it was a smile for her.

Rosalie put her wineglass down so quickly that the table shook. Papa glanced up at her with a frown. "What is it, *chérie?*"

"The wine," Rosalie said. "It's gone to vinegar."

Papa frowned. "Mattie?"

The servant looked at Papa with dismay. "It is the last bottle, *monsieur.*"

"Bring us another burgundy."

Mattie looked at him helplessly. "*Monsieur—*"

"Mattie cannot read, Papa," Rosalie said gently. She put aside her napkin. "I'll get another bottle."

"*Mon Dieu,* send another servant for it, Rosa."

"It will be quicker if I go." Rosalie started to rise.

"Let me," Jack said, getting to his feet. "Finish your soup, Miss Lafon. You've hardly touched it."

"But I—"

"Finish your soup." He looked at Papa. "Any burgundy will do?"

Papa shrugged. "It matters none to me."

"I'll get the wine." Jack left the room, and after he'd gone, Corinne went still with a sudden idea.

She would follow him. The thought of it . . . She remembered the night of the soirée, the way he'd cornered her then, his hands on either side of her, pressed into the wall. Corinne's heart pounded. Her hand was trembling as she picked up her glass of wine. Deliberately she brought it to her mouth too fast, tilted it a bit too much—

"*Mon Dieu,* I've spilled it!" she said.

Rosalie frowned. "And on your pretty yellow silk, too."

Corinne lurched to her feet and dabbed helplessly at the growing pink stain. The dress was ruined, but it was a small price to pay. "Oh, Papa, you must excuse me."

He waved her away. "Go, go. Fix yourself. And do not be so careless next time."

She was gone before he could say another word. She hurried out to the courtyard, through the sweet olive and the roses to the service wing. She heard the clanging from the kitchen, Monsieur LaFleur's raised voice as he yelled at Lucy that she had the brain of a turnip, *get me a skillet now!* Corinne crept past the opened doors, past the warm kitchen light that slanted into the courtyard. The wine room was just beyond. The door was open. The lamplight was dim.

She paused at the doorway. The wine room was small, and he was just inside, half kneeling as he turned the labels and read them in the poor light. His dark blue frock coat looked black; it hugged his broad shoulders, narrowing down his back to his hips, where the skirt of it dragged on the stone floor.

"You're getting dirty," she said softly.

She expected him to be startled, but he didn't even flinch. He glanced over his shoulder and then turned back to the bottle he'd pulled from the wooden rack. "Does your father know you're out here?"

"No one knows." Corinne stepped through the doorway. "We're alone, Jack."

He went still. Slowly he slid the wine bottle back into the rack. "You're sure?"

"*Oui.*" She breathed the word; her anticipation was so sharp, she saw every detail. She memorized the moment, the way his back was still to her, the brush of his hair against his collar—it was so straight and thick, it was nearly stiff—the almost imperceptible shift of his shoulder. She smelled that spicy scent of his, along with the must of wine and corks, the dampness of stone. She heard the scuff of his boot sole as he swiveled to look up at her. His eyes were such a pale blue.

"You shouldn't be out here," he said.

"Are you so dangerous, then?" she teased. She

tilted her head at him. "Should I be afraid you will steal my virtue?"

He swallowed. "Corinne—"

"I wish you would steal it, Jack," she whispered—such a bold thing, but the time had come for truth at last. "I wish you would."

His gaze was riveted to hers. "You don't know what you're saying."

"But I do. I do. I've wanted you, Jack, since I first saw you . . . but this is no surprise, *oui*? I have told you this before."

His eyes burned. Such heat—it caressed her, it made her bolder than before. Corinne stepped further into the room. Deliberately, without taking her gaze from his, she shut the wine room door. It thudded into place, and the latch clicked. He looked at it and then looked back to her. The moment held. She saw the tension in his jaw, the jump of a muscle.

"You should open the door," he said. His voice sounded tight and far away. He made no move to go to the door.

She leaned back against it and smiled at him. "Open it for me," she said.

"This isn't the kind of game you should be playing."

"*Should*," she said in disgust. "I'm tired of 'shoulds,' Jack. We have only a moment before they start to worry. Kiss me. You've wanted to. You know you have."

That burning gaze again. The quick swallow. He took a step toward her, and then he paused and closed his eyes. "Do us both a favor, Corinne. Go back to the dining room."

"Don't play the gallant for me. I know what I'm doing."

He laughed and shook his head. "Oh, no, you don't."

"But I do." Corinne stepped forward, because he would not, and she was tired of waiting. She grabbed his hand and held it to her cheek, pressing it so his fingers had to open against her skin. She held it there and stared up at him. "Believe me when I tell you I've dreamed of this moment. From the first time I saw you—isn't it strange how it works, Jack?"

"How what works?" His voice was hoarse. His fingers flinched against her cheek.

"Love," she whispered. "Did you ever expect it, Jack?" she asked. "When you first came here, did you expect to find love?"

"No."

"I have always marveled at how it happens. One moment you're yourself, and the next moment you meet someone's eyes across a room and everything is different."

"You can't . . . you don't love me."

"No?" She laid her hand on his cheek, which was rough and warm; she felt the softness of his hair against her fingertips. "Then what do you call this?"

She went up on tiptoe and kissed him. He staggered back, caught himself, and then groaned. She felt his surrender in the way his hand slipped from her face and curled around her neck, holding her tight. Corinne pressed against him. He plunged his other hand into her hair, anchoring her. It was a man's kiss he gave her, long and carnal, and it stripped her senses. She was aware of nothing but the feel of him and the taste—

He jerked away. It was so quick she felt the loss of him in sudden emptiness. Her hands met nothing; she nearly fell until he caught her by the wrists.

"What is it?" she asked. "What's wrong?"

His fingers were tight on her arms. When she tried to move closer, he held her away. "*This* is wrong," he said. His voice sounded broken, his breath hard. "We can't do this."

At first she wasn't sure she'd heard him correctly, but then his words sank into her, their physical weight, the dawning realization. "I . . . I don't understand," she heard herself saying, but her lips felt numb; it seemed impossible that she should say anything at all. "I thought—"

"You thought wrong," he said. "Good God, Corinne. I'm engaged to your sister." He dropped her wrists and looked away, down at the ground, and she followed his gaze, wondering in some vague part of her mind what he was staring at: the cracks in the flag-stones, or the moss growing at the edges?

Corinne squeezed her eyes shut. She felt tears pushing in a solid ache behind them. No, no, she wouldn't cry. She would not. "But Jack, I love you."

"I didn't mean for that to happen."

"But you . . ." What? *You flirted with me. You smiled at me. Idiot.* Corinne took a deep breath. "You like me, don't you, Jack? I wasn't wrong about that."

He looked up. He met her gaze. "No," he said. "You're not wrong."

"Then why?"

He exhaled, a rush of breath. "Your father," he said, and then, "Rosa. Damn." He turned away as if he couldn't bear to look at her. "I'm sorry, Corinne. I shouldn't have. It's just that . . . You're beautiful," he told her, as if it were an explanation.

"I'm beautiful," she said slowly. "But you don't love me."

"Yes," he said steadily.

She looked into his eyes, and he glanced uncomfortably away. "I don't believe you."

"I don't know how much clearer I can be."

She stepped toward him, and he backed away so hastily that his shoulder hit the wine racks. Bottles rattled. Corinne stilled. Suddenly something came back to her, something in his words, something wrong. *Rosa*. He had called her sister Rosa. Not Miss Lafon. Not even Rosalie. *Rosa*.

The deadening feeling inside her began to spread. She met his gaze. "This *is* because of Rosalie, isn't it? But not because you're engaged to her. Because you've fallen in love with her." He said nothing, did nothing, and Corinne felt a certainty that made her blood run cold. "Oh, Jack, she wants to be a *nun*."

"She's my fiancée."

Corinne turned on her heel. She couldn't help herself; it was too painful to stay there another moment. She pulled on the door, felt the scrape of it against her arm as she let it fly. It banged hard against the wall. She didn't look back at Jack as she fled the wine room. The shadows of the courtyard blended and wavered in her tears. She took the stairs to her room so quickly that her skirt caught beneath her heel and ripped.

Her room was blessedly dark, blessedly quiet. It wasn't until she reached it, until the doors were shut tightly behind her, that she let herself sob. And it wasn't until almost an hour later, when she felt hollowed out and too sad for words, that it occurred to her to wonder how it had happened.

Corinne had seen no evidence of a growing relationship between her sister and Jack. Rosalie's demeanor had not changed these last days. She still went to mass and the infirmary, still prayed over her rosary. If anything, it seemed she prayed more often.

Corinne sat up on the edge of her bed and stared into the blackness. Good Lord, could it be true? Could it be that Jack had fallen for her sister after all—and that Rosa had decided to give up the convent?

The ache in Corinne's chest spread to her stomach; she thought she would be sick. She stared through the wavy glass of the closed French doors at the blackness beyond. There were no answers there; she knew already whom she would have to ask to learn the truth.

Very well, then. Corinne nodded to herself. She opened the door, lifting her face to the balmy night air. It was fragrant with mimosa, with roses, and it touched the sweat gathering at her temples—her room had been sweltering.

From downstairs she heard voices, the clearing of the table, the men talking about cigars and port, Rosalie bidding them good night: "It has been a long day. *Bonsoir.*" Corinne stepped out onto the gallery. She

curved her hands around the railing—green in the day-
time, but black as shadow now. There was a slight
breeze that lifted the finest strands of hair from her face.
She waited until she heard the soft footsteps on the flagstones outside the dining room, the click of heels on the
cypress stairs. She counted each step. She knew exactly
when Rosalie neared the top.

Rosa slowed. "Corinne?"

"Dinner is over?"

"*Oui*. Are you all right? You didn't return—"

"I lost my appetite," Corinne said.

Rosalie nodded. She took the last steps and came
to stand beside Corinne against the railing. "Your
dress," she said. "You should have Paulette try to
remove that stain."

"I'm throwing it away," Corinne told her. She hated
the gown now; she hated that she was even still wearing it. "I won't wear it again."

"Such a waste," Rosalie murmured.

Corinne did not explain. She didn't expect Rosalie
to understand. Rosa still had dresses from three years
ago, somber colors without decoration, out of fashion—but then, they always had been, in their austere
way. Corinne doubted that any of them brought
unpleasant memories, but even if they had, she
couldn't imagine Rosalie throwing out a dress for that
reason alone.

They were so different. Sometimes Corinne wondered if Rosa could truly be her sister. But of course she
was. They looked so alike—their eyes, the shape of
their faces. Still, when it came to the important things,

to things like love and passion, they were as far from each other as two people could be.

"I am in love with him," she said quietly.

Rosalie turned to her. "What?"

"I'm in love with him," Corinne repeated.

"I don't understand."

Corinne stared out at the shadows in the courtyard. "I know Jack is your fiancé. You must have wondered why I've flirted with him so."

"*Non*," Rosalie said softly. "I haven't wondered."

"I asked you at the start if you wanted him. Do you remember?"

Rosalie nodded silently.

"If you'd said you did, I would have kept my distance, Rosa. You must know this."

"Of course I know it."

"And now . . ." Corinne took a deep breath. Her fingers tightened on the rail. "Now I wonder—have things changed?"

Rosalie stiffened—it was damning, had Corinne wanted to see it that way, which she did not. She could barely breathe waiting for her sister's answer.

"*Non*," Rosalie said. "Nothing's changed."

"You still mean to join the Ursulines."

"*Oui.*"

It was enough, Corinne told herself. But she didn't feel any relief. There was something else there, she knew. Something she felt and didn't want to question. *Take Rosalie's answers and forget the rest,* she scolded herself, but she could not leave well enough alone. She remembered Jack's eyes—if he was not telling the whole truth, he was not lying, either, and it was that half-truth Corinne wanted to understand.

"I want to be honest with you, Rosa. I want him. I mean to have him. Give me a reason to stay away from him, if you can." The words were out of her mouth before she could think, and Corinne prayed that Rosalie would not answer. She wanted no reasons. Without Jack . . . She shuddered to think of what Papa would do to her, what she would become. She was asking her sister for the truth, but Corinne was not sure what she would do if Rosalie told her something she did not want to hear. She could not bear to think about it.

Rosalie's sigh was hard and loud in the quiet. "I would ask only one thing, Corinne."

Corinne could hardly breathe. "What is that?"

"Be careful." Rosalie's voice was almost too soft to hear. "You do not . . . I—I've known men like him. I don't trust him. The things you will find yourself doing for him . . . the sacrifices you will make . . ."

Corinne exhaled slowly. "I'm not an innocent, Rosa. Do you think I have not been hurt before? I have, too many times to count. It is part of being in love. Without it . . . without it, where is the excitement? Where is the passion?"

"Do you think there might be a better kind of love, Corinne? A safer kind?"

"A safer kind? You mean God's love?" Corinne smiled. "You may have God, Rosa, and His pure love. I will take man, with all of his faults."

Rosalie was quiet. Together they stood there against the railing, and it seemed the pause stretched on forever between them. Corinne let it go for a long time. Then she turned to look at her sister. Rosalie was staring out at the courtyard, her face as tight as the chignon that pinned her hair.

Corinne touched her sister's hand where it was clenched on the railing. Rosalie's fingers were ice-cold in spite of the warmth of the night. "Tell me once again, Rosa. I want no sorrow between us. Are you sure you do not want Jack Waters for yourself?"

Rosalie shook her head. "I do not want him," she said, and though her voice was quiet, the words seemed oddly strong. "Not now. Not ever."

She's lying. The thought crashed into Corinne's mind, startling, unwelcome. She stared at Rosalie, and suddenly she saw her sister in clear relief. She saw the pain in Rosa's eyes, and she recognized it for what it was: Rosalie's vow to God at odds with her desires.

Corinne couldn't catch her breath; she couldn't put power to her words. "*Mon Dieu*," she whispered. "You *do* want him."

Rosalie staggered back as if Corinne had punched her. "I don't," she said. "I don't."

But Corinne did not believe her—in Rosalie's eyes she saw the truth. She did not know how it had happened, or when, but it was clear Jack and Rosalie were somehow drawn to each other. Somehow, there was something between them.

It couldn't be, it couldn't be. Corinne's desperation rose in her throat. In that moment she saw her future shatter before her. She'd been lying to herself. Things had gone too far; she had no other options. She had to take Jack Waters from her sister. And that need made her sick with herself, sick for Rosalie.

"Why didn't you tell me?" she heard herself saying, and even as Rosalie turned to her in confusion, Corinne whispered the words again. "Why didn't you tell me?"

She had never meant for this to happen. She did not want to ruin Rosalie's happiness. But it was too late. It was too late, and suddenly she hated her sister for putting her in this position, for not staying true to the vows she'd claimed to want so desperately. She could not stand the sight of Rosalie's pure and even features.

Corinne turned to go, breathing hard, on the verge of angry tears.

"Corinne, wait—don't go."

Corinne stopped.

"You must listen to me," Rosalie said. "You've misunderstood. I don't want him. In a hundred years, I would not want him."

Corinne turned to look into her sister's face. "Oh? Tell me, why is that, Rosa?" she whispered. "*Why?*"

She saw Rosalie go pale in the gaslight, saw her open her mouth to speak, but Corinne turned away quickly, decisively. Though she heard Rosa's weak whisper behind her, Corinne ignored it. She did not want to know. It changed nothing—it only made what she had to do so much worse.

She went to her room and closed the French doors tight behind her. The fine netting covering them was sucked in with the vacuum, catching on the latch so the doors wedged even tighter. She didn't care. She didn't care if her room grew sweltering with the night, if in the heat she couldn't sleep. She wouldn't sleep anyway. Because through all these years she had felt many things for Rosalie: She had been jealous of her, she had felt sorry for her, she had felt compassion. She had hated her sister's martyrdom and her usurping of Maman's role. But one thing Corinne had never thought: that she would be capable of deliberately hurting Rosalie.

Corinne sagged onto her bed and closed her eyes. She felt the fear leaving her, seeping slowly out of her body, and when it was gone she felt empty and shaken. The desperation was gone, but in its place was a new determination, a bitter wisdom that had not been there before today, a truth that squeezed her heart and colored every moment after. Because before today, she had never realized how far she would go to get what she wanted. And now she knew she would never be able to forget.

Rosalie did not sleep. The night drifted through her consciousness in interminable hours, darkness that stretched on and on until she imagined that there would be no morning. She lit her candles and prayed far into the night. When the sun finally began to rise, soft golden light that turned a brilliant pink and orange, she faced it with a troubled heart and no clear answers. Things seemed to be tumbling around her, falling so fast she could not catch them. And at the center of the chaos was Jack Waters.

She had been disturbed already, before Corinne had confronted her after dinner. Her meeting with Jack outside the bank had left her feeling uneasy. She had the feeling somehow that he could see inside her, that he understood things he could not possibly understand. How had he known her fear? He made her feel as if she was retreating from life, as if she were hiding.

But that was what she wanted, wasn't it? To hide, to be safe.

So why had her heart lurched so painfully when he said, "How lonely you must be"?

Because it was true. She was lonely. And she hated that he saw that. She hated how vulnerable she felt when she was around him, how aware she was that her guard was just a flimsy thing, a paper shield.

Rosalie squeezed her eyes shut. She had started something. Things had been put in motion, but she was not sure why she felt this way or what those things were. Corinne's wild-eyed expression haunted her, and her words had touched some truth Rosalie could not admit.

She felt as if she were hurtling toward disaster.

Rosalie pushed her anxiety aside, but still it nagged as she went downstairs to the dining room. It was very early, but Papa was seated at the table. The familiarity of his morning routine, his two newspapers, his café au lait, reassured Rosalie.

"*Bonjour,* Papa," she said, bending to give him a kiss before she sat next to him. "Did you have a good night?"

"*Oui, oui,* like always." He smiled at her, and then his eyes narrowed in a frown. "But you, *chérie,* you look tired. Are you ill?"

"It was a long night," she said.

His gaze sharpened. "Something is troubling you?"

"*Non.*" Rosalie shook her head, forced cheerfulness. "All is well with the world."

"If that is so, then I must have awakened in the wrong century." Papa leaned over. He covered her hand with his own. "What is it, *ma petite?* What has you looking so sad?"

"Nothing, Papa, really." Rosalie reassured him. "Corinne is upset with me."

Her father looked surprised. He took away his hand, sat back with a harrumph. "And this troubles you? Corinne is upset over something every day." Papa took a sip of his coffee. "Now, we are alone for a few moments, so you will tell me what you think of Jack now. Do you like him better, *chérie?*"

"I . . . don't know."

"No?" Her father raised his brows in surprise.

"He has not changed my mind, Papa, if that is what you're asking."

He nodded thoughtfully. "Well, then, answer me this: Do you trust him?"

"He's given me no reason to."

"Has he given you reason to distrust him?"

How could she say it? How did one describe a feeling, a moment, so someone else would believe? "*Non,*" she admitted finally. "He has given me no real reason to distrust him."

Papa smiled. "It is in your nature to worry, but you must not. Still—" He exhaled heavily. "I will not go if you think I should not."

Rosalie's heart tightened. She stared at him in surprise. "Go? Go where?"

"To the bay," he said. "Stephen Howard is vacationing there with his family. He is an important investor, *ma petite,* and there are some things I must discuss with him before the harvest season. I should not be gone long. Four or five days at the most."

Four or five days. He might as well have said a year. Rosalie fumbled for something to say. What could she tell him? *Don't go. Jack makes me nervous, and I don't want to be left here alone with him.* But if she said that, Papa would ask her why, and she would have no answer for him. He was right, after all; the only thing Jack had done in the last few days was prove he could be trusted to do what Papa told him. "Y—You won't take Monsieur Waters with you?"

"*Non.*" Papa shook his head. "Why do I need him? He has not learned enough at the bank to be helpful to me."

"I wish you wouldn't go."

"Why, *chérie?* You have taken care of the house before when I am gone. But . . . if you ask me to stay, I will."

Rosalie sighed. "*Non.* Of course you must go. I . . . we'll be fine here."

"You are sure, Rosa?"

"*Oui.* I'm sure."

"Very well." Papa pushed aside his coffee. "I will leave today. There is just one more thing."

"What is it, Papa?"

"You mentioned your sister. I have talked to Jack about her, and I am convinced he is not returning her flirtation. But he is a man, and Corinne is persistent. You will watch her, Rosa, *oui?* You will remind her that Jack is your fiancé. I would take her with me if I could, but this is important business."

Rosalie felt an uncomfortable twinge of guilt. She looked away. "*Oui,* Papa. As you wish."

"*Bien, bien.*" Papa rose, pulling his vest over his stomach and then taking out his pocket watch and glancing at it quickly. "I am late already. Give me a kiss, *chérie,* and I will see you soon."

"*Au revoir,* Papa," she said. She felt his kiss, and then he was striding toward the doorway. "Take your medicine," she called.

"*Oui, oui, oui,*" he said, each word fading with his footsteps into the hall.

Rosalie looked to the door. She had the sudden urge to follow him, to stop him. The sense of disaster she'd felt earlier came back with a vengeance. *Take him with you,* she wanted to say. *Make him leave me alone.*

But what frightened Rosalie most was the part of her that felt lonely at the thought of Jack's leaving—the part that saw his sadness and wanted to heal him, the part that denied Corinne's accusation, *You do want him,* so strongly . . .

Because she was afraid it was true.

❧ Chapter 15

Jack went with Garland to the bank to hear the old man go over last-minute details with Etienne, and every moment, with every passing word, he wanted to say, *Don't go. Don't leave me here alone.*

Jack sighed. All this because of a kiss. He had known, standing there in that wine room, that he would not be able to resist kissing Corinne if she touched him—it had been three long years since he'd held a woman—and still he'd disappointed himself when it turned out to be true.

He hated that she was a temptation, and resisting temptation was such a novel experience for him; there had been a time when he would have given in to it without a qualm.

That time had passed, thankfully, but still he didn't quite trust himself. He felt weak, too vulnerable. He was afraid of himself.

Just now was the worst possible time for Garland to leave. Jack wanted him there, in the house, at the table, bumping into him in the hallways. He wanted constant reminders of who he was and what was at stake. He wanted to erect walls between himself and Corinne.

Jack glanced toward the courtyard. He wanted distraction. He wanted to have coffee in some broken-down coffeehouse, bent over a table, so involved in conversation that the day passed by without worry or care. It had been years since he'd done anything like that. Years. He could hardly remember now whom he'd done it with. He'd had friends once; where had they gone? Had any of them stayed around to support him at his trial? Had a single one bothered to send him a letter in prison?

He couldn't remember. It was strange, but he couldn't remember a single face—just blond- and brown-haired heads whose features blended together, men his uncle had not approved of because they spent their days immersed in drinking and gambling and whoring. But friends? No, they had been drinking partners, nothing more. They had held contests over who could drink the most, they had placed bets on which of them would make love to the most women by the end of the night. But he could remember not a single deep conversation. No one who involved him. The only person in years who had intrigued him like that was Rosalie Lafon.

Except he didn't think of her that way. Not as Rosalie Lafon. He thought *Rosa*, instead, and it startled him a little that the wall of her full name had crumbled between them, though he'd used her nickname for the first time only the other day. He thought of her looking at him, the secrets behind her eyes.

Jack wondered what she was doing, where she was today, what prayers she was saying to the God she worshiped. He wondered suddenly if she might want to come with him to one of those coffeehouses—there was one somewhere that catered to women, wasn't there?

The idea became compelling; it became the only thing he wanted to do this afternoon. Once Garland drove off in the carriage, Jack hurried down the street in the opposite direction. It was still early, but he would have to rush to catch her before she went to mass.

It was hot, and growing hotter. The city had a smoldering, festering feel. There were funerals every day now, processions led by black horses, black-bordered death notices wrinkling in the bright humidity, tacked one over another on every post and tree and fence in the Vieux Carré. The cholera still. Yellow fever would come later, as it always did. Many of the Creole and American families who hadn't already gone for the summer were leaving now, off to spots where there was no sickness. The levees were packed every day with baggage and passengers waiting to leave.

The infirmary would be busy today. They would need her help. Jack sped his step. He turned onto St. Louis Street and was nearly to the Lafon house when he saw her coming out, properly veiled and covered, a gray shadow closing the door behind her and stepping onto the banquette.

"Rosa!" he shouted, wincing when he saw people turning to look at him. Then, more quietly, "Rosa."

She turned and waited until he came up beside her. "You're not at the bank," she said.

"No." He shook his head. "I'll go back this afternoon."

She tilted her head into shadow. He couldn't see her expression through the veil. "Hmmm." The sound was faintly chiding. "*Pardon, monsieur,* but I am on my way to mass—"

"Call me Jack. You did the other day."

She dipped her head again. He wondered if she was flushing beneath the veil. "It was a mistake. I was angry."

"Then be angry again. Just don't call me *monsieur.* We know each other too well now."

"Really, I'm late already—"

"Don't go."

She stopped, frowning at him.

"Don't go," he said again. "Come with me instead. I was going to get a cup of coffee. I could use the company."

She looked at him as if he'd suddenly turned into a frog before her.

He smiled at her again. "Are you still angry with me? Wait—no, you couldn't be. You called me *monsieur.*"

He saw the faintest shadow of a smile, and with it came relief—he had not realized how much he wanted her to bend, to agree to come with him. Even more than before, it seemed suddenly necessary that she agree. The smile was a start. He pressed his advantage.

"Rosa." He drew out her name, the rounded *O,* the soft hiss of the *S.* He liked the way it played on his tongue, whistled past his lips. "Come with me, please. I need a friend today."

She seemed startled. He heard the catch of her breath. "A friend?"

"I know it's hard to believe, but it seems you're the only one I have just now."

Another smile, a bit bigger this time. "I would hate to know your enemies, then."

He laughed. "Why, Rosa, you made a joke. You *do* have a sense of humor."

He was teasing, but her smile dried up instantly. She turned away from him.

"I can't. I'm sorry," she said. But her tone didn't sound sorry at all. It was prim and hard. "I have confession, and then the infirmary. Father Bara is expecting me."

He wanted to kick himself. "I was joking," he said.

"You don't know me well enough to know if I have a sense of humor," she said.

He'd hurt her. Just minutes earlier it had seemed impossible to have that kind of effect on her, to have any kind of effect at all, and that he had gave him hope again, almost more than her smile did. When she started to walk, he hurried beside her, falling into her rhythm.

"If you won't go with me, then at least let me walk you to church."

"Why?"

"Because I've offended you. Give me a chance to make it up to you."

She laughed shortly. "You haven't offended me."

"No? Then we can talk to each other instead of apologizing. We can get to know each other. I can find out if you truly do have a sense of humor."

She looked at him. "I've told my father I don't want to marry you. He refuses to listen—yet. But he will. So although I appreciate your efforts to . . . court me—" She made a face. "It seems only a matter of time before we go our separate ways. You don't need to pretend you want to be my friend."

There was a wealth of pain in that statement, though her voice was dry and brittle and coarsely blunt. It made him think of their conversation the other day, of his sense that she was like him. Because of that, he understood what she was doing: keeping him from getting close enough to see inside her, putting up a wall.

What surprised him was how much he didn't want that wall to be there.

"You can do whatever you want," he said quietly. "I have no intention of going away. Neither do I want a marriage where I can't talk to my wife. But I think we could truly be friends, Rosa. Frankly, I'd like that. I'd like to know that there's at least one person in this world who wants to talk to me."

"I don't want to be that person," she said.

Curtly. Baldly. It hit him hard so hard he stopped. She continued on, quickening her step. He was stinging, he was angry. *Leave her be,* he told himself. He didn't need to flagellate himself.

But . . . there it was again, that sense that if he gave up now he would be losing something. The feeling mystified him, and it made him race up to her again. It made him grab her arm and pull her to a stop, jerk her around to face him.

"What is it, Rosa?" he asked. "What is it about me that makes you think we can't be friends?"

He felt her stiffen. "I don't need any more friends," she said.

"It seems to me you do," he whispered. "Stop fighting so hard. I'm trying to be nice."

Her gaze rose to meet his. "I wish you wouldn't."

"Why? *Why?* What is it you're afraid I'll find out about you?"

She blanched. Even through the veil he saw it. The quick flutter of her eyelashes as she looked down at the street, her indrawn breath. "N-Nothing," she whispered. "I have nothing to hide."

"I don't believe you." He stepped closer to her. He didn't realize he was going to touch her until he'd already done it, until he'd lifted her chin so she was looking at him. He felt warm skin beneath fine lace, took in her softened features—he hated that veil, he thought again. He wanted to see her face. He wanted to see her expression. "What happened?" he asked softly. "What are you so afraid of that your God can't protect you from it?"

"Protect me?" She laughed bitterly. "It's not protection I'm looking for."

He frowned. He thought of her need for confession, her prayers, the rosary beads that even now her fingers were nervously worrying. "Forgiveness, then," he said. She flinched a little beneath his touch—ah, so he was right. It was forgiveness she wanted.

But for what? What sin could possibly be so big that it would require years of dedication to good works? What could Rosalie Lafon possibly have done to deserve a lifetime of contrition?

The question needled him. His curiosity itched on his skin; she was such an enigma that he felt blind when he looked at her. He found himself wanting to reach her, to affect her. "I thought God did not require so much."

"Perhaps not from most."

"You think God would punish you more than the rest of us?"

"Perhaps I've sinned more than the rest of you."

"I can't imagine that's true."

"Maybe you can't imagine a sin that great," she said. "But I assure you, I can."

She stepped back; his fingers fell. Once again she started to walk, and when he looked up he realized they were already near the cathedral. He saw the iron gates surrounding Jackson Square only a block away; the street opened to reveal the tall spire of the church. Her step quickened, and he felt a strange desperation, heard a voice inside him that said, *Don't let her go there. You'll lose her if she goes inside.*

He touched her. "Wait," he said. "Don't go to church. Come with me. We'll get coffee."

"I don't want coffee."

"Wine, then."

She gave him a look; he felt its sternness through the mist of her veil. "*Non.*"

She angled her arm so he was no longer touching her, and crossed the street. She was almost to the square. Once she was inside those gates, they would close behind her, he would never get her out again. He couldn't explain the urgency he felt; he didn't know why he wanted her to himself for just a little longer, why he was so unwilling to share her with her God, with her guilt. He only knew that he was. So he strode quickly until he could step in front of her and she had to slow to keep from bumping into him.

"Then come because of me," he said.

She frowned. He felt a heady relief when she stopped. "Because of you?" she asked. She looked at him as if she was trying to find something in his expression, as if he confused her. "Oh, Jack. Why not be honest with me? Why not tell me why you really came with me this morning?"

"I've told you already," he said. "I want to be your friend."

"Ah, of course." The words were caustic. "Because you are growing to care for me?"

"I don't know," he said honestly. "Maybe."

"I see." Her eyes glittered, but the effect was oddly softened beneath her veil. He thought she would turn away for good then; he thought that he would surrender and let her go if she did. But she didn't turn away. She looked past him, to the street, far away. "Do you know what it's like to challenge God, Jack?" she asked quietly. "To go ahead blindly with what you want even when you know it's wrong?"

"I don't know," he said. "What's wrong for one person may not be wrong for someone else."

She turned to look at him. He felt the intensity of

her gaze through the fine silk lace. "Who *are* you? Where did you come from?"

The question rattled him. Jack glanced away. His choices danced before him: a safe lie, an evasion, or . . . the truth. He'd wanted to find out the mystery of her, but his mysteries . . . he wanted them to stay mysteries. Still, he knew that his chance to win Rosalie Lafon—something that suddenly meant more to him than just the fortune she brought with her—had come down to this question.

He wasn't aware he had even made a decision when he heard himself answering her, but he heard the truth in his own voice. "I was in Parish Prison until two weeks ago, when your father found me sleeping in the street."

He didn't know what he expected from her. A gasp of shock, a turn away, a scream of terror. But she merely nodded, satisfied, as if she'd known it already and had only been waiting for him to confirm it, and he wondered how that could be, how she could make a decision about his character so surely when there were times he could not even reconcile himself to the idea that he was an ex-convict.

"What did you do?" she asked quietly.

"It's a long story."

Another nod. Then, "Why don't you tell it to me?"

They stood there at the corner of the street while people passed by close enough to jostle and carriages creaked and thudded past, raising clouds of dust. It seemed as if the whole of New Orleans was moving by this spot today, and Jack was aware of two things: that she was asking him the most intimate questions of his life where anyone could hear, and that he wanted to answer her, to explain. He had never got the chance to explain.

But now that the chance was here, he found himself fumbling. The truth was not pretty. The truth was hard to say to her. "A man died. It was an accident, but I went to prison for it."

"I . . . see," she said, though she sounded confused, as if she didn't see at all. "Then . . . you were not responsible?"

He looked at her. He wished again that her veil were gone; he could hardly see her eyes. He sighed and looked away. "My uncle and I never got along. When I was twenty-seven he kicked me out for the third time. I . . . had some friends who took me in. They were the reason Uncle Charles kicked me out to begin with. I'd been spending my time with them, drinking, gambling, whor—uh, 'throwing my life away,' as my uncle called it."

"What did you call it?" she asked.

Jack smiled bitterly. "Getting back at my uncle. He was so sure I could do nothing right. I didn't want to prove him wrong."

"So you turned to . . . debauchery."

She sounded as if it took all her will to say the word. Jack could not resist a smile. "What, Rosa, does it make you want to run and hide?"

She met his gaze evenly. "Not yet."

"One night we got especially drunk. I don't remember much of the evening, except that it was pitch black and foggy. The streetlights barely made a glow. It was late, nearly dawn, I think, and we decided to have a race."

"A race?"

"A carriage race." The memory had weakened with time, and it had never been entirely clear to begin with. "I don't remember what happened exactly, except that I was driving one of them. I couldn't see a thing, but I remember thinking those horses had to go faster if I was going to win the bet. There was . . . a man . . . walking his dog."

"So late at night?"

"Apparently he couldn't sleep," Jack said wryly. "I didn't see him. Not until the last minute. I tried to miss him. I thought I had. But, you understand, there was no room to maneuver. The streets were so narrow, and the other carriage was coming up on me. I remember thinking that if I tried to miss him I would overturn the carriage and crash into my friends . . ." Jack trailed off. "I caught the man with the wheel. We found him later, in the ditch. The dog was hovering over him, whining—a godforsaken whine . . . As long as I live, I will never forget the sound that dog made."

He looked past her, over her shoulder, lost in that singular memory, that poor dog's whimpering, the light from a nearby gas lamp lost in the fog, its shadows pooling on the dog's pale coat. When dawn came, only a few short minutes later, the shadows turned out to be its master's blood.

"It was an accident, everyone agreed," he said curtly. "A small bribe, and the police would have forgotten it ever happened. We all came from good families; the man was no one important. But my uncle refused."

Her eyes widened.

"He bought me three years of prison instead."

"Why would he do that?" she asked. "What did you do to him?"

It was, he realized, the question no one had ever asked. Jack told himself he should be offended—she assumed so readily that he was at fault. But he couldn't be offended, because she was right to ask the question.

Jack took a deep breath. He'd never said the words to another living soul. Not even Garland knew it. But for some reason, to Rosalie they were easy to say, a relief after so long a time. "That same night I'd stolen five thousand dollars from him."

Her expression did not change. "Why?"

It was strange now to think that it had all started because of a dream. A steamer company he'd wanted to start. Uncle Charles had objected. Too expensive, he'd said. Not enough return. *Earn the money yourself, Jack, and perhaps you'll understand that it's not so damn easy to come by.*

But the dream had had its hooks in Jack, and he could not let it go. He'd been young and stupid, still so naive. He'd thought that if he could get five thousand dollars, just five thousand dollars, he could double it in a night at one of the clubs he frequented. He was a passable gambler, and he'd been having a lucky streak. The dream had been so close he'd been able to see the first steamer in his mind, pristine white with brass trim. He could smell the oil and grease and steam. On its mast flew the company flag he had designed: bright blue, with a white *JW* set in a golden circle. The start of his brilliant future.

His brilliant future had lasted exactly one night. He'd gone to the lockbox at the brokerage before the week's deposit had been made and taken everything in it—just short of five thousand dollars. He had planned to replace it the next day with his winnings and still have enough to start his new business.

He'd lost nearly every dime.

Still, he'd refused to admit failure. He'd refused to think of the morning. He drank more and more. Then there was the race. The wager was two hundred dollars. In his drunken state he'd thought winning it would help, that it would somehow alleviate what he'd done, satisfy his uncle.

But no, of course not. Uncle Charles had wanted the five thousand paid in blood. Three years of Jack's life had been taken from him before he knew what happened. The travesty of a trial, his uncle's grim face and his words: *I hope this helps knock some sense into you, Jack. God knows, I've given up trying any other way.*

And then Parish Prison. Three years of a hell he could not have imagined before then. Three years of dreams rotting away, festering in his soul.

Jack shook his head, laughing bitterly. Her question should be so easy to answer. But it wasn't. There was nothing easy about it at all. Finally he said, "I wanted riches. I wanted respect."

"Riches and respect don't always go hand in hand," Rosalie said.

He looked at her. "Maybe not for everyone. But for my uncle . . . believe me, they do."

She tilted her head at him; he felt as if she was studying him, again looking for something. When she spoke again, there was something in her voice, something indistinct, vaguely chiding. "And do you have it now, Jack? You've landed on your feet, you have everything you've ever wanted. Your freedom, my father's fortune—"

He looked at her. "Not everything," he said. He felt the power of the words linger between them, saw her swallow and lick her lips before she glanced away.

"What is it you want from me, Jack?" she asked softly.

What did he want? What was he asking of her? "I don't know," he whispered raggedly, and the rawness of his longing left him weak. "I don't know."

She backed away, a half step, barely that. "You're . . . too close."

"You're afraid of me," he whispered.

"*Non.*"

"Oh, yes, you are." He stepped closer; he could not help himself. "Tell me why, Rosa. Tell me why. Was it the story I just told you? Did you want me to lie?"

"Perhaps." She took a deep breath. "I've . . . known men like you. Men who care only for themselves."

He could not see her expression, and he wanted to. He wanted to so badly that he reached out and lifted her veil over the brim of her hat. She flinched, and the movement caused the lace to fall again, but only halfway. The rest caught and held, so she was half masked now, a draping of lace angled over one eye, half of her cheek.

"You've known men like me," he repeated thoughtfully. "Is that your sin, Rosa? That you've known men like me?"

She didn't move and she didn't freeze, but the things that went through her eyes, the truth of it . . . it was astounding. It surprised him, the pain he saw there, the intensity of it; he felt he was seeing the core of her, and she was no saint at all, but just a woman. Just a woman . . .

He hardly knew what he was doing. Until he was kissing her, he didn't know he'd even moved. And it was a nothing kiss, a light brushing of lips, nothing more. It was the most chaste kiss he'd ever taken, and her lips were cold and tight.

She jerked away. She was trembling as she yanked the delicate lace over her face again. Then, without a word, she left him. She left him for the open gates of Jackson Square, for the God that waited within them. He stared after her, unable to move as the people and carriages around him began to come to life once more, and slowly the fog in his mind lifted. Slowly he realized what he'd done, what she was becoming to him.

And the depth of his feeling terrified him.

❧ Chapter 16

Corinne waited for Jack at breakfast. When he didn't come down, it seemed the day lost its glow; she could think of nothing to do. Rosalie was already gone, and in a way Corinne was thankful for that. She did not want to see her sister's face and know what she was about to do. She did not want to feel the guilt settling like a heaviness around her heart.

But it was there anyway. It was there as she wandered around the house, doing nothing, trying to find a way to keep her hands busy and her thoughts at bay. She hated knitting, and she was horrible at embroidery—her last effort, a bed pillow, had been so knotted that it left pits on her face whenever she slept on it, so she'd given it to Robert.

The list of things she would not or could not do was long. She had no fondness for digging in the dirt or clipping roses, as Maman had. Reading bored her after only a few paragraphs. Writing letters was torture; she been schooled in exquisite penmanship, and as a result, she wrote so slowly that she lost her thought before she had finished writing the first word. Rosalie ran the household, and she did it so efficiently that the last time Corinne had bothered to direct a maid, it had thrown off everyone's routine so badly that dinner was an hour late.

So she wandered around the courtyard, stopping now and then to smell a flower or kick a dry vine from the flagstones, and tried to remember what it was she'd done with her days before Jack Waters had arrived. She'd shopped and visited and spent her spare hours with Reynaud or someone else. It seemed already as if it had been a different Corinne who'd done those things.

She felt depressed and anxious, and so Corinne took a nap in the heat of the afternoon. When she woke, the house was still quiet. She was the only one at home, and that felt odd. She wanted noise now. She wanted company.

Finally she made her way into the parlor, to the piano. Seeing it there lessened the ache in her chest. She loved the way it looked, wood gleaming in the sunlight coming through the window, the tapestry runner laid across it just so, the vase of roses dropping pale pink petals that seemed almost white against the rich, dark wood.

Corinne ran her hand across it, so smooth, so warm. She trailed her fingers along the keys. They tinkled beneath her fingers, the lower notes resonating into her bones. She sat down and reached for the music and began to play.

It had been Maman who suggested that Corinne take piano lessons all those years ago. It had been the winter before Maman died, and Corinne had been so young then, only eight. It was planned for her to go to the convent school in the spring, but until then Corinne was to take weekly lessons.

How Maman had known she would love it, Corinne had no idea. But she did. She had loved music from the time she was just a little girl, and she remembered the first time she'd heard the piano. It had been at a dinner one day after mass—later Rosalie had told her it was at Ricardo Grimaldi's house, but Corinne had been very small, and the entire Grimaldi family had died that summer of yellow fever, so Corinne had never been back. She didn't remember the man who'd played at all, except that he had dark hair and long, beautiful fingers that stroked and flirted with the keys.

Even then, the piano had seemed to speak to her. She heard its voice in the beat of her heart. She'd been sitting in a chair next to Rosalie, and the music had pulsed into her fingers and her toes, had lifted her until she was out of her chair and dancing across the room, pirouetting and swaying before a crowd of surprised and tolerant people. When Maman had swooped down and scooped her up, Corinne had not wanted to stop. She'd cried to keep dancing.

But then she got her own piano and her own music teacher. There were days when it seemed the music that came from her fingers was the only thing that made her alive. After Maman died, Corinne had practiced every day, sometimes for hours, until Papa told her to stop: "*Mon Dieu,* missy, enough already! Make yourself useful, eh? Get me a lemonade."

She was grown now, and other things soothed her as well, but Corinne still loved the piano, and now she played until she lost herself in the music. She played for hours until she heard a sound and turned to see Rosalie coming through the door.

It was too late to hide—Rosalie had no doubt heard the piano all the way down the block. So Corinne let her hands fall silent on the keys and put a tentative smile on her face to greet her sister.

Rosalie did not even look up. She looked pale and anxious, her movements were nervous. In her light gray dress, she looked like a nun already, and Corinne felt a little pain in her heart.

"Rosa," she called softly, and Rosalie's gaze flew to hers.

"Corinne," she said nervously.

"I wanted to . . . apologize. For last night," Corinne said. "I did not mean to upset you."

Rosalie nodded. But she seemed distracted; Corinne wondered if her sister had really heard before Rosalie gave her a small, blank smile and hurried away again.

Corinne listened to her sister's footsteps fade, and felt a small stab of anger—it had been an effort to make the apology, and Rosa could have at least listened. But the truth was the apology had been meant for herself instead, an attempt to lessen her own guilt. When Corinne heard footsteps in the dining room and looked up to see Paulette standing in the doorway, that guilt grew until she could barely speak through the tightening of her throat.

"Tonight the night, *mademoiselle*," Paulette whispered. "There be a prayer—"

"Be quiet," Corinne hissed. "Who knows who could hear."

Paulette gave a slow, deep nod. "You dress for dinner now, *mademoiselle*."

Corinne swallowed and left the piano, following the maid up the stairs to her room. There was a dress laid out on the bed, one she'd loved once but never worn. She'd been grief-stricken over Papa's rejection of one of her old beaus—Jacques, she thought his name was—and so she'd lost weight, and the dress had never fit correctly. She looked questioningly at Paulette.

"No corset," Paulette told her. "You dress by yourself. There be a gris-gris in the pocket. I tell you, he be yours tonight."

The little maid withdrew. Corinne waited until Paulette was gone, and then she went to her mirror. She took comfort from her reflection; it made her remember who she was: Corinne Lafon, a woman who knew how to beguile a man, a woman who knew the power of desire. Reynaud used to tell her she was made for this, for love, for passion.

She turned away from the mirror and stripped off her gown and undergarments, throwing them to the bed. The muzzled light from the curtained doors was soft and white on her naked body. Then, slowly, deliberately, she dressed for dinner.

She had understood Paulette's message well enough, and so Corinne drew on her stockings and left her drawers crumpled on the bed. She left her corset off and put on only one petticoat. Then she put on the gown she had never worn.

It was a beautiful fabric, sapphire blue cabbage roses on an ivory ground, beribboned with blue.

When it was on, Corinne went to stand before the mirror again, and she smiled with satisfaction. Paulette had known what she was doing. Without a corset, the gown hugged her waist and molded to her breasts. It moved with her movements. She felt wicked in it, and that wickedness brought color into her cheeks, glittered in her eyes. She pressed the skirt into her thighs and felt the small, hard bag of the voodoo charm in her pocket. She leaned forward just a little so that her breasts swelled. He would never be able to resist her. In a hundred years, he would not be able to resist her.

When Mattie knocked softly on her door, announcing dinner, Corinne was ready. She opened the doors again, and the warm, humid air eased into her room— she had not realized how hot she was with the doors closed, how hard it had been to breathe. She stepped out onto the gallery and breathed deeply of roses and then she made her way down to the dining room.

Rosalie was already there, waiting. She seemed as nervous as she'd been earlier, and she had not bothered to change her gown for dinner. When Corinne came into the room, Rosa turned.

"*Bonsoir*," she said quietly, and then she frowned. "I haven't seen that gown before. Is it new?"

Corinne opened her mouth to answer, but it seemed Rosalie had already forgotten the question. She moved to the open doors without waiting for a response and stared out at the night courtyard. Her fingers tangled in her rosary; Corinne heard the rapid *click click click* of the beads.

"Are you upset tonight, Rosa? You do not seem yourself."

"I'm fine," Rosalie said, but there was distance in her words.

Corinne stared at her sister's back, at the smooth, tight chignon. She tried to gauge Rosa's mood—it was somber, restless, strange. Corinne wondered how much of it had to do with their argument last night and how much had to do with Jack. Whatever it was, Corinne tried not to care. Tonight she could not afford to care.

But then, suddenly, Rosalie stiffened. Her fingers stilled on the beads. It took Corinne a moment to hear what her sister had: the gentle close of the front door, the footsteps in the hallway. *Jack.*

Corinne's heart started pounding again. Her mouth went dry. Slowly she turned to face the door, seeing from the corner of her eye that Rosalie had done the same and that the rosary beads were wrapped tightly around her fingers. Her chin was raised, her face pale. She looked for all the world like a saint facing crucifixion.

Corinne forced herself to look away, but Rosalie's demeanor was oddly discomfiting. She could not get it out of her head, and because of that she was uneasy when Jack walked into the room. But at the sight of him she forgot her sister. He was too handsome; he took one's breath. Even though he looked tired and there were dark circles beneath his eyes, she felt his impact in her heart and her lungs, in the way her breath stopped, in the shiver over her skin. She could not bring herself to utter a single word—the things that she was about to do, the anticipation of them, stole anything she might have said.

"Good evening," he said, but the last word broke sharply because he saw her just as he said it. She saw the jump in his cheek, heard his pause of surprise.

And that brought her back to herself. Corinne smiled. She stepped forward and held out her hand. "*Bonsoir,* Jack."

She saw the way it disconcerted him. She had him off balance; that was as she wanted it. It meant that, in spite of his words the other night, he was not indifferent. Corinne's smile broadened. He was hers already; he just didn't know it yet.

"*Bonsoir,*" Rosalie said softly.

Corinne saw Jack glance at her sister. It was a quick glance, a nothing glance, but there was something in it that made Corinne's heart clench.

She stepped forward and put her hand on his arm, and when he looked down at her, she saw him swallow. She pressed into his arm—just slightly, enough to make him aware that she wore no corset. She saw realization flash through his eyes, and she felt him stiffen.

"Corinne—" he started.

She shook her head at him. "No words," she said softly, for his ears only. "I am sorry for the other night. I was not gracious, and that was unforgivable. Perhaps we can be friends?"

She knew just the right inflection to give the words—she had used them many times before. It was an art, to give a man the impression that you wanted more of him at the same time you played at being a virtuous maid. She saw their effect in the quick tightening of his jaw, the flare of his nostrils.

"You're forgiven," he said brusquely. He stepped away, not rudely, but just enough so that she had to release her hold on his arm.

Mattie came through the doors from the kitchen, carrying a steaming tureen.

"Dinner," Rosalie said, and there was relief in the single word.

Mattie was already ladling out the soup. *Gumbo z'herbes,* Corinne saw as she took her seat. She waited for Jack to sit beside her. He hesitated for only a moment before he pulled out the chair next to hers and sat down.

She felt his heat beside her, smelled his cologne. Corinne dipped her spoon into the soup. The bright greens tangled around the spoon handle, long and stringy, making it impossible to eat without slurping like a Cajun. She put it down again. She glanced at Jack, who was raising his spoon to his mouth. She leaned; beneath the table she put her hand on his thigh. He started. The spoon dropped with a splash.

Rosalie looked up.

"You don't like the soup?" Rosa asked.

Corinne felt Jack's shift in the muscles in his thigh. Slowly, lingeringly, she drew her hand away.

Beside her, Jack put down his napkin. He pushed back his chair. "Excuse me," he said, getting to his feet. "I find I have no appetite tonight."

"Are you ill?" Rosalie asked sharply.

Corinne caught the glance that passed between them. It was heavy and cryptic. She could not understand it at all. Jack looked away and shook his head.

"Tired," he said. "I hope you don't mind."

"Of course not," Rosalie said.

Jack nodded. He swept the table with an apologetic smile, and then he was gone, striding to the door, out into the courtyard night.

Corinne watched with a fluttering heart as he went. The night was not over, not yet. Corinne went back to her soup, but her appetite was gone now, too; in spite of her confidence, she could not banish her fear, the steady press of desperation. She could not look at Rosalie at all.

The courtyard brought no relief, just night shadows and blindness that accented scent and sound. The roses were loose and heavy, too sweet. Jack heard the trickling water from the cooling pond, the hum of mosquitoes, in the distance a dog barking. The air hurt where it scraped his skin; he was too sensitive, he was too alive. This place was strange to him tonight.

A cannon blasted. Jack jumped until he realized it was the curfew fire in Congo Square. It was nine o'clock, and it seemed much later than that, though the deep night music had not yet begun. He could not go to his room. Things pressed in on him there, and tonight he would never relax. Too, something called to him out here. It whispered in the banana leaves—a strange inevitability, a portent borne on the darkening night, and he tried to dissect it, to determine what it was, where it came from.

He walked into the middle of the courtyard and stood there, looking up at the dark sky, feeling night come upon him like a shroud. He was hungry, his mouth was dry, and he drank in the night as if it might quench his need. But it was like all nights in New Orleans; it only left him more ravenous than ever, and he stood there and stared helplessly at the sky. Not since he'd walked into Parish Prison for the first time had he felt so defenseless. The only difference was that then he'd been so naive, he hadn't even known to be afraid.

He felt the night's whispers all around him, their soft kisses, their ancient caress, and though he told himself he should go to his room, to bed, he didn't move—those whispers told him to wait. They held him in place until one of the servants brushed by him and murmured a startled "*Pardon*," and he realized that dinner must be over, that he'd stood here in the courtyard for a very long time.

Jack sighed. He turned toward the service wing, walked past the wine room and his memories of Corinne, past the washroom, where the sounds of dishes rattling against an old oak washtub rang along with the servants' rapid talk. He opened the shuttered doors to the stairway and disappeared into the darkness of the covered steps, feeling an odd urgency that made him hurry. When he finally reached his room, he closed the door behind him and leaned against it. He undid his tie and tore it from his throat, and then he shrugged off his coat and unfastened his shirt until he could breathe again.

He lit the lamp on the stand beside the door, and the room glowed softly with yellow light. The golden glow was haunting, like a dream—this whole night felt slightly unreal, so that the soft knock on his door was not a surprise, not unexpected.

He opened the door, and when he saw her there, glowing in the reflected light from his room, high-lighted against the darkness, he realized he'd been waiting for her.

In the light, she was a vision, a halo of blond hair and soft edges, skin that seemed impossibly fine, impossibly smooth. Her eyes were so dark he couldn't tell her expression, but he didn't need it; he knew why she was here.

And if there had been any part of him that doubted it, she put it to rest when she came into his room, her hand extended. "Jack," she whispered.

He looked at that hand, so pale in the light, and his gut clenched. He forced the words through a throat that was too tight to speak. "You don't know what you're asking," he said.

She smiled. "Love me, Jack," and that voice was low and quiet, as seductive as anything he'd ever heard. It grabbed hold of him and jerked him, so he felt as if he'd crashed into a solid wall.

He was paralyzed. When she stepped up to him, eased her arms around his waist, and lifted her face to his, he could do nothing. There was no man in the world who could resist this, he thought. Why should he even try?

But the reason was in his head, a vision so strong he smelled jasmine in the breeze. He saw a face half covered by fine lace, pain in a pair of dark brown eyes, words . . . *What is it you want from me, Jack?*

Jack squeezed his eyes shut. Corinne was against him, her warm body, the soft press of her breasts, and suddenly the desire he'd felt, the inevitability of this, faded. She was the wrong woman. She was not the woman he wanted to hold.

It was a moment before he realized something else, something so startling that he stared unseeingly into Corinne Lafon's beautiful face. For the first time since he'd come to this house, he had not thought of losing Garland Lafon's fortune, but only of losing Rosalie.

"Jack?" Corinne whispered, and the seductive whisper that had grabbed hold of him only moments ago was strangely unaffecting.

He looked down into her face. She was frowning up at him; there was confusion in her eyes.

"Jack?"

Gently he reached around his back and pried loose her hands, then stepped away from her. "I'm your sister's fiancé," he reminded her quietly. "Don't you think Rosa deserves better than this? From both of us?"

He'd startled her. She stepped back, her hand went nervously to her hair. "You—you're refusing me?"

"Yes."

"But . . . but you cannot!" She came closer; he

backed away until his knees were against the edge of his bed and he could go no further without falling onto the mattress. Jack held steady. She pressed her hand against his chest. "I don't believe this is truly what you want."

"Corinne—"

"Shhh." Her fingers shook as she pressed them to his lips. She stood on tiptoe, trembling as she moved to kiss him.

His hands went to her shoulders, holding her away. "No," he said softly.

He saw the pain that went through her eyes—and something else: fear.

She grabbed his wrists and held on to them tightly. "You can't mean this. I love you. I need you."

"You're in love with someone you made up, Corinne," he said. "You can't love me. We hardly know each other. I'm Rosalie's fiancé."

"Stop saying that!" She turned away from him, and he heard a small sob before she turned back to him again. She raised her chin, and slowly, slowly, her hands went to the buttons at her back. She began to undo them. "You want me, Jack. You know you want me. I can see it in your eyes. You want me. . . ." Her voice faded to a whisper. She was crying. "You have to want me."

He felt useless. There was a desperation in her he hadn't expected, didn't understand. He could not imagine where it came from. It made Jack uncomfortable; he didn't know what to do as she fell apart in front of him.

The dress fell from her naked shoulders; the fabric caught on her breasts, dipped lower. She stumbled into his arms, and Jack went rigid, uncertain, helpless. But she was sobbing into his shirt, and so finally he put his arms around her and held her close. He tried clumsily to pull her gown up onto her shoulders again, but it was caught, and so finally he let it go, he just held her there, and the urge to comfort her took over. He found himself smoothing back her hair, stroking her, whispering, "Shhh. It's all right, darling. You'll be fine. It's all right."

It seemed she cried like that for a long time—so long that he went silent. He caressed her hair and listened to her sobbing until finally it faded and he could hear the night sounds again. When she made the first move toward pulling away, he let her go, and she stumbled back, grabbing at her dress—but not before he saw the shine of moonlight on her skin.

"You are sure, Jack?" she asked.

"We aren't meant to be together," he said quietly. "Surely you can see that."

She nodded. "*Oui*," she whispered.

She stood on tiptoe and laid her hand against his cheek for a moment, a lingering touch, before she stepped away and looked toward the French doors.

"*Bonsoir*," she said.

She slipped into the night and was gone.

It was only a moment before Jack went to the door to watch her go, and she had already disappeared; there was nothing left of her but the scent of roses. She could have been a dream.

❦ Chapter 17

She was saying rosaries. Ten of them, in fact, and they were her own penance; she had not been able to bring herself to go to confession that day. The rosaries were as much for that as for courage. Rosalie had not known what to tell the priest; what could she say? Despite her prayers, God had delivered her greatest fear to her doorstep, and she felt betrayed and angry and afraid.

Rosalie buried her face in her hands, keeping the memories at bay with every ounce of strength she had. She had spent years burying these memories; she had made for herself a will of iron, she had become a virgin again in her mind. But then today, Jack's voice, his words, his kiss . . . they had made her remember, made her think of things she'd done once a long time ago . . . no, more than once, more than once. Rosalie closed her eyes against the images, but she tasted kisses and felt hands on her body, and they brought with them a bitter yearning—and that was why she could not go to the priests. She could not lie in confession; it was better not to go at all and risk God's wrath.

She knew, of course, that this was only another one of His tests. Father Bara had warned her the way would not be easy. God did not hand out simple tasks—that was why saints were saints. But there was a little voice inside her that said it was something more, that she was already damned, that this was God's punishment for that sin so many years ago.

She had prayed for forgiveness, she meant to dedicate her life to Him, but perhaps it wasn't enough—could it ever be enough for taking a life? Could she ever do enough?

She wanted to believe she could. She wanted to believe in forgiveness. But if she'd been forgiven, then why this? Why the temptation of Jack Waters? A criminal, no less. Had Papa known about Jack's background when he brought Jack to this house? When he'd affianced her to him?

She wanted to believe he had not, but there was a numbness inside her that told her Papa *had* known. That if she went to him in protest, he would tell her he already knew everything there was to know about Jack Waters. Her father had not come by his riches easily. He was a shrewd man. Age and illness had done nothing to impair that. And yet what frightened her most was not that Papa had known about Jack's time in prison, but that she knew . . . and she didn't care.

Rosalie raised bleary eyes to the solemn plaster faces of St. Catherine and St. Mary Magdalene. She said a last prayer, and then she blew out the votive candles and breathed in the smoke and the smell of wax in the seconds before they floated away. She was tired, but she knew sleep would elude her again tonight. Slowly she rose and went to the doors, pushing them open into the night, hearing their soft and familiar creak as they scraped along the gallery.

She stepped out and closed her eyes, taking a deep breath of the night air. It was sweet tonight; there was something blooming that had not been there before, though Rosalie could not say what it was. It reminded her of the night of the soirée, of Jack Waters, of his comment *Such a pity,* and Rosalie felt again that piercing, deep sadness, that sense that she had lost something, that it was gone forever.

She opened her eyes, meaning to banish the thought, and saw a light across the courtyard in the *garçonnière.* She stepped away from the twining wisteria to see better. Jack's doors were wide open, the fine muslin blowing slightly in the breeze, and there were shadows moving inside.

Rosalie told herself to turn away, but she found herself wondering why he was still awake, what he was doing. She wondered again why he had left the dinner table so abruptly tonight—though she had been relieved that he had. She wondered . . . had the kiss he'd given her been a real one? Or simply another attempt at winning her cooperation?

The thought seemed petty and strangely uncharitable, and so Rosalie abandoned it. She started to turn away, to leave him to his own lamplight and sleeplessness, when she caught a movement from the corner of her eye.

Corinne.

Rosalie froze. She saw her sister step from Jack's room, walking quickly. Even in the shadows, Rosalie could see the way the gown slipped from her sister's shoulders, the way the back gaped open to show her pale skin glowing in the moonlight.

Rosalie could not breathe. Corinne disappeared into the covered stairway, and Rosalie drew back into the shadows, watching as her sister reappeared again in the courtyard. Corinne hurried to her room. It was not until her doors were shut that Rosalie stepped from her hiding place.

Across the courtyard, the lamp in Jack's room was extinguished. Rosalie glanced up. She saw the last of his shadow. She heard the quiet click of his doors as he drew them shut against the night.

She was left alone in the moonlight.

She felt sick; her heart ached, though she told herself it should not. He was a better man for her sister, and she had given Corinne—however tacitly—her blessing. She knew Corinne was pursuing him; she should not be surprised that he was responding. Corinne was beautiful. She was perfect for him. She was everything Rosalie was not.

But still . . . still she felt a prick of anger, a mean little stab of envy. And along with that came the soft ache of wistfulness—no, not wistfulness. Not that.

Rosalie turned back to her room and shut the doors. She undressed and went to bed, but she did not sleep. She tossed and turned, and the images danced in her head: Jack leaning close to kiss her, Corinne rushing from his room with her dress falling from her pale shoulders, Corinne locked in his arms, touching him, holding him.

Rosalie was still awake when the sun began to

light the sky. She washed and dressed, binding up her hair before her reflection in the mirror, and for a moment she felt a weariness that made her drop her arms so her hair fell again, unbound, over her shoulders. She stared at herself, at the sleeplessness that made her skin pallid and her eyes too deep, and thought of everything she had to do today, and it seemed too much suddenly—it seemed just the same as every other day, and every future day. It stretched on and on before her eyes, into forever.

Don't think of it. Rosalie stared blearily at her reflection. She sighed, finished putting up her hair, and left the dressing table, left the night darkness of her room for the growing dawn. Already she smelled the cooking fires and saw Lucy adjusting her tignon as she hurried from the servants' quarters to the kitchen. She told herself it was reassuring to have everything just the same, exactly as it was every morning, and she headed to the kitchen herself.

Monsieur LaFleur was already at work. Steaming kettles rumbled on the stove, coals glowed in the stew holes beneath. She smelled baking brioches and brewing coffee. On the huge cypress worktable in the center of the kitchen was a bowl of pitted peaches.

"*Bonjour,*" Rosalie said as she stepped inside. Lucy turned from the huge fireplace with a little curtsy. LaFleur barely moved his oversize body to acknowledge her.

"Peaches this morning," he said curtly in French. "They are fresh and sweet—taste for yourself."

Obediently Rosalie took one of the pitted halves

and bit into it. It was perfect, as he'd said. Sweet and musky and fragrant—the kind of peach that left one awestruck at God's little details.

"Mmm," she said. "A pie, perhaps. Or a cobbler."

"I had thought a vacherin," the chef said stiffly.

"Of course," Rosalie said hastily. "As you think best."

"Or lemon tarts."

Rosalie shook her head. "The peaches, I think. And *monsieur,* my father thought Tuesday's étouffée was just the tiniest bit salty—".

"Salty?"

"He lacks a fine palate, you understand. But if, in the future, you would humor him in this . . ."

The chef harrumphed. Rosalie glanced over the other things on the table, the food the *marchandes* had brought to the kitchen very early that morning: a fresh redfish, glistening peppers, a basket of green beans. As usual, LaFleur had written out his chosen menu on a rough piece of paper, and Rosalie glanced it over. She decided against shrimp and suggested another sauce for the beef—one Corinne preferred.

"With that it is fine, *monsieur,*" she said. One task done, a hundred more still waiting. She turned to go.

Corinne was in the doorway. She looked drawn, a little pale, as if she too had not had any sleep, and Rosalie felt the swift bitterness of malice—no, that was too strong. But she did think how nice it was for once that Corinne did not look so beautiful.

"*Bonjour,* Rosa," Corinne said dully.

Rosalie stared at her sister. She tried to remember

if she had ever seen Corinne this way. "Are you ill?" she asked finally.

Corinne laughed shortly. "*Non*. Not ill." She came inside and reached for the coffeepot simmering on the stove. It was hot; she drew away with a little yelp, and Lucy was there in moments, pouring coffee, adding milk before Corinne had finished shaking her fingers from the pain. She took the coffee Lucy handed her and cradled it in her hands, blowing lightly over the top. "I had little sleep, is all."

The reason for that lack of sleep needled Rosalie. "Perhaps you should sit down."

"*Oui, oui,* that is my plan. To sit in the sun and stare up at the flowers all day." Corinne turned and stepped back out onto the flagstones. "Tell me, Rosa, do you ever feel as if the world is falling down around you?"

The words were so sad, so forlorn. They fell into Rosalie's head and made her ache, and suddenly she wanted to forgive Corinne everything. Rosalie forgot the sight of her sister running from Jack's room; she forgot the feelings she did not want to admit to herself. She touched Corinne's arm and looked at her sister intently. "What is it? What has happened?"

Corinne pulled away. "Nothing," she said. She walked slowly from the kitchen to the small iron table in the middle of the courtyard. With a sigh, she set down her coffee and pulled out a chair. The metal shrieked upon the flagstones.

"The brioches, they will come soon," Lucy said, handing Rosalie a cup of coffee. "You enjoy your breakfast, *mademoiselle*. The flowers, they make the mouth sing, *n'est-ce pas?*"

Rosalie took the coffee and followed Corinne into the courtyard. She took the seat across from her sister. "You must tell me what I can do, Corinne."

Her sister flashed her an inscrutable look. "Oh, you have already done quite enough," she said.

The words were a mystery, the bitterness behind them even more confusing. Rosalie frowned. "You are angry with me?"

Corinne was staring off into the roses. "Not angry, Rosa. It is just that sometimes I wonder—" She shook her head, then looked down at her feet. "I wonder why you do not enjoy life when you have so much."

It was a strange and disturbing thing to say. "I do enjoy it," Rosalie protested.

Corinne shook her head. "No, you don't. You don't even understand what I am saying to you, and that is a sad thing, Rosa. The things you worry about—I heard you in the kitchen. Who cares if the étouffée is salty? What would happen if the menu was not checked every day or if you missed a visit to the infirmary? Would God disown you if you skipped confession? Would the world fall apart? You do not live, Rosalie. I wonder sometimes if you even know how."

Rosalie looked down into her coffee, at the sun glinting rainbows on the oily skim. "Perhaps this . . . living, as you call it, is not as wonderful as you claim."

"How do you know if you never try?"

Rosalie glanced up. She met her sister's eyes. "How do you know I've never tried?"

Corinne said nothing. She simply looked at Rosalie as if she were seeing her for the first time, and her dark brown gaze was searching and oddly intent when she finally leaned forward.

"You are throwing everything away by joining the convent, Rosa. And I . . . I have it in my heart to stop you. But I will not. Because the things you have . . . You must understand me when I tell you that I need them more."

Corinne's meaning was incomprehensible. Rosalie frowned at her sister. "I don't know what you mean."

Corinne sat back with a sigh. "*Oui.* I know you don't." She closed her eyes. "Tell me, Rosa, why it is you will not have Jack. Tell me, so I understand."

The words sent a chill through Rosalie. She stared at her sister, at Corinne's perfect face, at beauty that would not die when she grew old, but would only heighten the delicacy of her expression. She thought of her own face. She and Corinne had the same nose, the same shape of the face, but Rosalie's eyes were not so fine, her face just a little harsher.

When Rosalie was young, she had wondered what life would be like if she were beautiful, if she were Corinne. For a time she'd thought she'd known. But no . . . it had all been an illusion.

Rosalie turned away.

"I want to know," Corinne said quietly, and Rosalie remembered the question: *Tell me why you will not have Jack. Tell me so I understand.*

Rosalie felt her sister waiting. When she looked up, she found Corinne's eyes open, her gaze settled and hard. Rosalie's mistake played in her mind, each detail perfect, intact. It had been years; the memory should not be so painful, it should not be so *there*. But it was, and the perfection of it was nauseating, horrifying. The darkness inside her spread; she felt its stain. *Unforgivable.*

"I—I had a vision," she managed finally. It took all her strength to tell her sister the lie, and as she spoke it, she prayed for forgiveness. "From God. I have a mandate from God."

The lie seemed so transparent, she was sure Corinne would hear it. But Corinne only watched her for a moment, and then she nodded as if she were satisfied.

"The brioches, *mesdemoiselles.*"

Lucy set a tray on the table. Rosalie started; she had not heard the servant. Now she looked at the tray—a plate of golden, steaming brioches, cream cheese sloshing gently in cream, orange marmalade, peaches—and her stomach tightened; she suddenly had no appetite at all.

Seemingly, neither did Corinne. She shook her head slightly at the tray and then rose in a hopelessly fluid motion. "I'm not hungry," she said with a sad smile. "You eat for both of us, Rosa, won't you?"

"Corinne." Rosalie stopped her sister before Corinne took more than one step. "What is it? Is something wrong?"

Corinne looked over her shoulder. "Wrong?" she asked. "Why, of course not, Rosa. Why ever would you think it?"

She walked away, and as Rosalie watched her go, her stomach tightened into such a hard knot she could hardly breathe; she felt the strangest sense of dread.

Jack was up early despite the fact that he'd had little sleep. When the first pale pink and purple light of dawn was coloring the horizon, he washed and dressed. He was on his way to the First Bank of New Orleans even before the *marchandes* began their daily rounds.

He walked slowly; the morning was still cool and quiet, but he felt the promise of heat in the air. Mockingbirds chirped and chased him; the trees themselves were alive and shaking with songbirds. When he got to the bank, the doors were closed, the windows dark. He half expected that the key Garland had given him would not fit the lock, but it did. It turned easily, and he went inside, hearing his footsteps echo from the beams of the vaulted ceiling.

Upstairs, his office—*his office*—was silent and dark. Here the heavy winter drapes still hung in the windows, blocking out light and sound, and he pulled them open and eased up the window sash to step out onto the gallery overlooking a small courtyard. The office still smelled of the last inhabitant, of macassar oil and sharp citrus cologne, but out here on the gallery there was no sign that the office had ever belonged to anyone but Jack. The bitter orange trees below were bent, with ivy twining in their branches.

The wisteria was bright green, heavy as a carpet along the railings and the walls.

The sun was rising now; Jack watched until its bright rays slashed through the greenery and reflected off his windows. From the street he heard the chatter of carriages, the cry of a woman selling buttermilk, the *tooo-shooo-ooo* of the cymbal man hawking his crullers. Below him, the bank begin to stir; he heard the rumbling that seemed to come from the very timbers of the building itself. *Time to work,* it called out to him, and the voice was heavy and rich. *One day I'll be yours. . . .*

He turned and went back inside. The bank books were still there on his desk, still open, but beyond them, balanced on the very edge of the desk, was a small framed daguerreotype.

Jack frowned. Garland must have put it there to remind him of his duties, he thought wryly; it had not been there before. He picked it up and glanced at the picture. It was a Lafon family portrait, and it had obviously been taken a few years ago. Garland's hair was mostly black instead of mostly gray; Corinne's face held a youthful, dimpled roundness. Of them, only Rosalie looked the same. She was unsmiling, stern-looking, her hair pulled back in a chignon, with a large black crucifix dangling against her breast.

The sight of her made him feel tight and strangely unsettled. Their conversation yesterday still haunted him; the kiss he'd given her had been so unlike him, he could not quite believe he'd done it. But he had— the visceral impact of it was with him still. Strange that he should feel so connected to her. She could turn him inside out with a word—from the start, she had been the one person in this household who confused him and kept him off balance.

When it came to Rosalie Lafon, he could never put his finger on just why he was doing anything. She irritated him, she intrigued him; he liked watching the emotions flicker across her face. She was beautiful, he decided, in a way different from Corinne. She was not like Corinne's sun; Rosalie was the moon instead, a reflected light, a beauty that was pale sometimes and vibrant others, that waxed and waned with every change in her eyes.

She was so sad, and he found himself wanting to comfort her, to reassure her. He wanted to take that wound inside her and heal it—and that amazed him. He'd never felt such a thing for anyone before. If he'd been asked, he would have said he was incapable of compassion, of seeing into someone, of recognizing dark places.

And yet he wanted to understand her, wanted her to understand him, felt a soft hunger for her that was as paralyzing in its way as his voraciousness for Corinne had been, and that was terrifying. It was not what he had planned. It wasn't even what he wanted.

What he'd wanted had seemed so easy: the chance to prove he was not a failure, to see his dreams shimmering again before him, possible at last. Beyond that, if Jack had bothered to think about it—which he had not—he would have expected he and Rosalie would go their separate ways. A marriage in name only. If they were lucky, they would find friendship.

But friendship was suddenly not enough, and he wasn't sure why. He felt exposed now, too vulnerable. He cared what she thought—too much. He wanted . . . too much. What had happened to the man who'd come to the house on St. Louis Street intent on securing his future? What had happened to the man who knew how to play all the angles?

He was gone, fading into nothing, and Jack grabbed after him desperately. He knew that man, he needed him. Without him, Jack was like every other idiot on the street: easily fooled, easily manipulated.

He had not felt anything like this since his dream of a steamer company had first lit a fire within him, when he had been willing to do almost anything to make it come true. For a long time he had forgotten what that felt like. It was as if those things had happened to another person; sometimes in those long, dark nights huddled against the stone walls of Parish Prison he had been unable to remember why he was there, unable to feel those few moments when he'd held that money in his hands and everything had seemed so possible.

It was the same sense he had today. That sense that things were not what he had expected them to be, that there was something he was missing, something he should understand. Last night had been the first sign of it, with his rejection of Corinne, of temptation. It was the first time in his life he could remember walking away from something he wanted. But the most surprising thing had been his realization that he hadn't really wanted it, that it was the walking away he needed more. It was disturbing somehow—he felt a slow, deep sense of dread, of change that he could not control, that he had no part of. What was happening to him?

Jack closed his eyes, felt the brush of a fragrant, hot breeze from the open windows, and told himself everything would be all right. Everything would turn out just as he wanted it.

But he felt for all the world like the man who had climbed down from a teetering carriage to find a dog whining at a lump in a gutter, its pale coat gone to shadows.

❧ Chapter 18

The bank closed for the day, but Jack didn't leave. He listened to the fading echo of employees departing, the clank of the doors, and glanced at the clock. Half past seven. Another hour and he would go. Two more hours at best.

But it was many more hours before he made himself look at the clock again. He realized everything at once: the single lamp on his desk struggling against the heavy darkness, the black shadows of the courtyard past the open doors, the cool, wet smell of night. He could not see the clock now; it was hidden in shadow. Jack turned the pocket watch dangling from a stand on his desk—another one of Garland's touches. He squinted at the time. It was three A.M.

He let his hand fall and accidentally brushed the Lafon family portrait he'd carefully turned to face away from him. The frame skittered a little; he had the sudden vision of those faces on the other side breaking into quick frowns, chastising expressions. *Where are you, Jack? Jack, I've missed you. Jack, you promised.* . . .

He rubbed his eyes, shook his head. By now Rosalie and Corinne would be asleep, and he realized that was what he wanted, that he had been delaying deliberately. He could not contain his relief as he closed the heavy ledger books and locked his office door behind him.

The bank was dark and quiet. His footsteps echoed in the emptiness, carrying up to the ceiling. It was disquieting; he hurried through the building to the doors, and when he opened them and stepped out into the night, he relaxed again.

The Vieux Carré seemed bigger at night, more wide open, the streets not so narrow. Shadows cast by the gas street lamps slanted against wrought-iron gates, rounded the corners of Creole cottages set flush with the banquettes. The world was black and white now, no soft colors, no crumbling plaster or battens hanging askew. It seemed grander, richer—it made him believe the Vieux Carré had not changed in the time he'd been gone.

But of course it had. There was a mansion not far from here whose owners had all died of yellow fever. There was an aunt in a Garden District house who would not even look on the face of the man she'd raised from childhood. There were gardens where there had not been gardens before, and weeds where once there had, and crumbling, vacant houses where once rich Creoles had turned up their noses at a young American.

Jack slowed. The night closed in front of him, behind him. He heard other voices, young Creole fops slurring drunkenly as they passed from one gambling hell to another, the faraway seep of music and someone singing, the eerie half silence of the dusty streets. There were few people, only shadows, the glow of gaslight across half-hidden features as they passed. New Orleans at night was not for the timid, but then, there had been a time when it had been familiar to him, when he craved it, and he felt comfortable in it now.

When he got to St. Louis Street, Jack hesitated. When he was standing below the huge pecan tree that bent over the porte cochere and the banquette, he paused. The windows were dark, the house seemed quiet. Everyone had already gone to bed. It was safe.

But he could not bring himself to go inside. He felt paralyzed standing there, and it seemed he hadn't moved long after he'd started walking again, away from the house, through the narrow, dangerous streets of the Vieux Carré.

His mind was racing. He couldn't clear his thoughts long enough to distinguish one from another. By the time the sun rose across the Mississippi River, spreading pink and purple into the sky, Jack had almost convinced himself that nothing had really changed, that he had imagined his strange feelings for Rosalie, that she understood him no better than anyone else. He could convince her to marry him and gain his fortune and still maintain the careful distance that made it possible for him to do what he would.

He waited until the sun was high in the sky, until New Orleans was awake, and he was jostled by people as he stood there along the edges of Jackson Square. The calls of the *marchandes* gave way to the talk of passersby, women going to market, servants adjusting their bright tignons as they followed after.

Slowly Jack made his way back to the Lafon house.

He paused outside the door, took a deep breath, and turned the lever to go inside.

And then wished he was still out walking.

He stopped in the hallway, waiting, listening. It was quiet; he thought for a moment everyone was already gone for the day. But then he heard the clank of silverware from the dining room. His stomach twisted, his mouth went dry. He did not want to see either of them. His feet felt like lead as he went in through the parlor, and when he saw her sitting there, sipping her coffee, he realized he was wrong. There was one person he wanted to see—he had not known how much until he saw her.

Rosalie.

He felt himself dissolve. His yearning filled his whole body, and as he went slowly to the high archway separating the dining room and the parlor, he hoped— he prayed—that she would look at him with a smile in her eyes.

Rosalie felt Jack's shadow before she saw him. She glanced up from her coffee, and despite everything she'd told herself, she felt breathless when she saw him there. Then she noticed how tired he looked, how drawn. He was still wearing his clothes from yesterday, and they were rumpled now, as if he'd slept in them— or as if he hadn't slept at all. She tried to remember what time she'd heard him return last night and couldn't, and her heart clenched again in her chest—a niggling worry, a question: Where had he been?

She made herself smile. "*Bonjour.* We missed you last night."

He hesitated, and then he took a deep breath and went to the sideboard, where covered dishes waited. "I was working late." He took a brioche, some coddled eggs, a peach.

He seemed oddly quiet, oddly distracted. Mattie had laid Papa's newspapers there at Jack's place, neatly folded, but when he came to the table he pushed them aside with his arm and poured a cup of coffee.

"What is it?" Rosalie asked. "Jack, is something wrong?"

There was a moment's hesitation, so short she wasn't sure if she'd truly seen it. He shook his head. "No, of course not."

It was a lie, she knew it completely. Rosalie waited until Jack looked up at her, until their gazes met. "Something *is* wrong," she said quietly.

"No." Then again, with more emphasis. "No. Rosa, about the other day—"

"It didn't happen," she said quickly. "It's forgotten."

He looked anything but relieved. "I didn't mean to upset you."

"Let's not talk of it again," she said firmly.

He was quiet for a moment. She felt his gaze on her face before he nodded slowly. "All right."

Two words, and it was gone. So easily dismissed, when it had caused her so many hours of unease, of heartache. It had truly been nothing to him, then, just as those first kisses had meant nothing to Gaston.

But then, she had meant nothing to Gaston, and Rosalie supposed she should be glad now that whatever had started between herself and Jack was over so soon. She did not like questioning herself, questioning her faith. It was much better this way.

She took a deep breath. The motion hurt her heart. Jack was still watching her, and Rosalie met his gaze.

"We are . . . friends, still?" he asked.

He looked worried, as if he was afraid she would say no, and she wondered why that should be. They were barely friends; if she said no, what would he have lost?

But—strange thing—she felt what he did. To say no was to send him on his way, and she could not—did not want to—do that. She nodded. "*Oui.*"

"Good." He smiled, and the smile was lightning quick. It was full and engaging, it changed his look completely. It took her breath, and for a moment Rosalie couldn't remember what they'd been talking about. "Now, tell me what I missed last night."

She found herself smiling back. "Nothing. Corinne played, I read . . . things were quite boring."

He split open his brioche slowly and deliberately. "And . . . nothing else?"

"Nothing else. We went to bed early."

"Where's Corinne?"

"Today's her calling day. She left early. But . . ." She paused. "I must admit I've been worried about her."

And then she felt that dread again. Because she had learned to see inside his eyes. She had learned to recognize his vulnerabilities, and so she saw the faint guilt pass his face before the shutters came down. His expression was carefully blank.

Rosalie's heart tightened. "Have you noticed? She's seemed . . . distressed."

A pause. And then, "Yes."

"She won't tell me what it is, but . . . I thought you might know something."

His face tightened almost imperceptibly, but she saw it. She felt it into her bones.

"What makes you think I would know?"

She did not know she was going to say it until the words came out. "Because I saw her come out of your room the night before last." Her voice was so calm— how could it be so calm when her heart was racing?

His gaze came up to meet hers, and she saw that guilt again. "Rosa—"

"I'm not blind," she said. "I've seen the flirtation between you. I've remarked upon it before."

"There is no flirtation," he said roughly. "Not anymore."

Rosalie frowned. "But—"

"She came to my room that night. I told her to leave. That was all."

"But her dress . . ."

He hesitated. "It was not what it seemed. Nothing happened between us, Rosa. You have to believe that."

She tried to read his gaze, tried to find the truth.

"Rosa, do you believe me?"

"Jack—"

"Do you believe me?"

"Wh-What does it matter what I believe?"

"It matters," he said, and then—so odd—he looked surprised. He sat back in his chair. "It matters."

Rosalie studied his face, looking for the emotions behind his eyes. He was watching her as if she held the promise of the world within her hands, as if her answer would break or redeem him, and she believed him.

It was that simple, suddenly, and that complicated. There was something he wasn't telling her, she knew that. But she also knew it didn't matter, because he was not lying about this, about turning away her sister.

Her relief was overwhelming. "*Oui,*" she said. "I believe you."

His breath came out hard. He closed his eyes for a brief moment, and when he opened them again, he said abruptly, "What are your plans for the day?"

"Papa's birthday is next week. I thought I would shop for a gift."

Jack looked up at her. "Oh? Can I come along?"

There was a part of her that wanted to say no, that didn't want him near her, distracting her, making her care. But there was a far bigger part that wanted him to go walking with her today—she tried not to think about why. She tried not to think at all.

She nodded. "Certainly, if you wish. I could use a man's opinion."

He smiled back and pushed aside his coffee. "Let's go."

They decided to walk, though it was a very hot day, and overcast. The air was heavy and wet, and Rosalie had no sooner stepped out the door of the house than she felt the cotton of her chemise and the silk of her dove gray gown sticking between her shoulder blades. The lace of her veil itched where it was pressed to her forehead by the brim of her hat, and for the first time in years she found herself wishing she could have left it at home. The veil blurred and grayed, and she wanted to see colors; she wanted sharp clarity.

But she was a Creole, and Creole women wore veils, and so Rosalie tried to ignore it as they stepped onto the banquette and Jack offered his arm.

"Where to?" he asked.

"Toward the river," she said. "There's a little shop there that Papa likes. I thought perhaps something for his pipe."

They started off—silently, at first; he still seemed distracted, and Rosalie had somehow lost her skill at conversation. She could not think of anything to say.

"It's beautiful," he said suddenly. Then, when she looked at him in surprise, "Everything. The colors. The smells. I never appreciated them before Parish."

It surprised her that he was bringing up prison—she had expected him to evade the subject, to tactfully pretend she was still ignorant of his past. It was not a good topic for polite conversation.

"It must be difficult," she said. "Losing three years of your life that way."

He stared off into the distance and nodded. "You're still living," he said. "That's what makes it so hard. You haven't lost anything but time, and yet it's the one thing you've suddenly got plenty of. You get used to looking at gray walls and ugly men. You know, when I first walked out, it was a beautiful day. The sun was shining, and I . . . I had to squint my eyes to look. The colors hurt. The smells were so strong they made my eyes water." He made a sound of disbelief. "I'd listened to the sounds of New Orleans every day. There was a window in the dining hall, and I used to press against it whenever I could just to listen. The everyday sounds—I would imagine those, because I couldn't hear them. The cathedral bells, carriages, people talking. I dreamed about hearing them again. But when I stepped out through those gates the funniest thing happened: All those sounds blended together. They were just one big noise."

He sighed. "I guess you get used to things quickly. By morning, it was as if I hadn't been away at all."

"So you've forgotten it already?" she asked gently. "Parish, I mean?"

He laughed shortly. "God, no. I haven't forgotten it for a minute. The day I left, the guard told me I'd be back. He said no one was ever gone for long once they'd been in."

He was quiet, and she didn't know what to say. When they brushed by a bush of viney jasmine tangling in a wrought-iron fence, he broke off a blossom. He brought it to his nose and took a deep breath, and then he twirled it in his fingers. "Jasmine," he murmured. He reached over and tucked it in the brim of her hat. "It suits you."

She smiled and ducked her head. It had been a long time since anyone had complimented her on anything other than the running of the household. It surprised and pleased her. "I've always liked jasmine," she said.

"I've always liked it, too." He looked down at her. "Rosa, take off that damn veil."

She put her hand to it. "I couldn't."

"Is your good name so fragile that it would be ruined if people saw you without a veil just once?"

The ease between them changed. Rosalie stiffened. She stepped away, putting distance between them, needing distance, but he grabbed her hand and held her there, and she heard his soft voice in her ear.

"Rosa, I'm not him."

She jerked up to look at him. Her heart thundered. His gaze was steady. It burned on her skin. "The man you're comparing me to," he explained. And then again, "I'm not him."

Her throat was so tight her words felt forced from it. "You're . . . very like him."

"How?"

She didn't know how to explain. So many things, so many ways. Gaston's face came into her mind, his smile, the light in his eyes, his intimate gestures. Rosalie swallowed.

"Let me help you," he said. He leaned closer. He smiled. "He was handsome?"

She recognized his teasing the way one might recognize a half remembered dream. Rosalie smiled weakly. "Oh, yes, handsome," she said.

"And charming, too?"

"Of course."

"I'll bet he didn't let you take yourself too seriously."

Something about what he said brought back the memory. It was startling in its intensity—a day she'd thought she'd forgotten, when she and Gaston had gone to the Market together. He had danced in front of her, pulling masks from a nearby vendor and making her laugh as he tried one on, juggling lemons. He had pulled a long, silky scarf in a rainbow of colors from another vendor's stall, wrapped it around her neck, and held her close with it, and she'd grown embarrassed and tried to wriggle away.

She felt his whisper in her ear even now, his warm breath, the wool of his coat beneath her hand. *Rosa, Rosa, Rosa, smile for me. You need to learn how to have fun,* chérie.

The memory shook her. Rosalie looked up at Jack, who was still smiling. Like Gaston.

"He was ambitious, like you," she said softly. "And . . . he knew the angles, too."

His smile died. "I wish to God you'd never heard that conversation."

"It doesn't matter whether I heard it or not," she said. "It only put into words what I already felt about you."

"What you still feel?"

She hesitated. Her heart said no, but her heart was so easily fooled. Her heart had not yet learned. "I . . . I don't know."

"What can I do to convince you?" he asked.

"I don't know that, either."

She heard him sigh. Then his hand was gone from hers, and she felt his fingers on her chin, pressing the fine lace of her veil into her skin, an immediate reminder of that kiss, and she wanted it again—such a shameful thing. But he didn't lift the veil aside; he didn't kiss her. This time he only smiled and whispered, "Oh, Rosa, what am I going to do with you?"

It seemed he didn't expect an answer, and she could not have given him one if he had. His hand dropped from her face. "Do you really want to go shopping today?"

Shopping. She had forgotten all about it, and now it seemed the last thing she wanted to do. She felt unbalanced, disarmed—she could not walk into Monsieur Louis's and look at pretty little boxes. Mutely Rosalie shook her head.

Again a reassuring squeeze. "Good. Will you come with me, then? There's something I want to show you."

"What?"

He shook his head, smiling. "Patience is a virtue, Rosa, or don't your priests teach you that?"

She found herself smiling wanly back. "Of course they do. Not only do I know the virtues, I know the seven deadly sins, too."

He slanted her a glance. "I never doubted that," he said dryly. "What you don't know is how to forget them. You need to learn how to live, Rosa."

An echo of Gaston's words. Rosalie tried not to hear it. "Surely you weren't taught that. Your aunt and uncle . . . they seem . . . certainly they took you to church?"

He shook his head. "The full extent of my religious training comes from a tutor who used the Bible as a textbook." He grinned. "I can tell you the story of the prodigal son, and I can see, my dear Rosa, that you are hiding your light under a bushel."

She flushed; she had not expected he could turn a discussion about the Bible into a gentle chastisement. For the time being she ignored it. It was a relief not to talk about herself; she was much more curious about him. "You mean you've never set foot in a church?"

"Of course I have. I went to mass with you."

That reminder, too, was disarming. "I meant before that."

He nodded. "Easter once or twice. Before that, my parents' funeral. I was only three. I don't remember it."

Three years old and parentless. Rosalie thought of her own mother's death when she was thirteen. It had been terrible, losing her then. How would it have felt at three? It made her sad to think of it. She squeezed his arm in an expression of comfort. "I cannot imagine. How did they die?"

"A boating accident," he said. "It wasn't so bad. As I said, I don't remember it."

"But you must have felt it then."

"Maybe." He shrugged. "What does one feel at three? They were there one day and then they weren't. My aunt and uncle were more parents to me than my own."

He went quiet. When she looked up at him, she saw his gaze was far away, his jaw tight, and she wondered if he was remembering the night of the soirée, his argument with his uncle, his aunt's snub.

Rosalie certainly remembered it. It seemed, when she thought back on it, that there had not been a day

since she'd known Jack Waters that she had not felt
sadness for him on some level, and that night—even
though she had barely known him then—his aunt's
snub had seemed heavy and mean, an extreme humiliation. Such deliberateness seemed too sad to be borne.

"It must be difficult," she said softly.

He started a little. "What?"

"Your aunt's forsaking you like that."

"She had a right, I suppose," he said mildly. "I
embarrassed her."

"She could not stand by you?"

"She was disappointed." He took a deep breath. "I
hadn't expected that, but I should have. In her own
way, she's as devoted to the social order as my uncle is.
She had always called me her son. It was . . . hard for
her when I was arrested. It made her look bad."

Rosalie looked down at the banquette. The bricks
were uneven here, catching at her toes. She found herself leaning into him for support. "Still, you say she
called you her son. She must love you. She should have
supported you."

"Is that what love requires?"

Rosalie nodded. "I would not walk away from my
own children, whatever they had done."

"No, you wouldn't, would you?" His voice was
thoughtful. "And your mother, was she like that?"

Rosalie smiled. "*Oui*. Maman was gentle and kind.
She understood so many things. If I could be half what
she was, I would think that God was generous."

"You are at least that, I think."

"*Non*."

"No doubt your father thinks so. Where would he be without you?"

His words mirrored thoughts she'd had a dozen times. Rosalie glanced away, fixing her eyes on the intricate curlicues of a fence they were passing, the pitchfork shadows stretching across the walk before them, and felt again that sadness, a sadness she'd had for a very long time. "My responsibilities are not what Maman's were. My life is easy. I have no husband, no children."

He was quiet, and Rosalie's heart clenched. She'd said too much. But no, of course she hadn't. Her words . . . she had revealed nothing. There was nothing to reveal.

"But you want those things, don't you?" he asked quietly.

Her throat tightened. "I am content with my life as God's servant." But the words felt unsatisfying, somehow. They did not hold the comfort they once had.

He didn't try to make her deny it. "Here we are," he said.

He had brought her to the levee. Rosalie looked at him in surprise. "Here? This is what you wanted me to see?"

He said nothing more as they crossed into the hustle and bustle of the busiest place in New Orleans. Now, in the middle of the day, it was more crowded than at any other time. Men shouting orders dodged drays pulling loads of sacks and barrels, and bales of cotton stacked too high to see over vied for space with steamer trunks and piles of luggage. Everywhere there were men loading steamers, slaves bent double beneath huge barrels of whiskey or rum or molasses, horses or mules straining against overloaded wagons. Here and there Rosalie spotted another strolling couple, a family, men deep in discussion. Beyond the wharves, the steamers spewed smoke into the air, blew their strident whistles as they finished loading, and churned up mud and water in their giant paddle wheels.

It was the heart of the city. It was impossible to stand there and not feel a singing in the blood, not feel life pulsing in the tips of one's fingers. Rosalie had not been to the levee for a long time, and now she stared at it, the shapes shifting beyond her veil, the colors muted.

Beside her, she felt Jack tense. She glanced up at him. He was staring out at the harbor, so intent it seemed he didn't even breathe, and suddenly she remembered his story about five thousand dollars and riches enough to buy a dream. "This is it, isn't it?" she asked. "Somewhere here is the reason you stole the money."

She'd surprised him, she could tell. He started and looked down at her, his brows coming together in consternation. Then he looked away, out toward the steamers.

"This is what I wanted to show you," he said. "Look out there."

She looked. At steamers lined up one beside the other, two and three deep. At a crowd of smokestacks belching smoke, brass fittings shining dully in the bright overcast, company flags lying limply against the lines. Some of them had just unloaded and were waiting for cargo. The decks of others were piled high. But they all seemed bright and promising as they waited at the dock.

"Your riches," she said softly.

"I wanted to start a steamer company," he admitted. "I wanted my name on one of those flags. I was sixteen the first time I set foot on a steamer, but I remember thinking it was the future. My uncle was not so enthusiastic." He laughed shortly, bitterly. "It seemed a natural extension to me. A cotton brokerage, our own steamer line. So much money to be made . . ." He sighed. "Ah, well. So much for dreams."

"You should mention it to my father," she said. "He's always looking for new investments—"

He cut her off with a look. "What are your dreams, Rosa?"

"I . . ." She searched for words. "I hardly know—"

"A husband?" he asked. "Children?"

"I—"

"What about life, Rosa? Life without God's minions telling you what to do or what you should feel. When was the last time you didn't feel guilty for simply enjoying the feel of the air on your face?"

She stared at him in confusion. "The air?"

He turned toward her, dislodging her hold on his arm. Before she could stop him, he lifted the hat from her head, tearing away her veil. He threw it into the air, and there was a breeze suddenly where there had not been one before. It caught the fine lace, twisting it away. It was gone, like wisps of cotton in the wind.

Rosalie looked at him. He was watching her, his eyes glittering, and in the glare his eyes seemed impossibly blue, his hair lit with gold. In that moment she realized she'd been looking through a haze, that she'd forgotten the sharpness of life, that she had taken refuge behind fuzzy lace. And now . . . now she felt naked. She felt air that was not simply her own breath, she smelled smells that were bigger and more intense than she remembered: sun-bleached wood and molasses and rum, oranges and bananas.

She stared at him, and he took hold of her arms and turned her gently around, so she was facing the steamers full on, the muddy waters of the Mississippi glittering before her.

"Look," he whispered behind her, down into her ear. "Look at that and tell me why it's so sad to lose your dreams, Rosa. Tell me why it hurts to think of what I threw away."

And she understood in a way she hadn't been able to see before; she knew what he meant. The dreams that had sustained her . . . where had they gone? She had not been living since they disappeared. She had not been living at all until he came through the door and reminded her of what it was like to love someone.

Chapter 19

"**Y**ou got no more time," Paulette said. "Soon nobody be believing this baby belongs to him."

Corinne lifted her gaze to meet Paulette's in the mirror. Her hand stilled on the brush. "I know."

"You should be having your hooks in that man already. The love charms work fast."

"Not fast enough. And apparently not well enough, either." Corinne laid her brush on the vanity with a sigh. "I've tried everything. I went to his room. . . ." She trailed off, hating to think of the humiliation of it, her own pitiful desperation, the hours she'd spent since then thinking, *What will I do now? What can I do?* The fear had been swelling inside her like a hard and painful little seed. "It didn't work."

"He has a will, that one." Paulette nodded. "We try something else."

"There's no time for that. You said it yourself. If I wait much longer, no one will believe me."

Paulette nodded again. She turned to the armoire and pulled out one of Corinne's gowns, smoothing it as she laid it on the bed, fingering the lace with a slow thoughtfulness. "There still be Mammy Zaza," she said quietly.

Corinne shuddered. "*Non.*"

"Your papa, he won't be liking it if—"

"I know," Corinne said abruptly. "Stop talking about it."

But she had never been able to order Paulette to do anything, and the servant kept on talking now. "They been seen walking together, *mademoiselle.* They lean close, they touch hands. Perhaps a kiss . . . it not surprising—"

"*Mon Dieu*, she wants to be a *nun*, Paulette!"

Paulette shrugged. "Maybe once."

"I can't believe she would have changed her mind. Not Rosa."

"You know her better than me, *mademoiselle.*"

"She still prays every night—doesn't she?"

"*Oui, oui*, she pray." Paulette looked thoughtful. "People pray for lots of reasons, *oui?* They not always self-righteous prayers."

Corinne twisted from the mirror to stare at her maid. "What does that mean?"

"She pray a lot. More than usual."

Corinne frowned. "So?"

"People who fear they be making a bad decision pray a lot."

Corinne felt a sinking in her stomach. She turned back to the mirror. "What should I do?" she asked quietly. "If he won't even take me to bed, how can I make him marry me?"

Paulette said nothing. She bent over the gown on the bed, straightened a piece of lace, fluffed a silk rose. Corinne watched her in the mirror, the deliberate movements, the slanting sunshine across the bright colors of Paulette's tignon.

"There be other ways," Paulette said finally, softly.

Corinne frowned again. "Not another love charm."

"*Non.*"

"But—"

"There be one way of getting what you want, *mademoiselle*. Your papa, he would not be happy to find Monsieur Waters been with you instead of Mademoiselle Rosalie."

"But I haven't been with him."

"You know that. Monsieur Waters knows it. Everyone else . . ."

Corinne felt a slow chill. "You're saying I should lie."

Paulette met her gaze steadily. "*Oui.*"

"I don't think I can do that."

Paulette shrugged. She picked up the gown and tucked it into her arms. "This need crimping," she said. She went to the door and paused, looked back over her shoulder. "You best think about who be better off in the convent, *mademoiselle,* you or your sister."

She left the room, but her words lingered after, uncomfortable, distressing. Paulette was right: Too much time had passed, and Corinne had no other options. Her pregnancy would become obvious before too long. When Papa found out, she would be en route to the convent before she had time to pack her things. Unless . . . unless she lied. Unless she told him Jack Waters was the father.

Corinne didn't want to think about it. She didn't

want to consider it at all. But there it was, planted now in her mind, hard to forget. She thought of how Papa approved of Jack, how Papa had made Jack his heir, how he'd given Jack to his favorite daughter.

Jack was the son Papa had never had, so why shouldn't he be delighted to find that Corinne was expecting Jack's child? Papa's first grandchild . . . The old longing for Papa's acceptance, for his affection, came back. Corinne's dreams blossomed in her head: She imagined Papa's arms holding her tight, imagined him telling her how happy he was that she had given him what he always wanted . . .

The dream wavered. He would be angry at first. He would not like the fact that she had stolen Jack from Rosa or that she and Jack had been intimate before marriage. He might not even believe her—

No, he would believe her. And Jack was a gentleman; he would not deny it. This child would change everything. She and Jack could have an autumn wedding. Papa would love her at last . . . if she did this right.

There would be no private conversations, no opportunity for Papa to dissuade her or send her off. It would have to be done with everyone there, so that Jack would be startled quiet, so that there would be no chance for protest until she'd been able to make it seem a wonderful, special thing. She needed to tie it up in pretty ribbons, to present it like a gift . . .

A gift. Corinne stilled. Papa's birthday was only a few days after he returned. This would be the perfect present.

She imagined it. The family seated around the table, laughing with each other, drinking wine. Papa opening Rosalie's gift, and next Jack's, and then turning to her, a question in his eyes: *Corinne, have you no gift for me?*

She would smile then, look at Jack, and say, *Papa, Jack and I are giving you the greatest gift of all. I am having a baby. . . .*

Corinne closed her eyes. She tried to bring it into her head, to feel joy and relief at the vision. But all she felt was sick and a little tired, and she wished Paulette had never put the thought into her head.

She wished she had the courage to refuse it.

It was the last night before Papa came home. Rosalie knew she should be glad; her father's presence had always given her a sense of well-being, of safety. She had always liked the constancy of the days when Papa was home, the routine that revolved around him, her feeling of efficiency. When Papa came home, she would no longer have time for afternoons spent just sitting in the courtyard, for walks to the levee. There would be much less time to spend . . . with Jack.

She told herself that was fine. She liked it better that way. He was disconcerting, and he reminded her of Gaston. And there was the vow she'd made, which she intended to keep. Why then, did she feel such sadness at the thought? Why did she feel that things were coming to an end just when they should have been beginning?

Rosalie hardly knew. It had something to do with yesterday, she realized. It had to do with the fact that, after Jack had gone, she had been unable to lose the memory he'd brought back to her—of Gaston at the market. She'd kept that memory, along with so many others, buried so deep that she'd forgotten the truth of those days. She'd wanted to believe she'd been foolish every step of the way with Gaston, that her passions had led her astray. She wanted to believe there had been nothing good about him, nothing to want again, nothing to wish for.

But that memory was good. It had been spring, and the sunlight had been warm and light, matching the glow in his deep brown eyes. She had felt carefree, as if her responsibilities had been lifted away for that one afternoon and she was just a sixteen-year-old girl in love with love, instead of sixteen going on twenty-six, a matron already, a substitute wife.

It made her wonder: Had she been wrong about everything? Were the memories of her love for her cousin Gaston so corrupted by what had happened after that she could not remember anything clearly?

She didn't know, and it made her uncomfortable that she didn't. She'd spent the last years under the heavy hand of caution, and to feel it lifting now, ever so slightly, panicked her. But she longed for it, too— there had been something about Jack yesterday, the way his hair had glinted in the sun, perhaps, or maybe it was simply the way he'd lifted her veil from her face. He raised that longing again inside her. The chance to see colors again, to breathe . . . She could not deny that yearning, even as it made her afraid.

She had prayed for guidance. She had spent hour after hour in her room, on her knees before her altar, rising stiff-legged and sore, but she felt her conviction falling away, just out of reach, and it did not seem so bad, suddenly. To have it leave her did not hold the terror it once had.

Rosalie found herself wanting to hold on to these last hours with Jack before Papa came home, these last hours of pure freedom. So when Jack started to excuse himself after dinner, she insisted he come with her and Corinne to the parlor. She wanted to hear him laugh, and she was still worried over Corinne's obvious depression. Her sister needed some diversion; she seemed too quiet, too thoughtful.

"A game of chess," Rosalie suggested as they went into the parlor. "Perhaps Corinne could sing while we play."

Jack looked at her bemusedly. "I didn't know you played chess."

"Oh, Rosa's quite good," Corinne said with a wan smile. "But I—I'd rather not sing, if you don't mind, Rosa."

"The piano, then," Rosalie suggested.

Corinne hesitated. She glanced at Jack, and it was a strange look, a disturbing one. But it was soon gone, and Rosalie forgot it as she led Jack to the big pedestal table in the middle of the parlor.

When he sat, she reached for the drawer beneath it and pulled out the chess set. It was an inexpensive set—Papa's from when he was a child. A thin painted board and rudely carved pieces. But she had a fond-ness for it. She liked the way the pieces felt between her fingers, how unfinished they were.

She set the pieces on the board and took the seat across from Jack. "Do you remember how to play?"

He nodded, studying the pieces idly, his strong, slender fingers playing with the worn nubs of the rook's crown. "I remember."

But then he was silent. And he was not a good player, she realized quickly. Or perhaps it was only that he was too distracted. She felt his preoccupation like a fog between them, unsatisfying, frustrating. This was not what she'd expected. It was not what she wanted . . . though she wasn't sure just what it was she did want.

Corinne was playing some somber, slow tune. It was depressing, and it jangled Rosalie's nerves. But even without her full concentration, she had Jack trapped within moments. In two more moves she would have checkmate. She waited for him to see the danger, to move his king, but instead he shoved a pawn forward.

"Your mind seems elsewhere tonight, Jack."

He glanced up at her. "I'm tired."

Corinne finished the tune with a crescendo of chords and then a loud *ta-dum*. The last soulful notes filled the room and then drifted away. Corinne rose from the piano with a sigh. She came over to the table, her rose perfume settling over them like a cloud.

"I am exhausted," she said. Then she glanced at Jack, and smiled dully. "*Bonsoir, Jack.*"

He looked up at her, and then away again, and he seemed uncomfortable. "Good night."

Corinne hesitated. "Rosa, it's late. Perhaps you should retire as well. Papa will be home tomorrow."

The reminder settled on Rosalie like a weight. "*Oui*," she said with forced enthusiasm. She moved her bishop across the board. "Checkmate."

Jack looked startled. He glanced down at the board. "My God, you've won."

She was disappointed. She'd hoped he could somehow find a way out, that they could continue the game. It was late, as Corinne had said, but Rosalie was strangely reluctant to go. The night felt strange: Corinne's sadness lingered, Jack's distraction worried her. Rosalie wanted a few moments more, perhaps another game, and she waited for him to suggest it.

He didn't. He sat back in his chair, and there was an odd tension in his face that made Rosalie hesitate even as Corinne touched her shoulder.

"Come, Rosa. *Bonsoir*, Jack."

Rosalie wished Corinne would go on. She started to suggest it, but she could think of no reason to stay, nothing to say. So she rose, said good night to Jack, and followed Corinne into the dining room.

There was still a tureen left on the sideboard from dinner—someone had forgotten it. Rosalie motioned for Corinne to go on and went to retrieve it. "I'll take this to the washroom," she said.

Corinne paused. Then she nodded and disappeared through the doors into the courtyard.

Rosalie picked up the heavy silver and turned—right into Jack.

"Don't go," he whispered.

She nearly dropped the tureen. He was so close—too close. She felt herself taking a step backward, but the sideboard was there, stopping her. Rosalie took a deep breath, struggling for calm. This was what she'd wanted, wasn't it? A few more minutes alone with him.

But there was so much in his words. *Don't go.* It frightened her, what she heard there, and so she pretended not to hear it. Slowly she turned and set the tureen back on the sideboard. Those moments gave her control again.

She turned back to him with a too-bright smile. "Don't tell me you would like another game."

"No," he said. "As you can see, I'm not that good."

"You said you were tired."

"That too." He looked past her, out the windows looking onto the side yard, and when he glanced back at her, she saw something flicker through his eyes. He motioned back to the parlor. "Will you come sit with me awhile?"

She should not allow her heart to leap in that way. But it did, and she could not help herself. She nodded and followed him back into the parlor, and when he poured himself a glass of port and offered her one, she took it.

The liquid was sweet and heady. She drank port seldom—Papa did not approve of it, and now it felt vaguely forbidden, a little licentious. Jack drank his quickly without sitting, and poured himself another, and after he capped the decanter he looked around for his glass as if he'd forgotten where he put it. It was as telling as every other gesture he'd made this evening.

"It's in your hand," she said gently. Then, at his sheepish surprise, "You *are* distracted. You've been distracted all evening. What is it, Jack?"

He shook his head slightly and sat in a chair across from her. But he didn't really sit. It was more like . . . hovering. He was barely balanced on the edge, and there was a restlessness to his movements. He went to put the glass on the side table, changed his mind, rested his forearms on his thighs and dangled the glass between his knees, then changed his mind again. He could not seem to sit still.

He was obviously not going to say anything. It was up to her.

"Things feel . . . strange tonight, don't you think?" she tried.

Her words seemed to arrest him. "Strange how?"

"As if there's going to be a storm."

"The skies are clear."

Rosalie leaned forward. "What is it, Jack?"

He seemed startled by her question. Then he looked at the floor. "There's something I have to tell you," he said. "Something . . . you should know about me."

The words made her uncomfortable. Rosalie suddenly wished she'd gone to bed. His tone was too serious; she knew she would not like what he wanted to say. She tried for lightheartedness. "What else could there be?" she teased. "You've already told me you were in prison. I am not sure my delicate constitution could take much more."

"What about murder?" he asked her.

She stared at him, confused. She thought of the man he'd hit with the carriage. "You told me it was an accident."

He shook his head. "Not that. Something else. Something that happened when I was in Parish."

She stilled. "I see."

"You remember that day at St. Anne's? When I told you I'd seen that house before?"

"*Oui.*"

"I worked at their plantation. On a chain gang of sorts, though we weren't chained—there was too much land to work, and the chains would have hobbled us."

She was used to terrible stories, to hard luck and bitterness. She was used to people's anger over their circumstances; she saw it every day—at St. Anne's, at the infirmary. But Jack's admission hit her hard, like a blow to the chest; she had the sudden image of him trudging beside the others, dressed in cheap, harsh prison garb.

If asked only a few days ago, she would have said she could picture him as a convict. But now the image jarred her; it seemed wrong, oddly unnatural. It did not seem to be him at all.

He laughed shortly. "I've shocked you."

"But that's what you meant to do, isn't it?" She met his gaze squarely. "Isn't it?"

Jack looked away again. "There was another man

on that gang. My cellmate. We had argued about something—I don't remember what. That night he came at me with a knife. In the morning he was dead, and I was the one with blood on my hands."

"You killed him," Rosalie said.

Jack nodded. He took a deep breath. "I spent the next two years in the workroom. In that time I saw the outdoors once. I didn't get a bath again for six months. God, it seemed sometimes that I'd forgotten what the sun looked like."

"You were trying to save your life. You did what you had to," she said quietly.

His gaze met hers. "Do you think God forgives us for that, Rosalie?"

"Of course."

Jack sat back in his chair, and his gaze when he looked at her was long and sad. "You believe it for me, Rosa—why don't you believe it for yourself?"

Instinctively she felt for her rosary. She saw his quick glance, and she stopped and gripped her glass of port instead. She felt unsettled, unsure. His gaze was so direct, it took her breath away.

"Tell me what this man of yours did to you."

The question was so unexpected that she gasped. It brought with it a familiar fear—all the good memories in the world could not make that fear go away. Rosalie was trembling as she put aside her port. But her hands would not stay empty. She reached for her rosary.

He was across the room and sitting beside her on the settee before she knew it. He grabbed her hand before she could lift the beads from her pocket.

"Don't," he said.

"But I—"

"Don't lean on God now, Rosa," he said. His voice dropped to a whisper. "I don't want a confession. I just want you to tell me what you really feel."

She felt a hundred things, and she stared at him in confusion, feeling alone and afraid—how had things changed so quickly?

He smiled, a small, friendly smile. "Come on, Rosa. You can do this. I know you can."

But she could not. She could not tell him. Too many years, too many broken-off confessions, too many fears. Her humiliation and her foolishness rose before her and cut her words dead; her sin lodged in her throat. She could not admit it to God—how could she admit it to this man, who made her face it all again, who made her heart ache with everything she had given up, everything she had vowed never to want?

She bowed her head and looked at his hand covering hers, his strong fingers. "I'm sorry," she whispered back. "The memory is mine to suffer alone."

She thought he would back away, that he would leave her. He had revealed his greatest sins to her; she expected him to be offended that she could not do the same. But he only grew very quiet. She felt the subtle flex of his fingers covering her hand.

"Don't be a martyr, Rosa," he said finally. "It doesn't suit you. You're no saint. Admit it. People make mistakes. I've made a hundred myself."

"Not . . . like this."

"I didn't go to prison for nothing."

"What you did is not the same." *Not the same as deliberately taking a life.* The words were so loud in her head that she thought she'd said them aloud, and she gasped in horror. But no, she hadn't said them, though, to her surprise, he answered as if he'd heard them, as if he understood.

"No," he said quietly. He squeezed her hand. "It isn't, is it?" He leaned close; she felt his breath against her temple. "But sometimes, darling, it's as you said: We do what we have to."

She looked at him in surprise. He was blurry—she had tears in her eyes that seemed to have come from nowhere. And then he was close, and closer still, and she felt his lips on hers—so soft, so dry and warm, barely brushing. The kiss lasted only a second, although she moved with him when he pulled away, and she found herself longing for more.

"I'm sorry," he said. "I didn't mean to make you cry."

No, no, it was not what she wanted. And yet at the same time it was.

She wiped her eyes. "You didn't. I . . . I'm just . . . foolish."

"You're no more foolish than the rest of us." He got to his feet, and suddenly he was impatient again, restless. "Are you all right?"

"*Oui. Oui,* of course." But it was a lie, of course. When Rosalie reached for her port, her hands were trembling; she nearly spilled it as she brought it to her lips.

He made a sound and turned away again. He put down his glass so hard that the lamp on the table rattled, the flame danced. "Good night, Rosa. I—I'm sorry."

He left her. Long after he'd gone, Rosalie sat on the settee, staring into the silence, watching the lamp flicker. And as the flame sputtered into dimness she heard his words circling in her mind, she saw again the effort it had taken him to say them. It was then that she realized two things: She cared for him much more than she wanted to admit, and the convent of the Ursulines seemed a long time ago, and very far away.

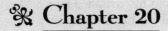
✽ Chapter 20

Rosalie waited anxiously in the parlor. Papa was due back at any moment, and instead of the relief she would normally have felt on such an occasion, she felt uneasy. Last night's conversation with Jack was still on her mind, puzzling, disturbing.

She did not think about it too much—in fact, she worked very hard not to. She did not want to wonder why he'd said such things to her, why he wanted so much to know her past, just as she didn't want to know why Jack's kiss, as friendly and unassuming as it was, had haunted her until she tossed and turned and dreamed of other kisses. Not just dreamed of—longed for . . .

She turned almost desperately to the roses on the piano, fumbling with them, sending loose petals falling onto the wood. She was picking them up with clumsy fingers when she heard the sound of the carriage.

Papa.

Her heart fluttered and her nerves tightened. She felt again her slow dread of yesterday. It was too soon. She did not want him back just yet.

But she hurried to the door and opened it just in time to see her father step from the carriage. He glanced up and saw her, and his wrinkled face broke into a bright smile. He held out his arms to her.

"Rosa!" he called. "Such a sight you are! After all those ugly men, it does my heart good to see you again."

Rosalie went into his arms. He held her tight, but she pulled away quickly. "I'm happy you're back," she said. "You took your medicine every day? You followed my instructions?"

He clucked. "You worry too much."

"Papa—"

"I did everything just as you said, *chérie*," he assured her. He put his arm around her as they walked to the door. "So tell me, how were things while I was gone, eh? Has the house fallen down around you?"

"As you can see, it has not."

"And Corinne? Don't tell me—she has found a new beau? Which silly *fainéant* must I rid us of this time?"

Rosalie shook her head. "If she has a new beau, she's kept it a secret."

"Oh?" Papa looked surprised. "What has she done with her days, then? Bankrupted me?"

Rosalie smiled weakly. "It's been only four days, Papa. But she seems to be . . . despondent."

"Ah, no doubt the dressmaker did not get new patterns." Her father sighed. Then his arm tightened around her shoulders, and he looked at her seriously. "And Jack. What about Jack, *chérie*?"

Her anxiety tightened. Rosalie took a deep breath. "He's fine, Papa."

He leaned close. "You like him better, eh?"

She twisted to meet his gaze. "You did not tell me the truth about him, Papa."

"The truth? What truth is that, *ma petite?*"

She gave him a chiding look. "You did not tell me about Parish."

His breath came out in a long sigh. "Oh, *chérie,* I was afraid of this."

"So you knew."

"Of course I knew. Did you think I picked him off the street? He is the nephew of my business partner, not some stranger. I made inquiries into his past before I brought him home."

"Did you think I would not find out?" she asked.

"I had hoped you would not," he said. He sighed. "Who told you?"

"Jack did."

His heavy brows lifted—another surprise. "Jack?"

"*Oui.*"

Papa looked thoughtful.

"I don't understand you, Papa," she said in a low voice. "What were you thinking? To bring a criminal into our home—to marry him to me without my knowing his past—"

"He is hardly a criminal, Rosa. A boyhood prank that ended badly. He is no murderer."

The word was vaguely startling. She thought of Jack's story last night, of the man he'd killed. "No," she agreed softly. "He's no murderer."

She glanced up to find her father studying her. When she caught his eye, he glanced hastily away.

"So tell me, Rosa. Do you hold this against him? Does this make your liaison impossible?"

"It is impossible already, Papa."

"But if it were not," he said, "if God decided it would be better for you to have a husband—"

Rosalie looked away. "Please, Papa."

"Then tell me, because I want to know. Answer my question, because I am an old man who needs reassurance. Do you like Jack better now, *chérie*?"

Again she thought of Jack's kiss, and of the intensity in his eyes. She thought of the peace she'd found at the levee, gazing at the steamers with him. But the question her father asked her was uncomfortable, and she could not answer without his reading too much into it, expecting too much.

"I've found nothing in him to criticize," she said finally. Then she changed the subject. "Now, tell me about your trip. Was it successful?"

Papa was quiet for a moment, watching her. Then he shrugged. "*Oui*. It was never in doubt, *chérie*, but I will tell you it is good to be home. These trips . . . they do not sit as well on an old body as they used to."

Papa went into the house. He stopped just inside the hallway, leaning his cane against the wall, taking off his hat. "Now, where is Jack?"

"Right here." Jack stepped from the parlor. He smiled—at the touch of his eyes, Rosalie felt warm all over. Then he looked to her father. "How was your trip?"

Papa moved past Jack into the parlor. "Fine, fine. How are affairs at the bank?" Papa sat heavily in his chair and motioned for Rosalie to come over beside him, but Rosalie felt strangely reluctant in the moment before she went dutifully to stand behind him. She rested her hand on his shoulder while he took hold of her fingers, holding her there. He had done this a hundred times, but this time Rosalie felt bound in place; she longed to pull her fingers away.

"Papa." Corinne came in from the courtyard through the dining room. She was breathless and distracted. "You're back."

She did not seem despondent, but neither was she her normal self. Rosalie frowned, and Papa stiffened beneath her hand. "What, no shopping today, missy?"

Corinne stopped beside Jack. She shook her head and gave him a small smile. "No, Papa. I've already got your birthday present."

"I don't need any more colognes."

"It's not cologne," Corinne said.

"Ah, that is good." Papa turned to Jack with a frown. "Now, go on, *mon ami*. You were saying?"

Rosalie barely listened to Jack's account of the last four days. She watched as Corinne went to stand by the piano; she saw the intent slant of her sister's gaze as Corinne looked at Jack. There was something about it that bothered Rosalie. She couldn't decide what it was: perhaps the nervous way Corinne fumbled with the tassels on the tapestry runner, or her seeming inability to keep still.

"Well, it seems things are under control," Papa was saying. He patted Rosalie's hand and got to his feet. "Now, Jack, you will stay here with me a moment, eh? Rosa, you and Corinne may leave us now."

Rosalie frowned at her father. A private conversation with Jack—it could only have something to do with what she'd said to him. Quietly, for her father's ears only, she said, "Do not be angry at him for telling me."

Papa drew away. His brow furrowed. "Oh, I am not angry, *chérie*," he said, and then he smiled, he touched her shoulder. "You go on, eh? Take your sister with you. Jack and I must talk."

Rosalie did not want to go, but reluctantly she dragged herself toward the doorway where Corinne was waiting. As Rosalie approached, her sister fanned herself.

"It's a warm day," Corinne said. "Some lemonade, Rosa?"

Rosalie nodded. But her step was lingering as she left the doorway, and she could not rid herself of the feeling that she should not have confided her conversation with Jack to her father—that she had made a mistake.

Jack eyed Garland speculatively. "You want to talk to me?"

"*Oui, oui.*" The old man nodded and sank again into his chair. He was smiling, but it was an inward smile, one not meant for sharing. "I have been speaking to Rosalie."

Jack tensed. "And?"

"She has told me something interesting, Jack."

"Stop the riddles, old man. What did she say?"

"She asked me why I had not told her you'd been in Parish."

Jack's heart stopped. "I . . . see."

"*Non,* I do not think you do, *mon ami.*" Garland smiled. He leaned back in his chair and steepled his hands before him. "You are a clever boy, eh? Just as I expected. I am thinking my trip away was the best thing I could have done."

"Why is that?" Jack asked warily.

"You have been courting her."

Jack hesitated. Strange how he had forgotten it was what he was supposed to be doing. *Courting.* He had been talking with her, getting to know her, needing her—"Yes."

"*Bien, bien.* Whatever you have done, Jack, it is succeeding." Garland's smile grew. "You should have seen her, *mon ami.* She is growing to care for you, I know this. She tells me you have been in prison—why did I not tell her? I say, 'He is no murderer,' and she agrees with me!"

The image of last night played in Jack's head: the look on her face as she sat across from him, her compassion. Even now the power of it weakened him. In the force of it, he could not remember what Garland had said or how he was expected to answer.

It seemed the old man did not need him to. He went on, and there was a gleeful look on his face—at any moment Jack expected Garland to rub his hands together. "Think about this, Jack. I asked her if she liked you better now, and her answer . . . her answer, *mon ami*, gives me a hope I did not expect to have. She says to me: 'I have found nothing in him to criticize.' Nothing to criticize! This is *after* she has found you are a convict! This is something, eh, Jack? This is . . . astonishing."

"She's a compassionate woman," Jack said quietly.

Garland shook his head. "This is more than compassion, Jack. She is bending, I know it. A few more days and she will give up this foolish idea of a convent."

"I wouldn't be too sure."

"Ah, Jack, you disappoint me! Look at what awaits you! This is what I want you to do, Jack—*mon ami*, do you hear me? You press a little harder, *oui*? She is halfway to you already. I want an announcement on my birthday. Such a gift . . . it is what I want, Jack, do you hear me?"

Jack said carefully, "I'm not sure I can promise that."

"You make it happen!" Garland demanded with a sudden scowl. "I tell you, she is changing her mind, Jack. If you cannot make her want you, then you are not the man I thought you were."

"I don't . . . She keeps . . ." *Something close to her heart. Something I can't touch.* The words unfolded in his mind, but he could not say them. They seemed suddenly to be an extraordinary breach of trust. Jack licked his lips and nodded shortly. "I'll do what I can."

Garland laughed. "*Bien, bien.* Ah, Jack, I am a happy man tonight."

The old man was jubilant. Jack wondered why he was not relieved over Garland's confidence, why he felt still unsettled.

"I'm glad," he said. "If that's all—"

"Jack?"

Jack turned back to the old man. "Yes?"

"*Merci.*"

"For what?"

"For being the man I thought you were," Garland said. "You are truly the partner I wished for, eh? I did not choose poorly."

Garland's eyes were shining with approval. Jack's discomfort wavered, then faded away. The last time someone had looked at him that way, he'd been standing in this parlor also, staring into warm brown eyes, and in that moment he saw Rosalie so clearly in Garland that they were almost the same person, and he felt warmed, the way he had then. Not alone. Suddenly he felt more a part of this life than he had since he'd first set foot in Garland Lafon's home.

"You didn't choose poorly," he assured the old man.

"*Bien,*" Garland said. "Let us hope it stays that way."

The warmth of that approval stayed with Jack as he left the parlor. He went down the hallway, toward the courtyard, but when he saw Corinne and Rosalie sitting out there, he hesitated, he backed away. It reminded him of why he should not feel complacent. Garland's approval was his now, but it was a fleeting thing, and Jack was too aware of the secrets Rosalie was keeping from him, the secrets that held so much power they could lead her away from him.

He turned and went back down the hallway, past the parlor where Garland was now pouring himself a drink, and out the front door. When he was there, he stood on the stoop, staring out at St. Louis Street, watching the people move by, the carriages, watching the New Orleans he had missed for three long years.

Those years came back to haunt him. Instead of the fragrance of mimosa, he smelled cold stone walls and sweat. Instead of colors, he saw only gray. He tasted the air in the dryness of his mouth. He felt somehow that if he could not change her, if he let those secrets consume her, it would be like prison again, a penance he could not face.

She had become important to him, and that made him nervous. He was drawn to her compassion; he needed her faith. Last night he'd been unable to go to bed without knowing he had it, without knowing that she had the whole truth about him. He had not been able to face a lie.

When had Rosalie Lafon become so precious to him? When was it things had changed? One day he was trying to win her because she held his future, and the next . . . the next he was yearning to see her laughter, wanting her to come alive beneath his hands, wishing for life to shine from her eyes instead of piety.

He wanted her secrets. He wanted to swallow them, to hold them tight within himself and tell her he understood. He wanted to be worthy in her eyes, because there was something inside him that told him she was worth being worthy for.

And so it was like that, day by day, minute by minute, that his future had become more than just a wish for riches and respect, but a yearning to see her dressed in springtime green. He found, to his surprise, that it was a future he wished for more than ever, that it, too, was precious to him, something he did not want to lose. Something he could not give up.

He didn't think beyond that, wouldn't let himself. Garland's faith in him was a heavy weight on his shoulders—Jack did not want to wonder what the old man's punishment would be if he could not convince her to turn away from this idea of atoning for her sins in cloistered silence forever, if he could not provide the present of Rosalie's conversion, all tied up in birthday bows.

Nor did he want to think of how he would punish himself.

❧ Chapter 21

"Non, non," Papa said. "No soirée, no ball. It must be a family affair, Rosa. I am old now, too old for celebrations, eh? Another year passes—what of it? It only means I am a year closer to my death."

Rosalie looked up from her market list. "What a thing to say, Papa."

"But true nonetheless. You are listening to me, *ma petite?* You hear what I am saying?"

"*Oui.*" Rosalie nodded and sighed. She put aside her pencil and looked up at her father as he stood beside her desk. "A family celebration for your birthday. It is a good thing, Papa, as it is far too late to send out invitations. Your birthday is tomorrow."

"I thought perhaps you were planning a surprise. . . ."

"*Non.*" she shook her head. "I've been far too busy."

"Ah?" He surveyed her with a smile. "Perhaps you should not be so busy, eh? Spend some time with your fiancé—" He raised his hand when she began to protest. "No, do not argue with me, Rosa. I am old, my heart is weak."

"I am beginning to doubt Dr. Wiley's judgment," she said wryly.

"I have been doubting it for years. Now, another thing: You tell your sister not to spend my money on a foolish gift. *Mon Dieu,* I hardly need another watch—" He frowned. "What is it, Rosa?"

Rosalie smiled wanly. "It's nothing."

"You are worried, I can see it."

"A little," Rosalie admitted.

"Ah, *chérie,* I have been old forever. It is nothing to fear." He leaned close, smiling as he chucked her under the chin. "Even you grow older, Rosa, *n'est-ce pas?*"

She winced and pulled away. "That isn't what worries me, Papa. It's Corinne."

"Corinne?" He took a step back, immediately uninterested.

"She seems not herself."

"Ah? Her friends are all gone to the bay for the summer. Send her there for a few weeks if it will make her happy."

"It seems more than that."

"Whatever you say, *chérie.*" Papa sighed, impatient as he always was when the conversation shifted to Corinne. He pulled his watch from his vest pocket and glanced at it. "She seems herself to me, but I will admit you know best. Take care of it as you will, Rosa. Now, I must go. I have an appointment."

She nodded. When he kissed her forehead and wished her good day, she murmured some response, and when he left her she sat at her desk and twiddled the pencil between her fingers. Her father's words didn't comfort her at all. The change in Corinne still disturbed her. At first she'd feared Corinne's despondence was due to illness—in a city rife with cholera, any sickness was cause for alarm. But it was clear Corinne wasn't ill. It was more that Corinne was not herself. She smiled and laughed, but there was something in her eyes that Rosalie could not dismiss. And there was the fact that Corinne was hardly eating, and that she was sleeping so late . . .

Nothing happened between us, Rosa. You have to believe that.

Rosalie put down her pencil. She looked out the window, but instead of the bright green leaves of the magnolia and the twisting wisteria, she saw Corinne hurrying from Jack's room, clutching her unbuttoned dress to her breasts.

The image was suffocating; Rosalie was struck with a close, hot envy she could not quite shake. She looked down at her market list again, trying to ignore the feeling, but it would not go.

Finally she rose from her desk, folding her list in half and shoving it into the pocket of her gown beside her rosary. Then she went downstairs. She'd just stepped into the courtyard when she saw Jack rising from the table where he'd been breakfasting. He broke into a smile when he saw her, a smile that warmed her so deep inside, she forgot the disquieting thoughts she'd been having and the treachery of her own feelings.

"Good morning," he said. "I was looking for you. Now you're too late. I've already eaten."

"I was talking with Papa. Planning his birthday."

"Ah, yes. How old is he this year?"

"I hardly know," she said. "He's been hiding his age from us since we were children. It's his one vanity."

"Only one?" Jack teased. Then he stepped back and frowned. "What is it?"

It surprised her that he should know her so completely. "Well, I . . . nothing."

"You don't hide your worry very well, Rosa," he said. He stepped closer. He touched her forehead, a soft touch, so light she barely felt it. "I can see it here. These little wrinkles give you away every time. And here." He touched her mouth, traced her lips to the corners. "You're frowning. Tell me what's troubling you."

She could hardly say it. How could she explain that she felt a change within her, a change she did not welcome, one she wanted to ignore? How could she tell him that when she looked at him she felt a little wish, the yearning for a touch that had nothing to do with comfort and everything to do with that passion inside of her, the Rosalie she was afraid of, the one who understood desire, who wanted it?

Rosalie swallowed and glanced away. "It—it's Corinne," she said, falling back on something she could at least explain.

Jack frowned. "Corinne?"

"Does she seem odd to you?"

He smiled. "Rosa, stop worrying. Your sister's a grown woman. She can take care of herself."

"Of course." Rosalie nodded. "*Oui*, of course."

"So easy?" he teased. "I expected it would take me an hour to convince you."

"Oh, but Jack, you've taught me well."

His expression grew immediately serious. "Have I?"

The air between them changed, just that quickly. Rosalie felt the touch of his eyes like fire; involuntarily she stepped back.

And the air changed again. He noticed everything; she saw the way his gaze followed her. He looked away briefly, and when he looked back at her, he was smiling again, this time, a tiny, self-deprecating smile. "Oh, Rosa, what am I going to do with you?"—a question he asked often now, and always with affection. He bent and gave her one of the kisses she was growing used to, a quick, soft brush of the lips, a warmth so fleeting she barely had time to grab it before it was gone. She missed it already.

"Your father asked me to pick up some papers for him this morning," Jack said softly. "Come with me?"

"I . . . cannot."

"Cannot? Or will not?"

"I have so many plans."

"Of course."

She thought he would leave her then, but he only looked over her shoulder toward the house, and his expression grew thoughtful.

"Your father thinks you're ready to give up this idea of the convent," he said slowly. He did not look at her.

She spoke with the confidence of old habit. Quickly, too soon for thought. "*Non.*"

"No?" His laugh was low and soft. It cut into her heart.

She foundered. "That is, I—"

"He wants an answer for his birthday." He looked at her. His eyes were piercing. "It's the gift he's waiting for, Rosa. Your acquiescence. Will you give it?"

Her throat felt too tight to speak. He did not look away from her. He was demanding an answer, and she supposed he had a right to it. He had a right to know where he stood. But there was no answer. "Do you think I can?" she asked miserably. "So soon? Do you think my conviction is so fragile, then?"

"No." He shook his head. "No, I don't think it."

"I cannot just give him what he wants. I—"

"I understand."

"I don't know the answer!" She blurted the words, and they tumbled out between them, too loud, too desperate, too fast. When Jack stared at her, she wished she had not said them; she wished she did not understand the importance of them, the admission that she was uncertain, that she was afraid.

It gave him too much power, and she waited for him to use it, to take the last bit of her strength from her, the way Gaston had done once so long ago, to push her into a decision she was too vulnerable to make.

But Jack did not move. He said nothing. He stared at her, and then he stepped away from her and sighed. "More time, then. Rosa . . . I don't want to take you from your God."

They were the most beautiful words she'd ever heard. They calmed her in a way she could not remember ever feeling. They soothed until the ragged edges of her fear were worn away. Rosalie squeezed her eyes shut and bowed her head. "*Merci*," she whispered.

His touch on her chin was infinitely gentle. He lifted her face to his, and she opened her eyes to find him standing so close she could smell him, she could almost taste him. His blue eyes were startling, and what she saw there took her breath away.

His kiss was slow, as gentle as his touch had been. She felt the warmth of his lips, the soft pressure, and this was what she'd wanted only a few moments before—*more*. More than a friendly kiss, more than an affectionate gesture. She felt him and she knew him, and when he stepped away from her again, she felt as if she might fall without him.

"I want you," he whispered. "I'll make no secret of it. But if you don't want me . . . if you never want me, that's all right, too. All I ask, Rosa . . . all I ask is that you're honest with yourself."

She was trembling inside. She was trembling so hard she could not hear her heartbeat. "P-Papa will not be pleased." Such a silly thing to say. So irrelevant.

But that little smile came across Jack's face again, and he nodded. "You let me take care of your papa. Now I have to go. I'll see you at dinner?"

"*Au revoir*," she said softly.

He stepped away and with a final smile was gone, crossing the courtyard. She watched him until he disappeared.

❦ Chapter 22

The day of Garland's birthday dawned hot, and it grew hotter with every passing second. There was a thin layer of clouds in the sky, holding the humidity tight to the ground, and it was so warm and wet a man could feel the sickness in the air. The people who ventured out walked huddled beneath veils or with noses buried in collars, close to the camphor bags they wore around their necks.

The cholera had spread. Along with everyone else, Jack watched the sky, dreading every humid, cloudy day, feeling a heavy uneasiness in his gut whenever he heard the trumpets of a funeral procession. He wished Rosalie would stop working in the infirmary—but he knew her so well already. She would only laugh at him and say that if God intended her to die of cholera, she would be dead already.

Her faith was touching, but it was not his. And Jack had no illusions about God's compassion—or His tendency to play games.

There hadn't been a minute that passed since his talk with Garland that Jack didn't expect to find his whole world crumbling around him.

He had told Rosalie yesterday that he would take care of the old man, but the truth was that his confidence had been a facade. He had spent the hours since his conversation with Garland going over every word, wondering if there'd been a threat, feeling as if there had been. He could not give Garland the gift he'd wanted—what would be the consequence?

Yesterday Jack had hoped that perhaps she was ready. But she was not, and he would not force her. He'd known that for certain when she'd looked at him with those big brown eyes full of confusion and pain.

She was the only real friend he'd ever had, and so he was inexperienced at this and cautious. He'd set out to make her want him, but what he hadn't expected was his own reliance on their relationship, the comfort he took from her, the ease he felt in her company. He looked forward to her smile each day, and to her laugh, and if sometimes there were shadows in her eyes, they were there less and less often. One day, he knew, they would be gone forever, because he would make them go away.

But until then there would be that wariness in her, and he knew the slightest misstep would put distance between them again. She was fragile; he didn't want to crush her. He'd made the right decision, for once in his life, but still he could not escape his foreboding as he hurried home from the bank on Garland's birthday.

He left the doors of his room open as he dressed for dinner, with the muslin curtains hanging across the opening like a veil. When he heard the family gathering in the dining room, he pulled on his frock coat. There was a part of him that wanted to stay in his room, and another part that nearly ran across the courtyard to see

Rosalie again. When Jack stepped into the dining room and saw her there at the far end, dressed again in that blue gown from the soirée, he waited, heart pounding, for her to turn and look at him. When she did, when she smiled, he felt a relief so overpowering it was all he could do to keep from closing his eyes.

He started across the room to her. Corinne stepped in front of him.

"Jack," she said. Her smile was a little hesitant, but her eyes were shining.

He was instantly wary. These last few days Corinne had seemingly forgotten him, and he was grateful for how quickly she'd managed to recover. It was true what Garland had said about her at their first meeting all those days ago: Corinne's heart was like a flower, always blooming anew.

He was relieved at that, but still he doubted he would ever be truly comfortable with her. She reminded him too strongly of his near disaster, of what he had nearly thrown away.

She was stunning this evening, luminous, but he could not remember what it was about her that had held him so in thrall. She seemed easily resistible, even though she held a suppressed excitement, a smile she could not quite keep at bay.

"Corinne," he said. "You look—"

"Better?" She laughed. "I feel better, Jack. Oh, I feel much better."

There was a meaning there he couldn't grasp. "That's wonderful."

"The future is going to be so good, Jack."

Jack smiled as if he understood and looked past her to Rosalie, who was waiting for him. "Is it?"

Corinne smiled broadly, reached out, and squeezed his hand. "Don't worry, Jack. I hope you'll be part of it."

She turned away then, leaving him standing there, confused and uneasy. Such a cryptic statement; what the hell did she mean? He had no time to ask her. He heard the clinking of a knife on crystal. Garland was at the head of the table, calling them to attention.

"Come, come," he said. "Dinner is ready, and I am starving."

There was no time to talk to Rosalie, either. She smiled at him again before she went to her seat across the table from him, and Jack felt a hunger for her talk that was almost painful. He sat beside Corinne.

Garland lifted his glass for a toast. "To my birthday. Long may I live, eh?"

Rosalie laughed. "*Salut,* Papa."

They drank the wine, and then the courses began. Beside Jack, Corinne squirmed. They were not touching, but Jack felt her fidgeting so much it was hard to concentrate on the conversation. Garland was going on about something—something to do with the bank, Jack thought, but he wasn't sure. He took another sip of wine.

Garland spooned into the oyster stew with enthusiasm. "The bank's new *dix* is finally designed, Rosa. I am like King Louis in it, surrounded by the sun. It is a good likeness, *n'est-ce pas,* Jack?"

Rosalie glanced at him. Jack smiled at her. "It's very good," he said.

Her answering smile warmed his blood. She

spoke to her father, but she didn't take her eyes from Jack. "You must be pleased, then, Papa. Finally you're king of something."

Garland laughed. He speared a whole oyster and put it into his mouth. He swallowed it almost without chewing and turned to scowl at Corinne. "You are sitting over there as if the chair is made of pins and needles, missy. You're making my stomach jump, and it is ruining my appetite. What is it?"

Corinne smiled, a tight, close little smile. "I've a surprise for you, Papa."

"Well, then, out with it."

"Oh, not yet, I think," she said.

Jack glanced at Corinne, and she smiled at him, too, and the smile was so . . . intimate, he decided finally. As if the two of them shared a secret. But he hadn't spoken to her for days. Again he felt the chill of foreboding.

This time Jack did not even attempt to follow the conversation. He turned back to his dinner with no appetite. When Mattie brought the other courses—beef in some sauce, a duck with currants, too many other things to remember—he only poked and picked.

He was relieved when dessert was served—Garland's favorite, bread pudding with whiskey sauce. Dinner was almost over, thank God. When Rosalie brought out a tissue-wrapped gift, Corinne seemed unable to sit still.

"Here you are, Papa," Rosalie said, sliding the box across the table toward her father. "I thought you would like this."

Garland paused in the midst of his bread pudding. He looked at her with a little smile as he reached for the box. "What could this be?" he asked. He shook it slightly. "A new pair of socks, perhaps?"

Rosalie smiled.

Garland opened the box. It was a gold tobacco box that glinted in the candlelight. He turned it over in his hands, opened the lid, exclaimed over it as if it were the royal jewels. "It is lovely, *chérie*. A thoughtful gift. I will treasure it." His gaze shot to Jack. "And you, Jack? What have you brought me for my birthday?"

The words were heavy with meaning. Jack glanced at Rosalie and then back at Garland. "I'm afraid—"

"Papa, please. I would like to go next."

Corinne's voice was a relief. Jack exhaled slowly when Garland turned to look at her.

Corinne sat up straighter, her hands trembled as she laid them flat on the table, then took them back again, folded them in her lap. She was practically quivering. "What I have for you, Papa," she said softly, "is very special indeed."

"Eh?" Garland barked.

Corinne licked her lips. She looked around the table, and her gaze stopped on Jack. Her smile widened. "Jack and I are going to have a baby."

There was a part of him that heard what happened next: Rosalie's gasp, Garland's thunderstruck silence. And then there was a part of him that heard nothing but the blood rushing into his head like water crashing over him, suffocating him, drowning him. He saw Corinne's glittering smile and the plea in her eyes, and the shock of her words shook him and shook him; his future crumbled into dust before his eyes.

But that wasn't the worst of it. The worst of it was that he opened his mouth to deny it, to say, *No! She's lying!* but then he glanced at Rosalie and saw the leap of belief in her eyes, and it kept him silent; it rocked him so he could do nothing but sit there while her name pounded in his head. *Rosalie. Rosalie.* He wanted to reach for her. Corinne had just taken his future and destroyed it, and all Jack could think as he stared unseeingly at her was that he was in love with Rosalie. That he loved Rosa, and this could not be happening to him.

At first Rosalie could not believe she'd heard the words. Corinne actually must have said something else instead. She could not have said, *Jack and I are having a baby.* She could not have.

But then Rosalie saw Jack go still, and the images flashed through her head—Corinne leaving his room, her strangeness these last days, the words Rosalie had forgotten: *I love him, Rosa.* Suddenly Rosalie couldn't breathe. No, it couldn't be true. It was a lie.

There is nothing between us.

But why would Corinne lie?

Papa's fist came down on the table so hard the dishes rattled. He was apoplectic, shaking. "*Mon Dieu*, missy, this had better be a joke!"

Corinne drew back. "No, Papa, it's—it's no joke."

Papa swiveled to face Jack. "Well? Is this possible?"

Jack took a deep breath. Rosalie waited for him to look at her, but he didn't, and she was glad, she was not sure she could have borne it. She reached for her rosary, tangling the hard, cold beads in her fingers, reaching for the comfort of prayer, but the words wouldn't come, the Hail Mary, the Our Father. She couldn't remember a single one.

Corinne put her hand on Jack's, speaking before he could. "Rosa, I'm sorry. I did not want to hurt you, but I . . . I warned you—"

"Shut your mouth!" Papa thundered at her. "Look what you have done, you stupid girl! He was for your sister! You have ruined everything!"

"But Papa, w-we could have a wedding," Corinne stammered. "I-In early autumn—"

"You stupid girl! There will be no wedding! Do you think I would allow you to marry this man now? After the lies he has told me?" He turned back to Jack. "You! You get out of my house! Tonight—right now! I do not want to see your deceitful face again!"

Corinne went white. "Papa, you can't mean it. He is your heir—"

Papa lunged at her. The table stopped him. His wineglass toppled, sending wine spraying across the table and across Corinne's face and neck, staining the bodice of her dress like blood.

Jack got to his feet. "Enough," he said quietly. He had angled his body, shielding Corinne in a motion Rosalie would have thought admirable if her heart had not been breaking.

But it was the motion, too, that gave her strength again. Rosalie hurried to her father's side, grabbed his arm. He was red-faced and trembling. He tried to wrench away from her, but she held his forearm tightly, grabbed his shoulder, and tried to force his considerable bulk back into his chair.

"Papa, please, sit," she said in his ear. "What's done is done. Remember Dr. Wiley—"

He threw her off. "I want him out of my house."

Rosalie glanced at Jack. His gaze met hers; she felt the weight of it, the sorrow of it, deep into her heart. "There's time to talk about this when we've all calmed down," she told her father.

"Get him out."

Yes, go, Rosalie's heart cried. She didn't think she could bear to look at Jack again. She focused on getting her father into his chair.

Corinne put her face in her hands. Rosalie felt her sister's pain in the quiet sobs that filled the air, and it was that, finally, that took the spine from Garland Lafon. Papa sagged into his chair, but the thunder didn't leave his expression. He pointed to Jack. "Get him out of my sight," he said slowly.

Rosalie exhaled. "It would be best if you left," she said quietly to Jack.

Jack nodded. But at the doorway he paused and looked at her over his shoulder. She saw the pain in his eyes, the regret, and something else, something that pulled the heart from her, that made her look away because it was too unbearable.

Too late, the voice inside her whispered. It was

too late, and he was everything she had first thought he was. A man like Gaston. A liar and an opportunist.

But even so, her heart hurt—she had forgotten how badly it could hurt. And as Corinne went running from the room, Rosalie looked at her father, whose anger still blazed, and she felt her future like a living, breathing thing, a prison closing around her, the gates that had begun to open clanging shut again, blocking out the sun.

Silence fell into the room like the clanging of bells, loud and sudden, weirdly jarring.

Papa's face was in his hands. She thought he would stay like that for a long time, but it was only moments before he looked up at Rosalie. "Did you know of this, Rosa?"

She rested her hand on her father's head and shook her head. "*Non*, Papa. I didn't know."

"A demon," Garland muttered. He reached up and took her hand, holding it there. "I should have known. *Sacre bleu!* I should have known. Ah, Rosa, I am sorry. I had thought . . . But you were right about him. What are we to do now?"

"There has to be a wedding, Papa." Her heart ached so with the words she could barely say them.

"*Non.*" Her father shook his head stubbornly. "I will not allow it. He has betrayed me. He has betrayed you! Would you really have me reward him? I will not marry your sister to this . . . this fortune-hunter. Does your own experience not tell you what would happen?"

Rosalie went hot. "It's not the same," she said tightly. "There is a baby—"

"We will send her away," Papa said. He reached for his wine, his fingers were trembling. "To my sister. She can have the baby there. We will give it away then." He looked up at Rosalie's gasp. "I am not heartless, Rosa. There are orphanages there, eh? A convent we can pay to take care of this for us."

Rosalie's heart squeezed. She felt she might cry. "Papa, you can't do that—"

"Why not?" Her father shrugged. "She can still be some use to me, *oui*? I have always had in mind for her an advantageous marriage, and who would marry her with a child?"

Rosalie drew back her hand. She stepped away from her father, and it seemed the room was swirling around her. Suddenly she couldn't breathe. "But Jack is the father, Papa. He is the best choice. Surely you must see that."

"It is already decided," he said.

"But you can't do this to Corinne—"

He waved her away. "You will talk to her, Rosa, *oui*? Explain things to her. I have faith you can make her see reason."

Rosalie started to protest. But she looked into her father's face and knew there was nothing to say. He had decided. He had declared Corinne's future the same way he'd decided hers all those years ago.

And Rosalie felt the resentment she'd buried for so long rising in her again, building until she could not stop it, filling her heart. She turned away from her father, said, "*Oui*, Papa," in a whisper because she was choking, and went to the doors overlooking the courtyard.

It was still light outside, but the day was winding down; the world was lazy and heavy and somnolent. She heard Corinne's sobs coming from some faraway place, and she glanced back over her shoulder at her father sitting in his chair. Like some giant spider throwing out his web, she thought, and then she left him there alone. She went to comfort her sister.

❧ **Chapter 23**

Jack paced the courtyard. He heard the low talking in the dining room, though he could not hear the words because his ears were buzzing. There was a pounding in his head that grew with every step he took.

But he could not stop walking. Over and over again he relived that single moment when Corinne told him—them—she was going to have his baby. The panic had not abated since then, it had only grown. He felt desperate—God, could no one stop the clock? He prayed for impossibilities with a vehemence that astounded him. He wanted to go back in time, back to those few seconds when they had all turned to him in disbelief, when he could have said, *No! It wasn't me!*

He wanted still to be the kind of man who could have said it, who could have humiliated her in front of her family. But he was not. He had seen Rosalie's face, and her belief had stung, and somehow that had fed some newly developed sense of honor within him. He would not embarrass Corinne by denying it. If this was to be settled, it would be between the two of them. It would be because she told the truth.

Jack clung to that one hope. She had lied; certainly she would not drag him to the altar based on that. She would admit the truth, and he would have his future again. . . .

Ah, damn. Jack sank into one of the benches by the cistern, then sprang to his feet again, unable to be still. He paced to the roses—the smell sickened him—then to the far side of the service wing, back again, aimless walking. What to do, what to do? His choices narrowed before him; he could not even make sense of them. Urge Corinne to confess, talk to Garland, beg Rosalie's forgiveness, marry Corinne . . .

Marry Corinne. He felt desperate at the thought. The future narrowed to a tiny pinprick of light; he could not move within it. He felt the constraints like the stone walls of Parish. He could not face the future without Rosalie, and yet he wondered what kind of a future they could have if she was so willing to believe the worst of him.

He heard footsteps, and Jack turned to see Rosalie leaving the dining room. She looked worn, tired; her shoulders were slumped, her expression resigned.

Rosa. He'd thought it was in his head only, but she looked up as if he'd called her, then closed her eyes as if the sight of him was too much to bear, and that was when he really hurt—that was when he felt his loss in a pain that caught at his heart and his breath.

He went to her before he knew what he was doing. He took her into his arms before he thought, and when she melted against him he held her there as tightly as he could, afraid to let her go, pressing his face into her hair, drinking in her jasmine scent, feeling the bones of her body against his hands.

"I'm sorry," he whispered, and then wished he hadn't said anything, because it seemed to startle her away from him.

She drew back and looked up at him, and her fine eyes were so stark with pain that he felt he couldn't live with himself another moment for putting it there.

"You didn't answer Papa's question," she said softly. "Is it possible? Is it . . . true?"

"Would you believe me if I said no?"

She dipped her head. "I saw her coming from your room—"

"Rosalie—"

"She has never been a liar," she said to him.

Jack felt the trap slamming shut. He could barely say the words. "Then what kind of a man would I be, Rosa, if I called her one?"

Her gaze jerked to his. She swallowed hard, and that—that evidence of her misery—brought an ache into his heart he could barely breathe around.

"I'll say only this," he whispered. "You believed in me once, Rosa. Nothing's changed since then."

She searched his face. He had no idea if she saw there what she wanted to see, but finally she pressed her lips together. Softly she said, "Papa wants to send her away. But you'll . . . if she needs you, you'll marry her, won't you?"

Her voice was like funeral bells: stern, solemnly righteous, signaling an ending. Jack closed his eyes. She was separate from him suddenly, as far from him as she had ever been.

He nodded. "If she needs me, yes."

She took a deep breath. "*Bien*," she said, and then without another word she turned away and went up the stairs.

He watched her go to Corinne's room, knock softly, go inside. The door closed gently behind her.

And it was strange, but his panic was gone; the desperation that had made him pace had faded. He felt drained now, resigned. Now that the decision had been made, there was nothing else to do. He waited a few more moments, gathering courage, or rather, giving himself one last chance, giving God— or Satan, or whomever—a last moment to save him from this. He waited for Rosalie to come running from Corinne's room to tell him Corinne had told the truth. It didn't happen, and there was no movement at Corinne's door, and so finally Jack went to the dining room.

He paused outside the doors. Garland had left the table. He was collapsed in one of the chairs near the sideboard, cradling a glass of port, his eyes closed.

Jack stepped inside. Garland opened his eyes.

"I thought I told you to leave," he said.

"You did." Jack nodded. He came fully into the room.

"Then why aren't you gone?"

"I thought we should talk."

"I have nothing to say to you," Garland said slowly. "But perhaps you will tell me, Jack, why you risked everything for this. What was your plan? How was this to make things better for you?"

Jack smiled humorlessly. "You're so eager to

believe the worst of me. You and my uncle must have gone to the same school."

Garland's brows rose. "Come, Jack, you disappoint me. Do you tell me this is not what I think it is?"

"What do you think it is?"

"You have betrayed me."

"You made a devil's bargain to begin with, old man. You didn't care about Rosalie's wishes when you brought me into this house, and you don't give a damn about Corinne now. It occurs to me that you probably get just what you deserve."

Garland waved his hand dismissively. "Go on. Get out of my sight."

"Not quite yet."

"What?"

"I'll marry her."

Garland looked at him in disbelief. "You what? You must be insane to think that I will allow it."

"What else do you propose?" Jack asked. "What do you plan to do about this, Garland? Send her away? Bring her back in a year with a 'niece' or 'nephew'? Do you think anyone will believe whatever story you tell?"

Garland's eyes narrowed. "And what is my choice, eh? To let you marry her and accept you into my home as my son-in-law? My own snake in the grass? Do you think I am a fool?"

"We'll get our own house," Jack said stubbornly.

"And have all the Vieux Carré accuse me of allowing my daughter to live in poverty?"

Jack smiled bitterly. "Then give us money, old man."

"Tell me, Jack, what my compatriots will think of me if I allow my daughter to marry an ex-convict, a criminal." Garland's voice was so cold it sent goose-flesh over Jack's skin.

"I've been a criminal since I came to this house. It didn't seem to matter when I was Rosalie's fiancé."

"Ah, but it was different then," Garland said. "Rosalie is a paragon. People would have said she had forgiven you, that you were a changed man. Because of her, you would have been welcome, you would have been respected. And I thought you were clever enough to have made them believe those things of you. But you are not so clever now, eh, Jack? And you have out-lived your usefulness to me. So leave my house before I have you thrown out."

Jack hesitated. His instincts told him to go. He could gain nothing here. But then he thought of Rosalie's face, the way she'd looked up at him, the soft plea, the quiet resignation in her expression, and he had the sudden, sinking feeling that she knew Corinne had lied. He should have been relieved, but he wasn't. Because now he realized that even if Corinne admitted the truth, he could not walk away from this. Corinne needed help. She needed protection—Rosalie knew that, too. Marrying Corinne was the right thing to do, when he had never done anything right in his life.

"I'm going to marry her," he said softly. "There's nothing you can do to stop me."

"*Non?*" Garland laughed. "Do you know, Jack, how long it will take to get the auditor here to the house?"

Jack frowned. "An auditor?"

"I can have him here within the hour. What do you think he will say when he looks at the bank books on your desk? Do you think he will find it odd that the ledgers do not reconcile?"

"I don't understand you."

"You disappoint me, Jack. Such a simple thing to understand. Do you think the auditor will find it strange that there is three thousand dollars missing, that a ex-convict is involved?"

Jack felt hot. His collar was too tight. Images danced through his head: a trial where he was allowed to say nothing, his aunt's tears, the clanging of the gate at Parish Prison. Three long years, two of them without seeing the sun. Two years of darkness . . .

He was choking. "You've set me up."

"A little insurance." Garland shrugged. "After all, *mon ami*, I hardly know you. What do you say, Jack? It is your choice. The street . . . or Parish Prison."

Garland swirled the drink in his hand as if the words meant nothing, and it was that, finally, that told Jack the old man would do it.

The honor he'd clung to slipped away. So easy. It slipped into that place inside him where his uncle's words lingered: *You want respect, Jack? Show me you can be respected.* In the end, honor was too hard; he was not made for it. Jack felt his worthlessness deep into himself.

"You win, old man," he said softly. "I'll leave. Just let me get my things. And . . . say goodbye."

Garland said nothing. He looked away, into his

drink, and Jack felt the old man's dismissal into his bones. He turned away, leaving the dining room, stepping into the quiet sunset of the courtyard. The day was not quite over yet, and it seemed both too long and too short to bear. It would be dark soon, and he had no place to go. There was just the street to welcome him.

All these months, and he was back where he started. Except . . . He saw Rosalie's face before his eyes, her soft confidence—jarring now, torturous. She would be disappointed in him, and in a way it was easier knowing that. Knowing that she would always be disappointed, that he would never have to prove anything to her again. *I want you to be a better man,* she had said. Well, he was not. It was time she knew it.

Corinne heard the knock on her door through her sobbing. She turned onto her side and whispered, "Who is it?" and hoped against hope that it was her father coming to apologize. Papa, sitting on the edge of her bed, smoothing back her hair, kissing her forehead, and saying, *I lost my head,* chérie. *I am so happy you are having my grandson.*

But she knew it was not. That dream had shattered, along with every other one she'd ever had about her father, and reality pressed hard and heavy on her heart. Her father would never love her now. She had disappointed him beyond reason. She had failed, and she should have known. . . .

"It's Rosa." Rosalie cracked the door and peered around the corner. "May I come in?"

Corinne's guilt welled up so that she couldn't look at her sister. She had not only ruined her life, she had ruined Rosalie's. It was too much to bear. She buried her face in her arms again. "I don't want your prayers, Rosa. Or your forgiveness. I do not think God will help me now."

There was a pause. Rosa's voice was very soft, very quiet. "You have my forgiveness anyway."

It was such an unequivocal statement that Corinne looked up again from the cradle of her arms. Rosalie was a dark shadow haloed by the light coming through the doors—like an angel, if angels existed. Corinne frowned. Her sister came over to the bed and sat on the edge, and Corinne felt Rosalie's hand smoothing back her hair, a gentle, comforting touch that was more reassuring than she wanted it to be.

"I cannot explain," Corinne said, but the words spilled out anyway. "I thought . . . I thought Papa would be happy. I knew he would be angry at first, but he respects Jack so, and I was so afraid, and I thought . . . perhaps this would make Papa love me. But he hates me more now than ever."

"Papa doesn't hate you, Corinne."

"That is easy for you to say, Rosa, when he dotes on you. You have never known his displeasure."

"I've known it," Rosalie said softly.

Corinne shook her head. Her despair washed over her again, bitter and black, along with new tears. "Oh, Rosa, you don't. You can't. He has never loved me, and that was all I wanted. I wanted him to love me. Ah, what does it matter? I am ruined now. I have nothing."

"You're not ruined."

"Oh?" Corinne looked bitterly at her sister. "I am expecting a baby, Rosa, and I have no husband. Do you think I will be welcomed in any home now?"

"Papa has a plan for you," Rosalie said softly.

Corinne snorted. "What? To send me away? To lock me in a convent for the rest of my life?"

"Don't be absurd."

"Then what?" Corinne asked miserably.

"He wants you to go to Aunt Louise's. To have the baby there. Then he'll bring you back. He has in mind a suitable marriage."

Corinne heard a reluctance in her sister's voice. It brought with it a bleak dread that grew with every word. Corinne waited until Rosalie stopped talking. She waited until she caught her sister's gaze.

"What about the baby, Rosa?" she asked slowly. "What man would marry me with a bastard?"

Rosalie paused. Corinne's dread grew until she could hardly breathe.

"He wants me to give it away," she said—if she had not been sure of it before, she was the moment she saw Rosalie flinch. "*Mon Dieu*, he hates me so much that he would give away his only grandchild."

"Corinne—"

"What have I done?" Corinne hugged herself tightly and rocked back and forth; it was the only way to keep from screaming. "How could I have been so stupid?"

"There is another choice," Rosalie said quietly.

Corinne felt her sister's hands on her shoulders, holding her steady, stopping her panicked rocking.

"Listen to me, Corinne. Jack will marry you."

Corinne recoiled. "*Non*. He won't. Rosa, you must understand . . . I did not want to hurt you. But I was afraid, and I knew Papa would be angry. . . ."

Rosalie frowned. "What are you saying?"

"Jack is not the father," Corinne said miserably. "I lied. I wanted him to think he was the father, and so I . . . I went to his room. I tried . . . but he . . . he rejected me, Rosa. He doesn't want me. He doesn't love me. I have lied to you, too."

"Corinne, I already knew this."

"But how can you know? He told you?"

"*Non*." Rosalie shook her head. "He has not said a word."

"Then . . . how?"

"Because I know him."

The words shocked Corinne into silence. She stared at her sister. "*Mon Dieu*, Rosa, you do love him. How can you ever forgive me this? I tried to take him from you. I lied to protect myself."

"That doesn't matter. He'll protect you, Corinne. He'll marry you."

"But I don't want him to!" Corinne burst out in panic. The thought of it made her sick inside. Marrying a man who didn't love her, who would always hate her for trapping her, for lying. Having this baby, who would look like Reynaud, a man her father hated. Losing her father forever—and she *would* lose him. Whatever chance she had of his love would be gone when he knew what she had done, once she had this baby he hated. This baby . . .

She pressed her fists into her stomach, hating the child, hating her own naivete. How stupid she had been. She had lost everything.

Rosalie shook her. "Corinne, listen to me. It's the best thing. You have to listen to me. Jack will marry you. The two of you can live here in the city. Papa will come around."

Corinne met her sister's eyes. "Rosa. When was the last time Papa changed his mind about anything?"

Rosalie went quiet.

"He will hate this baby forever, won't he?" Corinne asked. "Even if I tell him it is not Jack's . . . he hated Reynaud, too. He will never accept it—or me, as long as I have it."

"Corinne, we can make him accept it."

"You are being ridiculous," Corinne said wearily.

Rosalie's hands tightened on her shoulders. "Listen to me. You don't understand. You mustn't give this child away, Corinne. You will regret it forever if you do."

"I'm not going to give it away," Corinne said. She lifted her face to her sister's, and suddenly she knew what she would do—she felt it with a little relief, a strange, numbing comfort. "I'm not going to have it."

Rosalie went absolutely still. "What?"

"I'm not going to have it."

"But—but . . ." Rosalie's hands dropped from Corinne's shoulders, and Corinne saw something that looked like pain cross her sister's eyes. "You can't mean it."

"I do."

"*Mon Dieu,* Corinne, no, please . . . this is not the answer. Trust me when I tell you it is the wrong thing to do. Marry Jack. Live your life here, love this baby—"

"How can I love it, Rosa, when I know Papa will hate it so much?"

"It's not Papa's life!" Rosalie's vehemence was surprising, but against Corinne's numbness, it only fell away. "It's your life, and I'm telling you that you will regret this. Forever, Corinne . . . please . . . oh, please, listen to me."

"I don't want it. No one wants it. Not Jack, not Papa, not me."

Rosalie's eyes looked teary. "Then *me.* I'll take care of it."

Corinne shook her head. "*Non.*" She disentangled herself from Rosalie, backed off her bed. Now that the decision was made, she wanted to do it now, right now, before she had time to think about it, before she had time to doubt. The child was a mistake. Papa hated it, and she didn't want it. It was only a symbol now of everything stupid she'd done, a symbol of her failure. She would never be able to look at this child without thinking of what a disappointment she was to her father, of how he would so easily give away a grandchild she'd given him. She didn't want to remember. Once this baby was gone, she would be able to believe again that one day Papa might love her.

"I'm going to find Paulette," she told Rosalie. "Her aunt—"

Rosalie grabbed her hand and held on so tight it hurt. "Don't do this."

Corinne jerked away. Distractedly she went to the doors of her room and glanced out onto the courtyard. "I think she lives out on the bayou."

"There's no one out there," Rosalie said, and there was a strange desperation in her voice. "Corinne, listen to me!"

Corinne turned back to her sister. "I'm done with listening! This is my decision, Rosa, and I've made it. Why should I not do it?"

"Because I'm asking you not to. I'm asking you to trust me when I tell you you'll regret this—"

Corinne laughed bleakly. "It's not enough. It's my life, as you've said. This is what I want. Either help me or leave."

"Corinne—" Rosalie hesitated, and Corinne heard the plea in her sister's voice, and something else, too, some force behind the word, a lingering, as though there was more Rosalie wanted to say.

Corinne waited. She saw the struggle in Rosalie's face. "What is it? What?"

Rosalie didn't answer right away. She hesitated, she opened her mouth. But in the end her face tightened, her eyes went dark and fathomless, and her voice was completely without emotion when she said, "You must promise me to think about this a few days. Please, Corinne, it's all I ask. A few days only."

Corinne stared at her sister uncertainly. Rosalie looked tired and suddenly old, worn beyond her years, too wise.

But even this sad stranger could not stop her now. Rosalie did not understand. She would never understand. So Corinne lied to her. She said, "As you wish. I'll wait a few days," and felt a great relief when Rosalie closed her eyes.

"*Merci*," Rosa said. There was a wealth of emotion in the words, a world of relief. It was curious, and distressing, and Corinne felt an odd fear, a strange premonition. She shook it off and faced Rosalie with equanimity as her sister rose.

Rosalie smoothed her skirt nervously, and then she put her arms around Corinne and pulled her tight—and that, too, was so odd. "I'll leave you, then," she whispered. "Things will turn out well, Corinne, you'll see."

But as Corinne nodded an agreement and watched her sister leave, she could not ignore the voices in her head telling her it would not be all right. Nothing would be all right again. Her decision was made. Waiting a few more days would not make that decision clearer.

Her determination was like a heavy ache, and Corinne's throat closed with tears. She waited until she heard Rosalie's door shut, and then she eased out of her room, crept down the stairs and across the courtyard to the service wing. To the servants' quarters, and Paulette.

He didn't hurry as he went up the stairs to his room. He gathered his things, careful to take nothing he hadn't come with. Garland would be watching, he was sure, and Jack didn't want to be awakened from a refreshing sleep beneath the wharves to face a constable armed with a theft charge.

He changed his clothes, back into the ones he'd worn when he first came to this place, back to his prison stench. He had never bothered to unpack his bag; it was shoved beneath the bed, unopened, and he took it out now. It held only his greatcoat, a signet ring that no longer fit and which he didn't want to wear in any case, a comb, and a brush.

He left his room and walked slowly across the courtyard again, then climbed the stairs to the upper gallery. He went to Corinne's room first, because she was the easier one to leave—and he grimaced at what kind of a man that made him. He paused just outside her room, wondering what to say to her. Better not to agonize over it. He knocked and waited for the answer.

There was silence. Jack frowned. He knocked again. "Corinne?" he called. Then, more softly, "Corinne?"

Nothing. The door was ajar; he pushed it open. The room was empty. She was gone. Jack frowned and backed away, and it was then he saw the light in Rosalie's room. Perhaps Corinne had gone there. He steeled himself, went the short distance to the door, and knocked.

"Rosa?"

There had been movement inside, but it stopped at his soft whisper. Jack's gut tightened. He waited for her to open the door, and when she did, when she cracked it open and stood haloed against the light of her room, he felt the enormity of what he was losing in a blow to his senses. It was so overwhelming that for a moment he couldn't speak.

But Rosalie frowned. "What is it?" she asked.

"Corinne's gone," he managed. "I thought she might be with you."

"With me?" She shook her head. She came out, and looked down the gallery toward her sister's room. "But I just left her. She must be there."

"She's not."

The sound of horses, the rattle of a wagon, thundered from the stables. Jack turned around. He caught a glimpse of two figures huddled together on the seat before the wagon disappeared into the porte cochere.

"Who was that?" Rosalie asked, and there was something in her voice—terror, he thought. "*Mon Dieu*, who was it?"

Mattie was crossing the courtyard. She called up. "Mademoiselle Corinne. And Paulette."

"Corinne and Paulette?" Rosalie pushed past Jack. She looked panicked as she leaned over the railing and called down. "Mattie! Where are they going? Did they tell you? Do you know?"

Mattie shook her head. "*Non*. They said nothing. Robert, he want to take them, but they tell him no."

"*Mon Dieu*," Rosalie said again. So breathless, so . . . afraid. She turned to Jack, and her eyes were wide with fear. She grabbed his arm, tried to pull him with her. "We have to stop her, Jack. We have to stop her."

He held firm. "Stop her from what? Where has she gone?"

Rosalie looked wild. Tears sprang into her eyes, and when Jack saw them, a dull certainty tightened his heart. "Where did she go, Rosa?" he asked again. "Why did she take Paulette?"

Rosalie was trembling. She grabbed his hands; her delicate fingers squeezed so tightly it hurt. "Paulette's aunt practices the voodoo," she whispered. "The baby . . ."

It was all she needed to say. "Where?" Jack demanded.

"I don't know." Rosalie was crying now in earnest. "I don't know. The bayou . . . Corinne said the bayou."

"Who would know?"

"I . . . I . . . Robert, perhaps."

Jack nodded. He squeezed her arm, and then he left her. He raced for the steps, for Robert, and he prayed he could get to Corinne in time.

❧ Chapter 24

T he fog was rising along the dips of the road, eerie on any night, but especially tonight, as Corinne and Paulette left the familiar streets of the Vieux Carré for the countryside. The shadows of the trees quivered and shook even though there was no wind, and the familiar birdsongs of the quarter gave way to the lonely, echoing calls of owls, the screech of cicadas.

Corinne glanced at Paulette, huddled in her cape as she handled the reins. The night was settling quickly, the only light was from the lantern hanging from the wagon seat. Its glow made the darkness beyond seem even darker, and the shadows took on a menace that made Corinne shiver.

"How far?" Corinne asked.

"Not too long now, *mademoiselle,*" Paulette told her. "You ready to do this?"

Corinne nodded. "I'm ready."

She could barely see, but she could smell the swamp beyond the road, the heavy, green smell. She was glad she could hear nothing beyond the creak of the wagon wheels and the jangle of the harness; she did not want to think of the things that lived in this swamp, she did not want to hear the soft splash of alligators or see the ripple of water moccasins through the water. When she was a child, Mammy Titi had filled her head with tales of the *letiche*—the soul of an unbaptized dead child, who haunted those still living—and the Cajun werewolves, the *loups-garous*. It had been years since Corinne had thought of those stories, and she was an adult now, a full-grown woman, but those tales came back to haunt her now. The howl of a faraway dog made her jump.

"Not far now," Paulette said again. The road curved; they drove into a curtain of Spanish moss draping a huge tree, and suddenly there were no more open spaces. The swampland hugged them close, the road became narrow and winding—too narrow for a wagon. The wheels caught, splashed in muck, tangling in vines. Beyond the wagon, Corinne saw pools of water that were nothing but inky blackness, with darker shadows of cypress knees. Moss draped into her hair; she felt its lacy, sticky touch like spiderwebs, and she imagined huge spiders falling into her hair, down her collar—

"How close, Paulette?" she asked again—she could not keep the panic from her voice. She wanted to turn around, to go home, somewhere safe. But home was not safe.

"The wagon don't go here," Paulette said matter-of-factly. The truth was, the horse wouldn't go, either. The poor thing shied at some sound and tried to back up into the wagon. "We have to leave it for now."

"We can't leave it," Corinne said.

"Mammy Zaza just around this corner up here," Paulette reassured her. The maid hopped fearlessly down from the wagon—no doubt she'd made this trip a hundred times. She adjusted her tignon and reached for the basket they'd stowed in the bed of the wagon. "Come, *mademoiselle*. You be safe with me, I swear it."

Corinne hesitated. She glanced down; swamp water was seeping over the wheels and onto what was left of the road. She glanced up to see Paulette tying the skittish horse to a tree.

"She be safe here, too," Paulette said, nodding to the horse. She beckoned Corinne to follow as she grabbed the lamp from its hook on the seat. "Follow me."

It was either follow her or stay there in the darkness with the horse. Corinne jumped from the wagon. Her feet went ankle deep into ooze, but there was solid ground beneath. She hurried away from the side of the wagon, back onto the road, shuddering when a trailing vine grabbed at her arm.

She raced after Paulette's light. Without the rattle of the wagon, she heard those noises she had not wanted to hear. They seemed loud, and her senses were tuned to every one: plopping water, ripples, the hush of wings in the darkness. They were not alone here. She felt watching eyes everywhere. Corinne pulled her cloak tighter about her, huddling against the night. She should have listened to Rosalie. She should be home now. She should have—

"There," Paulette said with satisfaction. She pointed ahead into the trees. "Just there."

Corinne squinted. She saw it then, just beyond, the faint glow of light through the closing trees, the shroud of moss. A little house.

A shack, really, she realized as they neared it. It was closer than she'd thought, a broken-down hut with a sagging lean-to. The yard was littered with shadows, and as they went closer Corinne saw them in the light: a rusted plow, a broken lantern. Her feet scattered a pile of chicken bones near the steps, and Corinne shuddered as she followed Paulette onto the moss-covered stoop.

"Mammy," Paulette called, knocking on the door. "Open up."

The door jerked open. Corinne blinked in the sudden light.

"Why, if it ain't my Paulette."

A woman's voice, and then a woman, a huge shadow in the door. Paulette was swept into her arms, and then the woman stepped back. She frowned, and the expression was horrible in the half-light. "Who you with, girl?"

Paulette glanced back at Corinne, and then she whispered something in Mammy Zaza's ear. Corinne tightened her cloak about her; suddenly she wished she had not come. She felt a growing dread, a fear that made her sweat. Better not to think of why she was here. Better not to think at all.

She waited. The woman stared at Corinne steadily, measuringly. She rubbed the bridge of her wide, flat nose and stepped back from the doorway. With a jerk of her head, she ushered them in.

Corinne followed Paulette. The house was small, one room and another darkened one just beyond. The furniture was old, frayed, and there were scarves at the window that had once been bright but were faded now, their patterns softened. The room was warm, and the stove held a bubbling pot that smelled of some faintly foul stew. On shelves behind a scarred table were clay pots jockeying for space with a half dozen plaster saints and glass jars holding dusty herbs or liquids that shimmered in the light. A painting of Jesus on the cross held a place of honor at the far end of the room, and surrounding it was a makeshift altar: candles, a sculpture of the Virgin, draped scarves, a heavy black rosary, a chicken foot, and the dried skin of a snake.

Corinne shivered. The old woman closed the door. Her hand was still on the handle when she turned to Corinne.

"So, you Corinne Lafon, eh?" she asked.

Corinne nodded.

"An' you got yourself in a pot of trouble."

Don't think. Don't think. Corinne swallowed. "*Oui.*"

"What you got for me?"

Paulette held out the basket. "Some oysters. Fresh this morning."

"What else?"

"A good beef roast." Paulette smiled. "The best the Lafon money can buy."

The woman hesitated. Corinne felt her scrutiny, and she tried not to bow beneath it. But this place . . . it felt strange, and it smelled stranger, and she was afraid.

But then the woman nodded. "You sure 'bout this, missy?"

Corinne swallowed. She thought of Papa, and it gave her strength to nod. "*Oui.*"

"This ain't no easy thing. But I think I can help you out."

"I would . . . appreciate it."

The woman laughed. She grabbed the basket from Paulette and stowed it beneath the table as if she was afraid they might steal it back from her.

"You best get comfortable," she said, turning her broad back as she looked at her laden shelves. "Spells . . . they take some time."

Corinne glanced at Paulette, who looked somber as she sat on a torn and sagging settee against the wall. Corinne joined her, sitting gingerly on the edge. Her stomach was churning; she felt her nerves tingling in her fingertips. Whenever her courage waned, she thought of the disappointment and anger in her father's face, of the sacrifice Rosalie had been ready to make. Corinne pressed her hands against her stomach, feeling for any telltale sign—but no, it was as flat as ever. It was hard to believe there was a baby in there, and she couldn't stand thinking of it. She hated it. She would have no regrets when it was gone. When she thought of having this child, of bearing her father's contempt for the rest of her life . . .

No, there were no regrets.

Mammy Zaza was humming as she reached for jars. Her ample hips shook to the muttered words of some song. "Git ready, git ready, tall angel at de bar . . ."

Corinne squeezed her nails into her palm. "Is it ready yet?"

The old woman laughed. "Not so quick, missy."

She went on mixing. It seemed to take forever: a pinch of this, a few bits of that, some liquid from another jar. Finally it seemed all the ingredients were there, because she fitted a lid over the top and shook it until the mixture bubbled in the dim light. Then she turned to Corinne and held it out.

"Here it is. You take two spoonfuls tonight, another two tomorrow. Take it slow, missy, or it be bad for you."

Corinne lurched off the settee and grabbed the jar. It was cool in her hands. She looked into it and nodded. "*Oui, oui.* Two spoonfuls."

"In a week, all you troubles be gone," Mammy Zaza assured her.

Corinne glanced up at her. "What about a spell?"

"A spell?" The woman shook her head. "What spells there be I said into it, missy. You pay 'tention now, you hear? Take it slow."

Corinne clutched the jar in her hands. "*Merci,*" she said. "*Merci.*"

"Oh, you come anytime, missy," the woman laughed. "You bring me a beef an' you can come anytime."

Corinne barely heard her. She was trembling, and she held the jar tightly, afraid she would drop it as she went out of the little shack, into the warm, wet darkness of the marsh. But this time the swamp didn't frighten her; she barely heard the sounds. The horse they'd left tied shied a little at some noise, and Corinne hurried to it. She heard Paulette following behind.

The horse was spooked. It pranced as they approached. Corinne climbed into the seat as Paulette calmed the horse with a caress and a few whispered words.

"I'm going to take some now," Corinne said.

Paulette gave her a small frown. "You'd best wait 'til we be home, *mademoiselle*."

But to wait another minute . . . it seemed too long. Corinne wanted this taken care of, she wanted it to be over. She pried off the cap of the jar, grimacing at the smell. It was astringent; it burned her nose. She held her breath as she lifted the jar to her lips, but even then the bitterness stung her tongue. She nearly gagged as she took one gulp, then another, and a third for good measure before she could not stand it any more.

She gagged, turning her head away, squeezing her eyes shut so she wouldn't vomit.

"You all right, *mademoiselle?*" Paulette asked.

Corinne nodded. Her eyes were watering, her nostrils stinging. "*Mon Dieu,* that was terrible!" she said as she caught her breath.

But already she felt better. She felt the potion coursing through her veins, felt its warmth in her stomach, felt it churn. It was working, she knew, and that filled her with a relief she could hardly contain.

She clutched the seat as Paulette maneuvered the wagon from the muck. The jerking nauseated Corinne; she clutched the seat harder and held on to the jar with her other hand. When the wagon was back on the road again, she tried to relax, but she was tense, and the night was getting chilly. Corinne wrapped her cloak tighter about herself, but the cold cut deep into her bones. She could not get warm. Such a cold night for July—it was usually so warm . . .

They had hardly gone far at all when she started shaking. Her teeth were chattering; she could not keep her body still.

Paulette sent her a sideways glance. "You be all right, *mademoiselle?*"

Corinne nodded. "*Oui.*"

But she didn't feel all right. Her stomach was cramping, a small ache at first that grew into a stab of pain. But with every yard they traveled it grew greater and greater.

"*Mon Dieu,*" she gasped.

Paulette frowned. "*Mademoiselle—*"

"Ah, it hurts!" Corinne heard her own voice, the panic in it, the whimper. It was as if there were a hot knife twisting in her gut. She doubled over, grabbing her stomach, dizzy now with pain. "*Mon Dieu, mon Dieu* . . . Paulette, stop the cart. Stop it."

Paulette shook her head. She gave Corinne a frightened glance. "Something be very wrong."

"*Non, non.*" Corinne could not catch her breath. She was being torn apart inside. "I'll . . . be . . . fine. One . . . moment only. Stop. Please, stop."

Paulette slapped the reins. The horse went faster. The wagon jostled, and Corinne could not hold herself upright. She clutched at the seat, but the pain . . . It seemed the world was closing around her, a dark veil . . .

"Get in back," Paulette hissed at her. "*Mademoiselle,* get in back.*"

Corinne nodded. She pulled herself from the seat, biting her lip against a scream as she fell into the wagon bed. She dropped the jar, heard it roll and jostle, and she couldn't care. She curled up in the corner, holding her knees to her chest, groaning as the pain swept over her, wave after wave. She angled herself up just in time to vomit, and in the darkness it looked black, it smelled like something had died within her.

And something had. Corinne lay down again, trying to avoid the pool of vomit, but it was there; her hand flopped into it, but her body hurt so much that she didn't care. Some giant hand was punching her hard. . . . She felt a gush between her legs, something warm and wet.

"We almost there, *mademoiselle,*" Paulette said.

Corinne heard Paulette's voice with only part of her mind. The little maid sounded terrified, panicked, but what had she to be panicked about? Was she feeling this pain, too? How could she be? She had not tasted the potion. . . .

The jar rolled around the wagon bed, sloshing, hitting Corinne's back and rolling away again. Another wave of pain hit, and she dug her fingernails into the wagon bed, she heard her own cry—it seemed sharp and loud, and the wagon was swaying from side to side, jerking and bouncing. Every bounce made her groan.

"Stop, Paulette!" she begged, she cried. "Stop!"

And then, finally, they did. With relief, Corinne sagged into the splintery wagon floor. She was sweating now, and the pain was so great that she could no longer feel the waves of it—there were no waves. It was just constant pain, a single, unending cramp wrenching her whole body.

"*Mon Dieu*, Corinne!"

Rosalie's voice. But how had Rosalie got out here, into the swamp? How did she know?

"Papa, help me. Robert! Robert, come quickly! Hurry, hurry . . ."

Many voices now, like a dream. A dream with touch and movement. Corinne felt hands on her, she felt herself being lifted, and in some far place in her mind she wondered—was she dying? Was God taking her to heaven? Or was there no heaven for someone like her?

Her breath went out of her as she was jack-knifed over something hard—a shoulder. She groaned.

"Hush now, hush." Rosalie. A firm, warm hand took her own, squeezing it tight. "You'll be all right. I promise."

But no, she wasn't all right. She hurt. She dug her fingers into Robert's arm. She heard his quick intake of breath, but he kept his hold on her.

His body moved, and then she was falling, falling into something soft, something fragrant . . . her bed. She was in her bed. . . . Corinne curled up, clutching her stomach. The knife again, digging into her, twisting. More wetness . . .

"Miss Rosalie! Miss Rosalie!"

Then there was nothing but blessed blackness.

•   •   •

Rosalie hovered over her sister's bed. Years of comforting the sick, of nursing in the infirmary, should have prepared her for this, but she felt curiously unprepared. She bathed Corinne as her sister lay there silent and unmoving. She spooned broth between Corinne's lips and prayed for each swallow. Rosalie did everything she knew to do, everything Dr. Wiley told her. And still, that first, endless night, she was aware of her uselessness with every passing minute.

The darkness settled around them. There was only herself, her sister, and a dim light that cast a golden light on Corinne's pale, bloodless skin. Papa had gone white at the sight of Corinne's blood coursing onto the sheets, and now he was drinking alone in the parlor. And Jack . . .

Jack was out somewhere, looking for Corinne. Jack had not yet come home.

Rosalie bathed her sister's forehead with a damp cloth and wrung it out in the basin beside her, then dipped it again. Then she caught sight of it: the stain of blood, a drip she'd missed, sticky on the bedframe, and her strength left her suddenly. She dropped the cloth and sagged, burying her face in her hands. This could not be happening. Not to Corinne. Not to her beautiful Corinne.

She heard the front door, then voices: Papa's, then a low and rapid voice. Then someone racing up the stairs, two at a time, and a knock on the door that was barely perfunctory before it burst open and Jack came rushing in, breathless, sweating.

"What happened?"

Rosalie reached for the cloth again. She wrung it out slowly, then again bathed her sister's forehead. She could not look at him; she was afraid she would fall apart if she did.

"Paulette brought her home a few hours ago," she said tonelessly. She heard him waiting for more, and so she nodded to the jar setting on Corinne's dressing table. "She took that."

He looked at the jar, picked it up in his hands. "This," he said. "A voodoo potion?"

"She's lost the baby, Jack," Rosalie said quietly.

He set down the jar again, hard enough to make the table shudder, and came over to the bed.

Rosalie felt him behind her, his presence soothing. She should not want him here beside her so much. She closed her eyes against the feeling.

"Has the doctor seen her?"

Rosalie nodded. "She's very ill. It was poison of some kind."

"But she's going to be all right?"

Rosalie felt the tears behind her eyes, the burning ache. She bit her lip. "He doesn't know."

"My God. My God." It was a whisper. He paced to the doors open to the courtyard and stood there, raking his hand through his hair. "I would have married her. Did you tell her that?"

"*Oui.*" Rosalie hesitated. "But she didn't want it. She . . . she told me the truth, Jack."

He turned away from the doors, and in the half-light he went so still it nearly broke her heart. "The truth?"

"That you weren't the father."

His voice was very quiet. "Oh. That truth." He hesitated. "But you knew already, didn't you? I wasn't . . . wrong to think you knew."

"You weren't wrong." Rosalie dropped the cloth into the basin and stared down as it unfolded in the water and floated there. "I'm sorry," she whispered. "I'm sorry."

"For what, Rosa? Why are you sorry? What could you have done?"

Too much. Not enough. Rosalie's guilt rose in her throat. All the things she could have said to Corinne, what she could have told her. *Don't do this. I know what it's like.* But she had not been able to bring herself to tell the truth, and now this . . .

She stared at her sister's face, then let her gaze fall to the pulse beating in Corinne's throat, a tiny flutter, so faint. *Please, God. Please, if You will do nothing else for me, save her.*

She heard Jack move, and then he was behind her, his hands solid on her shoulders. As much as she derived comfort from it, she wished he would not touch her. She did not want the proof of her feelings; she wanted to forget that there could have been other reasons why she didn't tell Corinne the truth. She wanted to forget her sister's words, her sister's misery: *You want him, too.*

The door squeaked behind them, and there was a heavy footfall. Jack took his hands from her shoulders—she felt the loss of his touch in relief and sorrow—and Rosalie twisted in her chair to see her father come into the room.

Papa looked haggard, suddenly too old, older than he'd looked after his illness all those weeks ago. His movements were heavy and slow, his vest unbuttoned, his pocket watch hanging loose, dangling against his hip. He said nothing to Jack; Papa seemed not to see him as he moved to the other side of the bed. He stood there, his hands behind his back, staring down into Corinne's face. She looked so peaceful, it was hard to remember her screams of pain only a few hours ago. She looked as if she were sleeping—but how could sleeping bring so much blood? So much of it . . .

Papa closed his eyes. When he opened them again, there was so much sadness in them that it hurt Rosalie to look at him. "Ah, Corinne," he said softly. He shook his head slowly and sighed before he glanced up at Rosalie. "Do you remember, Rosa, the night she was born?"

"I was only five, Papa."

He shrugged. "But who knows how much someone remembers? I thought I had forgotten it until now, but I have not. It comes back to me as if it were yesterday." He sighed heavily. "Your *maman,* she was confined to bed that last month—Corinne wanted to be born early. She was like this even in the womb, eh? Rushing into things. She has never known what is best.

"When she was born, she was so loud I thought she must be a boy—what kind of girl has such lungs? Now, you, Rosa, you were a good baby. One could put you in a corner with a storybook and you would stay all day. But Corinne . . . she was always putting things in her mouth, getting into trouble. She was a nuisance from the day she came into the world." He smiled wanly. "Such trouble from such a pretty package, *n'est-ce pas?*"

Rosalie said nothing. Her father's words, his memories, made her sad for no reason she could say. Thinking of Corinne as a little girl . . . She remembered her sister toddling in pink lace dresses with ribbons in her hair. Maman had given them some old necklaces, and Corinne had worn them everywhere. When Maman said, "You are so beautiful, *ma petite*," Corinne had smiled and repeated, "Booteeful . . ."

On the other side of the bed, Papa reached out. He laid his hand against Corinne's cheek, a gentle caress. She stirred in her sleep and smiled, pressing her cheek into his hand.

"*Ma petite*," he murmured close to her. "Ah, my beautiful girl."

Corinne's eyes flickered open. She smiled. "It's gone, Papa," she whispered—the words were barely there. "Do you think you can love me now?"

That was all. Just those words, and then Corinne relaxed; she was unconscious again. Papa looked stricken. He pulled his hand away from her face, and he was shaking and pale.

"*Mon Dieu*," he murmured. "Is that what she thought? Is that what she thought?"

Rosalie met his gaze. She said nothing, but he must have seen the answer in her eyes, because he cursed beneath his breath and turned away. His shoulders sagged.

"Get Wiley here," he demanded. "He will stay with her around the clock if he must. She will be fine, *oui?* She is not going to die. *Non, non,* do not send someone. I will get him myself. That way there can be no argument."

He strode from the room. The force of him lingered after, vibrating in the air, disturbing the peace. *Too little,* Rosalie thought. *Too late.* But she struck those words from her mind. No, it was not too late. It could not be too late.

She turned to find Jack, but he was gone, she was alone in the room. She wondered when he'd left, and then realized he would have removed himself soon after Papa arrived. The moment had been so private, after all. Even Rosalie had felt an intruder.

It should have been a relief, having him gone, but she only felt more alone than ever. With a sigh, she picked up the cloth she'd dropped, wrung it out, and laid it over her sister's forehead.

Corinne's eyes flickered again. "Rosa," she sighed.

Rosalie's heart squeezed. She felt the start of tears. "Oh, Corinne. How do you feel?"

"It . . . hurts." Corinne swallowed with difficulty. Her smile was weak, a shadow of her other smiles. "I . . . I'm going to . . . die?"

"*Non, non.* Of course not. Papa's gone to get Dr. Wiley."

But the words were too desperate; Corinne must have heard Rosalie's worry in them, because she turned her head away. Corinne's fine hair spidered on the pillow, webs of golden silk, and Rosalie ran her fingers through it. Numb fingers; she wanted so badly to feel the softness of Corinne's hair, and yet she felt nothing. "Of course you aren't going to die."

"I . . . should have . . . gone to mass . . . more . . . often."

A little smile. Rosalie saw the edges of it and felt the tears pool in her own eyes. She looked away, not wanting Corinne to see, blinking away her sadness. "I'm sure God forgives you."

"*Oui.*" It was a hush of sound, a sigh, and then Corinne was quiet. Her sister's silence settled in Rosalie's chest, and with it was a regret so big and heavy that Rosalie wondered how her heart could keep beating around it. The things she should have done, the things she should have said. She heard Jack's words again in her mind: *What could you have done?*

Rosalie squeezed her eyes shut. She felt Corinne move beneath her hand, and when she opened her eyes it was to find her sister staring up at her. Rosalie tried to smile.

Corinne swallowed—again, such a hard thing to watch, such effort. "That . . . feels good," she said.

"Then I won't stop."

Corinne sighed. "Rosa . . . I . . . I'm sorry."

"For what, *chérie?*"

"For hurting you. For . . . lying." It was a whisper, hard to hear. Corinne's lips barely moved.

Rosalie bent close. Desperately she kept stroking her sister's hair. "You were afraid."

"It was not . . . a good . . . reason. . . ."

"Shhh, shhh. Not now, *chérie*. Now you must rest."

"Oh, I have been so stupid." Tears started at Corinne's eyes, and her words broke on a sob that seemed to take all her strength. "So . . . stupid."

Rosalie's hand stilled. She looked into her sister's face, into that beautiful face that was so pale now, so sharp with pain and sorrow and regret. A face she recognized, because once it had been her own. *Tell the truth. This time, tell her the truth.*

And in the end, it was not such a hard thing to do. Not a hard thing at all.

Rosalie reached down, weaving her fingers through Corinne's, holding her sister tight.

"Not so stupid," she whispered back, squeezing Corinne's hand. "Corinne, let me tell you a story about another stupid girl. . . ."

Corinne lingered until late the next morning. They were all gathered around her bed, waiting for Dr. Wiley, when that faint pulse in her throat stopped beating. The noon bells of Angelis were just beginning their chime.

Rosalie knew she would spend the rest of her life hating their sound.

❧ Chapter 25

They let out the story that Corinne had died of cholera, and no one questioned it. But every time Jack saw one of the black-bordered death notices fluttering in the breeze, the words "of the cholera" leaped out at him, and he felt a tired regret, a guilt that he had not done enough, that he had walked away.

The days he'd spent in the Lafon household seemed long ago, and yet they had not left him. Whenever he woke from his makeshift bed beneath the wharves or huddled against the loading dock of some warehouse, he was always disoriented until he realized he was not in his bed in the *garçonnière,* that Rosalie was not waiting for him to come to breakfast.

He'd left the morning Corinne had died—his time there was over then, and he knew it. There was no reason for delay. He'd left Rosalie a note saying goodbye, but that was all—there was no need to add his sorrow and regret to her already heavy burden, though he had wanted so badly to stay. He'd wanted to touch her and comfort her. He'd wanted to hold her tight and feel her sorrow into his bones.

But if there had ever been a time for that, it wasn't now, and so he'd gone. Even after Rosalie had told Garland the truth, the old man had wanted him gone, and Jack had not wished to ask Rosalie to take a stand against her father. He'd stayed away, too. Until today. The day of the funeral. He knew he should not go—he did not want to bring her more sadness—but he couldn't. He had liked Corinne, in spite of what she'd done to him. Perhaps some of the fault had even been his. He had flirted with her. He'd wanted her. Now, he needed to say goodbye, even if he was no longer welcomed as one of the family.

Even, for that matter, if he was no longer welcomed at all.

It was oppressively hot. There was a storm coming; the dark clouds were lingering at the edge of the horizon, slowly creeping in. It reminded Jack of the first day he'd come to the Lafon household. It seemed like only yesterday that Corinne had leaned into the table and smiled at him and said, "I love storms."

He followed the funeral procession, the black Lafon carriage, as it wound its way through the Vieux Carré, and the silence was deafening. It seemed that all of New Orleans was mourning, because the colors had faded to pale next to the stark black of the funeral horses, the black coaches, the heavy black clouds moving now into the sky.

She was to be buried in St. Louis Cemetery #2, in the family vault. The remains of the most recently deceased Lafon—Garland's brother—had been placed in the lower chamber of the tomb, the upper chamber readied for Corinne, and as the mourners followed the casket into the cemetery, all Jack could think was that he was glad she wasn't to be buried in the ground. He preferred to imagine her lying peacefully at rest, her beauty gently fading the way it would have if she'd lived. Year by year—or at least until the next Lafon took his place in the family vault.

He walked far behind the family, with the rest of the nameless and faceless. Garland walked ahead with Rosalie, and the man had never seemed so powerless and unintimidating as he did now, leaning on her arm. With each step, his weight sent his cane sinking deeper into the marshy ground; he gripped the head with white-knuckled strength. The air grew heavier, too; Jack felt the first drops of rain as they walked by the tombs in silent procession. The names passed through his consciousness in one long liturgy of the dead: de Bore, Plessy, de Marigny, Duran . . .

He heard the weeping around him, and the melancholy of the cemetery settled on him in heavy somberness. When they were gathered around the elaborate Lafon tomb, he stood back, allowing others to come closer to the family—not his family, not any-more. He had no real place here. He heard the priest's words, the low, smooth Latin, heard the clank as the wrought-iron fence surrounding the tomb was opened, the rusty grind of metal on stone as the bolts holding the marble slab inscribed with her name were put into place. He heard a voice reciting a prayer, and for a moment he thought it was Rosalie's. But it was not; it was some woman he didn't recognize, her voice breaking as she prayed, "Eternal rest grant unto them, O Lord . . ."

He looked up and caught Rosalie's glance. It

shook him to his bones. She looked tight and drawn, sallow in black, alone even surrounded by her family. He was stunned at the intensity of his feeling. He wanted to hold her so much that it hurt to look at her. But the right to comfort her was not his, and there was this sorrow between them now, and so Jack looked away again, trying not to think beyond this moment, not wanting to think of any future past five o'clock today, when the rest of his life began. Since he'd left the Lafons, every moment had been only time passing until this funeral. He had not wanted to think beyond it.

It started to pour. It rained until they were all soaked, big, fat plopping drops that steamed up again from the ground when they hit. By the time the service was over, Jack was up to his ankles in mud. He stood while the family filed past him; he heard Rosalie's soft, reassuring whispers as she tried to comfort her father, Garland's stoic silence. None of them looked at him. Not even Rosa.

It was time to go, to leave this all behind, and yet he could not. He thought he would follow the mourners to the house after, and then he would leave. But when he was there, watching the house grow full, watching people milling about behind the windows, he couldn't walk away. Just one more moment, to see her one more time . . .

He went into the house with a group of others. Garland was at the door; Jack eased by him, hidden by a very tall man in a curly beaver hat, and then he was inside, breathing deeply of the fragrances of the house, listening to the mourners speaking their condolences, murmuring about how lucky it was that the rest of the family had not been taken by the dread cholera.

Jack's throat tightened. He had been here only moments, and already the secrets of this house seemed too much to bear. He couldn't breathe—it had been a mistake to come.

He eased away, into the courtyard, out near the stables, beyond the cistern. The climbing roses there were sweet now, their fragrance diluted by the heavy rains, but still there, still . . . roses. Jack closed his eyes and took a great, deep breath, knowing that the scent would forever remind him of her and that he did not want roses growing in his own yard, not even cut roses in his house. He did not want the reminder of his complicity in her death. He did not want to remember how he had saved his own skin and agreed to walk away.

That was it, then. In the end, he was just the kind of man his uncle had told him he was: selfish, worthless. *I wish you were a better man,* Rosalie had once said to him. Well, he wished it, too.

He turned away then, away from the roses, though the whole courtyard was full of them—he cursed whoever it was who loved the flowers so much they'd planted a whole gardenful. The scent filled his head, along with everything he had thrown away, everything he had lost. His dreams. Respect and riches.

Rosalie.

Ah, that hurt. He felt the pain of it clear into his soul. And then, just as he'd thought it, he saw her. She had left the dining room and was walking quickly, as if afraid she would be discovered. She took the stairs to the upper gallery, to her room, but she didn't reach it. She stopped only feet away from her door, as if she could not go another step, and buried her face in her hands.

Her back was to him, but he saw the shaking of her shoulders; he felt her grief even down where he stood. Jack didn't think; he only did what he had wanted to do since Corinne had died, what he'd been afraid to do. He rushed through the courtyard and took the stairs two at a time until he was behind her, beside her.

"Don't cry," he whispered. "I can't stand to see you cry."

She did not seem surprised to see him. She turned, looking up at him, and he took her into his arms. She collapsed against him, and he wrapped his arms around her and held her tight—so tight; he didn't want to let her go. Her body shook; her sobs were great, gasping things. Jack buried his face in her hair, he stroked her. But he said nothing. He only held her hard, and for a long time—until her sobs faded and she was limp against him, until he felt her pull away and had to let her go reluctantly.

"I . . . I'm sorry," she said. She looked at her feet, not at him as she wiped her face with her sleeve. "I didn't mean to—"

"It's all right."

She raised her tearstained face to his. "I saw you at the cemetery. *Merci.*"

"For what?"

"For coming."

Her voice was politely distant, as if he were nothing more than one of those mourners filling the dining room just now, and she held herself stiffly. He didn't think he could bear it. It was hard to believe that only moments ago she'd been sobbing in his arms.

"Good God, Rosa, I had to come. Don't tell me you thought I wouldn't."

"I wasn't . . . sure."

Such pain. Jack swallowed hard and looked away. "I'm not just one of those 'friends' crowding the parlor today, Rosa. Believe me, I know that if I hadn't been in this house, none of it would have happened."

Her gaze jerked up to his then. He saw the flash of pain in her eyes, and he wished he hadn't said it.

"If I could change it, I would. I would change everything."

"It wasn't your fault," she said. "None of it was." She gave him a painful, weak smile. Then she looked over the railing. From below came the buzz of talk, punctuated with the occasional "I'm sorry" and "So sad to lose one so young." She made a small sound.

"They are all so sorry. Everyone has lost someone to the cholera, and so they think they understand." Her eyes teared again, and her next words were a whisper. "But how can they understand? How can they know how much I blame myself?"

Jack frowned. "You blame yourself? How could it possibly be your fault?"

"She came to me. She asked me for help. I knew . . ."

She stopped, as if she could not bear to say more, and the tears were in her eyes again. She took a deep breath before she went on. "I knew what she wanted to do. About the baby. I could have told her . . . I could have told her . . . and I didn't."

The last words ended on a sob. She turned away, moving quickly to the end of the gallery, where the rail disappeared beneath vines of wisteria, a solid border of leaves. It was as if she were trying to escape him, or the world, or both, but she could not go farther. The boundary was there, and when she reached it, she sagged. She grabbed hold of a vine as if she could tear a doorway through it.

Jack was beside her in only a few steps. He took her arm, spun her around to face him. "What could you have told her, Rosa?" he asked, and it seemed that question was suddenly the most important one he could ask. It held all her secrets, everything she'd kept from him. It was the wall between them.

She looked away. "Nothing," she whispered.

Jack took her chin in his fingers. Gently, he forced her to look at him. "There is nothing you could say that would make me hate you. There is no crime that great."

"You don't know. . . ."

"I do know," he contradicted her. "Now tell me, Rosa. I've waited long enough. Tell me what you could have told Corinne. Tell me why you think you're to blame for this."

She closed her eyes, and he released her. She stepped back and crossed her arms. Her fingers were white where they dug into the black wool of her dress. She seemed hopelessly frail at that moment, and his feelings for her were impossibly tender.

"Tell me," he whispered again.

Her eyes opened. She looked at him for a long moment, and then she turned, but not away from him; she wrapped a thin tendril of vine around her finger.

"I was sixteen when I met him," she said slowly. She laughed softly, sadly. "Sixteen . . . it seems so young. It was a hundred years ago. I was just a girl, but Maman had been dead for three years, and I had not really had a girlhood. Corinne dreamed of handsome lovers, but me . . . I dreamed of taking Maman's place so no one would suffer her loss—especially not Papa."

She paused, staring at the vine twirling around her finger. But she seemed not to see it at all; her gaze was very far away.

"When Papa told me Gaston was coming to stay with us for a while, all I thought was that I must make him comfortable. He was my cousin, you understand, though I had not seen him since we were very small."

She sighed. "I did not know it, of course, but Gaston was coming to stay with us because he had been in trouble in Baton Rouge. He'd been in a duel over a woman he was having a liaison with. A married woman. Papa didn't tell us this. I knew nothing about him. So when he came . . . He was handsome. He was charming. And I . . . I fell in love with him."

The way she said it squeezed Jack's heart. There was tragedy in the words, a dull regret. One's first love should hold happier memories than this—his own did, though it had ended badly. But there was no wistfulness in Rosalie's voice, no lingering sweetness.

He said nothing. He leaned back against the wall of the house and watched her, waiting for her to continue.

"I was so innocent," she whispered, shaking her head. "I didn't know what kind of man he was, that he was only playing a game because he was bored and restless. I thought he was honorable. I thought he loved me. It turned out that neither of those things was true. He was—" She looked at Jack, and the words she'd spoken only a few weeks ago hovered between them.

Jack parroted them back to her. "Like me."

She flushed and shook her head. "I thought that was true, but it isn't. Gaston would have left here long before now. He would not have stayed for Corinne's funeral. He would not be here now, listening to me."

It was some relief, anyway, knowing that she no longer compared him to this man. But still Jack's throat tightened; her faith only made him think of how much she didn't know about him, how much he *was* like this Gaston. He took a deep breath and looked down at the planks beneath his feet.

Rosalie went on. "I—this is hard to say."

He looked up at her. "This is me, Rosa. It's only me."

She looked embarrassed, but she held her gaze as she said, "One night he . . . came to my room. And I . . . I didn't send him away. I didn't send him away then or in—" Her voice faltered, lowered to a whisper. "—any of the nights that followed."

She looked at him as if she expected him to run away. Then she took a deep breath and went on.

"I was in love, you understand, and I had all these dreams. I thought we would be married, that we would have children. I wanted those things. Gaston asked me to keep our affair secret, and so I did, but I was so happy, I wanted to share it with the world. So when Papa told me he was sending Gaston to Charleston, to work with one of his business partners, I . . . I told him he could not. I told him I was in love, that I intended to marry Gaston."

She laughed bitterly. "Of course Papa was horrified. He offered Gaston one hundred dollars to leave New Orleans forever. And Gaston took it." She looked up at Jack—there was still so much anger in her eyes, after so many years. "When Papa told me, he was smiling. He thought I would be relieved to find out what a villain Gaston was."

"It's not a crime to be a fool, Rosalie," Jack said softly. "It's not unforgivable."

She went on as if she hadn't heard him. "What Papa didn't know was that I was with child."

With child. Pregnant. Jack stared at her in shocked surprise. "You were—"

The tears came into her eyes again. "Gaston knew, and he left anyway. I was afraid. I couldn't tell Papa, and Gaston . . . I saw then what kind of man he was. I was afraid, and I was sixteen." She squeezed her eyes shut. "There was a servant here, a scullery maid. She knew a voodooeine, a priestess out by the Bayou St. Jean. I was desperate, you see, and I had nowhere else to turn, and I was . . . foolish. I didn't know what it would be like. But she . . . she took me there. And for a redfish, the woman gave me a potion. It was . . . much like the one Corinne drank. But I . . . I didn't die. . . ."

She swallowed; her tears ran down her cheeks. "I didn't die, but the baby . . . the baby was gone. . . ."

"Good God," Jack breathed. It stunned him. He had never suspected; it was the last thing he would have thought she would do. And he understood. He realized then why Rosa went to church every day, why she dedicated her life to God, what she was searching for, what she thought she could never have.

"I—I've shocked you," she said. Her voice broke on a sob. "I'm sorry."

She tried to move past him. Jack grabbed her arm, stopping her. "No."

"But . . . you must see . . . how can you want me now?"

"How can I not?" he asked. He took her arms and turned her to face him. "Rosa, Rosa. Is that the sin you're so afraid of? Is that what you think God will not forgive you for?"

She looked up at him. Her tears shone on her face. "You don't understand."

"I do. I understand. Surely God does, too. You did what you had to do, and there's no crime in that."

"If only it were so simple."

"Why can't it be?"

She shook her head. "Because . . . there is Corinne."

"You think you could have stopped her?"

"*Oui*. I could have told her. But I . . . I was too afraid, and so I . . . I allowed her to die."

"You think telling her would have kept her from going?"

She closed her eyes and nodded.

"I don't think so," Jack said. "Rosa, darling, when did you last see Corinne as something other than a child? She made the decision. You couldn't have stopped her."

She looked slowly up at him. "Perhaps. But whom do you think God will hold accountable?"

"Maybe no one. Maybe He is kinder than that."

She tried to smile, but it wavered, it crumpled.

It hurt to see the pain in her eyes. Jack took her hands and pulled her close. He linked his fingers with hers and felt her delicate strength. He held her so tightly he felt her swallow, and he stepped back, meaning to smile at her, to whisper to her that it would all be all right, that they would survive this.

But she looked up at him with those luminous dark eyes, and he saw himself reflected there, along with every dream he'd ever had. And it seemed suddenly that they had all—every one—included her.

So he kissed her.

He had meant only to comfort her. He'd meant it only to be a kiss like all their other kisses: soft and simple, easy to step away from. But he was hurting and grieving, and he loved her, and so when she pressed into him, when she didn't pull away, he deepened the kiss.

He moved his hands to her hair, held her tight, explored her mouth, tasted wine and grief, the salt of her tears. He felt her hands on his back, at his neck, he heard the groan deep in her throat as she kissed him back, and he felt his passion for her explode inside him. He could not get enough of her.

Still, he forced himself to break the kiss, to step back. "I'm sorry," he murmured. "I—"

She clutched at him, keeping him close. "*Non,* don't be sorry. Just . . . make me forget, Jack. Make me forget everything."

He knew that what she was asking was impossible, but he was willing to help her try, more than willing; he was burning for her.

"Are you sure, Rosa?" he asked hoarsely.

She answered him by standing on her toes. She reached up and pulled him down to meet her mouth, and he was undone. All he'd ever wanted, all he needed, came down to this kiss, her breath. *Rosalie . . .*

Before he knew it, he was moving her backward, toward her bedroom, pushing through the open doors, tangling in the muslin curtains. His breath was mingled with hers, there was an intensity to this he could not break, didn't want to break, and suddenly they were in her room, and he was aware of darkness and the smell of wax and incense, an overriding scent of jasmine.

Her bed was just beyond, and they fell onto it, grabbing at each other. His hands tangled in her hair, and he pulled loose the pins holding it—first one and then another. He dropped them on the bedspread, desperate to feel her hair spreading through his fingers, desperate to see it loose around her. It was long and straight and heavy; it spread like a veil beneath her, so beautiful.

He pulled away, just for a moment, to look into her eyes, and when she looked back at him he saw a passion there that matched his own, a passion that inflamed him. He fumbled with the buttons on her gown, and she pushed his frock coat over his arms and off, then fumbled with his shirt. His own fingers tangled in the laces of her corset—tight knots, impossible to undo, and so he left them, he pushed her gown over her shoulders until he saw her skin. Creamy and white, unmarred. He had her gown to her waist and he could not go farther. Her armor kept him at bay.

His frustration made him fumble. Jack reached for her skirt, her petticoats. He yanked them up, over her legs, to her waist, and she lifted her hips and helped him, she groaned into his mouth and spread her legs beneath his hand.

And when he thrust inside her, she opened her eyes and looked at him. Dark eyes, liquid eyes, so full of emotion that he paused. His tenderness for her washed over him again; he slowed and kissed her gently. He traced her jaw with his finger, the line of her cheek. He followed the trail with his lips.

"Rosa," he whispered against her mouth. "Rosa, Rosa . . ." *My love . . .*

The rest was as gentle as their kisses had been

rough. She was soft and yielding beneath him; she arched against him, she urged him on. She tangled her hands in his hair and held him close, and her breath came faster and faster as he moved within her. And when he came, she was there with him, too; he felt the soft throbbing of her body, her gasp, then her sigh.

And as he collapsed on her he wished it weren't over. He never wanted it to be over.

They lay there for what seemed like a long time, silently listening to the sounds outside, the call of birds, the low talk downstairs, the clink of glasses. The muslin wavered back from the open doors, caught by the faint breeze.

Jack listened to her breathing, and he closed his eyes, pulling her rhythm inside him, holding his breath so he could feel it in the rise and fall of her breasts. When she sighed, he rose on his elbows and looked down into her face, smiling when she smiled, stroking back her hair from her face.

"Maybe you're right," she said in a whisper. "Maybe God is kinder than I think. I would like to believe it."

"Believe it," he said. "At this moment, how can you believe anything else?"

She smiled again, but it was wistful, sad. He felt the light push of her hands, and he eased off her. When she started to rise, he grabbed her hand, pulling her down again to kiss her.

"Rosa, don't go. Stay with me."

"I have a house full of guests," she said.

"They won't miss you. But I will."

Again, such a sad smile, and it startled him . . . it sent a stab of doubt into his heart. She pulled away and fumbled with her gown, pulling the sleeves up her arms. She reached back to button it, and gently he moved her hands aside and took over, fastening each jet button into its loop. He could not remember undoing so many, but he had, and he had been careful—not a single loop was torn.

She bent her head when he was done. Her hair cascaded over her shoulders, and he ached when she grabbed it and twisted it into a knot. In the bedspread she found one pin—the others had disappeared—and she speared her hair neatly. He saw his Rosalie disappearing, motion by motion. When she was done, she sat on the edge of the bed, her back to him, ramrod straight.

"What will you do now, Jack?" she asked quietly. "Where will you go?"

No words of love, no pleas to stay. It hurt. He tried to ignore how much it hurt. But he knew nothing had changed—nothing except that he loved her more than ever. He could not imagine leaving her. He could not imagine how he could live another moment without her.

"Come with me," he said.

She looked at him in surprise. But she didn't do what he wanted her to. She didn't smile and say *"Oui"* in that rush of breath, as if she'd waited her whole life to say it to him.

In that moment, that hesitation, he knew that his dream would never happen. He felt the disappointment of it deep inside him, a bruise on his heart.

"I . . . can't," she whispered.

"Why not?"

"I have vows to keep."

He stared at her in shocked surprise. "You can't mean it. You can't mean to—"

"I do."

"How can you?" he asked bitterly. "Doesn't what just happened show you how unsuited you are for a convent? What about your life? What about the things you want for yourself? You wanted a husband once, Rosa. You wanted children." He heard the plea in his voice, but he didn't care.

She looked at him with that soft wistfulness in her eyes. "That was a long time ago."

"Rosalie," he whispered. "Don't tell me you don't still want it. Listen to your heart. When was the last time you let it decide?"

She looked startled, then sad—so terribly sad. "When I was sixteen," she said, and then she rose from the bed. She was going to leave him.

She was at the door when he said the words he'd promised himself not to say, when he called, "Rosa. I love you."

She paused. Her back was to him, and she didn't turn around. He heard her voice in a low murmur, a whisper he couldn't forget even though he wanted to.

"I can't love you."

Then she was gone.

✦ Chapter 26

After Rosalie left him, Jack went out through the porte cochere, past the carriages lined up there, blocking the tunnel to the street. On the banquette outside the house he stopped. He glanced back at the soft pink plaster glowing golden in the rain-fresh sun. He saw people moving behind the windows, black shadows. He heard the rustle of the pecan tree above his head. The first time he had stood like this, outside this house, his future had glowed before him.

Now it only seemed dark and empty.

Jack took a deep breath. He turned away from the house and began to walk, and the images from the past weeks drifted through his head: Garland Lafon leaning over a table in a coffeehouse, his eyes glinting as he made his proposal; Corinne standing by the window in pale green, her hair shining in the light; Rosalie arching against him . . . Too many memories. He wondered how long it would take him to forget them, if he ever would. How long before his life became his own again?

It seemed years ago now that he'd first stepped from the gates of Parish and faced the street without anywhere to go. Years since he'd spent that first night huddled on the loading dock at the cotton brokerage with his greatcoat as a blanket, waking with the dawn and the mockingbirds, scrambling away when he heard the first worker come through the gate.

He was back where he'd started. The decision he'd been putting off until after the funeral, the decision about what to do with his life, could no longer be delayed. He'd spent the last three nights huddled beneath the wharves, and he didn't want that to be his future. But that was the only thing he knew. The rest, what to do, who to be . . . those things he didn't know.

So he kept on walking. It seemed he walked for a long time, slowly, aimlessly, and when he finally looked up to find himself on lower Camp Street, he realized it had not been aimless after all. It had been more than three years since he had made the daily walk from the Vieux Carré to his uncle's house, but it seemed his mind still knew the way.

He stopped. He told himself not to go there; what was the point? His aunt would have nothing to do with him, and his uncle Charles would only laugh in his face and say, "I told you so." But it was the only home Jack had ever really known, and he supposed, in a way, he needed to see it again. He just wanted to look at it for a few moments, and then he would be on his way. Then he would decide what to do.

He had the luxury of time now. There was no place he had to be.

So he walked. It took a long time, longer than he remembered. He was sweating hard by the time he reached the house. The neighborhood had not changed; somehow he had expected that it would have. He felt so different that he expected the world around him to take on new colors. But it had stayed the same—the same wrought-iron gates in the same patterns, the same Negro women scrubbing the same front steps with brick dust that floated pink and heavy on the breeze. The flowers had not changed, still bougainvillea and mimosa. Still the faint, muddy scent of the river. He felt as if he had been lost in time somehow, that things had been moving so fast around him, and yet here the hours had stayed still. He felt again like the young man who had watched as the workmen built his uncle's house. Beam by beam, every nail . . .

But he was not that man. And this was no longer his home.

Finally he stopped before his uncle's house, the showcase Charles Waters had built six years ago. The sweet olive trees were taller now. The rosy crape myrtles Jack had spent months nurturing were bent now against the columns, and Spanish jasmine climbed the wrought-iron gates. Still fragrant and cool and regal, hardly changed.

He stared up at the second story, at the lacy shadows cast by the filigreed iron gallery, at the sun glinting off the paned French doors. He thought he saw movement behind the glass, perhaps the flicker of skirt, of his aunt's favorite pale yellow satin. But when he looked again, there was only the bright reflection of the sun.

Time to leave, he thought, but he didn't move. He

stayed there and thought back to the night of the soirée. He remembered his aunt and uncle's arrival, Rosalie's sorrow and compassion over his aunt's snub.

Jack closed his eyes. He supposed he deserved what had happened to him. *There wasn't a situation made that you didn't find all the angles to it*—yes, that was he, and he wished now that it wasn't. His manipulations had brought him nothing but grief, nothing but . . . nothing. A better man would not have given in to temptation, would have told Garland Lafon what to do with his offer, would have married Corinne despite the threats because she was afraid and needed someone.

A better man would be holding Rosalie Lafon in his arms right now.

Jack stared at the house where he'd spent so many intolerable hours and so many happy ones. He remembered his aunt's simple faith in him, her comforting smiles after each of his uncle's tirades about his ineptitude. Such belief she'd had in him. So much love. And he'd disappointed her in spades—funny how he'd never thought of that before. He'd always only felt his hurt over her abandonment. Never before had he thought that maybe it was he who had abandoned her.

I want you to be a better man. Rosalie's voice came to him, a whisper on the breeze, and he felt its touch on his cheek, he felt the way it swirled around him. He had lost her, but perhaps . . . perhaps there was a way to hold on to her still, to restore his faith in himself and so keep precious the memory of her smiles.

It was a startling thought, an idea he had never had before, had not thought to want. Jack swallowed. He looked up at the big house before him, and slowly he reached for the gate.

The latch caught on his hand, the sharp edge grazed his palm—a little scratch. He wiped it on his frock coat and let the gate clink shut behind him, and then he took the steps to the front door slowly and deliberately.

His heart pounded as he knocked on the door, and it didn't ease as he waited, as he listened for the heavy, rhythmic steps behind. They came, finally, and the door creaked open, just a crack. A familiar black face peered out.

"Sissy," he said, and when the servant made to close the door, Jack put his hand on it, holding it steady, holding it open. "I know she's angry with me, but if you could just tell her I'd like to talk to her for a minute—"

"It don't matter, Master Jack," Sissy said, shaking her head. "She don't want to see you."

Jack licked his lips. "Tell her . . . tell her I need her help. Tell her I want to be a better man. Tell her . . . tell her I love her."

Sissy paused.

From behind the door, Jack heard a step. He looked through the crack, to the stairs beyond, and saw the edge of a yellow skirt, a strip that grew wider and wider as his aunt came down the stairs. Sissy stepped back from the door, opening it wider, and there was Aunt Agatha, standing on the bottom step, her face still and hard. But her eyes . . . he recognized her eyes, he saw the hope there.

"A better man, Jackson?" she asked softly.

"Please," he said, and he felt the truth of it growing like a desperate seed inside of him. He held out his hand to her. "Please."

She nodded to Sissy. "Let him in."

Jack went weak with relief. Sissy stood back, holding the door wide open, and the smell of the house drifted out to him, such familiar smells—lavender, citronella, fine wood. He glanced up at his aunt, who was watching him warily, and he smiled at her as he stepped through the door and into the hallway.

"We heard about the Lafon girl," she said quietly. "Is the household affected? Is that why you're here?"

The household affected. He stared at her in confusion until he realized she was talking about the cholera. It was on his tongue to tell her the truth, but then he thought of Rosalie, and he held his tongue. "They're fine. It seems to have skipped over the rest of the family."

She nodded. An awkward silence fell between them, and then, distractedly, his aunt motioned for Sissy to leave. They were alone, and he felt the loss of the intimacy between them like a brush of cold air.

"I've . . . I've left Lafon," he said finally. "Uncle Charles was right about everything."

"Your betrothal?"

"It's ended."

She gave him a shrewd glance. "Why are you here, Jackson? Is it because you've nowhere else to go?"

He deserved that, he supposed, but still, it hurt. Jack shook his head. "I don't expect you to believe this, but . . . if a man can truly change, I'd like to give it a try."

The words seemed to have some effect. His aunt melted a little; she looked away, and then back at him, and then she said, "We've been looking for you these last days. Where have you been?"

He stared at her in surprise.

She didn't explain. Instead she nodded down the hallway toward his uncle's office. "Why don't you tell him what you've just told me?"

He went cold. It was one thing to talk to his aunt—she, at least, had always loved him. But Uncle Charles . . .

I want you to be a better man.

Jack took a deep breath. He glanced at his aunt, and she nodded again toward the office, but she didn't follow him when he went down the hall. When he paused at the door and glanced back at her, she had not moved.

Slowly, quietly, Jack knocked.

"Come in, come in."

Uncle Charles sounded distracted, and Jack hesitated for a moment before he pushed open the door. His uncle sat at his big oak desk, surrounded by books and papers. The lamp was lit even though it was still daylight, the netting at the windows was drawn completely back, and Uncle Charles was bent close over some ledger, his spectacles falling halfway down his nose.

He didn't glance up until Jack closed the door. Then the quiet click seemed to rouse him. He looked up, frowned, adjusted his glasses. Then he sat back in his chair.

"Jackson," he said with a sigh. "You're not lost after all."

"I suppose that depends on whom you ask."

Uncle Charles nodded. He looked down at his hands. "I received a message from Garland Lafon a few days ago. He said he'd thrown you out of the house, that you'd betrayed him."

"I don't imagine you were surprised," Jack said bitterly.

"I had hoped for more."

Jack frowned. "You what?"

His uncle sighed again and pushed back his chair. He rose slowly, and his joints creaked when he did; he had to put a hand to the desktop to get to his feet. Such evidence of his uncle's age startled Jack—he had to remind himself that three years had passed, and that his uncle had not been a young man when he went into prison.

But then Uncle Charles clasped his hands behind his back and walked to the window, and once again he looked stern, imperturbable. He was once again the man Jack had always thought was ageless, too strong to ever die.

"I had hoped for more," Uncle Charles repeated. "Did you never wonder, Jack, how it was Garland Lafon happened to find you?"

The night of the soirée came back to Jack. He

heard the same question, different words. He shook his head. "It didn't seem important then."

"I sent him after you," Uncle Charles said.

Jack looked at him in confusion. "You?"

"Garland and I had . . . an agreement. He had a daughter he wanted married. I had a . . . son . . . who needed to learn responsibility. It seemed the perfect answer."

"I don't understand."

"You tell me, Jack, what I was supposed to do. You were, for all intents and purposes, my own son. My heir. But you seemed determined to destroy your life. It may seem hard to believe, but I . . . loved you. I love you still. I am not an easy man to live with; I know this. Your aunt tells me I'm too hard, and there are times when . . . well, I find myself saying the wrong things, doing the wrong things. I'm sorry for that. You don't know how sorry. Perhaps I was partly to blame for who you became—I'm willing to admit some culpability for that."

Uncle Charles did not turn around. He spoke his words to the window. "We had despaired of you, Jack. Drinking until all hours, carousing, such debauchery . . . I thought—your aunt and I thought—that we had to do something, but you seemed unreachable. Then that terrible night . . ." He shook his head slightly, the sun sparkling off the gold rims of his spectacles. "That terrible night. When I came back to the office and found the money gone, I knew who had taken it. I knew I had to do something. The accident . . . that poor man . . . it seemed heaven-sent."

Heaven-sent. Jack looked away. *Heaven-sent.* "You let them send me to prison," he said.

Uncle Charles turned from the window. "I begged them to send you, Jack. I didn't know what else to do. I thought a few years there might do for you what I could not seem to."

"You could have sent me to New York instead," Jack said bitterly. "To one of your offices there."

"Don't think it didn't cross my mind," his uncle told him. "But let me ask you something, Jack. Answer me honestly, if you will. What would you have found in New York? Newfound responsibility? Or better gambling hells?"

Jack went silent. He didn't have to think back to those years to know what the answer was.

Uncle Charles nodded. "As I thought. Your aunt and I wanted this to succeed. We believed that if you thought we had washed our hands of you . . . Well, it didn't work. We had reports of you in prison. Arguments on work gangs, altercations with your cellmates, a murder . . ."

"You could not have any idea what kind of hell it was," Jack whispered.

His uncle looked at him, and there was sorrow in his expression. "No, we could not have. We made a mistake sending you there, I realize this now. There were other things I could have tried. Better things . . . But at the time we were desperate." He paused. "Then, just a few months before your release, we received a letter here at the house. From one of your old friends."

Jack went still.

"We had no hope you had changed, Jack, you must realize this. We were afraid you planned to rejoin your friends, to return to what you had been, and these three years would have been for naught. I could not let that happen. So I applied to my business partner."

"Garland Lafon."

"Yes." Uncle Charles nodded. "We came up with a plan. I would disown you. He would make you a proposal you could not refuse. I had hoped that marriage, responsibility . . . Ah, well, things didn't work out the way I'd wanted them to, did they?"

"No."

Uncle Charles unclasped his hands. He took off his spectacles and rubbed the bridge of his nose before he put them back on again and squinted in Jack's direction. "Why are you here, Jack? What is it you want from me?"

Jack looked down at the rich, dark, intricately patterned carpet at his feet. He tried to find a single thread, to follow it through, and then realized there wasn't one, that his life was like this rug—a hundred wrong steps, twisted pathways. Did anyone ever really live the kind of life they wanted to live?

He looked up at his uncle, who was watching him carefully. "I wanted your help to find my own dream, Uncle Charles," he said quietly. "It was all I ever wanted."

"Jackson—"

"It doesn't matter." Jack held up his hand, shook his head. "I don't know what it is I'm meant to do,

Uncle, or who I'm supposed to be. Perhaps you didn't get what you intended—I'm not married, I'm here without a penny to my name and nothing to show for the last three years. But I don't want to be the man I was, I can promise you that. I don't think I even have it in me anymore."

Uncle Charles watched him.

"I'd like a job," Jack said. "If you'll have me."

"My God." Uncle Charles took off his glasses again, squinted at him in the bright light of the room. "Should I believe this?"

Jack said nothing. He waited.

"Jackson . . . what happened to you at Lafon's?"

What hadn't happened? Jack looked at his uncle, and he could not keep the melancholy from drifting into his tone. "It was God, Uncle Charles. I suppose you could say it was God."

❧ Chapter 27

October 1856

Rosalie moved through a fog. For days after Corinne's funeral, and then weeks, and then months, she took care of everything. She made sure Papa got his medication twice a day, she conferred with the chef, she kept the household running smoothly. She was the model of efficiency; she was just as she had always been.

But there was a hole in her life now. She felt it always, an ache that wouldn't go away, a void. Perhaps it had always been there and she had merely ignored it before. It was hard for her to remember.

But then again, no. Surely it had not been there all this time. It had been ten years since Gaston had left her. Ten years . . . The words seemed longer than the time felt. She felt hopelessly old when she thought of it that way. *Ten years.* It seemed impossible that it had been that long.

Yet it had. Ten years she'd been mistress of this house. Every day the same. She woke to café au lait and brioches. She dressed, she washed, she approved the menus before she went to have a proper breakfast with her father. When he left for the day, her chores began: the servants to oversee, the marketing, the bills. There was the infirmary, the asylum; there was Corinne.

And those things had not changed—except for one.

Rosalie sighed and turned away from her window. No, things had not changed. But there had been a time, she knew, when the sameness of her days had brought reassurance and satisfaction. She was the cog around which the entire house ran; that knowledge had always been with her, her raison d'être. It had been all she needed.

What about the things you want for yourself? When did you last let your heart decide?

She squeezed her eyes shut against the words. Sometimes she thought she heard his voice—she would be halfway to the parlor before she realized she hadn't heard him at all. Sometimes she thought she saw him on the street. She would see a man with blond hair, with an easy, confident stride, and her heart would jump in fear and joy before she realized it was not him at all.

She had heard of him, of course. Here and there she'd heard the talk, and she knew he had gone back to work for his uncle and that things were going well for him. It made her happy that he'd made amends with his family, that he was gaining the respect he'd wanted so badly. But it made her sad, too, because it seemed he'd forgotten all about her.

She told herself it was the way she wanted it. She had been the one to turn him away, after all. She had other plans for her life, plans that seemed more vital than ever after Corinne's death. And if there was not a day that passed that she didn't remember his hands on her body or the rasp of his breath against her ear, she did not let herself think on it. She preferred to think of it as a brief interlude, a momentary insanity. For a few moments, an hour, Jack Waters had made her believe she could escape her guilt, that she could find happiness.

She should have realized that God would demand nothing less than her dreams as payment for her sin.

She was ready to pay the price. She wanted peace at last. Papa seemed to have come to terms with her decision now that she'd found a nurse to care for him, an older woman he liked and Rosalie trusted, and there was no one else to prevent her. Her three months had ended. All that remained now was Father Bara.

She heard Papa's voice downstairs. He was home from the bank, though it was early. Lately he'd been at the bank more often than he was home. Rosalie shook away her thoughts and went to greet him.

He was standing at the window, staring out on the Rue de St. Louis, and he seemed diminished somehow as he turned to see her.

"I saw your bags on the carriage," he said. "So, then, today is the day? You are leaving me?"

Rosalie nodded. "After I speak with Father Bara."

"And I cannot hope to . . . change your mind?"

"*Non.*"

"As I thought." He sighed and looked back at the window. "Rosa, I am an old man. And today I look at the street and see that things have changed so much that I do not recognize them. It seems strange to say 'Jackson Square' when all of my life I have called it the Place d'Armes. To speak the street names in English . . . These things I had never expected to do. It seems, sometimes, I do not recognize even myself."

"Papa—"

"You must let me speak, *chérie*. I may never have the courage again. You see . . . I have loved you too much. And I have been too proud. For it, I have lost one daughter. I do not wish to lose another one."

Rosalie felt the ache of tears. She looked down at the floor, and the carpets blurred before her eyes. "You are not losing me," she said quietly.

"Oh, Rosa. Rosa, I have lost you already."

She looked up at him in confusion. He was still staring out the window. "I lost you ten years ago, when I did not let you follow your dreams. I have often thought I should not have stopped you from marrying your cousin."

"But—but you said he didn't love me."

"How did I know? Perhaps he did. Perhaps he would have. Do you know where Gaston is now, Rosa? He is married. He has two children, a home in Philadelphia. A respectable man, I hear."

Rosalie's heart clenched. "How do you know this?"

"He wrote me some years ago. He asked about you, *chérie,* and I told him you wanted to be a nun. It seemed to satisfy him. He never wrote again." He turned to look at her. "Should I have told you this, too? Rosa? Was I wrong to keep it from you?"

"*Non*," she whispered. "He hardly matters to me anymore."

"But he did once."

"A long time ago."

Papa sighed. "I should have let you fly, Rosa, and now I regret that I did not. When you wanted to go, I kept you close to my heart. And now . . . I fear now that you will never be happy."

"I'm doing what I want now, Papa," she said. "I'm following my dreams."

He looked at her, and then he smiled sadly. "*Oui*. I suppose that you are."

Rosalie felt unsettled, strangely reluctant to go even though the sun was high now in the sky—if she did not go soon, she would have to wait until tomorrow. But she didn't want to wait. She wanted no more opportunities for someone to stop her, no more delays.

Her father must have seen her hesitation, because he beckoned her to him. When she came, he held her close, she felt his kiss upon her hair. "Go, Rosa," he said. "But know that I love you. If you ever need me . . . ."

"I know, Papa," she said.

She left him there. She went to get her hat and her veil, and her fingers trembled as she fastened them in place. Her father's words had shaken her. His regret, his news of Gaston . . . *I should have let you fly.*

She was flying now. She was ready to do what her heart had been demanding of her. As she'd told her father, this was her dream. She had wanted it with a singular determination all these years.

But her trembling didn't cease as she went out the

door and started on her way to the church. Nerves, perhaps, or simply excitement. Yes, it was excitement. The day had never seemed so bright and luscious—a warm, beautiful autumn day, the kind not meant for staying indoors, for kneeling at an altar—

Rosalie pushed away the thought. She hurried her step. When she finally got to Jackson Square, she paused outside the iron gates and stared up at that majestic spire.

It's impressive, isn't it?

Rosalie caught her breath, turned . . . but he was not there. His voice had been so loud in her ears, how could he not be there? But the only person near to her was the driver of a mule cart on the street. She was alone.

She turned back to the square and went through the gates. Deliberately she sped her steps, counting each one. *One step closer to God, two steps, three . . .* When she was finally at the doorway of the great cathedral, she felt a kind of breathless relief. At last it was over, this indecision, this fear. At last.

The church was quiet. Whispered prayers, muffled footsteps. Rosalie closed her eyes and took a great, deep whiff of God: His smell lingered in the candle smoke, in the cloistered air. Then she hurried to find Father Bara.

She found him in one of the little offices. When she knocked on the door, he looked up with a smile. "Rosalie," he said, rising to welcome her. "I have been expecting you."

His words flustered her for no reason she could fathom. Rosalie smiled weakly and stepped inside the room. "Could we . . . could we walk, *mon père?*"

He only smiled again. "Of course, my child."

He said nothing else as they went into the sanctuary. Their footsteps echoed in the hallways, and the sound was disturbing; Rosalie felt the vastness of space like a strange heaviness on her heart. It was as if the good father understood her discomfort, because he led her from the cathedral and out into the garden behind. It was quiet there, and beautiful. The statue in the center—the Sacred Heart of Jesus—seemed to be holding out his arms to welcome them.

It wasn't until they were there that the priest turned to her and said, "You have made your decision, Rosalie?"

Her voice seemed to lodge in her throat. Rosalie nodded.

"You have thought carefully on this? You have prayed?"

"*Oui, mon père.* I have prayed."

"And?"

"And . . ." Rosalie closed her eyes. "I am ready to take the veil."

She heard Father Bara's sigh like a soft breeze, and when she opened her eyes, he was looking at her with such an expression of sympathy that it nearly broke her heart.

"Rosalie," he said quietly, "tell me why it is you wish to join the convent."

"I . . . for the love of God."

"The love of God," he said thoughtfully. "Is that all?"

"And to continue service in His name."

"And?"

"And . . ." Rosalie fumbled. "And for peace."

He nodded. "A few months ago we talked about a man—"

"He's gone."

"Gone?"

"*Oui.*"

"Have you reconciled your feelings for him, then?"

"I was . . . confused, *mon père.* But now I know what I must do. I am ready to do penance and devote my life to God."

He gave her a curious look. "You think of this as penance?"

"*Non,*" she corrected hastily. "I—I misspoke—"

"Rosalie." The father took her hand and patted it—such a warm, dry touch, and her hands felt so cold. "Rosalie, my child, tell me: These last months, since this man has gone, have you found solace in the church?"

"*Oui.* Of course—"

"Shhh," he whispered. He smiled. "Think on it a little longer, Rosalie."

"I don't understand."

"I think you do," he said kindly. He looked toward the statue. "God's arms are always around you, my child, even when it seems they are not. There is nothing you do that does not hold His forgiveness—all you must do is ask for it."

"Oh, *mon père,* I would like to believe that."

"Then believe it. Do you think God means for you to be unhappy?"

She looked miserably at their hands clasped together. "I don't know."

"You have been running from happiness for a long time. God has been counseling you, but you have not been listening."

"You . . . you don't know what I've done."

"But God knows, Rosalie. God knows."

"That is what I'm afraid of."

Father Bara squeezed her hand. "Those sins have only the power you give them. Do not make them worse by adding another to the list."

She looked up at him in confusion.

"Do not give away the life you were meant to have because you think God demands it of you. If you do not feel the call in your soul, Rosalie, do not pretend you do. The church is not a place to hide."

"But—"

With his other hand he reached out and laid his fingers gently against her heart. "Listen to your heart, Rosalie. There you will hear God's voice."

Listen to your heart. When was the last time you let it decide?

The tears came to her eyes then. The flagstones blurred before her as she looked at the ground. These last months . . . The sadness of them washed over her, and she could do nothing but squeeze her eyes shut and think of them. Such regret, such pain, and yet . . . there had been happiness, too. Suddenly she remembered the last time she'd seen Jack, how he had asked her to come with him, how he'd told her he loved her. She remembered the colors of the levee, the shadows of her past that had—for an afternoon—drifted away. But then there had been Corinne, and her own failure, and now those things were gone forever.

Not forever.

It was a whisper, a touch of a breeze. Rosalie started—the words were so loud in her head it was as if she'd heard someone say them. She opened her eyes and looked at Father Bara, who was watching with a soft, compassionate smile.

And the message was there. She heard the voice inside her; she knew what it was asking. She remembered again that day with Gaston at the market. The words she had spoken then came back to her, words she'd forgotten: *Oh, Gaston, if tomorrow I am not so happy, remind me of today. . . .*

She should not have forgotten them. There were too few tomorrows. That had always been true, and yet Rosalie had been biding her time, wasting each one. She felt their loss now like a wound inside her. She had been afraid to risk again. But Jack was not Gaston, and life was so fragile, so short. Perhaps God would take her tomorrow.

Where were her todays?

Behind her she heard the closing of a door. She heard voices as people came into the garden. She looked up at Father Bara, who was waiting patiently.

"I have to go," she said quietly. "There's . . . something I have to do."

He nodded. Then he smiled. "You have always walked with God, Rosalie, my child. Never forget that—and go with Him now."

❧ Chapter 28

Jack closed the door of the brokerage behind him. The sun was beginning to set, the sky full of orange and rose and purple, and the air was cool now, though it had been a hot and breezeless day for October. His shirt was sticking to him, and he would be glad to get home, to wash the dust of the day from his neck and his face.

He glanced once again over the building and turned the key in the lock. It made a satisfying click— he would never have guessed he would find such pleasure in the sound, in the responsibility of locking up for the night. The streets were quiet around him; everyone had already gone home for the day. He felt the heat of the sunset on his back, watched the golden light soften the buildings and the street around him before he shoved the key in his pocket and started toward his uncle's house.

The walk was easier now than it had ever been. These last months had been difficult; despite his uncle's words and his aunt's quick acceptance of him, so much time had passed, and they were starting over. But Jack had applied himself—there was nothing else for him but the brokerage now, and whenever things grew too unbearable, he thought of Rosalie standing on the levee, the veil torn from her eyes. He thought of his dream to own a shipping company and how she hadn't laughed or scorned the idea. She had made it possible.

And that possibility was enough. He didn't have her, but he had his dreams again, and this time he was not so impatient to get them. There was time enough— he had worlds of time. Slowly, slowly, things were changing. And if there were still days when Uncle Charles railed about Jack's ineptitude, well, Jack had learned to take that in stride.

He was gaining some success, and that gave him hope again. But still, there was a restlessness in him, a wish that never went away. To see her face again, to see her smile. To feel her in his arms.

It hurt to think of those things, so he tried not to think of her, yet he still could not resist the images that came into his head: the light in her eyes, her laughter, the way she'd tilted her head at him when he made some asinine move on the chessboard. And he never went by the jasmine at the side of the house without stopping to breathe in its scent.

He knew he had to stop doing it. It was time to get on with his life, and he didn't expect to see her again, though he watched for her—how ludicrous, that Rosalie Lafon would ever set foot in the American part of New Orleans. He couldn't help himself. How long did it take to get over a love? It was a question he asked himself every day.

She was like a long-distant memory already, an ache he kept close to his heart, and so, as Jack approached his uncle's house, he didn't recognize at first the carriage in the street outside the wrought-iron gates.

Even when he came close enough to think it seemed familiar, he didn't believe it—not until he saw Robert sitting on the driver's seat, his hat angled back on his head as he waited.

Jack's heart jumped. He stopped short. He was seeing things. It was only because he wanted so much to believe . . . But this could be anything. It could be Garland. The probability that it was Rosalie, that she had come to him . . .

He didn't allow himself to believe it.

He could barely breathe as he opened the gate and walked to the front porch. When he stepped inside the house, he heard voices in the parlor. His aunt's voice, and then another voice, a lower one. But definitely female. Definitely . . .

Rosalie.

Don't think, he told himself. It was nothing. Perhaps he'd left something and she was only returning it to him. Perhaps she was running an errand for her father. But despite his warnings, he could not slow his step. He hurried down the hall, and he was breathless when he stepped into the parlor.

"Aunt," he said, and then, when the woman on the settee turned to face him, "Rosa."

She was the most beautiful thing he'd ever seen. She was without a veil—she wasn't even wearing a hat. Strands of her dark blond hair were loose around her face; not deliberate, he was sure, but beautiful nonetheless.

She smiled uncertainly, and there was a question in her eyes. "Jack. *Bonjour.*"

Aunt Agatha rose from the settee. "I'll see to the tea," she said, but as she brushed by him, she touched his arm and smiled. He read the message in her eyes. She wouldn't be back until he called her.

When she was gone, he turned back to Rosalie, who was rising from the settee. She looked nervous; her fingers twined together, and he noticed with a start that there was no rosary dangling from her skirt. She laughed a little. "I imagine you didn't expect to see me."

"No," he whispered.

She motioned around the room. "You . . . you've made peace with your uncle, I see."

He could not take his eyes from her. Every movement she made seemed to ache inside him.

"I have heard that you . . . that you're doing very well."

"Not so well, Rosa," he said quietly—the truth at last. "Not so well."

She started. Her gaze came up to his, and he saw the hope that flared there. It was too much; he didn't dare believe it. When she turned away from him, he was not even sure he'd seen it. She moved around the room, touching, lingering, taking inventory with her hands: the wax flowers, a macramé runner, painted miniatures in gilded frames . . .

"I talked to Father Bara today," she said. Her voice was quiet; he had to strain to hear. And she kept moving as she spoke, she didn't look at him.

He couldn't take his eyes from her. "Yes?"

"I—these last weeks, I've been preparing to take the veil. I hired a nurse for Papa. I reconciled all our accounts." She was talking aimlessly, and it shook him—she had always been so economical with words. It worried him. He was so tense he could feel his skin.

She went on. "But I—at the last minute I . . . Father Bara agreed that it would be best if I didn't join the convent." She laughed bitterly, running her finger along the edge of a frame that held a miniature of his father. "It seems I am not meant for the Ursulines."

He heard the pain in her voice, and he wanted to hold her, to soothe her. But he held himself in place, limiting himself to just words. "I'm sorry." So inadequate.

But she nodded as if she took comfort from them. "I'm sorry, too. I'm sorry I've spent all those years . . ." She inhaled slowly. "But then I tell myself it was what I wanted. I wanted to be isolated. I wanted to be safe."

She looked up at him. The pain in her eyes stole his breath. "But I wasn't safe at all, was I, Jack? I was just numb."

"We do what we have to, Rosa," he said slowly.

"That's what you said before."

"That's what I believe."

She nodded and looked back down at the miniature on the desk as if seeing it for the first time. She picked it up, studied it. "This is you?"

"My father."

"You look very like him."

"I wish I'd known him," he said, and then he realized it was true, that it was a small regret of his.

"He would have been proud of you."

"Somehow I find that hard to believe."

"Do you?" She smiled softly, a little wistfully. "But Jack, you are the wisest man I have ever known."

That startled him. When she saw what must have been obvious shock in his eyes, she laughed.

"You told me once that I needed to learn how to live. You were right. And you told me something else, too."

"I'm a font of wisdom."

She smiled. "You told me I was not to blame for Corinne's death."

His heart hurt. "You were never to blame, Rosa."

"*Oui,* I know that now." She paused, setting the miniature down very carefully, looking out the window onto the yard, the crape myrtles. "Today I realized that for the first time. And Jack . . . I listened to my heart again. And I . . . I wanted to live."

Jack swallowed. He waited, he hoped.

She turned back to him. "When you asked me to come with you, I was afraid. But now . . ." She took a deep breath, then blurted out the rest in words too fast to stop. "Now I wonder, do you still want me?"

Jack squeezed his eyes shut. When he opened them again, he expected her to be gone. This was a dream, just a dream. But she was still there, and watching him, and he saw her fear in the sharpness of her features, in her eyes.

"I've never stopped wanting you," he said. He stepped toward her, and it was as if his movement released her, because she came to him, she went into his arms, and he was holding her again, burying his face in her hair, filling his nose with jasmine, feeling her warm, slight body beneath his hands.

"Rosa, Rosa," he murmured into her hair. "What am I going to do with you?"

She looked up at him, and there was a smile in her eyes. "Show me how to live again. I—I've forgotten how."

But he knew, as he held her there, tight against the world, that they would have to learn together. Because before this moment, life had only been a meaningless game.

Before this moment, he had never lived at all.